DEEP AND MEANINGFUL DIARIES
FROM PLANET JANET

Dyan Sheldon

CANDLEWICK PRESS
CAMBRIDGE, MASSACHUSETTS

PLANET JANET

PLEASE NOTE:
GLOSSARY FOR THE UNINITIATED
IN THE BACK OF THIS BOOK

For Erika T
and with special thanks
to Gayle Donnelly

THURSDAY 21 DECEMBER

Talk about self-centered! Me! Me! Me! Me! ME! That's all anybody in this house cares about. I was trying to have a normal conversation over supper (the way people do in films, etc.), not some Great Intellectual Discussion (I know my family's limits, believe me), when I realized that no one was listening to me. I stopped dead right in the middle of explaining about what happened at lunch (which was v dramatic and emotionally stressful), and no one so much as glanced my way. Sigmund (my male parent) was messing around with his electronic organizer, as per usual, and the Mad Cow (my female parent) was staring at him with her eyes squinted like she was trying to work out whether or not he was going to blow us all up. Also as per usual, my parents' OTHER child was reading some book like the rude, antisocial boil that he is. (Tomato sauce was dripping down his chin in a particularly revolting way. You'd think at his age he'd at least be housetrained.)

*   *   *

Anyway, I just sat there watching them for a few seconds.
They were chomping away like lions round a dead zebra,
oblivious to anyone but themselves (for a change, right?!!).
And it suddenly hit me not just how Spiritually Alone I am,
but how easy it would be for me just to **GIVE UP** and
become like them: shallow . . . superficial . . . more boring
than asphalt. I recovered from this **DEVASTATING**
realization and asked them very sweetly if they were aware
of the fact that I was trying to have a conversation. I'd've
got more of a personal response if I'd farted. Still staring at
Sigmund, the Mad Cow asked him did this mean he was
going out again tonight and, still staring at his organizer,
Sigmund said he was just checking his schedule, and was
that a crime now or something? I could tell that they were
about to start another fight, which is pretty much the only
thing they do together lately. If you ask me, it's just as
well Sigmund's hardly ever home, or the flat would be like
war-torn Beirut or one of those places. So, for the sake of
Peace, I cleared my throat and tried again. "Hello? Hello?"
I shouted. "Is anybody there?" Which was when Justin
suddenly looked up and made his one joke about Planet
Janet trying to communicate with Earth. That, of course,
caught the parents' attention. The three of them laughed
like a pack of demented hyenas.

It's **TOO MUCH**, if you ask me. I'm at a v crucial time
in my life when I should be encouraged to express myself

1

and explore my feelings and experiences, and what do I get instead? I get, ooh, Planet Janet's trying to contact Earth, that's what I get. So I said that I didn't see what was so bloody funny and the Mad Cow told me to watch my language, as per usual. Sigmund's contribution, also as per usual, was to quote the only poem he knows—the one about seeing yourself as others see you. Too right, I said, and I removed myself from the kitchen in a meaningful way. I was **REALLY** irked. I mean, I listen to them all the time, not that any of them ever has much to say. (Yadda yadda yadda the government . . . yadda yadda yadda guess what happened in the supermarket . . . yadda yadda yadda . . . yadda yadda yadda . . . I mean, **BORING** or what?)

So that's why I decided it's definitely time to start the Dark Phase. Disha (*My v Best Friend in the Universe and Forever*) and I have been talking about it since September. I **REALLY** don't want to end up having a trivial life like everyone else, especially everyone I'm related to. I want to **LIVE**, not just exist. I mean, life isn't about what's on telly or who left the toilet seat up, is it? It's full of **ANGST** (meaning suffering and deep emotions) and **PASSION**. I want to be in touch with the **REAL** stuff. The **DEEP** pain and joy. The **TRUE** Essence and Substance. I have a *Questing, Artistic Soul,* and if I don't get away from all this mundane crap, it will wither and die like a flower in a desert.

* * *

3

Anyway, I was lying on my bed thinking about all of this when I remembered this diary. Sappho (aka my aunt Hannah) gave it to me as a winter solstice present. (Sappho doesn't give presents for Christmas because it's a Male, Capitalist, Consumer Bloodbath; she gives winter solstice presents instead.) It's called *The Lives of the Great Feminists Diary*, and it's packed with facts you never wanted to know about women you've never heard of. For instance, Fusae Ichikawa founded the Women's Suffrage League of Japan in 1924! I was **REALLY** glad to learn that! At last my life has meaning! Anyway, I was going to wait a couple of months and then throw it out without the Mad Cow noticing, which is what I usually do with presents from Sappho, but now I've changed my mind. Instead of trying to converse with people who don't want to listen, I'm going to seek solace and self-expression in the written word. I reckon that way I can get in touch with my **DEEPER SELF**. And also it should help my chances of finally getting a story published in the school magazine.

Rang Disha after the kitchen was finally evacuated by the peasants. She was suitably shocked by their behavior, though not, of course, surprised (she's known me a long time and knows what my family's like almost as well as I do). D says she reckons the Mad Cow squints like that when she's really trying to focus on something, though I can't imagine why she'd want to focus on Sigmund. I asked D where she gets this stuff from and she said from books. D's ready for the Dark Phase too.

I was going to tell you what happened at lunch, but I'm so emotionally depleted now that I can't exactly remember what it was.

FRIDAY 22 DECEMBER

Last day of school before the Christmas break, so it was v intensely busy. On top of everything else, I had to race to the shop during lunch because I left all my Christmas cards at home (the Mad Cow was nagging me this morning, as per usual, so I totally forgot about them). I got fifteen cards (including one from Ms. Staples, my English teacher and a constant source of inspiration to me), and a present from Siranee, who's going up north for the holidays.

Went round to Disha's after school to discuss the Dark Phase. Disha agrees that since we both turn seventeen next year (D's Libra and I'm Scorpio), it's an excruciatingly important time for us and if we're ever going to REALLY LIVE and not just go through the motions like our parents, we'd better start preparing for it now. Also we're both very *Creative and Artistic*, and it's the

Great Artists and Writers who have always known how to suffer. If they're not killing themselves or hacking off body parts, then they're full of 𝖉𝖔𝖔𝖒 𝖆𝖓𝖉 𝖌𝖑𝖔𝖔𝖒 and muttering about how awful everything is (Disha says she reckons Shakespeare was always in a Dark Phase). We owe it to ourselves to explore the Deep End of the Pool of Life. D and I decided the Dark Phase will begin on the 𝕾𝖙𝖗𝖔𝖐𝖊 𝖔𝖋 𝕸𝖎𝖉𝖓𝖎𝖌𝖍𝖙 on New Year's Eve. We're going to be intense, serious, intellectually and spiritually curious and adventurous, and spend a lot of time nurturing our *Souls*. To do this we're going to read poetry and great literature, really get into art and serious films, and wear mainly black clothes and makeup so everyone will know how deeply we experience things, etc. I'm v glad I changed my mind about chucking this diary. The Dark Phase and all its revelations, understandings, and epiphanies MUST be recorded!!!

The Mad Cow and Sigmund were arguing again at supper. (If things go on like this much longer, I'm going to demand combat pay.) The MC was all wound up because when Sigmund said he'd take her Christmas shopping tonight she didn't think he was going to bring along half of the single parents group he runs as well (this, of course, was a GROSS exaggeration on the MC's part; it was only Mrs. Kennedy). Anyway, when they broke for air, I took the opportunity to make my announcement re the Dark Phase. It really is the season of miracles, because for once (to my utter amazement) they were all listening. Sigmund said, "Does this mean you're leaving Earth's orbit for good?" The Mad Cow said I could forget getting any money from HER for a new wardrobe (as if!), and Justin, keeping to his policy of being as difficult and bloody-minded as possible, said that it wasn't the Great Artists and Writers who understood suffering; it was the poor sods nobody'd ever heard of. CAN YOU BELIEVE IT? My brother the philistine Neanderthal. Justin said that if I wanted to get in touch with the deepest levels of human angst I should try living on the streets! I didn't even stay for pudding after that. I went straight to my room. Obviously I'm starting the Dark Phase not a moment too soon!!!

SATURDAY 23 DECEMBER

Disha and I did some last-minute Christmas shopping today. (Except for D, I'm giving everyone either v cool candles or v cool picture frames that I got in the market.) We ran into David and Marcus. David wanted us to help him find something for his sister. This proved a little difficult. She doesn't read, she doesn't have any hobbies, she never writes letters, she has no interest in plants, and EVERYBODY always gets her bath oils, etc. (I ask you— what choice do they have?!!) On the basis that, if nothing else, David's sister must eat, Disha suggested food, but that was also out since David's sister's always on a diet. I finally cracked it and he got her a gift voucher at the video shop. (David thinks I may be a genius, but modesty made me point out that I am related to a psychotherapist.) To celebrate, we all went for lunch at this v cool Japanese noodle place. I was going to get another little present for the Mad Cow because Disha remembered that I gave her a candle for her birthday, but I spent more than I'd meant to on lunch. So we went for coffee instead. (Marcus and David, being male, don't really like shopping anyway. They find it v stressful and largely boring. D and I discussed it later and we agree that it's something to think about. I mean, they can play the same computer games for HOURS ON END, which we find EXCRUCIATINGLY TEDIOUS, yet when it comes to something that's actually quite intellectually demanding and stimulating they either get pissed off or fall asleep. Disha reckons it must be genetic.)

The Mad Cow dragged the Christmas tree in from the garden this afternoon, complaining the whole time like it was as big as the one at Buckingham Palace or something. (Defying all natural laws, it's exactly the same size it was last year, which isn't exactly enormous.) Sigmund's meant to do the lights, but he wasn't home so I got stuck with the job. Of course, the MC nagged me to check them before I put them on. None of them worked, but I put them on anyway. I don't have HOURS to waste testing every bloody bulb. Alice Bestler's having a bunch of us over to watch Christmas videos tonight.

LATER

Had a v good time at Alice's (her parents were smashed, so we helped ourselves to the eggnog), but came home to find the MC still up. Redecorating the Christmas tree. She was even grumpier than usual because she'd had to rush out to Woolworth's to get another set of lights. I told her the lights were working fine when I tested them, and she believed me. She's really not that bright.

SUNDAY 24 DECEMBER — CHRISTMAS EVE

When I was little, Christmas Eve was *Magical*. I'd wake up practically tingling with excitement. (One time I even threw up all over the kitchen table, I was so jazzed!) I'd lie awake for hours, listening for sleigh bells and singing angels and stuff like that. Oh, youth! How brief it is, and how deluded! (I know I'm only sixteen, but I already get a bittersweet feeling when I think about my childhood.) Now Christmas Eve is about as exciting as Groundhog Day (but with presents). The same people. The same food. The same arguments. To show you what I mean, Nan arrived this afternoon just in time for lunch (as per usual). The first thing Nan says *every year* is, "Doesn't the tree look beautiful?" And then she starts complaining about the ride over or her arthritis, etc. I said hello to Nan, and then I said I had to deliver my Xmas presents to my friends and got out of there **FAST** before Nan started banging on about God. When I got back, my mate David was waiting for me. The MC was force-feeding him her home-baked biscuits (which are more like pressed sand than what you buy) and Nan was going on about Why We Celebrate Christmas as though he'd never heard the story before. David was trying to smile and act interested and hungry and all, but I could tell that he was **V GLAD** to see me. There was definitely sweat on his forehead, which was excruciatingly attractive in a v virile way. I sort of go in and out of fancying David, but right then I was absolutely more in than out. In fact, I really wished it were snowing, because then we could have gone for a walk in a winter wonderland and had a snowball fight, which I know from films is a *v Romantic* thing to do. (And also v Christmassy, of course.) But since it wasn't even raining we went to my room.

David and I had a v interesting conversation about the hypocrisy of adults. Do what I say, but not what I do. Yadda yadda yadda, God and Peace on Earth and Goodwill to Men, but it's really all about selling as much crap as possible, and then the prime minister even tells everybody not to give anything to street beggars. What's that supposed to mean? I'm not on the God Squad or anything, but even I know that Jesus was v into helping beggars and people like that. I said maybe Nan should go round and read the PM the New Testament, because he seems to have missed a couple of crucial chapters. David agreed. David's pretty intelligent. He says his family behave even worse at Christmas than they do the rest of the year too. And they never give him what he wants. I said I was thinking of painting my room, and David said he'd help. (Even if I fancied doing the whole thing all by myself, I would've accepted—think how sweaty he'll get painting!!!) Then we exchanged our presents. I bet he got me something from the Body Shop. Even though he wrapped it himself to throw me, you can tell from the shape. And, anyway, boys aren't exactly imaginative shoppers, are they? David guessed I gave him a photo frame. He said he hoped there was a picture of me in it. What a brilliant idea! I wish I'd thought of it before I wrapped all my presents.

CHRISTMAS DAY

It was just us today. Sigmund, the Mad Cow, their other—less successful—progeny, and Nan. Which was even more dire than it sounds. The only bright spot was that Nan and the MC *loved* their candles (I guess she forgot what I gave her for her birthday—that's gratitude for you!), though this was more than made up for by the fact that Sigmund and Justin acted like I'd given them something secondhand. By lunchtime Nan was well into God mode and the parents were well into the Xmas booze.

There was a major row. Even worse than last year. Sigmund's under orders not to argue with Nan at Christmas because it's her favorite day next to Easter, but how long he holds to that depends on how much he's had to drink. Today he lasted till it was time to say grace. (Nan *always* has to say grace, even when it isn't Xmas. Even at breakfast, for God's sake!) For the first time since I've known him, Sigmund volunteered for the job. The Mad Cow gave him one of her Death by Laser Looks, but Nan was delighted. (You'd think she'd know better; he's been her son for more than half a century!) Sigmund closed his eyes and bowed his head, all solemnlike, and then he started thanking God for the millions of people in the world who suffer hunger, poverty, oppression, torture, injustice, etc. "We're all very grateful that it isn't us," said Sigmund. "Very, very grateful." Justin (who has less of a sense of humor than he has brains if you ask me) thought it was hilarious, but neither Nan nor the Mad Cow so much as cracked a smile. Nan said there was a lot of evil in the world, and it had nothing to do with God, and Sigmund said how did you get to be the Supreme Creator

and not have anything to do with evil? Nan said man had
a **weak and wicked** side, and Sigmund wanted to know whose
fault that was. Sigmund said that if God *had* created man,
then He'd made a pretty big mess of it, hadn't He? But Nan's
not one of those meek Christians. She started snapping and
bristling and reminding Sigmund how long she was in labor
with him (two weeks, apparently). Sigmund took his plate
and a bottle of wine into his office (or the Bunker, as the
MC's started calling it, because he spends so much time there
lately). He stayed there for the rest of the afternoon, which
didn't exactly kill the party. At least we got to finish eating in
Peace. Sappho came round after we'd eaten because she's a
vegan as well as a pagan and she won't sit in the same room
as a turkey unless it's alive and extremely well.

Here's what I got for Christmas:
(1) **A MOBE**! This is the best present I ever got in my
ENTIRE life! Especially since it came from Sigmund.
Last year he gave me a gift voucher for Marks & Spencer
(how tacky is that? He said I could use it to **BUY
UNDERWEAR**—as if!!!) and this book called *Freud for
Beginners*, which I dumped in the book bank. Sappho said
giving a teenager a mobile phone was the equivalent of
giving her a spear or a bow and arrow in more primitive
cultures. Everyone laughed like she was making a joke,
but I think she has a point. Must discuss with D.
(2) Besides the mobe, I got a phone card for fifty quid's
worth of calls! That should last me **EONS**.

ß

(3) A well wicked pair of knee-high black leather boots with the most incredible heels that the Mad Cow only got me because she said she wouldn't have any peace if she didn't. (I really had to turn the screws for this, believe me. I even had to GO with her to get them, because I knew she'd never buy them for me if I wasn't there to goad her on. I had enough trouble just getting her into the shop!)

(4) A T-shirt that says JESUS LOVES YOU from Nan (all four of us got the same thing). It's a slight improvement on last year when we all got pocket Bibles, but mine was in Korean.

(5) A book on yoga from Justin. I'm not exactly paralyzed with joy by this one. Either Sigmund put him up to it, or Justin thinks it's funny to torture and torment me like this. What I really wanted was money for a class. Ms. Staples goes to one at the yoga center, which she says is v cool. I even bought this v wicked neon-purple leotard and matching leggings in case there were any deeply spiritual but excruciatingly attractive blokes about, but Sigmund refused to pay for the course. He said my piano, swimming, computer, and pottery lessons cost him THOUSANDS, and all he has to show for it is a piano nobody ever plays, an antique computer no one uses, and a bowl with a round bottom that he keeps his paper clips in.

(6) Two lots of bath stuff from the Body Shop. (One from Marcus and one from David. They must have asked Disha what aroma I like because they're both Raspberry Ripple. This could be a problem, because Raspberry Ripple doesn't exactly fit with the Dark Phase. White Musk would be better.)

* * *

What I didn't get was an electric razor. God knows I dropped enough hints. And I practically **BLEED TO DEATH** every time I shave my legs. But I suppose I should've known I had as much chance of getting an electric razor as I had of getting a car. Even though Sigmund throws a **MEGA** wobbly every time I borrow his razor, and is **ALWAYS** championing women and blathering on about what a feminist he is because sometimes he washes the dishes and stuff like that, he isn't v interested in female things. (I once asked him to get me some pads while he was in the chemist's and he practically went into cardiac arrest!) And I get no sympathy for that sort of thing from the MC either. Not only is she related to Sappho (who has hair under her **ARMS**!!!), but she's so far beyond being a sexual object that she's pretty much into the chimp look herself.

Oh, yes, and I also got (7) this excruciatingly cool top from Disha (it's black with the outline of a bat in purple glitter—**V DARK!**).

TUESDAY 26 DECEMBER — BOXING DAY

Disha had to go to her aunt's for dinner and her father made her leave her mobe at home. (D says getting a mobe isn't exactly the modern equivalent of getting your own spear because nobody was going to take your spear away from you because you used it too much, were they?) Anyway, since I'm stuck all alone in the **House of Horror** I reckon this is a good time to put you in the picture re ME!

VITAL INFORMATION ABOUT ME:
Name: Janet Foley Bandry.

Age: Sixteen years and almost two months.

What I'm Like: I'm outgoing, but I can be quiet and v thoughtful—I don't consider myself superficial at all. I like to think about life and all the BIG questions a lot. Everybody says I have a wicked sense of humor. (I believe laughter is v important. I mean, what do you have if you don't have laughter? You have tears.) I'm interested in EVERYTHING, except things that are BORING. I'm pretty sure I'm heterosexual, even though there's lesbianism in the family and Sigmund's cousin Bryan is married to a bloke named Ethan. But I'm not just a thinker. I'm an action person too and I am planning a life that is full of *Romance and Adventure*.

Parents: Jocelyn Bandry, aka the Mad Cow, forty-five if she's a day, teacher (it's just like they say: those who can't do anything, teach); and Robert Bandry, aka Sigmund, fifty-five, some sort of psychotherapist.

Siblings: Justin Bandry, eighteen, dweeble and general cosmic fungus.

Favorite Colors: They used to be red and blue when I was younger, but now that I'm more mature and about to embark upon my Dark Phase they're **black and purple**.

Favorite Foods:

(1) Hamburgers with lots of stuff on them.

(2) Roast beef and Yorkshire pudding.

(3) Chips (esp. with gravy).

(4) Fried chicken.

(5) Smoked salmon with cream cheese. I've only had this once, at Disha's, because it's too excruciatingly sophisticated for my family (who think a shred of paper towel is a serviette), but I really loved it (proving yet again that I was meant for greater things!).

Favorite Subjects in School: English and art.

Favorite Things in the Universe:

(1) *My Best Friend,* Disha Paski.

(2) Books.

(3) Films.

(4) Music.

(5) Hanging out with my mates.

(6) Exploring other dimensions and stuff like that.

(7) **LIFE!!!**

(8) Cats. It's no mystery why the Egyptians worshiped them, is it? They're not soppy and weak like dogs, but strong and v independent, qualities I definitely admire.

(Other things I really like are rainy nights, the moon, plain Bounty bars, tortilla chips, triple chocolate mousse, really big jumpers, silk, cold sheets, watching telly in the dark, pigs, etc.)

Most Hated Things in the Universe:

(1) PE and the Anti-Barbie (Mrs. "Don't Get Your Knickers in a Twist" Wist, my PE teacher).

(2) Science.

(3) Maths.

(4) Anything boring.

(5) Catriona Hendley.

(6) Cruelty and injustice.

Life Ambition: I'm not sure yet. I reckon I can work that out once I'm at university—if I go. I may go to art school instead, even though Justin goes to art school, which is hardly a recommendation. (Personally I think calling what Justin does art is pushing it. I mean, anybody can take a photo. We've got **ALBUMS** full of the bloody things, to prove my point. People don't queue for hours to see the Mona Lisa because da Vinci had a good camera, do they?) But I, of course, do not merely take photos; I'm a painter, so art's still a v definite possibility. On the other hand, literature is also a possibility. (I lean more towards literature because there are quite a few Great Women Writers but all the Great Artists are men. I don't see much point in entering a field with such limited potential.) On the other hand, maybe I'll travel and find myself in India or Australia or someplace like that instead, which is something both artists and writers often do.

Some Things That Really Annoy Me:
(1) My family.
(2) Women with pushchairs (you can't move without tripping over one).
(3) Pop music.
(4) People who pick their noses on the bus, etc.
(5) People who talk to themselves out loud in public.
(6) People who never listen to what other people are saying (esp. if the people not being listened to are in their teens).
(7) Catriona Hendley.

That's not absolutely everything, and I do change my mind (which is, of course, a sign of personal growth as well as a *Creative Nature*), but it gives you a rough idea.

WEDNESDAY 27 DECEMBER

Two whole days of family festivities is about all I can bear without applying for citizenship in another country, so since Disha was dragged to Kent to see some old gene sharer, I sought refuge at Sara Dancer's. Sara Dancer lives with her dad because she had this **GINORMOUS** fight with her mother in the summer, and her mother said that if she hated it so much living with her she should go and live with her father. Sara says her father's not exactly

COOL (he's an accountant) but it's a lot less stressful living with him than with her mother because he doesn't give a toss if there are dishes in the sink, etc. Sara says the difference between living with a male parent and a female parent is like the difference between buying your groceries in a superstore and in the corner shop. Sara Dancer says she thinks she may DO IT soon. She says she can't stop thinking about sex, so why not? I said because she never has more than two dates with the same boy, and she agrees that this is her MAJOR stumbling block. And also she reckons that though it would be easy to do it with the Johnny Depp of *Sleepy Hollow*, and maybe with Russell Crowe, she's not so sure about anyone she actually knows. Which is probably just as well since Sara's mother would kill her if Sara did it and she found out.

Talked to D on my mobe after she got home from her mission of mercy, which was (surprise, surprise) incredibly boring. (D says she doesn't know how ANYONE could live anywhere but London but I pointed out that true *Creative Spirits* can draw inspiration from anywhere. Look at van Gogh—he was always doing flowers.) Wound up having a v intense conversation. D says it's no wonder that Sara can't stop thinking about SEX since it's always being pushed in your face. Songs about sex, ads using sex, films about sex. It just goes on and on . . . Disha says she reckons if everybody had good sex (or even bad sex) on a regular basis they wouldn't need to talk about it all the time. I asked D if she thinks it's man's nature to deceive himself, and she says Shakespeare's always banging on about that. D says I'm definitely going to be a natural at the Dark Phase.

I think I must have what Sigmund calls "a low libido" (apparently another thing I can thank the Mad Cow for), because I'm not sex mad at all. What I think about a lot more than sex is *Falling in Love*. I want it to be like Romeo and Juliet or Jane Eyre and Mr. Rochester. I want to be swept away by *Passion,* a hopeless fool for *Love*! (Not like Sappho's friend Samantha, who seems to get swept away every time some bloke buys her dinner.) Disha agrees with me about love and passion, of course, but she says she's afraid we may have a long wait before we find men who inspire those feelings. She says look at the boys at school—most of them couldn't inspire a drop of water from a rain cloud. I said not even David or Marcus? Disha says she likes them both as people, and she does see that each in his way is more attractive than most of them, but she once saw Marcus run a piece of dental floss from one nostril to the other, which pretty much deleted passion from that menu. And she's not **TOTALLY** sure about David, but at least he doesn't wear trainers, which is so très passé. (I mean, really, the parents both own a pair!)

THURSDAY 28 DECEMBER

Went to get the paint for my room today. Disha couldn't
come because her mother was pissed off about something
and made her stay in to help her with the housework.
(At least that's one thing the MC wouldn't even consider!
She learned her lesson the time she made me do the
vacuuming and the Hoover caught fire.) There was this
V OBNOXIOUS man on the bus who told me off
because I was talking to Disha on my mobe. I couldn't
believe it! He said I should get a life instead of spending
my parents' hard-earned money telling my friends I was on
a bus. I told him I already had a LIFE, and it included
being part of the age of communication, and that he was
the one who should get a life instead of butting in on
someone's private conversation. People are TOO MUCH!
Really. It's no wonder the sensitive suffer.

Stopped at the bookshop on the way home. I reckoned
this would be a good time to read one of the books Ms.
Staples is always talking about. Deep, meaningful, angst-filled
modern classics are her speciality. I got *The Outsider* by Albert
Camus because Ms. Staples says he was into the absurdity
of life, and because I definitely identify with the title (the
Spiritually and Creatively Gifted are always on the outside,
aren't they?). And also because it was about three thousand
pages shorter than *Ulysses* (another of Ms. Staples's favorites).

FRIDAY 29 DECEMBER

I'm absolutely exhausted! Marcus and David came round to help me and Disha paint my room today. I could only find two rollers, so Disha and I did the woodwork with brushes. It looks well wicked! We did the walls purple and the woodwork black. It's v sophisticated, but powerful and moody at the same time. You can imagine someone sitting in it, writing poetry and listening to jazz. (Which, of course, is what I plan to do!)

My family has the aesthetics of wildebeests—which probably isn't v fair to wildebeests. Not one of them appreciates the new decor of my room. The Mad Cow said it reminded her of a whorehouse. I asked her if she was saying this from previous experience, or if she was just basing it on her wide knowledge of whorehouses in general, and she told me I wasn't half as funny as I thought I was (how original is that?!!). Nan said that she would never have been allowed to get away with painting her room like that When She Was a Girl. I said I was surprised she could remember that far back.

Started *The Outsider*. The narrator's mother dies on page one, which seems promising. I fell asleep though before I could get any further. Thank God I didn't get *Ulysses*, or I'd be reading it for the rest of my life!!!

MONDAY 1 JANUARY

A NEW YEAR BEGINS!
WE EMBRACE LIFE ANEW!

D and I were invited to a Bruce Lee Festival at Marcus's
for New Year's Eve but we declined. Even though I find
boys can be pretty interesting on their own, when you get
a few of them together their maturity level collapses in
a v alarming way. They think a car chase is intellectually
challenging. Disha agrees. She says it sometimes strikes her
as Absolutely Amazing that all of the Great Thinkers are
men. It doesn't really seem possible.

So since Disha's parents went out last night, D and I spent
a quiet New Year's Eve at hers. In anticipation of this
momentous upcoming year, we both wore black jeans and
tops, and black lipstick and eye shadow. The effect was
excruciatingly DP. There was a bottle of white wine in the
fridge, and Disha said we could take it because her parents
had had so much to drink over the last week they wouldn't
notice. I'd nicked a couple of fags from Sigmund's **LAST**
pack (this time he says he really is giving up for good). We
don't smoke, of course (never mind the heart disease, etc.,
have you **SEEN** what nicotine does to your **TEETH**?),
but we reckoned it was a special occasion so we should
try it the once. (And also **MASSES** of Great Artists and
Writers have been addicted to tobacco as well as alcohol,

24

so we reckoned it was fitting for the beginning of the Dark Phase.) Disha managed a whole one, but I was coughing too much to exactly enjoy it, and it made me feel sick to my stomach. But the wine was great. (If I have to be addicted to something because of my *Creative Spirit*, I would definitely prefer white wine to something that could give you cancer and ruin your smile. Plus Sappho says white wine's **NOT FATTENING,** and everything else I like is!!! We lit a bunch of candles and some incense, found a jazz program on the radio, and sat on the floor of Disha's room. We talked for **HOURS**. Mainly about life. It was all v deep and intense, and v intellectual. Disha said it was too bad the wine wasn't one of those bottles in a straw basket, since that was much more Dark Phase than chardonnay, but I said wine was the drink of intellectuals no matter what it was in. D puked in her waste bin in the middle of the night, but the wine must've knocked me out because I didn't hear her. Neither of us even had a headache today. But Disha told her mum she thought she had a touch of flu, so she didn't even have to clean out the waste bin herself.

I don't believe in making New Year's resolutions. I believe in constant and continuous personal growth. My parents, being très mundane, make resolutions every year—and usually break them by noon on January first. So, this isn't a resolution, but one thing I am going to do this year is listen to more jazz. Disha and I really enjoyed the program on the radio last night, even though a lot of the time there wasn't any tune you could actually recognize. But that's because jazz is the music of the intellectual, so it's meant to be like that. In our house all that's usually played is the music of the bourgeois (Sigmund's Capital Gold and the MC's classical tapes) and the depraved (the noise Justin listens to). And also I'm going on a diet. It's not like I'm **OBESE** or anything, but artists, writers, and intellectuals in a Dark Phase tend to be lean. (Disha said that's because they're usually too poor to eat, but I pointed out that the artist who sold her bed to the Saatchi Gallery isn't poor, and Disha said that just because someone put your bed in a gallery didn't make you Rembrandt, who anyway was **FAT**. I hope she's not going to spend the Dark Phase being argumentative.)

When I got back to the **House of Horror**, the MC and Sigmund had had another **MAJOR ROW**. I knew as soon as I got into the flat because the MC was muttering darkly on the phone to Sappho. Sigmund only emerged from the Bunker for supper, and they didn't say a word to each other for the whole meal. Personally I prefer it when they're not speaking since at least it's quiet.

TUESDAY 2 JANUARY

Life really is v ironic, isn't it? (This is something I've been noticing more and more lately.) Every morning during term I drag myself out of bed and listen to the news hoping that a small fire's closed my school for at least one day, but when it's the holidays I'm **BORED OUT OF MY MIND**!!! Disha, of course, feels exactly the same. She says she's finding the holiday stultifying (meaning it's turning her brain into oatmeal). I asked her where she got that word from, and she said that just shows how bad it is, doesn't it? She's started reading the dictionary for fun. Thank God Marcus rang up and said everybody was hanging out at David's this afternoon if we'd like to come along. Do birds like to fly? Not only were we **DYING** to get out of the house, but this was our Dark Phase debut, so to speak. (Disha got a red leather jacket for Xmas, which is unfortunate since even though it's cooler than ice it **RUINS** the effect. Thank God my boots are black.) The Mad Cow wanted to know if I was going to a funeral (is that funny, or what?!!), and Sigmund said no, it was just the way creatures on my planet dress (surely I must've been adopted!). It took me and D so long to get totally ready that by the time we got to David's, Marcus had already gone home! After inviting us and everything. It's too much, really.

*   *   *

Except for David (who said we looked *v* 𝕸𝖔𝖗𝖙𝖎𝖈𝖎𝖆 𝕬𝖉𝖉𝖆𝖒𝖘), none of the others even noticed our new look! They were too busy stuffing their faces and playing the PlayStation game David got for Xmas, which was V BORING, esp. if you were practically starving to death. It made me think about the power of telly and stuff like that. Their reality's totally distorted. You should've heard them banging on about tactics like they were crack SAS troops and not teenage boys who can't get across London without an A–Z. My feet were hurting a bit from my new boots and my stomach was starting to growl (all I'd had all day was ONE slice of DRY toast and two v small apples) and D looked like she might fall asleep, so we decided to leave. Fortunately I've had new boots before, so I'd thought to bring a pair of shoes with me. I changed as soon as we got out of the house and was able to walk home without doing my feet any permanent damage, even though I didn't look as cool. I was RAVENOUS by the time I got home, of course. I stood at the counter and ate half a packet of water biscuits, which I reckon is OK since they don't have any fat in them. Not so sure about the cheese.

WEDNESDAY 3 JANUARY

I think the Mad Cow's really starting to lose it (she is pushing fifty). If she's not picking fights with Sigmund,

she's picking them with me! I sat down to have a cup
of tea with her this afternoon while she was cooking
something, and she went BERSERK because I sniffed the
milk. I just wanted to make sure it hadn't gone off. Is that
a crime? I swear that I am not going to become grumpy
and senile when I get old. I'm going to have a *Young
Heart and Soul,* even when I'm sixty. And maybe plastic
surgery.

D says it sounds to her like the MC must be
MENOPAUSAL!!! She says she's heard of cases where
the woman either won't come out of her room for months
or does weird things like painting the entire flat bright
orange (sometimes on the OUTSIDE!!!). When her nan
went through the menopause she thought that ghosts were
after her and kept climbing into the washing machine
because she thought she'd be safe there (it was a top
loader).

THURSDAY 4 JANUARY

Went with Disha to exchange my two gift sets of
Raspberry Ripple for two sets of White Musk, but the sales
assistant wouldn't exchange them because I didn't have the
receipts. I asked her where else she thought they came
from, since they say Body Shop on them, but she was a

right stubborn cow. Disha says I can always use them as presents for other people, as long as I don't give her one.

The Mad Cow was sitting in the kitchen, sniffing into a cup of tea, when Disha and I got back. I couldn't tell whether or not she'd been crying, but she looked like she was getting into one of her 𝕸oods. We made ourselves scarce. Disha says the MC seems V TENSE lately, but I explained that it's just her hormones. She's up and down like a staircase. You never know what mood she's going to be in. D says she hopes that if we ever get that old they'll have invented some drugs to combat it.

FRIDAY 5 JANUARY

Andrew "the Missing Link" Jeffers, Justin's best mate for reasons that will become obvious, accosted me in the kitchen while I was making myself a cup of tea. He wanted me to know that he thinks my friend Disha is v fit. I said that's because she works out and has a black belt in karate, and he said that wasn't what he meant. (Really? Um, duh. . . ! I didn't know that!) He said to tell her she has great tits. I told him to tell her himself.

SATURDAY 6 JANUARY

According to The Lives of the Great Feminists, Virginia Woolf is famous for saying that every woman should have a room of her own. You can tell right off that she didn't live with my family. I woke up this morning to find the child my parents should **NEVER** have had standing over my bed taking pictures of me! (I wouldn't sleep in the nude in this house in a heat wave.) It's all the Mad Cow's fault for getting him that new camera for Christmas. (She's always spoiled him!) Now he's started taking pictures of US again. Of course, the MC's on his side, as per usual. She says Justin doesn't mean any harm; he's just obsessed. Possessed, more like. Then she went off on one of her tangents, yammering on about how talented Justin is and how proud she is of him. (For pushing a button!) The MC says that Justin wants to experiment more with style, now that he's made a bit of a name for himself. I said and what would that name be? Shithead? She thought I was joking. Personally I think she's delusional. (I can only assume that my father the shrink hasn't noticed this because he's not home or they're fighting or he's in the Bunker pretending to be working but really sneaking fags.) It was soooo excruciatingly **BORING**. I was tempted to tell her that Justin takes pictures of her and Sigmund sleeping as well, but I decided to use the information to blackmail him instead. I need the money.

*   *   *

31

Talked to Disha for **EONS** last night. It's so civilized, being able to lie on my bed in privacy and have a conversation without everybody eavesdropping on my business or constantly interrupting to tell me the time or that they're waiting for a call. I'm going to need another phone card soon.

SUNDAY 7 JANUARY

Disha and I hung out with the others at David's again this afternoon, and this time Marcus managed to stay for more than two seconds. Marcus suggested we go for a walk and then David said he'd come too. Marcus got us laughing so much I had to go into a pub to use the loo. I pretended I was looking for my mother. After Marcus and David went home, Disha and I went back to mine. Justin and Andrew were in the kitchen. I went to the loo and Justin went off to get something and can you believe it? The Missing Link **DID IT**! He actually **DID IT**! He told Disha she had great tits! And then he tried to **TOUCH THEM**! I lied about Disha being a black belt, but she did take a self-defense course from the police last summer because her parents are refugees. She flipped Andrew over and he crashed into the fridge. Disha and I didn't stop laughing for **HOURS**. I got yelled at by the MC for knocking most of the magnets off the fridge, of course. Like it was **MY** fault,

32

right? And then she made ME pick them up, not Justin! Talk about INEQUALITY between the sexes! I should ask Sappho who I should complain to.

MONDAY 8 JANUARY

What an excruciating relief to get back to the real world after all that time imprisoned in the House of Horror! And also, of course, I was glad to see my many friends and Ms. Staples (my English and FAVORITE teacher). There was a lot to catch up on! Catriona Hendley spent most of the day boring everyone with tales of her excruciatingly wonderful holiday in NEW YORK (of course! Where else would she go; they're not selling tickets to Mars yet, are they?), and all the famous people she met, and all the amazing restaurants she ate in, and all the astounding things she did (like shopping till—cue hysterical laughter here—she couldn't shop anymore!!!). Step aside, Columbus. You'd think SHE discovered America, the way she went on. It was TOTALLY revolting. Not all was gloom and doom, however. Disha, Siranee, Alice, and I all noticed that Catriona had put on a few pounds eating in all those amazing restaurants. Her chest bones aren't protruding as much as usual. Unfortunately this also means that I'll NEVER be able to go to New York unless I lose at least a stone beforehand. And so far I apparently haven't lost a gram. I'm going to have to stop my diet until the MC buys a decent set of scales (i.e., ones that work). What's the point of starving if every time I weigh myself I'm heavier than I was the time before?

Wore my new boots to school for the first time today. **EVERYONE** admired them. Even Catriona Hendley said they were *très* cool and asked where I got them. Wiping a tear from my eye, I sadly had to tell her they were the last pair in the shop. Which is why they're a little tight (though I didn't tell her that, of course). I was starting to limp by the end of the day, but I don't think anyone noticed.

TUESDAY 9 JANUARY

I asked Mr. Belakis, my art teacher, why there aren't any Great Women Artists, and he said what about Frida Kahlo, to name but one. Then he told me to read some book by Germaine Greer. Found Germaine in my diary. Apparently there are **HORDES** of Great Women Artists, but no one ever tells you about them. Then I found Frida in my diary. Apparently she had one eyebrow, a mustache, and slept with **TONS** of people of **BOTH** sexes.

Had to soak my feet when I got home because of the blisters. Despite the pain I was in, the Mad Cow threw a

MAJOR wobbly because I used the stew pot (it was the largest thing I could find). She said why didn't I use the mop bucket? I didn't know we had a mop bucket, but even if I had I wouldn't have put my feet in it. (After she's used it to wash the floors?) Disha says I can probably stretch them (the boots, not my feet).

I mentioned Frida Kahlo to Sappho, so she'll know I'm finally using something she gave me. Sappho said Frida's husband (who was also a famous artist) had a mustache and slept with TONS of people too, so what was the big deal?

WEDNESDAY 10 JANUARY

There really isn't any justice in this world, is there? The school magazine met this afternoon, and the next issue's going to have TWO poems by Catriona "God Died and Left Me in Charge" Hendley that she wrote about New York. One's called "Skyline" (how très original!) and the other's entitled "Invisible People" (about the poor—like she's ever met any). They're both really stupid poems if you ask me. Esp. the one about the invisible poor. All I can say is New York must be v different to London. Here poor people are right in your face. And you can't move down the street without tripping over their blankets and dogs, etc.

*   *   *

Meanwhile, **NOBODY** liked the story I submitted before Christmas. They found it confusing. But isn't life confusing? I talked to Ms. Staples about it in private. She had some v constructive things to say (*good imagery! nice use of language! gripping idea!*), but she says I need to work a bit harder on my plots. I told her I thought plots belonged in gardens, and that to conform to rigid rules about stuff like that stifled my *Creative Spirit*. Ms. Staples laughed and said that she hoped I didn't take that line when it came to my GCSEs because the education authority likes plots.

I could never be a teacher. It must suck the *Soul* right out of you (e.g., Jocelyn Bandry, though it is possible that she never had a soul in the first place). I feel bad for poor Ms. Staples, who, unlike my female parent, does have a *Passionate Soul* and a questing, intelligent mind despite the personal lack of talent that must've driven her into teaching. How depressing it must be to work for people who don't understand literature or art or the true nature of life! I told her I'd do my best. She gave me a grateful smile. It's a **BIG** responsibility, having to keep Ms. Staples's level of hope up, but I feel I'm old enough now to handle it. After all, that's part of what life's about, isn't it?

36

THURSDAY 11 JANUARY

What a day! I don't think any more could go wrong if
I tried! The Mad Cow forgot to iron the gray skirt I was
going to wear, so I had to find something else that fit my
mood. It took **EONS**. I missed my usual bus, of course,
and then I couldn't find my pass. I took *everything* out of my
bag, but it wasn't *anywhere*. You should've heard the driver
moan about how much stuff I carry around with me.
(What's it to him? He's not my mother!) I asked him if
he thought I was lugging around all these schoolbooks to
get a free ride! I mean, really, if there was ever a man in
DESPERATE need of a life, this was the man.

When I finally got to school, Disha turned up wearing
almost the exact same shirt I was wearing, so we went
back to hers so she could change. We were really only
seconds late, but Stalin (aka Mr. Wilkins, our tutor)
wouldn't listen to our perfectly reasonable explanation and
gave us detention. (Power corrupts, and absolute power
corrupts absolutely. I can't remember where I heard that,
but it's true.) Then it turned out that besides forgetting to
iron my skirt, the Mad Cow forgot to remind me to take
my PE kit again. I told Mrs. Wist that I had cramps so bad
I thought I was giving birth, and she let me go to the
library instead of running around the field having my shins
clubbed. The bad news was that the sight of me reminded
the librarian, Mrs. Higgle, that I still had two books

outstanding. I tried to explain that I thought I'd brought them back, but she said that was what I said last time. It'll be a note home next, and then Sigmund will get on my case, yadda yadda yadda. The man can talk you into unconsciousness. I hope the Mad Cow can find the books.

LATER

OH, TRAGEDY! OH, DARK DAY OF HORROR AND GLOOM! I CAN'T FIND MY MOBE! And I thought nothing more could go WRONG today! How ironic is that? Why does everything happen to ME? I must've dropped it on the bus this morning, which is understandable considering all the trauma I was put through! The last time I remember having it was when I rang Sara Dancer at the bus stop. The parents will dehydrate me if they find out.

FRIDAY 12 JANUARY

I'm meant to be tidying my room. ("If you want to go to Disha's tonight, you'd better tidy that room!" I don't know why she doesn't put it on a tape loop and save herself the trouble of saying the same thing OVER AND OVER.)

The good news is that I thought I heard her coming to check on me (she was definitely a prison guard in one of her previous lives), so I dived under my bed in cleaning mode, and guess what I found? The yoga book I got for Christmas! I'd forgotten all about it. The woman on the cover is sitting cross-legged and smiling. There are dozens of quotes on the back from ordinary people who say that yoga changed their lives. It looks pretty easy. I can smile, and I can sit cross-legged, so what could be so hard? Maybe I'll give it a try. I can see yoga fitting in v well with the Dark Phase. Ms. Staples does yoga and she says it's *v Spiritual*, as well as healthy. I wonder if you can lose weight doing yoga (since dieting obviously doesn't work).

SATURDAY 13 JANUARY

Had a v good time at Disha's, as per usual. Her parents aren't as obtrusive as some. We were going to have an **Exploring Other Dimensions Night**, but I left the book on witchcraft at home and Disha couldn't find the tarot cards I gave her for Christmas (you've got to be given them; you can't buy them for yourself), so we decided to have an Intellectual Night instead. We were going to get out this brilliant Japanese film Ms. Staples told us about, but Blockbuster didn't have it. We were going to listen to intelligent music and read poetry instead, but we couldn't find the jazz station. All was **FRUSTRATION AND DOOM** until Disha remembered that Mrs. Foster next door (who is civilized and has cable) lent her a copy of *Clueless* last year that we never watched. Ms. Staples says *Clueless* is based on a Jane Austen novel, so we reckoned that was just as good as something in Japanese. We finally found it under some stuff on the floor of Disha's wardrobe. But then frustration and doom turned to **AMAZEMENT AND SHOCK**! Someone who was probably Mr. Foster taped over *Clueless* with an **ADULT MOVIE**. We're not naive—we've seen the magazines on the top shelf in the news agent's and stuff like that, of course—but both Disha and I come from homes where pornography is frowned upon. Even Sigmund and the MC, who are major believers in free speech, say it's demeaning to women. Sappho said if she ever found Justin with porn she'd make him eat it, and not even Justin would think that was an idle threat. As for the Paskis, they were both arrested for disorderly conduct when someone tried to open a sex shop in their old neighborhood. (Mrs. P whacked the store owner over the head with a sign that said CHILDREN LIVE HERE.) We didn't watch much (you don't have to watch much to get the idea, and after that it's sort of boring). Disha says now she'll never be able to see the Fosters (esp. Mr. Foster) without feeling embarrassed. We talked a bit about the boys we know and whether or not they're into porn, which is a bit weird and creepy to think about. Then Disha said could I imagine either of our mothers straddling a chair in black lace suspenders with tassles hanging from her nipples and her tongue out like that, and we practically died laughing.

When I got back to **Bleak House** this afternoon, the Mad Cow was lying in wait (and not in suspenders and tassles, believe me. She might be into S&M though. I have no trouble picturing her with a whip). I barely got the door shut before she started in. "What did I tell you. . . ? What did you promise. . . ? I thought you were going to clean up that pigsty before you went out last night!" Same old same old. Then she literally dragged me over to the sink so I could see all the plates and stuff she'd found under my bed. **AND** she actually made me count them: six glasses, seven mugs, two plates, nine spoons, three bowls, and Great-Grandmother Rose's **WILLOW PLATE**!!! (Was I **INSANE**? How could I treat a family heirloom like that?) I told her to chill out. "A woman your age shouldn't get so excited," I told her. "You'll give yourself a stroke." For a minute there I thought she was going to forget about her commitment to nonviolent parenting and give *me* a stroke, but instead she asked me to let her know when my planet was ready to receive transmissions from Earth so she wasn't just wasting her breath all the time. And then she told me to **GO AND TIDY** my room, and not to come down till it was done. I may spend the rest of my life up here. (At least I would if I had a phone!)

SUNDAY 14 JANUARY

Disha wanted to know if I managed to stretch my new
boots. I groaned out loud! Disha'd said I should wet them
before I stuffed them full of newspaper so they'd be more
flexible when I stretched them, so on Wednesday I filled
the mop bucket with water and left them in it in the
garden shed. I TOTALLY forgot about them! Disha said
when she told me to soak them, she meant for an hour or
so, not nearly a WEEK. What a DISASTER!!! I must've
been cursed at birth or something. They look all funny,
and the heel came off the right boot. Disha said I could
take it to a cobbler, but I was too depressed to ask her
what a cobbler is.

I hate my brother more than anyone has ever hated
ANYONE or ANYTHING in the history of the world.
As if it wasn't enough that my new boots are TOTALLY
RUINED, I was just trying out some new makeup
(Sorceress Black) when the door to my room was flung open
and there was Justin and his bloody camera (we at 73A
Wooster Crescent live in a virtually lockless world). He got
me putting on eyeliner. I really think it's time they had
him put down. You can't bite into a crisp in this house
without being photographed. It's like living with the
paparazzi (but without the champagne and stuff). Poor
Princess Di! I really feel for what she went through. Death
must've been a kind of release. (When I told that to Disha,

she said maybe it's not just the *Creative* who suffer—the famous do too. I never thought of it like that. I mean, you can be **MEGA FAMOUS** and have the *Soul* of a cow pat, can't you? But D says one has to make a distinction between physical suffering and spiritual suffering. Spiritual suffering is what the creative do. I don't think it's premature to say that the Dark Phase is v successful so far!)

MONDAY 15 JANUARY

Sara Dancer says her mother's boyfriend is into porn, which Sara says is pretty understandable, since her mother isn't exactly Madonna (she looks like a dinner lady). Sara even found magazines with names like *Sex Slaves* and *She's Gotta Have* It under the rug in the bathroom. She won't take baths anymore. Sara's mother doesn't know it, but Sara's little brother watches porn all the time on cable. And also on the Internet. Sara watched it there once, out of intellectual curiosity, and it was pretty gross. She says she's searched her dad's flat for signs of Solitary Sexual Activity but all she turned up was a packet of condoms, which she took as a good sign even though she doesn't think he has a steady girlfriend. Sara says there's no way she'd put up with a room without a lock in her mother's house—not even when she's just there for a visit. She says it's like living with wild lions. You never know when their primitive nature is going to take over and they attack. I said you don't think your mum's boyfriend would **DO SOMETHING,** do you, and she said no, of course not, but you can't be too careful, can you? Look at all the articles in the papers about people molesting minors. Maybe newspapers aren't as **BORING** as I've always thought. (And also reading papers might be good for stimulating the 𝕯𝖊𝖕𝖗𝖊𝖘𝖘𝖎𝖔𝖓 𝖆𝖓𝖉 𝕾𝖊𝖓𝖘𝖊 𝖔𝖋 𝕾𝖚𝖋𝖋𝖊𝖗𝖎𝖓𝖌 of the DP. At least they're faster to read than most of Ms. Staples's books!)

I don't see how I can go another day without a phone. It's like having a limb amputated. I can still feel it pressed against my cheek. I can still see the special purple case I bought for it. I can still hear its distinctive call (some Beatles song). I reach out for it and it isn't there. My fingers touch the air and I wonder why. Why? Why has this happened to me? (I reckon I must be learning an important life lesson in loss—you know, that **NOTHING** lasts forever—but I still wish I could've lost something else. Like Justin, for instance.) D says maybe I should've checked lost property, but everybody knows that anything good that gets lost gets nicked, so why bother? Now I have nothing to do when I'm waiting for buses or walking down the street on my own. It's **SO BORING**! And also it's torture.

*   *   *

44

Since I can't just lie on my bed and talk to Disha, I was going to watch some telly to relax before I started my homework, but Nan turned up. I was just about to open the living-room door when I heard her say, "Ask yourself what Jesus would do in this situation, Jocelyn." God knows what they're on about now, but I should think it would be hard even for Jesus to be in the place of a menopausal madwoman. I beat a hasty retreat.

TUESDAY 16 JANUARY

THIS IS TOO MUCH!!! You want to know how **TOTALLY INSANE** the Mad Cow's getting? Now she's going through the rubbish. **REALLY!!!** I asked her if she's planning to become a bag lady when she finally retires from making my life hell, and she said she was actually thinking of joining MI5. She said she was looking for evidence of Sigmund still being a closet nicotine addict. You'd think she'd remember from last time that he always sneaks the rubbish from the Bunker into someone else's bin so we can't accidentally find his butts. Anyway, she went through the rubbish and she found the boots. She went **BALLISTIC!** I mean, they're only **BOOTS.** They can be replaced. If you ask me, she's way too materialistic. She should try nurturing her spiritual side a bit more.

WEDNESDAY 17 JANUARY

Sigmund was banging on about work, as per usual,
while the rest of us were trying to eat our supper. I wasn't
really listening (I mean, who *does*?), but I heard him say
something about matrophobia. I hate to ask Sigmund
questions (because he always gives such v long answers
that by the time he's finished you don't have a clue what
you actually asked in the first place), but the Dark Phase
is one of intellectual curiosity, so I risked it. Sigmund said
matrophobia is when you're afraid of turning into your
own mother. Justin spoke one of his first full sentences
of the new year then. He asked Sigmund what it would
be called if he was afraid of *Sigmund* turning into *Nan*.
Everybody laughed except me. I was practically turned
to stone. It never even occurred to me before that such
a thing could happen. I know I worry about becoming
as shallow and pointless as the rest of my family, but it
never occurred to me that I could actually turn into MY
MOTHER. I asked Sigmund if that sort of thing was very
common, and he said it was much more common to turn
into your own mother than to be afraid of it. I couldn't
believe it! Me, turn into the Mad Cow?!! I'd have to kill
myself! I mean, really, what other option would I have?
Now I'm feeling Deeply Depressed. All the years they make
you go to school to memorize a bunch of crap that you
immediately forget, but nobody ever tells you anything

REALLY IMPORTANT. It doesn't seem fair. Are we mushrooms that have to be kept in the dark?

D agrees that no one ever tells you anything REALLY IMPORTANT or even worth knowing. She says the more she finds out in the DP, the more she realizes that it's practically a miracle that EVERYBODY isn't depressed. TOO TRUE! It almost makes you admire people like my parents, who manage to exist on such a superficial level that the slings and arrows of Outrageous Fortune miss them entirely. But can you truly experience REAL joy or meaning by floating on the surface of the Lake of Life and never diving down to the depths? Disha and I don't think so.

THURSDAY 18 JANUARY

There is a God! There really is! And He's ON MY SIDE!!! Sigmund caught Justin getting ready to take a picture of him while he was peeing (Sigmund, not Justin) and he went BERSERK!!! You'd never believe Sigmund makes his living being reasonable in this dead calm way if you'd seen him waving the roll of film about. He would've had the camera too, but the Mad Cow snatched it away just in time. I think she thought it was funny, because she left the room v quickly after that. I thought it was hilarious. Sigmund got so worked up that he got one of his migraines and had to go to bed.

Thursday nights I usually mind Mrs. Kennedy's twins, Shane and Shaun, while she goes to her computer class and then out for a drink with her mates, but tonight she rang to say she had a cold and wasn't going out after all. Mrs. Kennedy is in several of Sigmund's groups (including the wives of men in prison support group and the low self-esteem group), and now, under the guidance of a man who can never find his car keys, she's getting her life together. At four quid an hour, she can get everyone's life together for all I care. Not that the twins are easy. But God knows I could use the money (getting money out of Sigmund or the Mad Cow is harder than putting your eye makeup on in the dark); I could also really use the break from them, though. Children definitely don't fit into the DP. From what I can tell, most of the Great Writers and Artists didn't have that much to do with children—if anything. Not even the women. D agrees. She says Shakespeare had the twins and all, but she doesn't think he took them every other weekend or anything like that. On the other hand, the MC doesn't like Mrs. Kennedy, so me going over there usually winds her up (one has to snatch bits of happiness where one can in this life!). The MC says she doesn't like Mrs. Kennedy because she shows right-wing racist tendencies (she votes Tory and once asked the

MC what her ethnic background is), but I reckon it's really because Mrs. Kennedy's v attractive in an *EastEnders* sort of way, and the MC (being about as attractive as bog roll) resents her. It's a pretty common syndrome.

FRIDAY 19 JANUARY

Disha and I had another long talk about **MEN AND LOVE** this afternoon. Should I go after David? Should I go after Marcus? It's a big decision to make. Marcus is a v good artist, which gives us a *Spiritual Connection,* but he's got a v square face and only one eyebrow and isn't as good-looking as David. David's v sexy (D and I agree it's his eyes—his lashes are longer than mine when I'm wearing lash-lengthening mascara), and though he isn't a painter, he is v literary. (One time when we were all at his and excruciatingly bored, we played his parents' Trivial Pursuit and David was incredible! Even Disha was impressed, and you already know how much she reads!) But he did start a food fight at Lila Jenkins's Halloween party, which was v juvenile, even though he did get Catriona Hendley smack in the face with a handful of jelly, which was pretty hilarious and ruined her hair! Sometimes I think that if I could put David and Marcus together I'd have the perfect man. After all, if you do end up having sex with someone, you get to be on pretty intimate terms with his penis, don't you? I don't think I'd be able to be on intimate terms with the penis of someone less than close to perfect. And also I do worry that there's no real *Frisson,* as the French (who seem to know a lot about *Passion and Romance*) would say. There's no real chemistry, no explosion of *Souls.* On the other hand, a little practice might not hurt. Maybe passion's something you have to work up to. As Disha says, you don't jump into the deep end of the pool the first time you try to swim, do you?

SATURDAY 20 JANUARY

GOD LOVES ME! He really does. Or maybe my karma's better than I thought, because wait till you hear what happened tonight. My whole family evacuated the premises after supper. Together! I think they were going to some exhibition at Justin's college. The parents were pretty presentable looking, but Justin is NEVER presentable looking; he always looks like he lives on the streets. The Mad Cow asked me if I was coming and I sighed and told her I had too much homework this weekend (which is pretty much true). Having the flat to myself is about as rare as seeing a flock of pigs flying over north London, so I decided to take advantage of this unexpected opportunity and as soon as they left I had a look for the Mad Cow's mobe. (Sigmund did all his Christmas shopping in one shop this year—he even got a mobile for Nan that has large numbers so she can see them and that plays "Amazing Grace.") I finally found it in her desk, looking pathetically untouched. She never uses it, so she'll also never know it's gone.

Read another page of *The Outsider* (to be honest, it's not exactly what I thought it would be from the title), TWO poems by this French guy Ms. Staples recommended, and the introduction to my yoga book tonight. The Dark Phase is going REALLY well. I almost can't remember what it's like to be a child anymore.

SUNDAY 21 JANUARY

Disha just rang. We had a v interesting conversation. D wanted to know if I remembered her brother's friend Elvin. (Disha's brother, Calum, is younger than Justin— he's in the sixth form at our school—but he's about two million years on in evolutionary terms. For one thing, he can speak.) Disha says I've seen Elvin a couple of times. He's the one Calum met on the special film course he's taking. I said, "Blond?" Disha said no, he's the one with the longish black hair who wears cowboy boots. I said, "Oh, HIM!" Anyway, Disha was alone in the kitchen with Elvin just now, and he'd been asking about ME! Elvin's a naff name, but Disha and I agreed that he's pretty good-looking. ALSO he wears black turtlenecks and his hair is just long enough to make him look like a Beat poet. (We discovered the Beat poets when one of them died and Ms. Staples told us how they were an intellectual movement and everything. Ms. Staples says they were pissed off with the system and the middle-class lifestyle long before the punks—True Artists always are.)

Disha says Elvin's at film school and he's already won a prize for some film he made about cats (at least Disha thinks it's about cats; she isn't TOTALLY certain). A filmmaker is v cool—sort of a combination between an artist and a writer. I reckon I didn't really notice Elvin before because he's older. I know lots of girls like older men. (One of the maths teachers left over Christmas to fulfil her biological destiny and has been replaced by Mr. Plaget, who looks young enough to be a sixth-former except GORGEOUS, and you wouldn't believe how many girls who can't add up without a calculator are talking about doing A-level maths!!!) I, however, don't see the attraction. Older men make me sort of nervous. I think you have to suspect their motives. (I mean, why can't they get a woman their own age? Is there something wrong with them? Are they afraid of being with an equal? Do they think a younger girl would be easier to push around?) Elvin's different though (he's not that old—in fact he's probably the same age as

Justin, but MUCH more mature). Disha and I agree that this is v exciting.

On a more mundane note, Sara Dancer's having second thoughts about DOING IT. She was talking to some girl who started having sex the day before she turned fifteen, and this girl reckons Sara should hold out for a bed as well as a real boyfriend. The first time this girl did it was in a garden shed (she had a rake handle in her back the whole time, but it was over pretty fast so it wasn't too bad). She says she's never done it without her clothes on or lying down—unless you count the back seat of her boyfriend's father's car, which none of us do. Sara says it doesn't sound much like in films. And I said it was just what I was always saying, wasn't it? Where's the *Romance*? Where's the *Passion*? Where's the overwhelming desire to merge your *Soul* (and a couple of body parts) with another?

MONDAY 22 JANUARY

Mentioned to David at lunch that I'm reading *The Outsider*. He was impressed. He said he admires Camus's clarity of intellect, philosophical optimism, and hopeful love of life. This doesn't sound much like the book I'm reading, but I said I did too. I reckon the optimism and hope must come after page three.

The yoga isn't as easy as it looks on the cover. I'm sure some of the positions are only possible if your bones are made of Plasticine or you're double-jointed or something. I was trying to do the Chakrasana (the Wheel, to the layperson) because it says in the book that it strengthens your thigh and stomach muscles (I reckon it beats going on another diet). I got into it OK, but then I got sort of stuck. It was either call for help or crash. I made the wrong choice. I screamed and Justin raced in, but of course he wasn't alone. He had his stupid camera with him. He snapped me just as I fell. He'd better hide that bloody thing, because if I get my hands on it I'm throwing it into the loo.

WEDNESDAY 24 JANUARY

IT HAS TO BE TOLD!

Five Reasons Why I Hate Catriona Hendley:

(1) She's **ALWAYS** had a big head because her mother writes for the *Guardian* and her father is some excruciatingly ginormous big deal at Channel Four.

(2) When we were in primary school, Catriona Hendley always made up dumb games for us to play, and I was always the dog.

(3) When we got to secondary school, Catriona Hendley asked me in front of everyone if I was a Taurus, but I

didn't know anything about astrology then and I thought she said tourist and I said no, I was born in London. It took **EONS** to live it down.

(4) One day last summer we were all hanging out in the park and Catriona was telling some incredibly boring story. I was lying on the ground, watching the clouds, and I sat up to ask Disha something, and Catriona told me to lie back down and eat another **BAG OF CRISPS**! Like I'd already eaten one! In front of everybody! (Disha said that was not what Catriona said, but I think Disha was just trying to make me feel better. Disha's v loyal.)

(5) **CATRIONA HENDLEY'S AFTER ELVIN WHATEVER-HIS-NAME-IS!!!** I can hardly believe it myself. I mean, I know the world's a global village now, but it's still not **THAT** small. How does she even know him? He doesn't go to our school, she doesn't have an older brother, and she's not big mates with Disha. But the Eyes Don't Lie. There I was, minding my own business and waiting for Sara after school (Disha had to go to the dentist's), when who should come riding through the gates on his bicycle but Elvin! Now that I know he's interested in **ME,** his face has been burned into my brain and I recognized him immediately. He looked even cooler than I remembered. I reckoned he was meeting Calum, and I was just getting ready to go over and say hello in a hey-don't-I-know-you sort of way when Catriona Hendley came flying down the steps behind me like a bat out of hell (nearly knocking me over) and practically tackled him

as he got off his bike! If Catriona Hendley was built like a real woman (like some of us) and not a wood sprite, she would have floored him. Then she dropped her books. **ON PURPOSE!** (This is the twenty-first century. Can you believe it?) What could he do? He had to help her pick them up. And, anyway, she was practically standing on his feet so he didn't have much choice. This really isn't fair! He saw *me* first! If she'd batted her eyelashes any more, she'd've given him a **RASH**.

Rang Disha on the way home to tell her what happened. She's going to see what she can find out. I hope Nan's right and there is a hell, because it would really make my life to know that Catriona Hendley will be going there. Then we'd see how cool Ms. "So Trendy You Could Break Your Teeth on Her" really is.

THURSDAY 25 JANUARY

It took ages to get Mrs. Kennedy's twins to bed tonight. They must have visited their dad at the weekend, because they were all wound up about him. Dad this . . . Dad that . . . Dad . . . Dad . . . Dad . . . Boring or what? I think they're confusing him with someone who isn't doing time for armed robbery. Shane said their dad was coming home soon, and I reminded him that soon was nearly a year

56

away. Children have no real sense of time. I had to keep interrupting my conversation with Disha to tell them to chill out, and it was a v important one. (Disha managed to get the information that Catriona Hendley used to live across the road from Elvin, so that's how they know each other—I'm not sure if I think this is good news or bad news.) I had to tell the twins to be quiet so many times that in the end Disha said she'd rather have a bath than listen to me screaming at Shane and Shaun, so we just hung up.

Rang Sara Dancer. Now she's having third thoughts. She says she's going to have to have sex sometime, so why not now? And also she says it's like putting off a haircut. I don't think so. There's nothing even remotely romantic about having your hair cut. Sara says maybe she'll meet somebody Saturday night. She's going to a party.

The MC was polishing off a bottle of wine when I got home. (On top of **EVERYTHING,** now she's started drinking as well! I don't know why, but it irritates me when she gets really inebriated.) First she told me what time it was and that these late nights had better not affect my schoolwork. Then she wanted to know where Mrs. Kennedy went tonight. Doesn't she know they have pubs and cinemas in London and she doesn't have to go to Bristol for a drink after her computer class? I felt like telling her to get herself on Prozac **IMMEDIATELY.**

It's bad enough she's always on at me, but extending her attacks to the neighbors can't be a good sign.

FRIDAY 26 JANUARY

I had a nightmare last night that Johnny Depp was my brother and Catriona Hendley was going out with him. Every time I turned a corner, there they were frantically exchanging saliva and flu germs. It was so scary, it woke me up. On the other side of love, the Mad Cow and Sigmund were shrieking at each other in the kitchen. You'd think they were trying to wake the dead the way they were carrying on. I wish they'd go back to just ignoring each other like they usually do. It was two in the morning, for God's sake! I mean, **REALLY**! One minute she's angry with poor Mrs. Kennedy for staying out after her class and ruining my sleep, and the next she's started World War III practically next door to my room! And also they're always telling me I never think about anyone else! I got my Discman and plugged myself in so I could get some sleep.

Tomorrow Disha's going with me to the yoga center to buy a mat so I don't slip over again. I have to pay for it myself, of course. Sigmund wouldn't give me the money because he says it'll just wind up with a bunch of plants on top of it like the piano. The Mad Cow can usually be

worn down eventually, but she wouldn't cough up either
this time. She says she paid for the leotard and the
leggings, and that was enough. What did I think she
was—MADE OF MONEY? I'm beginning to think
she's made of toxic waste. I wonder if I should suggest
hormone replacement therapy.

SATURDAY 27 JANUARY

OH MY GOD!!! YOU ARE NOT GOING TO
BELIEVE THIS!!! Disha and I were coming out of the
yoga center with my new mat (lilac because they didn't
have black) and a Tibetan meditation CD (to help me get
in the right mood, which is v important) when, as if
drawn by the invisible forces of the universe, we happened
to glance through the window of the veggie café next
door. Sitting right in the middle of the room was Elvin.
I was struck anew by how excruciatingly attractive he is.
(I'm amazed it never really hit me before.) I swear, my
heart LITERALLY skipped a beat (a sure sign of the first
stirrings of *Passion*). And then my heart hit my kneecaps
when I saw who was sitting with him. You could have
knocked me over with a crisp wrapper. OH YES!!! None
other than Catriona Hendley. She's like a germ the way she
gets everywhere. Elvin and the Hendley were eating salads
and having a v intense conversation. At least she was. She

was leaning over so much she was practically in his lap! (It's just as well she doesn't have boobs or she would've suffocated him.) And then it hit me! Elvin and the Hendley have something in common besides being ex-neighbors! Everybody at school knows Catriona Hendley is the biggest vegetarian since the cow because she's always banging on about it (you'd think she'd invented it, the way she goes on). But I'd no idea about Elvin. I could see it all clearly. Catriona was trying to worm her way into Elvin's life through lettuce and herbal teas. I asked Disha why she hadn't told me about Elvin being a **VEGETARIAN** Serious Filmmaker, and she said that since she didn't hang around trying to see Elvin eat, she couldn't possibly know a thing like that, could she? She said she didn't think it was important anyway. (I'd like to know what she thinks *is* important!)

Nobody else at home tonight. Justin sloped off as soon as he'd stuffed his face, and then a while later Sigmund and the Mad Cow rushed off shouting at each other. Isn't life ironic? If I'd known I was going to have the flat to myself, I'd've stayed home and enjoyed the luxury of all the peace and quiet, but I'd already planned to go over to Disha's. So, to take some advantage of this *Gift from the Gods*, I helped myself to some of the politically correct bath oil Sappho gave the Mad Cow for the winter solstice (which is tested on nothing except chemists and is more expensive than plastic surgery) and had a long soak before I went. (Can you believe how childish my mother is? She hid the bath oil behind the tinned vegetables because she thought I'd never find it there!) The bath was bliss! Oh, how I long to live on my own! When I can't sleep and I don't feel like a *Romantic Fantasy,* I plan my entire flat. I choose the furniture and the kitchen units, everything. I even plan dinner parties.

SUNDAY 28 JANUARY

Desperate times call for desperate measures, and if starting to *Fall in Love* with someone who is being stalked by Catriona Hendley isn't desperate times I don't know what is. So even though the book says that constructive spells (like making someone have a hormone rush every time he sees you) should be made during a full moon, I called an **Exploring Other Dimensions Night** last night. It was a new moon, so I decided to think laterally the way Sigmund is always telling me to. I reckoned we could trick the Other Dimensions into thinking there was moonlight. We rounded up every candle we could find (including a Frosty the Snowman one left from Christmas, a pack of birthday candles, and Calum's skull candle, which he wouldn't be needing since he wasn't home). Then we waited till Disha's parents went to bed so we didn't have to worry about being interrupted. That got us to one in the morning. Disha's mother is a phenomenal snorer (MUCH worse than Sigmund). Her snores are to ordinary snores what a nuclear bomb is to a slingshot. We left the transom over Disha's door open, and as soon as we could hear the earth-shaking snorts and wheezes that meant Mrs. Paski had passed out, Disha started lighting the candles while I started lighting the incense. The candles were going out as fast as she was lighting them, so we shut the window (Disha's father believes in AIR the way my father believes in Freud). Her room looked well wicked when we were done. Holding hands, we sat in the middle of the floor with our eyes closed. I started the incantation. "Pray to the moon when she is round—" But I didn't get any further, because Disha told me to be quiet and listen. I didn't hear anything. Disha said that was exactly what she meant. Her mother had stopped snoring! Disha has a more pessimistic nature than I do. She immediately decided that this meant her mother was getting out of bed to come and check on us. I said not necessarily (if I didn't have such an *Artistic Soul,* I might consider being a solicitor, since I also have a very logical mind). I said maybe Mr. Paski rolled her out of bed to shut her up. That's what the Mad Cow used to do to Sigmund (though lately she just makes him sleep on the couch, which is pretty bloody inconvenient if you want to sit up late watching a film).

Anyway, Disha started blowing out the candles in a frantic sort of way. We just got them all out when a sound even more horrific than Mrs. Paski's snoring shattered the peaceful silence of the night. Disha clutched my hand. Her palms were already sweating. "Oh my God!" she whispered. "We're being burgled." I told her that it definitely wasn't the house alarm. I'm an authority on house alarms. Ours was always going off till Sigmund ripped it out in a fit of temper, so I know what they sound like. This was more like an air raid siren. It wasn't easy getting to the light switch because of all the candles. Every time we took a step we knocked another one over. We were still groping around in the dark when Mr. Paski started running through the hallway shouting, "Fire! Fire! Everybody get out of the house!" We didn't need to be told twice. I once put the iron on my hand (I was thinking of something and wasn't looking), and Disha once set her shirt on fire with a candle, so we both knew the agony of burning flesh. We trampled over the candles and hurled ourselves through the door. Mrs. Paski had a blanket over her shoulders and a pair of high heels on her feet, but Mr. Paski was just wearing pajama bottoms, a ratty old Pink Floyd T-shirt, and one sock (God knows what he'd been up to!). We all ran into the road to wait for the fire engine. Every time we heard a siren, Mr. Paski shouted, "There they are!" But they weren't. Disha wanted to go back inside to save her new leather jacket, but her mother wouldn't let her. There was a bit of an argument about that, but then Mr. Paski started ranting and everyone finally shut up.

After a while Mrs. Paski said she didn't see any smoke. Mr. Paski told her that was the most dangerous kind of fire, the kind without smoke. Mrs. Paski pulled her blanket tighter and sniffed. She didn't smell smoke either. Mr. Paski said he smelled smoke. He asked me and Disha if we smelled smoke, and we said we guessed so since agreeing was a lot easier than disagreeing. Mr. Paski started standing on one foot. I wondered if he'd ever done yoga. After another while, one of the neighbors poked his head out of an upstairs window. Mr. Paski explained about the fire. The fire engine was there in minutes. Apparently, in all the confusion, neither of the parent Paskis thought of actually ringing the fire department!!! By then half the road was out on the street. Disha and I were just about to go next door for a cup of tea when a fireman came out of the Paskis' with Frosty in one hand and the skull in the other. Apparently the smoke from all the candles set off the alarm in the hall. Mrs. Paski mumbled something, and then she started laughing. Mr. Paski didn't laugh. (He didn't laugh later either, though Disha and I did.) Mrs. Paski told him to look on the bright side. If Calum had been home, he would have been filming the whole thing.

The MC and Sigmund weren't laughing either when I got home. Nobody told me, of course, but Nan broke her elbow falling off a bus yesterday. Apparently that's where they went rushing off to last night—the hospital. They had to put a pin in her elbow to hold it together. I didn't quite get the whole story. Sigmund and the Mad Cow were busy moving their stuff out of their bedroom so

Nan could sleep in there, so all I got was a garbled account from Nan. She kept laughing and saying I should've seen the other guy (I presume she meant the pavement). They must've given her some heavy drugs for the operation. The major part of the story is that Nan has moved in with us until her elbow's healed enough for her to be on her own (which could take MONTHS considering how old she is). Her arm's all wrapped up in plastic like a hunk of meat. It looks really GROSS. Sigmund's wigged out completely. "Is this what Jesus would do if He broke His elbow?" he kept asking. "Move in with His son?" I hope he remembers this when he's old and feeble and wants to move in with me!

MONDAY 29 JANUARY

Sara Dancer's father twisted his ankle on Saturday night so Sara stayed home to look after him instead of going to the party. I think this may be an excuse. It's only an ankle, for God's sake.

Back in the land of the sexless, there was so much trauma at home last night because of Nan (Sigmund and the Mad Cow are both sleeping on the couch now, which is not exactly an optimum situation) that I forgot all about doing

65

my spell again until I was getting ready for bed. It was raining, so I reckoned it didn't matter if the moon was full or not. I mean, who's going to see it anyway? I lit some candles and sat cross-legged on my bed in my underwear so I'd be more in touch with my primitive self. I closed my eyes and REALLY concentrated. At first I had to keep checking to make sure I was saying it right, but after a while I started to get into it. I swear I could feel the **Spirit of the Female Goddess** filling my room. I started rocking gently back and forth and chanting, "Queen of the Moon . . . Queen of the Sun . . . Queen of the Heavens . . . Queen of the Stars . . ." (I didn't plan to do this. It just happened! It was well wicked!!!) I forgot about who I was, and where I was. I was an Aztec maiden or an ancient druid. I was drifting in the cosmos like a particle of light, unfettered by the chains of the material world. At least I was until Nan screamed, "Praise be to Jesus! It's the devil's spawn!" I came back to Earth pretty sharply at that. My first real spell and I had a manifestation! The devil's spawn! How brilliant can you get? I opened my eyes, shouting, "Where? Where's the devil's spawn?" Turns out there wasn't any manifestation—Nan was actually talking about me! Can you believe it? Her own flesh and blood! I was well disappointed. It took EONS to calm her down (it's a good thing I wasn't naked). The Mad Cow put a sign on the bathroom door that says BATHROOM in case Nan gets confused again. I demanded that the lock on my door is fixed, but Sigmund isn't having it. He gave me twenty excruciatingly boring minutes on why he doesn't believe in locks (he doesn't know how to fix them himself and he's too cheap to pay someone else to do it is why).

TUESDAY 30 JANUARY

Late again for school. Mr. Wilkins gave me another detention. (According to the papers, teachers are leaving the profession **IN DROVES,** but not Mr. Wilkins, of course. Probably he knows he'd never get another job.)

Disha discreetly pumped Calum for more information on Elvin. (There's not a doubt in my mind that Disha is my cosmic sister. I know in my *Soul* it's no coincidence that we were born in the same year, in the same borough of the same city, and go to the same school.) Anyway, besides being a veggie, Elvin (according to Calum) is very concerned about the state of the planet. He feels filmmakers have a responsibility to show the world as it really is and to help protect it (so at least there's no danger that if I do *Fall Madly in Love* with him he'll go running off to Hollywood). Elvin's anti-hunt, anti-vivisection, and anti-international globalism (he's anti so much that even Sappho would approve). I asked Disha what international globalism was, since it's one of those terms that everybody uses but no one ever explains. I thought it might have something to do with the age of communication and being able to e-mail anywhere in the world in a second, but Disha said it had something to do with those riots they have every spring. So she isn't sure either. But whatever it is, Elvin was nearly arrested outside McDonald's at the riots last year. No wonder Catriona Hendley's after him. She's always protesting about something. She's practically London's answer to Joan of Arc. Besides all that, Elvin's taking some sort of Eastern martial arts course (for the philosophy, not the ability to break a brick wall with one hand, of course), but Disha couldn't remember which one. And also his star sign's Leo. I don't know anything about Leo. I'll have to ask Sappho.

The police were round at ours when I finally got home this afternoon! At first I thought they must be looking for Justin, but they were there to talk to Nan. Apparently she didn't fall off the bus; she jumped after some guy who'd grabbed her bag. She downed him, but he got away (*sans* said bag). The police were v impressed with her quickness of mind and body. Nan said it was the way she was trained in the war. She's obviously still suffering from the drugs.

GET THIS!!! Geek Boy overheard me telling Disha about the police and everything, and he said Nan REALLY WAS in the war. I said right, in an air raid shelter (which D thought was v funny), but Justin said no, not in an air raid shelter, in France! He said she was some sort of spy. Disha and I nearly choked, we were laughing so much,

68

but later I asked Sigmund and he backed Justin's story. He said not only did they give her a medal for bravery, but I'd seen it at least a million times because it's up on her mantelpiece, next to Grandad's ashes. So then I asked the MC, because although she has a lot of faults, winding me up isn't one of them. Plus she doesn't have a sense of humor. The MC said if I visited Earth more often, I might have some idea of what was going on around me. Which I took to be confirmation of Justin's story. My grandmother the spy. I REALLY can't believe it. The MC said that's because I think Nan was born OLD, which she wasn't. I said did she mean unlike her, and she said she took it back; I should stay on my own planet or she might have to kill me. Didn't I say she has no sense of humor?

WEDNESDAY 31 JANUARY

The Mad Cow was in a prize bitch mood this morning. If she got paid by the moan, she'd be a millionaire. All I did was ask where my black trouser-skirt was and she went mad. "I'm not your skivvy, young lady! If you want it washed, get off your bum and wash it yourself!" Justin shuffled in right then, asking about breakfast (one of the few verbal communications he can be relied on to make), and she rounded on him for a change. She told him he could do his own laundry from now on too. (How unfair is that? He only changes once every couple of weeks, whereas I change at least twice a day!) After that I didn't feel much like eating, so I made my escape. I was **HOURS** early, of course. It would've served the MC right if I'd been raped by some drug-crazed psychopath on his way home from a night of carnage. That's what I was thinking as I turned into the road the school's on. I was imagining my mother weeping on television, begging the nation to tell the police if they knew anything that could lead to the arrest of the heartless killer of her only daughter. I was practically crying myself. And what happened next? All of a sudden I heard a mobe go off behind me. It was playing the *Star Wars* theme song. The *Star Wars* theme song is definitely not something you'd expect a normal person to have on their mobe. It really took me by surprise, but I managed to calm myself down. (Psychopaths are like dogs—they can smell fear.) Besides, I was fairly certain a drug-crazed psychopath wouldn't remember to take his mobe with him. I mean, who would he call? Psychopaths don't have friends. And even if he did, what would he say? "Hi, I'm on the street and I'm just about to attack this attractive young woman with a bum like Jennifer Lopez's who's walking on her own." I looked round. It wasn't a mobe. It was a high-tech bicycle bell. And on the bicycle (which was also high-tech) was **ELVIN**!!! Electricity shot through me as if I were a metal pole (the metal pole of *Love*!). I couldn't believe it! What was he doing here?

70

What if I hadn't left early? What if I'd been **LATE**? I half expected Catriona Hendley to drop out of a tree and ruin it all.

Elvin said, "Hi. It's Jan, isn't it?" I admitted to being Jan. He got off and walked the rest of the way with me. He was meeting Calum to give him something before school. I mentioned that Disha and I saw him in the café on Saturday, and he said we should have come in and said hello, so I explained that we were just going to our yoga class and didn't have time. He said he'd always been interested in yoga. I said it had changed my life. I told him we went into the café a lot (which is a slight exaggeration, but we do pass it quite often on our way to the video shop). I said we went there after our yoga class for herbal tea and stuff like that because there aren't that many places that cater for veggies. He said he didn't know I was a vegetarian too. I am now.

Bought a lock for my bedroom on the way home. If I'm going to really get into my yoga, I can't live in fear that Justin's going to burst in to take more photos. It destroys my concentration.

Disha asked Calum if he met up with Elvin this morning, and Calum didn't know what she was on about. So Detectives Bandry and Paski now know that meeting

Calum was just a feeble excuse. Elvin was there to see ME! I actually TINGLE when I think of it.

THURSDAY 1 FEBRUARY

I made my announcement about turning veggie at supper tonight (last night we had sausages, which is one of the few things the MC can actually cook properly, so I reckoned I might as well have one last meal as a meat eater). As per usual, I had to wait for Sigmund and his wife to finish their argument, but as soon as they took a break I pushed my plate away and went for it. "I can't eat this," I said. The Mad Cow turned her venomous gaze on me and wanted to know why not. Justin said he'd have it. Sigmund didn't say anything, because he'd already stormed off to go to one of his groups (Sigmund's got more groups than Columbia Records). I explained that I had become a vegetarian and would only be eating fish, chicken, and soya burgers from now on. "And you'll be cooking them yourself too," mooed the Mad Cow. "I'm not making special meals for *you*." I pointed out that her sister, Sappho, was a VEGAN and she didn't have to cook her own meals when she came round. The Mad Cow said I could go and live with her. And they talk about teenagers having attitude!

*　　*　　*

I was going to mention to Mrs. Kennedy that the twins have been a little overactive lately. But I never got the chance. As per usual, she was flapping all over the place getting ready and banging on about what a great person Sigmund is and how lucky I am to have him as my father. I always agree. I see no reason to burst her bubble.

FRIDAY 2 FEBRUARY

Cinderella Bandry (that's ME) was fixing herself a veggie burger for supper tonight when the oven mitt caught on fire. I reacted immediately. (I was v impressed!) Without a second's hesitation, I swung around and hurled the mitt into the sink. This was obviously the most intelligent thing to do, but of course the Mad Cow was in my way and the mitt hit her instead. You'd think I'd shot her (and except for a little singed hair she wasn't even hurt). Now she's changed her mind about me cooking my own food. Didn't I say she's menopausal? What more proof do you need, I ask you? She's up one minute and down the next like an oil pump.

I think I'm starving in the clinical sense. The incident with the MC and the oven mitt distracted me so much that the burger got burned and all I had for supper was vegetables. It's like living on water. But I'm not giving up. The

Hendley has enough advantages with Elvin. I can't let her have that one too. And all I had last night was a cheese sandwich. I had to stop at McDonald's on the way to school this morning, I was feeling so faint. I ate two boxes of those chicken things (I couldn't eat duck—you know, because ducks are so cute—but chickens aren't very attractive so I reckon they're all right). But coming home on the bus tonight was this depressed-looking giant chicken (wearing Reeboks), and I wondered if it was some sort of sign and started feeling guilty.

Disha says she was once given a bag of baby carrots by a giant rabbit on Parkway. She says he was really grubby and there was even a stain on one of his ears. She threw the carrots away.

SATURDAY 3 FEBRUARY

Sigmund thinks my decision to show respect for other animals and turn veggie is the sign he's been waiting for that I'm not just getting older; I'm growing up as well. He's delighted to see me thinking for myself and accepting responsibility for my own life. (I don't understand why he sounded so surprised.) Then he said that at least I was doing better than the "bloody government." I bet the bloody government isn't as hungry as I am though. I finished off the shepherd's pie Mrs. Kennedy left for the twins' supper on Thursday before I remembered about being a vegetarian. I reckon it's all right though, because she used mince and that doesn't really count as meat either.

Disha said the giant chicken wasn't a cosmic sign. She said he stands in front of that new chicken restaurant, handing out flyers. I said I didn't think he really was a chicken (he was wearing trainers!); I just thought maybe the universe was trying to make me feel bad by putting him on my bus. Disha said he was just going to work. Which is probably why he looked depressed. I thought about that, and I can definitely understand it. What must it be like, getting up every morning and putting on this bright yellow chicken suit, knowing tomorrow you're going to get up and do the same thing, and the next day, and the day after that . . . maybe for your whole life? (And I bet he's paid chicken feed!) I will never take a job as a giant chicken, no matter how desperate I am for cash.

Sappho came over this afternoon with her new girlfriend, Mags (she seems nice), and a Congratulations on Becoming a Vegetarian present for me. I was braced for some more feminist propaganda (never mind the winter solstice, for my birthday she gave me this huge book on the history of the suffragettes—she couldn't expect me to read it, so I reckoned I was meant to use it as a weapon), but what it was was this excruciatingly cool pair of purple combat trousers. Sappho said that every woman should own a pair, since they're in combat most of their lives. I would've liked them a teeny bit darker, but last time I commented on something Sappho gave me, she took it back, so I kept quiet. I think Mags must be a mellowing influence on Sappho.

Nan and Sappho are usually kept pretty much apart, because Nan thinks lesbians are really un-Christian, and she made sure Sappho knew how she felt right from the first time they met, which was at the parents' wedding. On that first, historic occasion, Sappho got melodramatic and stopped the band in midsong by loudly demanding to know why it was all right for Jesus to hang out with whores but not with gay people. On this occasion, however, Nan got a lot of sympathy from Mags for her broken arm, which kept her happy. And even Sappho was impressed with Nan's story (**HORRIBLY EXAGGERATED,** of course) of how she nearly caught the perpetrator because of her training in the war. Sappho said Nan was a closet feminist, and even Nan laughed.

So anyway, we got through giving me my present and showing Mags the flat without too much trauma. But as soon as we sat down for tea Sappho started banging on about female sexuality (not that anybody asked). It was so très boring. Especially if you've heard it all about six million times before. I was practically asleep when Nan suddenly shot to her feet, shouting, "I never had one of those things, and it didn't do me any harm!" It was pretty dramatic, with the sling and all. I had no idea what "things" she was talking about, but she definitely had my attention. Sappho put on her best professor of women's studies voice and said, "Mrs. Bandry, are you saying you've never had an orgasm?" This is not a word I've ever heard spoken aloud in our kitchen before. (In fact, I reckon it's not something that's happened very often in our house. If ever. The only sounds I've ever heard from the parents at night are either arguments or Sigmund's snores.) I wasn't alone. The Mad Cow spat the biscuit she was chewing right across the table. I thought she was going to choke to death. Mags asked if anybody wanted more tea.

SUNDAY 4 FEBRUARY

Disha and I went to Camden Market this afternoon. I got my nose pierced! I've been thinking about it for **EONS** and today I just went for it. Never mind the pain or possible disfigurement. (Even Catriona Hendley doesn't have her nose pierced!) Disha isn't sure how she feels about self-mutilation, so she just got two more holes put in each ear. We spent hours wandering around the market. It was well cool (aside from all the wicked clothes, we saw someone throwing up outside a pub, and someone else being dragged off by the police). I bought this Chinese skirt and these really cheap wind chimes (they're meant to be very calming, and with Nan in the flat I need all the calm I can get, so I bought three). Disha left me on my own while she went to get some fried noodles since I'm back on my diet today. Even though I don't eat ANYTHING now that I'm a vegetarian I seem to have gained two pounds! (D says if crisps were made of pork I'd be all right.) Anyway, I was looking at the bowls on one of the stalls when the bloke said to me, "So what do you like?" I said I thought the blue fish bowl was nice, and he said that wasn't what he meant. I don't know why I always smile when someone says something I don't understand, but that's what I do. He smiled back. "Well?" he said. "Eees . . . weed. . . ? Maybe a hip girl like you wants something a little more exotic. . . ?" I couldn't believe it! It must be the nose ring. No adult has ever tried to sell me drugs before. Disha was furious that she missed it!

The only member of my family who noticed my nose ring was Nan. She thought I'd joined a pagan cult. She said she'd always known something like this would happen. Sigmund told her to put a sock in it; it was only a ring. And then all of a sudden Justin decided to join in. He wanted to know if I realized that the nose ring was a symbol of slavery and servitude. For cows and pigs, I said. Justin said for women too. Traditionally, if a woman wears a nose ring it means she's owned by a man. I said it was

78

no such thing; it was a fashion statement. He said I'd be having myself circumcised next. (See what I mean by stupid? It's boys who get circumcised! Everybody knows that!) If you ask me, his parents should have thought about how their son would be affected by the ravings of a militant feminist during his formative years.

MONDAY 5 FEBRUARY

I couldn't believe it! I came out of art with Marcus and there was Elvin! As soon as I spotted him, I started laughing, even though Marcus wasn't saying anything funny. It was brilliant! Elvin looked well surprised. He'd come to see Mr. Belakis. (I can't believe Disha didn't find out that Elvin used to go to our school! She said I could have asked him that myself when I was talking to him the other day. Always an excuse!) Marcus wanted me to go to the high street with him, but I said I had things to do after school.

Later, I came out of the library just as Elvin walked past on his way out. I said I thought he'd be on his bike, and he said he wished that he was. He said it was the only way to travel in London, and I said too right. So when he asked me if I had a bike I automatically said yes (not a total lie— I used to have one; I just haven't had one for a while).

And **GUESS WHAT**? He asked me if I wanted to go riding on the heath with him sometime! Do leaves grow on trees? I don't remember much after that, although I'm sure everything he said was v intelligent and witty. I know it sounds weird, but I almost wished he hadn't got on my bus. I really wanted to ring D and tell her all about it and everything he said, etc. But then he said he was dropping by Catriona's on his way home, and straightaway I wished he wouldn't get off.

You're not going to believe this, but Sappho says women *can* be circumcised! I said but we don't have a penis, and she said, "You really do live on your own planet, don't you?" (Ha-ha-ha, right? You can see why no one's ever accused feminists of having a great sense of humor.) I said well, we don't have penises, and she said maybe it would do me some good to pay some attention when people are talking to me now and then. Phoned Disha and she didn't know women could be circumcised either.

TUESDAY 6 FEBRUARY

Because I made One Little Comment about the nut cutlets she fed me last night (and they really did taste like cardboard), the Mad Cow went into one of her **MEGA** mood swings. After she calmed down she gave me thirty quid to buy myself some vegetarian food. I said I didn't know why she couldn't just pick up stuff for me when she's doing the carnivores' shopping and she said she has enough to do without trying to guess what I want to eat. Is that **LAZY** or what?

Disha went shopping with me after school. Neither of us has been in a supermarket for **EONS**. It was pretty horrifying. Not only is it as big as an airport terminal, but it was **ABSOLUTELY PACKED** with shoppers! Disha said you'd think they were giving the food away. We couldn't work out where all these people came from. Don't they have jobs? Don't they have lives? There's practically a whole aisle for crisps, a whole aisle for sweets, another aisle for biscuits, and yet another aisle for breakfast cereals. No wonder the Mad Cow spends hours getting the groceries. Disha said if she had to do the food shopping she'd probably spend the rest of her life trying to decide which packet of rice to buy. It took us an hour just to find where they hide the vegetarian stuff. After that it was easy since they hardly have anything. They've got more varieties of pizza than vegetarian meals. Then we had to queue for another eon. And what thanks do I get for wasting precious hours of my life doing the Mad Cow's job for her? **NONE!!!** She was all pissed off because I didn't bring back any change! I really should have a word with

Sigmund about getting her on hormone replacement therapy. That or Prozac. I don't see how I can be expected to live with her lack of rational thought.

WEDNESDAY 7 FEBRUARY

I think Marcus thinks I like him (well, I do like him, but at the moment I'm not sure how much). Marcus, David, Sara, Lila, Nick, Disha, and me all went down to McDonald's after school (I had the fish thing, of course). We were sitting by the window when who did I see coming out of the video shop across the road? Calum and **ELVIN**! I wasn't sure what Elvin was doing outside McDonald's last spring that nearly got him busted, but I was pretty sure he wasn't queuing. And all of a sudden it hit me that I probably didn't want him to see *me* in McDonald's, even if I wasn't eating a hamburger. So I ducked under the table. Marcus (who was sitting next to me) looked down and asked me what I was doing. What I was doing at that very moment was kneeling in some ketchup trying to unhook my nose ring from his trousers without unhooking my nose as well. I didn't want to explain about Elvin, so I just said the first thing that came into my head. Which was that I wanted to give him a foot massage. And he said, "Why don't you come back to mine and give it to me there?" in a v suggestive way. I hope his mother can get the blood out of his khakis.

Revolting glop is oozing from the hole in my nose. I don't think this can be right. I just hope I don't have to be rushed to emergency in the middle of the night.

THURSDAY 8 FEBRUARY

TOTAL HUMILIATION! And it's all Mrs. Wist's fault. It was pissing down, so we got to stay in and play volleyball. What a treat! I told the old bag I was feeling crampy and wanted to go and get a pad, just in case, but she wouldn't let me leave the class. "I thought you had terminal cramps last week, Janet. How can you be getting your period *again*?" She was well sarky. Catriona Hendley laughed louder than anybody else. (Disha says I should've said that I was afraid of getting hit on the nose by the ball. Which would have been true. It already hurts like hell.) Anyway, I said that last week's cramps were a false alarm, but she wasn't having any of it. Mrs. Wist forced me to play, and of course I started bleeding like I'd been stabbed—right in the middle of the game. It was so gross! Blood was dripping down my leg. Everybody started shrieking. You'd think that with PE being the last class of the day, Mrs. Wist would have let me go home after that, to avoid the rush, but **OH NO,** she let me go and get a pad and clean up and all, but then she made me stay right to the gruesome end. I didn't want to go on the bus because I was feeling really stressed by then, so I went to Disha's to call the Mad Cow to come and get me. And who do you think was sitting in the kitchen, eating a cheese sandwich? Elvin! Who else? Of all the billions and billions of people in the world—many of whom I wouldn't mind seeing me traumatized and smelling like something slaughtered—it had to be him. I would've swooned, but I was on automatic panic. This was my big chance! My chance to sit down and have a cheese sandwich with one of the most desirable men in London while we discussed the merits of being vegetarian. Only I Couldn't Take It because I felt so gross. I didn't even say hello. I just turned straight round and collided with Disha. I nearly trampled her getting out of the room. What a day!!!

Three Reasons Why Disha Paski's *My Best Friend:*
(1) She's intelligent and loyal.
(2) We're into all the same things.
(3) Disha told Elvin that the reason I ran off like that yesterday was because I suddenly remembered it was the afternoon I worked in the local Oxfam shop. It was a pretty brilliant lie. She said he was suitably impressed, being the serious sort. I just hope he never asks me where the shop I work in is, since I haven't a clue. Except for

when the MC used to take me to charity shops when I was little and didn't know any better, I've never been to one in my life. They smell. And also Siranee's sister's friend got bugs from a secondhand jumper once.

FRIDAY 9 FEBRUARY

I think I may start keeping a list of Most Unromantic Sexual Encounters. Forget the garden shed and the back of a car. Boris Becker knocked up some model in a broom cupboard. I couldn't believe it either, but it was on the radio so it must be true. He was in some well posh Japanese restaurant, and between courses or something he followed this model into the cupboard, and nine months later he's a dad. Boris Becker! He's always dressed in white, so you sort of think of him as a good guy. I'm beginning to think that if you're going to have a role model you should probably pick someone who's already dead so they can't disappoint you. Disha says not to forget President Clinton when I start my list. She says she knows power's meant to be a turn-on, but she doesn't think the Oval Office with armed guards outside and all those phones would put her in the mood.

Lila's parents are going away for a romantic weekend so Lila's decided to have a valentine party tomorrow night, despite what happened last time. I wish Sigmund and the

Mad Cow would go away for a **LONG** romantic weekend, but even if they weren't **AT WAR** and might possibly do such a thing, they'd have to take Nan with them, so there's no use hoping. Marcus asked me if I was going to Lila's and I said yes, of course—even though I have **NOTHING** to wear. He's going to pick me up so we can walk over together. I said that was great. I told Disha to meet us at mine.

Disha's had a **BRILLIANT** idea! She thinks I should send Catriona Hendley a valentine and make her think it's from David. Lila, who's a v good friend of Catriona's, told Disha that Catriona used to have the hots for David, but even though he hangs out with her a lot (because her parents own a heated pool and a snooker table!), he's never asked her out. That should take Catriona's mind off Elvin for a bit. Disha said what we should do is write a D on the card, and then partly cover it over with a sticker so it looks like he started to sign it and then tried to hide it. Then she said we should send David one from Catriona too. Disha shows a remarkable talent for subterfuge.

Even though my nose still looks a bit red and has a tendency to leak, I went over to Disha's this afternoon because Elvin was going to be there. I was very cool. This time I didn't run out of the kitchen; this time I sat down. Elvin and Calum are going to make a film together, probably in the summer if everything works out right.

86

(Apparently there's much more to making a movie than putting film in the camera.) They talked a lot about it. I think it's sort of a documentary about people. We fixed toasted cheese sandwiches. Elvin and I made a great deal of eye contact. He even asked me a couple of questions: why I became a vegetarian, what my favorite subject is, and if I have a brother (because the meat industry is irresponsible and motivated only by profit, which is what Sappho always says; art and English, but I wish we had a film course; and, yes). He said he thought he'd heard of my brother. I told him that was virtually impossible. I'm well chuffed that I had the sense to hide in McDonald's, even though I have no idea how to get ketchup out of my combat trousers.

David rang for a chat. As you know, I usually flirt with David, but I was still thinking about Elvin and didn't have the energy. It's funny, isn't it? When you have no single object of your desire, you can flirt with anyone, but as soon as your heart begins to yearn to see that one face, you lose interest in the others. At least that's the way it is for me. And also my nose really hurts. You don't feel like flirting when your nose really hurts.

SATURDAY 10 FEBRUARY

Went shopping with Disha this afternoon. She wanted to
get something to go with her red skirt for the party tonight
(we reckon we can be exempt from the DP just this once—
after all, even Great Artists and Writers do *Fall in Love*,
even if it's only **TRAGICALLY**). I, of course, could buy
NOTHING. I have to save all my money for a bike, and
no one else would give me any. (Not even Justin. He's left
the photos of Jocelyn and Robert Bandry sleeping at
Andrew's, so it's my word against his.) I offered to do
errands for Nan for a nominal charge, and she accused me
of being worse than a moneychanger in a temple. I even
tried to borrow a tenner from Justin, but he wasn't having
it either. He said that I still owed him fifty quid from the
summer. I pointed out that I'd only borrowed a fiver that
time. He said it was fifty quid with interest. (Rest assured,
the skies over London will be choked with pigs before he
sees any of that!!!) Anyway, Disha and I went to the West
End. I was so distraught over my poverty that I forgot to
bring my mobe and Disha's was at home charging, so she
had to use a phone box to ring her mother and find out
what it was she was meant to pick up for her. You couldn't
even see out of the box, there were so many cards plastered
all over the glass. And they're not like minicab cards (you
know, name, phone number, and maybe a drawing of a
car). They're full-color photographs with whips and stuff

like that. Disha said she doesn't know why they bother putting porn magazines on the top shelf of the news agent's when the phone boxes are wallpapered with the same sorts of pictures. She said Sappho must never come to the West End, because if she did there wouldn't be a box left standing. I asked Disha if she thought they were **ALL** prostitutes, or if some of them really were masseuses and personal trainers. Disha said she hoped I was joking. It was just that there seemed to be **SO MANY**. Disha said well, there would be, wouldn't there? You don't need any qualifications, you make more than you would working in Woolworth's, and you don't have to pay tax. All you have to worry about is not catching some fatal disease or being beaten up or murdered. I think prostitution in general has to go on my Most Unromantic Sexual Encounters list. It makes the giant chicken job look good if you ask me. There's obviously a lot more to sex than you'd think. Or a lot less.

Walked past a bike shop on the way home. I couldn't believe the prices! I could buy a motorized scooter for that! Disha said I should look for a secondhand one in Loot.

When Sigmund saw the hole in my door where I tried to put on the lock, he lost it completely, as per usual. Yadda yadda yadda. It's hard to believe he gets paid to **LISTEN** to people. I've never heard him keep his mouth shut for more than two seconds. He says I've **TOTALLY** ruined the door and that now he'll have to get a new one—and God Knows How Much That's Going to Cost. I said to make sure he got one with a lock.

I practically rubbed my fingers to the bone trying to get the ketchup out of my new trousers, but you can still see it, so I bought a bottle of black dye to hide the stain. It looks pretty easy. You just dump it all in the washing machine.

SUNDAY 11 FEBRUARY

Marcus was late picking us up last night, which was just as well since I had to change **FIVE** times before I found something presentable to wear. I tried on the Chinese skirt I got in the market, but it must've shrunk or something because it was too tight. Ditto my pink Lycra. Even Disha said I looked like an overstuffed sausage. I can't possibly be gaining weight, even though I'm not **STRICTLY** on my diet anymore because I don't really eat anything but vegetables. Finally remembered the MC's black silk skirt (mercifully she was out), which is both casual and sophisticated and went **PERFECTLY** with the bat top.

When Marcus arrived he was wearing a pink bow tie and carrying a single red rose. (Even Disha said he looked pretty good.) I acted overwhelmed. "For ME?!! Oh, you shouldn't have!" He said, "Sweets for the sweet; roses for the thorny." (He can be pretty funny.) Marcus said that if he'd known he was escorting two devastatingly beautiful women to Lila's and not just one he would've bought another rose. He reckoned he could've got a deal on two. We were just about to leave, when David turned up. (I forgot he also said he wanted to walk over with me.) David was wearing a red shirt (no tie), but he had a rose too (they must've been giving them away at the end of the road). I think he thought Marcus's rose was for Disha, because he whipped it out of my hand and thrust it at her. And then he gave me the one he'd brought.

It wasn't until we got to Lila's that I understood why I'd been SO PARTICULAR about what I was wearing. My psychic self must've been picking up messages from the Earth Goddess because guess who was already there when we arrived! Yes! Oh YES YES YES!!! Fate is with me! It was none other than Elvin Whatever-His-Name-Is. My heart did a double flip and the rest of the room faded around him. I was glad the lighting was low, because I could feel myself blushing (which is something I usually only do when I'm out in public with members of my family). Elvin was talking to Catriona. (Of course! She would've known he was going to be there, wouldn't she? She's not one to miss an opportunity! It doesn't even have to knock. She sees it coming, opens the door, and hauls it in.) There were a bunch of other people with them at the back of the room. I pretended not to see them and gave Marcus my jacket to stick in the bedroom. David said he'd do it, and whipped it out of Marcus's hands. Marcus snatched it back and marched off. Within seconds, Elvin was coming towards us (towards me!). I was practically *Swooning with Happiness,* but I didn't let it show. Still acting like I hadn't seen Elvin, I stood as close to David as I could without actually hugging him. (If a bloke's interested, he'll be even more interested if he thinks he's not the only one. I'm not sure where I read that, but Sara Dancer says it's true.) It sort of worked. It was definitely a V AWKWARD moment. Only it wasn't Elvin who started to bristle like a dog that's just seen another dog—it was David. I could feel him get taller. And then Marcus came back and latched himself on to my other side. I felt like I was wedged between two Roman columns or something. Elvin (being a sensitive Leo) must've realized that D and M were being all male territorial because I've been friends with them for so long, because after the usual friendly greetings, instead of bringing up the bike ride or anything like that, he asked me if Marcus was my brother! Marcus wanted to know if he *looked* like my brother, and Elvin said he wouldn't know since he's never met my brother. Elvin and I thought that was v funny. As soon as Elvin went back to Catriona and her motley crew, Marcus asked who he was. Then he mumbled something about Elvin always hanging around. Disha and I watched Catriona

and David (subtly, of course) to see if they made eye
contact or anything. **AND GUESS WHAT?** It was all
we could do not to laugh out loud! David kept looking
over at her so much that he barely kept up with the
conversation, and she cast more than one thoughtful look
his way too. I suppose it was just as well for everybody's
concentration that Elvin left early and Catriona left the
room (though not the building, sadly). But despite the fact
that Elvin left really early and I didn't get a chance to talk
to him again, I had a pretty good time. At Lila's Halloween
party the only person who danced with me was her cousin
from Glasgow, whose concept of dancing was to jump
straight up and down in the air like a Jack Russell. This
time, however, I had two boys to dance with—usually,
as it turned out, together. They're both **REALLY** good
dancers. I found it very exhausting, though, so when
Marcus went into his John Travolta routine, and then David
went into his, I slipped away and sat down. It took them
EONS to notice.

Mr. Burl next door was backing his scooter out of his front
garden as we got to my house. I closed the gate for him.
Then Marcus and David came in for a cup of tea. After they
left I told Disha how hostile Marcus and David were to
Elvin. Disha thinks they both thought they were going to
the party with me. I said she was mad. I'd remember if
one of them asked me out. Anyway, what about David
and Catriona? Their eyes were drawn to each other like

magnets. Disha said she'd forgotten about David and Catriona. So maybe it was just Marcus after all. D said it would serve me right for practically licking his boots in McDonald's the other day.

The Mad Cow's having dinner with Sappho and Mags, Sigmund's grouping (left-handed redheaded dyslexic unwed fathers with one blue eye probably), and Justin's gone out, leaving me grandmother-sitting, **AS PER USUAL**. Fortunately Nan's nodded off in front of the telly, so now's my chance to dye my combats without her telling me how Jesus would do it.

MONDAY 12 FEBRUARY

Found the roses Marcus and David brought under the table in the hall, still in their wrappers but already withered and dead. *Love* and Death. I reckon they're the two greatest themes in art and literature—as well as in life. And it made me realize how short life really is. We are all born to die (I don't know if some poet wrote that line before I did, but I think it's pretty good). At least the roses had their moments of beauty. (That's more than my mother ever had!) I took a couple of petals to press in my diary, and then I chucked them in the bin.

*   *   *

Last night I dreamed that I was at this barbecue (like in Texas or somewhere like that). There were whole cows turning over the coals. And you should've seen the burgers! They looked like meteors! I was sweating when I woke up. It's weeks since I became a vegetarian, and all I've had besides vegetables is fish and chicken (and that little bit of mince). And my parents think I don't stick to anything!

There must be something wrong with the washing machine. The combats didn't exactly come out the way I thought. The trousers are brilliant, but the stitching didn't take the dye, so I've got these really cool **BLACK** trousers with almost **WHITE** stitching. It is v passé. And not exactly my image.

TUESDAY 13 FEBRUARY

The Mad Cow nearly got arrested in the supermarket for nicking a birthday card that somebody left in her trolley (at least that's her story!!!). Apparently there was a **MEGA** scene with the manager, and **HUNDREDS** of shoppers were standing around watching. Sigmund said considering how much money she spends there each week they should be giving her **BOXES** of free cards, not persecuting her. The MC said it was nice of him to take her side for a change, and they nearly got into another row. (I'm beginning to think that rowing's what they do instead of having sex.) Justin said the MC was really unlucky to get the only conscious security guard in London. Nan said she should sue for defamation of character (which, let's face it, would be **REALLY** hard to prove). The MC says she can never go back there again, in case somebody recognizes her. I told her not to worry about that since nobody remembers what women her age look like. And then she got angry with **ME**!!! She says she hopes she's still alive when I'm her age so at least she can die laughing.

D reckons I can cover up the white stitching on the combats with a laundry marker. If you ask me, she should consider a career in fashion. She has a real talent.

VALENTINE'S DAY

To celebrate this day of *Love,* the boys who sit at the back in Mrs. Gumpta's maths class let loose a bunch of inflated rainbow-colored condoms while Mrs. G was writing on the board. She thought they were balloons. It was excruciatingly hilarious. Disha said you could bet that if we'd had Mr. Plaget, he would've known what they were!

I GOT MY FIRST VALENTINE! It was waiting for me when I got home this afternoon. It's one of those really naff ones with a red satin heart trimmed with lace. I love it! I put it on my bureau so the Mad Cow will see it when she patrols my room and know that someone loves me. That should wind her up. Here she is, finishing her life as a woman, and I'm just about to begin mine. Dare I hope that my secret valentine is Elvin? Was that moment when he smiled at me in Disha's kitchen the moment when he thought, I think I'm *Falling in Love* with Jan?

THURSDAY 15 FEBRUARY

So what's the **FIRST** thing I see when I get to school this morning? Nothing less than Catriona and David chatting nonchalantly just inside the gate!!! Were they discussing their valentine cards, one wonders? I gave them both a **BIG** greeting, and David got a distinctly pink tinge to his complexion, as though I'd come across them snogging or something. Naturally I acted like I didn't notice. David did eat lunch with us, but I'm sure it was just to divert suspicion. He was definitely preoccupied, and even though Marcus had the rest of us in stitches, David hardly cracked a smile.

Since no one sent her a valentine, the MC bought herself a bottle of sparkling chardonnay. It didn't help her mood any, though. She was all sarky because I was going to Mrs. Kennedy's (as per usual!) and wanted to know if The

Woman ever stayed home. I said what happened to Female
Solidarity and being supportive of single mothers? The MC
said maybe I should ask Mrs. Kennedy about Female
Solidarity. God knows what she was on about. She really is
gong through the CHANGE—from human to witch.

The MC must've gone round to Sappho's for more wine,
because she wasn't in the flat when I got home from Mrs.
Kennedy's. Nan was asleep at the kitchen table. She's not
getting older; she's turning into a cat. No matter where you
put her, she nods off. Even in the middle of supper (though
not before she's said grace)! Disha says it's better than her
grandmother. Her grandmother doesn't remember anything
unless it happened seventy years ago. She calls Disha Paula
and is always asking her if she liked the chocolates.

FRIDAY 16 FEBRUARY

Caught David and the Hendley with their heads together
in the library today!!! Made a point of going over to say
hello. Did David look **EMBARRASSED** or what? He
gave me some crap about history homework. Yeah, right.
Like I was born yesterday.

The Mad Cow had another **major trauma attack** tonight because
her whites came out gray. Sigmund and Justin had vanished,

as per usual, and Nan was passed out in front of the telly (also as per usual), so she came straight for me. She wanted to know what I'd been doing in the washing machine. "Nothing," I said. "Washing clothes." She started waving a finger in front of my face. Hysterically. "Then what's this, Janet? What's this?" she kept shrieking. It was black dye. She said if this was my clever way of getting out of doing my own laundry, I could forget it. She suggested I read ALL instructions before I did anything. She said if it EVER happened again, she was going to send me to Indonesia to work in a factory until I'd earned enough to buy a new machine. She reckons it would take till I'm thirty.

Everybody else had spaghetti Bolognese for supper tonight, but all I had was a cheese sandwich because Nan threw out the soya mince. She thought it was dog food and we don't have a dog. How is it possible that I'm related to these people? I hope I'm not getting anemic.

Found myself in the kitchen with my parents' other child tonight. I was ignoring him as usual when he suddenly told me I should give the MC a break. I said what? Her leg? Her arm? Her neck? He said it's not a joke. Can't I see the state she's in? I said it would be pretty hard for me to miss it, since I'm the one who gets most of her shit. Thank God, our conversation got cut short by Sigmund barging in, looking for the corkscrew (the MC was over at Sappho's again so he couldn't ask *her*). Justin didn't even look at him; he just mumbled something about it being about time that I joined the human race, and left the room.

SATURDAY 17 FEBRUARY

I woke up this morning looking like I'd been bitten by the King Kong of mosquitoes. My whole nose is red now. And swollen! The Mad Cow says it's infected and made me take the ring out. Thank God it's half-term or I might end up going to school with a bag over my head like Katie Jamers did that time she dyed her hair pink and her father went INSANE and SHAVED IT ALL OFF! Sappho gave me one of her herbal remedies for my nose. At least it smells OK.

Since looking like something deformed has made it impossible for me to go out in daylight, I read another couple of pages of The Outsider and did some yoga. I was feeling in a pretty reflective mood after that, so I wrote a poem about being Here while everyone else is There. Disha said it was v deep, which is what I thought. So maybe it was important for my nose to go septic for me to assimilate what the DP has taught me so far.

SUNDAY 18 FEBRUARY (Sara Dancer's advice about locked doors proves prophetic!!!)

Three Reasons Why I Hate My Brother:
(1) He's ugly and stupid.
(2) He tore up my best coloring book when I was four.
(3) This afternoon I was practicing yoga to my new CD (the chanting does help, though there's a bit when they suddenly start blowing trumpets and banging cymbals that comes as a surprise the first time you hear it) when the stereo just stopped playing. I wasn't going to go through all the bother of finding a new fuse and putting it in and all that, so, since Justin wasn't home, I went to his room (otherwise known as the Black Hole) to borrow his stereo, which is like going into a house where someone's just died of bubonic plague. His room isn't just untidy—it SMELLS. I couldn't see his stereo, so, holding my nose and trying not to gag or touch anything with my skin, I started kicking piles of clothes aside. And what do you think I found? MY LEOPARD-PRINT BRA!!! That's what I found!!! Are you revolted? Multiply that by about a trillion and you'll know how I felt! I picked it up with my sleeve and brought it downstairs to show the Mad Cow. (I don't want to think about what he was doing with it!) The MC was less than horrified. She said there's probably nothing unhealthy about it (there is for ME!), and that Sigmund will "have a word with Justin." Well, that should help. (Sigmund never has less than a thousand words with

101

anyone, and Justin will stop listening completely after "talk to you.") And also she refuses to buy me a new bra. She says I'm being melodramatic and I should just wash it. She says it probably just got mixed up in the laundry, which is another good reason we should each do our own. I may have to burn it.

There must be more to Sappho's picking-wild-sage-when-the-moon-is-full routine than I thought. The swelling's gone down and my nose has stopped aching.

Disha was suitably AGHAST when I told her what Geek Boy did. She says it just proves that you never really know anyone, not even the people who are closest to you. There are always depths. D says it's sort of scary when you realize that EVERYBODY has a secret, inner life. I said not everybody. As the child of Robert and Jocelyn Bandry I can say that with CERTAINTY. And as far as Justin goes, I don't know if I consider nicking my bra a DEPTH exactly, even if it is true that I wasn't expecting it. It's more like a Cesspool of Shallowness.

MONDAY 19 FEBRUARY (Half-term. Can I use the break? Do I need to breathe?)

Sigmund made Justin apologize for nicking my bra. If you count uttering one word ("Sorry") from behind a camera an apology. Justin said it was Andrew's idea. (Andrew is the fourth reason I hate my brother.) According to Justin, they just wanted to see how it worked. What for? Are they planning to wear one? I'm going to make a list of every bra I own so I can check whether any go missing in the future.

The Mad Cow and Nan were all atwitter when I got home from Disha's this afternoon. I reckoned there must've been another excruciatingly exciting incident in the supermarket, so I wasn't really paying attention till I heard Nan say that she thought it might be a good idea if we set up a neighborhood watch. Nan said she doesn't know what the world's coming to. In her day (like she can remember that far back!) people looked out for each other and knew how to take care of themselves. I thought Sigmund must've had another car stereo nicked (number five!), but it turned out that Mr. Burl next door was robbed. Somebody took his scooter last Saturday night! My mobe was charging, so I raced to the kitchen phone to tell Disha that we'd actually witnessed a robbery in progress. Disha said hadn't she said Mr. Burl looked like he'd lost some weight? I said no. (I certainly don't remember that.) She thought maybe the police would want to question us. The only person who wanted to question me was the Mad Cow. She'd been listening to my whole conversation, of course (I couldn't have less privacy if I lived in a doorway). The MC was HORRIFIED that I actually *saw* someone going off with Mr. Burl's bike and didn't say anything. I asked her what she wanted me to say. Anyway, how was I meant to know it wasn't Mr. Burl going for a moonlit ride? It was dark. She said she hoped I realized that at some point in time I was going to have to take up residence on Earth, and advised me against going into any career that required even an insignificant amount of thought.

TUESDAY 20 FEBRUARY

Another v interesting day!!! Went shopping for general maintenance supplies (shampoo, conditioner, etc.), and who should I spy with my little eye but Catriona and David! They were coming out of the record shop near the tube. They weren't holding hands, but they were walking V CLOSE!!! I really am a creature of impulse, because I suddenly decided to follow them. They strolled along just looking in windows for a bit, and then they went into Woolie's, Agent Bandry right behind them. Woolie's was crowded and it wasn't easy to keep them in sight and stay out of sight at the same time. I was sidling past the kitchen stuff when I realized David and Catriona weren't the only ones being followed!!! I was being closely observed by a youngish man in a Nike sweatshirt. I dived down the sweets aisle, and he popped up at the other end. I knew instantly that it wasn't lust or anything like that, though. He had undercover security guard written all over him. The last thing I wanted was to follow in the footsteps of Jocelyn Bandry and get accused of shoplifting. Especially with the Hendley about (spreading sensational news stories is in her blood after all). I suppose I could simply have left, but I didn't think of that until later. Instead I was attacked by genius once again! I went straight to the manager and told him a pervert was following me around the store. Naturally, the manager didn't want to admit that it was the store detective, so we got into a v intense discussion. Perhaps acting is my real calling, because I definitely got into my role of Victimized and Innocent Young Woman Alone. The manager finally offered me a five-pound gift voucher to appease me, which I generously accepted. The downside was that by the time I returned to my quarry they were gone. Decided to save the voucher for Nan's birthday.

Came home to find the female parent **IN MY ROOM**! She was lying on my bed! I was highly indignant, I can tell you. Not only was this a **MAJOR** breach of my privacy, but her eyes were all red and she was sniffling like she was coming down with something. She'd better not be infecting me with her germs. She said she was taking a break from Nan, but I know her better than that. She knows I got a diary for the winter solstice, and she probably wants to read what I say about her (though I can't imagine why, since even SHE must realize it isn't going to be good!). Time for a move!

Sigmund and Nan had an argument tonight. For a change! This one was about war as a method of settling differences. Sigmund doesn't think it's what Jesus would do. Nan said the Bible said an eye for an eye and a tooth for a tooth. Sigmund said it also said turn the other cheek. Nan stomped off muttering that the Word of God is the Word of God, and Sigmund shouted after her, "Even when It contradicts Itself?" The Mad Cow told him if he didn't stop winding Nan up she was going to kill the two of them. I know she was only kidding, but Disha's words from the other day came back to haunt me, and I stared at her for a few seconds like I'd never seen her before. Maybe D's right and EVERYBODY—even my mother—has an inner, secret self. Maybe, deep down in her inner, secret self, Jocelyn Bandry (primary school teacher and graduate of the St. John Ambulance first aid course) really would kill someone. People do, don't they? You see it on the news all the time. The neighbors are always well shocked. Usually it's a man slaughtering his wife and children, but it could go the other way, couldn't it? And even if the MC's not a serial killer waiting to happen, lots of housewives go into prostitution for extra money (this is well documented in films and TV programs). And there was this suburban wife and mother in America who it turned out was wanted by the FBI for being a terrorist in her youth. I know none of these seem likely for my mother, but it did make me think. I must've got lost in my thoughts because she suddenly started shrieking, "And what are you looking at?" So I said I was just wondering if she really had the potential to murder someone, and she said not to provoke her. I beat a hasty retreat, but I couldn't stop thinking about how you never **REALLY** know **ANYONE**. It's all through literature and history. Betrayal. Treachery. Deception. It's even in comic books and films, for God's sake! After a while, though, I got really **tired and depressed** thinking about all this so I went and watched telly with Nan for a while, but her soap was pretty **RIFE** with betrayal and deception too (who knew the Dark Phase was going to be **THIS** dark?!!), so I rang Disha. D says Shakespeare was totally obsessed with treachery, betrayal, and deception. She says it just proves we really are probing the **DEPTHS** of human experience. She says now she **TOTALLY** understands that poem about ignorance being bliss. And I said our *Souls* must be even *Deeper and More Creative* than we thought. D agreed. Now I feel oddly at *Peace*. I reckon we've reached another spiritual plateau!!!

WEDNESDAY 21 FEBRUARY

Justin has a black eye. He won't say how he got it.
Probably walking into a lamppost or something. He's
always hurting himself (last time it was a broken ankle).
Not only is he the clumsiest thing on two feet, but he's
practically comatose most of the time. Sigmund said he
hoped Justin wasn't doing anything dangerous. Like what?
Eating hamburgers? Crossing against the light? (This isn't
exactly the young Indiana Jones we're talking about here.
Justin hasn't even ridden a bike since he was hit by a
police car.) Nan said thank God he wasn't hurt worse, and
the Mad Cow muttered something about nothing being
more important than human life (although I can think of
several things that are more important than Justin's life).

THURSDAY 22 FEBRUARY

Made another attempt at my story for the school mag this
morning, but writing is **A LOT** harder than it looks. I was
pretty relieved when David rang up. He was bored too. So
in the end I hung out with Marcus, David, Siranee, Disha,
etc. at David's. I took the opportunity to try and get some
information out of him about what's happening with
Catriona when we had a few minutes alone. I started out
by asking him if he got any valentines and he actually

blushed! Busted!!! (It was really *v Sweet and Endearing*. Like when you see some guy built like an American football player with a baby. I don't know why that should seem so sweet—I see dozens of women with babies every day and all I think is that's their youth and figure gone.) I said I got one too, to encourage him, and he didn't say anything. Then I asked him who he thought his was from, and he smiled (he has one of those v attractive lopsided smiles) and said he had an idea but he wasn't going to say. I was about to start wheedling when the others came back. Better luck next time.

Disha said did I notice that Marcus and David seemed a bit cool to each other, and I said no. D said **REALLY**? I asked her if she was trying to make some point, and she said no, she was just saying because the DP has got her into the habit of thinking and noticing things. I reminded her that we're meant to be noticing things with profound significance, not mundane details.

I've spent a lot of the half-term going through all the possibilities, and I really think my valentine must have been from Elvin. It was too soppy for Marcus. And I **KNOW** I'm right about David being interested in the Hendley. Who else is there? This is the first time anyone's sent me one, and it's the first time I've known Elvin. The logic seems pretty irrefutable to me. So, since he obviously is interested in me (having more or less said so), I've decided to be one of those new women you're always reading about in the color supplements and not wait for him to ring me about the bike ride. After all, maybe he forgot. He is a filmmaker. You wouldn't expect Spielberg to remember he once asked you to go on a bike ride, would you?

I don't think being twins can be healthy. Either S&S don't speak to me at all because they live in their own little Twin World, or they won't shut up and talk in stereo. Tonight they were banging on about their father again. Apparently he's bigger than my father, stronger than my father, cleverer than my father, and even better looking than my father. God they're exhausting! I ask you, who would be young? How tedious and infantile their minds are. I tried to ignore them. After all, I couldn't really argue with them—they are mere children—and, anyway, since I've never met their dad (because he's been inside all the time I've known Mrs. Kennedy) they may be right as far as I know. (The DP is also helping me develop an open mind.) Then Shane said their dad could beat my dad up, and Shaun said too right. I asked them why he would want to do that, and they said **BECAUSE**. Could I ever have been like that? It really doesn't seem possible. Sigmund was still up when I got back, so I told him how weird they've been lately. I reckoned, since he's Mrs. Kennedy's therapist and all, he'd be interested, and he was. He went into this long yadda yadda yadda about the way twins relate, and their imaginations, and how you can't really believe much they say, especially twins who have been through as much as Shane and Shaun and have to pretty much make up a father. And he thinks I talk a lot!!! As per usual, I was v sorry I'd brought it up. I said all I really wanted to know was if he thought they could be on medication. Sigmund said the only person he suspects of being on medication is me. You can see what I'm up against. And he expects me to have serious conversations with him!

FRIDAY 23 FEBRUARY

Since the McDonald's incident, I've been reluctant to hang out with the boys anywhere too public, just in case we run into Elvin (which, with my LUCK, would be bound to happen), because even though it does men good to think that other men are interested in you, I don't want to overdo it. You know, I don't want it to backfire and actually DISCOURAGE him. But today I broke down and said I'd go to the bookshop with David. He said if I'd finished the Camus, he could recommend something else. It was a tricky situation. If I said I'd finished The Outsider I'd have to tell him what I thought of it, but if I said I hadn't he'd think there was something wrong with me since it's not exactly LONG. But then GENIUS struck! I told him I'd finished it but was going to read it again, so I could fully appreciate all its subtleties. I said I didn't feel I could discuss it after just one reading. He seemed v impressed. No sooner did I hang up than Marcus rang. What was I doing, yadda yadda yadda? I said I was going to the bookshop, so he said he'd come too. Then it occurred to me that I could **EASILY** bump into Elvin in a bookshop, so I asked Disha if she wanted to come too. When we got there David was pretty quiet, but I reckoned that was because he was in literary mode (you should've seen the book he bought—it's thick as a brick!). Anyway, Marcus was in good form so we had some laughs. And we didn't meet Elvin.

My good mood evaporated almost as soon as I got in the flat. The MC was in my room **AGAIN**! This time she said she had a migraine (which might've had a shred of truth in it, since she didn't exactly look like a piece of art) and it was the only place she could lie down in *Privacy and Peace*. I said what about Justin's room; he hasn't sold his bed, has he? And listen to what she said!!! She said Justin needs **SPACE** because of his photography. And what about me?!! I'm an artist, or maybe a writer. I said how am I ever going to finish my story for the school magazine if I don't have any **PRIVACY AND PEACE**? And then you know what she said? She said J. K. Rowling wrote the first Harry Potter in a café so she didn't see what I was making such a fuss about!

SATURDAY 24 FEBRUARY

Is this injustice or what? Apparently, when Justin got his black eye he also lost his new camera. And is Justin being punished for this carelessness? Is he being treated like a pariah? Is he scorned and grumbled at and told OVER AND OVER how much things cost and how no one's ever going to buy him anything again? NO, HE ISN'T! He's been bought another camera! Sappho's right. There is no equality between men and women. Not in this house at least!!!

SUNDAY 25 FEBRUARY

Finally got around to hanging my wind chimes outside my bedroom window. They're absolutely brilliant! I lie on my bed, looking up at the glow-in-the-dark stars on the ceiling and listening to my chimes as though I'm camping in the Himalayas, watching the night sky and hearing the temple bells ringing in the distance. As someday, perhaps, I will!!! (Must check out what the scorpion situation is in the Himalayas before I go, though.)

MONDAY 26 FEBRUARY

A black star hangs over me! The curse of a whole coven of witches envelops me! You doubt that? Well, guess what's happened now! I'm the bold, innovative trendsetter who has her nose pierced and gets a dangerous infection as a result—and Catriona Hendley goes and gets a ring put through her lip like she invented body piercing! (You will notice that she did it **DURING HALF-TERM**—probably on the first day!!! That way, if it went septic and her lip swelled up like a zeppelin, no one would ever know. Talk about **deception and treachery**. I'm sure if William Shakespeare were to come back to life and run into Catriona Hendley on the high street, he'd think she was Lady Macbeth in a short skirt and knee-high boots. "Gadzooks!" he'd cry. "You're back!") Everybody was hanging around talking about Catriona's lip before the bell. I told them about facial rings being a sign of slavery and oppression. I said I took my nose ring out as soon as I found out. Catriona said she reckoned lips rings were different. She said she wasn't really sure about kissing with it though. Someone said he'd be happy to help out if she wanted to practice, and everybody laughed, including David. He's obviously a better actor than you would have thought! It's good news about the kissing though. That should slow down her moves on Elvin a bit too.

TUESDAY 27 FEBRUARY

Disha had some V DEPRESSING NEWS. Elvin came by hers last night with Catriona Hendley! How could he do that? I feel as if someone's Rollerbladed across my heart. He knows Disha's my best friend! Did he think I wouldn't find out? That I wouldn't be excruciatingly hurt? That the *Hopes of My Love* wouldn't be dashed against the craggy rocks of Catriona Hendley's common good looks? Disha says it wasn't like they were holding hands or anything. He just brought her along because they're such OLD friends and he wanted to show her his award-winning documentary on cats, which (apparently) he left with Calum. I am not consoled. That's how these things start. One day they're joking around like brother and sister, and the next he's sticking his tongue down her throat.

WEDNESDAY 28 FEBRUARY

I think Justin must have a girlfriend because a girl called asking for "Just" (I was so surprised I said, "Just what?"), and when I asked him who it was, he said, "No one" (which is pretty ironclad proof if you ask me). The MC says I'm getting carried away by my vivid imagination (as usual!!!). She says this girl's probably just a friend. She says Justin has lots of female friends. Strange but true!!! Geek

Boy's always had lots of girls hanging round him, but he's never gone out with any of them. I said I reckoned it must be time that changed. Why else was he nicking my underwear? And, anyway, as hard as it might be to believe that **ANYONE** from the human species could be interested in Justin, there was something in this girl's voice that sounded **POSSESSIVE**—and also suggested **SEX** (and if that isn't a thought to sober up every wild party in London, I don't know what is). I know from waiting at airports, etc., that some of the most unattractive people imaginable find partners (look no further than the parent Bandrys for proof!!!), so I think we have to accept that— though grossly improbable—it is not impossible that a female might be interested in my brother. She's probably a right tart.

FRIDAY 2 MARCH

Went to Disha's after school (again) hoping I might run into Elvin but he wasn't there. The good news was that Calum wasn't there either. I had another attack of genius. Maybe Calum had Elvin's phone number written down somewhere. Disha said looking in Calum's room for Elvin's number was a waste of time. (Was I mad? He's a **BOY,** for God's sake. Did I think he kept an address book?) But I was convinced it was worth a try. She was right about the address book, but Calum, being a Serious Filmmaker, does keep a notebook! It was in his desk. Elvin's number is written on the inside cover. Disha said it was too bad Calum didn't keep a diary. She'd give her red leather jacket (which, obviously, she **LOVES**) to read it. I said that even if Justin knew how to write, I wouldn't want to read his diary. I'd be afraid to. Knowing the superficial Justin Bandry is creepy enough without finding out his **deepest secrets**. Disha said yeah, but think of the v interesting bets we could make each other about what we would find in our brothers' diaries. Disha said she bet Calum is seeing an older woman. I bet her that Justin has boils on his bum. We laughed so much we thought we were going to gasp our last!

We found two other **V INTERESTING** things in Calum's desk: **DRUGS** (there was a lump of hash in a tin on top of his notebook) and **ELVIN'S MOVIE** (Purr Love—a film by Elvin A. Zagary). We debated what to do about the dope for about half a second, and then we decided that it should definitely be part of our intense, experience-seeking Dark Phase, so Disha hacked a bit off with Calum's Swiss Army knife and wrapped it up in a few of the Rizlas that were also in the tin. She hid it under the rug in her room for future use. Then we watched Elvin's movie. It really is about cats(!!!)—feral cats and the people who feed them. I have to say that I learned **A LOT** from it. You wouldn't believe how many people there are skulking around with carrier bags of cat food and bowls and stuff. D said she not only found it très depressing, but she also felt she now knew more than was necessary about the relationship between loneliness, madness, and felines. I, however, found it a disturbing but V MOVING and thought-provoking commentary on our times.

SATURDAY 3 MARCH

Awake half the night worrying about where I can hide my diary. I've been keeping it in my laundry basket, under my dirty clothes, but it doesn't seem very secure. (With her mood swings, the MC could suddenly decide to do the lot herself, never mind what she said about not being anybody's skivvy.) I don't know why I didn't think of it before. I mean, not only have I got the Mad Cow lying on my bed and snooping round when I'm not home, but I've got Justin bursting in whenever he feels like it to take pictures and nick my underwear and Nan wandering in when she forgets where the loo is. It's like King's Cross Station at rush hour. It goes without saying that NONE of these people respect my right to privacy. And also, in case you haven't noticed, Sigmund still hasn't got me my new door. Unless I rip up a floorboard, I can't think of any place that's REALLY safe to keep my diary. I have temporarily moved it to my closet, under a pile of stuffed toys. Even the MC doesn't go in there since the time she opened the door and was buried under an avalanche of clothes. (Well, where did she think I was going to put everything? If it would all hang in the closet, it wouldn't have been on the floor, would it?)

SUNDAY 4 MARCH

I DID IT!!! I rang up Elvin and asked him when he wanted to go for that bike ride. (Thank God he answered the phone. I've had just about enough of mothers! I'm not sure I could cope with another one, even if she is the woman who gave birth to such a remarkable son.) Elvin said we couldn't go today, because it's raining. So NEXT SATURDAY, weather permitting. I'm a little wary of trying a weather spell since obviously neither D nor I have enough *Peace and Privacy* in which to make one. Maybe I should get Nan to ask Jesus to make sure it's not pissing down.

Had a v intensive self-improvement day in preparation for next Saturday. I even read Sigmund's *Observer* so I'll know what's happening in the world if it comes up in conversation. (I reckon I don't actually need to read up on the cinema, even though it's Elvin's great passion, since I've been watching films from before I was born.) And also I bought a jazz CD (*Masters of Modern*), partly because jazz is the music of the intellectual and partly because it was v cheap. I even did **TWO** sessions of yoga! I felt absolutely brilliant afterwards, but nobody tells you that yoga makes you fart, do they? You wouldn't believe how much **NOISE** can come out of one body. How can people do it in a class? It must smell like any room Justin and Andrew have been in for more than five minutes. I reckon that's why they burn incense.

MONDAY 5 MARCH

Late for school this morning because I fell back to sleep when I was doing my yoga (lying dead still is v relaxing!) and the Mad Cow didn't wake me because she was busy! What sort of mother is so busy she forgets her own child?!! (What am I going to do if I **DO** turn into my mother? How will I ever live with myself?)

TUESDAY 6 MARCH

I'VE BEEN MUGGED! Can you even believe it? I HAVE BEEN MUGGED! IN BROAD DAYLIGHT!!! I hate to say it, but Nan's right. What **IS** the world coming to? Here's what happened. I went to see

this bike that was advertised in Loot after school. It's not
exactly state of the art (it's white, pink, lilac, and rust), but
it was only twenty quid (which seems to me a reasonable
price for something you have to pedal). I took the
overground after I bought the bike because it was MILES
away and there was no way I was getting all sweaty riding
it home. I was talking to Disha on my mobe as I came out
of the train station. (Lila's NEVER allowed to have
another party because this time someone threw up in the
ficus. They'd covered it up with dead leaves, but Mrs.
Jenkins smelled it.) We were trying to work out who the
mysterious barfer might be. I had to stop for a second to
get my bearings, and then I went left through the tunnel.
That's when it happened. Two boys were coming towards
me, and I had to swerve a bit to avoid running into them.
The bike sort of wobbled, and I was dealing with that (not
easy with only one hand!) when two more boys came up
behind me. One grabbed my mobe and the other gave me
a shove. I tore my best tights. The stripy ones Sappho gave
me for my birthday. I was so traumatized by falling over
with the bike and all that, I didn't even know my mobe
was gone until I'd calmed down. No one came over to
help me up or anything, of course (this is definitely the
age of selfishness!!!). And the irony is that I could have
been saved. David wanted to go to the library to work on
our English project, but I said I couldn't. Well, I couldn't. I
HAVE to have a bike by Saturday or I'm really going to

have a problem. But if I could have that moment back, I'd make David come with me to see the bike. I'm sure he would've done it. He's very accommodating.

I must've caught her on one of her **UP** swings, because the Mad Cow was excruciatingly sympathetic about my mugging. She wanted to take me for an x-ray. And she wasn't even angry about me losing my phone. She just kept saying, "You poor thing. . . Are you sure you're all right?" over and over. Nan tried to cheer me up by reminding me that God Works in Mysterious Ways. Justin, of course, was his usual insensitive, uncaring self. He said I was the only person he knew who'd fallen off a bike without ever getting on it. I said at least I hadn't ridden in front of a police car. I wasn't as stupid as *that*.

Justin had three phone calls tonight—and they were **ALL FROM HER**!!! The Mad Cow answered the first time, I answered the second, and Nan answered the third. Nan has no shame, so she asked her what her name is. You won't believe this!!! It's Bethsheba!!! I knew she couldn't be **NORMAL** *and* interested in the Bandrys' other child. I usually spend some time before I fall asleep imagining all the brilliant things that are going to happen to me once I've left secondary school, but last night I spent it wondering what Bethsheba could possibly see in my brother. I know girls are different to boys. Boys see a short skirt and a big pair of tits and they go into meltdown.

122

(I think it has something to do with male hormones, but Sappho says it's because men can see better than they can think.) Girls, however, are attracted by other things, like intelligence, talent, character, and personality. But Justin doesn't possess intelligence, talent, character, or personality any more than he possesses looks, for God's sake. I reckon Bethsheba either lost a bet or is a nymphomaniac with no standards whatsoever.

WEDNESDAY 7 MARCH

MEGA trouble at the Rancho Bandry!!! When I got home from school today the Mad Cow had a surprise for me. She'd decided to GIVE ME her mobe. She said she never used it, so she didn't see any reason why I shouldn't have hers. I tried to talk her out of it. I said I was pretty shaken from the attack and wasn't sure if I wanted to walk around with something that was so popular with thieves. As per usual, she paid ABSOLUTELY no attention to me. She said as long as I was careful and paid attention to where I was she'd actually feel better about me going out on my own if I had her phone. She went to get it. She was gone for eons. I crossed my fingers and sipped my tea. Maybe she'd totally forgotten where she'd put it. She hadn't. She returned in screaming mode. "Where's my phone? Did you take my phone? Did you go through my things? How would you like it if I went through your things?" (As if, right?!!) Yadda yadda yadda. I didn't break down though. I've been her daughter for sixteen years; I know how to do it. I just kept saying that I had no idea what she was talking about. What could she do? She's too lazy to dust for fingerprints. The whole time this was going on, Nan was sound asleep at the kitchen table. She only woke up when the MC started screaming that it was her phone I lost yesterday. "Tell the truth, Janet. It was my phone, wasn't it," she kept shrieking. "Trust in the Lord!" cried Nan. The Mad Cow said He was probably the only person in this house you could trust.

THURSDAY 8 MARCH

Disha, being of a v thorough (and, to be honest, less creative) nature, thinks it would be a good idea for me to try out my new bike BEFORE the weekend, but this seems a little reckless to me. I mean, what if I *do* get hit by a police car? (If you belong to a family like mine, you realize at a young age that you haven't exactly been born under a lucky star.) It would be bad enough if I had an accident *after* my ride with Elvin, but I don't want to be in traction when I should be with him. I reminded Disha that you never forget how to ride a bike, no matter how long it's been. That's a fact. She said she reckons it really is a fact, since her grandmother can't remember where she is most of the time, but last summer at the family barbecue she jumped on some child's bicycle and rode all over the garden, singing.

The MC was still up and in one of her anti-Mrs. Kennedy moods when I got back from baby-sitting tonight. She wanted to know where I'd been till nearly midnight, and I said across the road—where did she think I'd been? She said she thought Mrs. Kennedy, having children of her own, would realize that Thursday is a school night. Then she wanted to know if she was usually drunk when she came home in the middle of the night like this. Did she say where she'd been? Did she go out on her own or with friends? (I really think the MC must've played a v key role in the Spanish Inquisition in one of her previous lives.) I said so now you're Mrs. Kennedy's mother too. She said no, she's just my mother and that's hard enough. I pointed out that paranoia is also a symptom of the menopause, and she said not to forget that infanticide is too. I said it's lucky she doesn't have an infant then, and she said that's not what it means.

FRIDAY 9 MARCH

Marcus rang wanting to know if I fancied going to the cinema at the weekend. I said Disha and I were planning to see that Chinese film on Sunday and he could come along if he wanted. Then David rang with the same question, so I invited him to come along too. I consider this v fortuitous! It could be my chance to find out what's happening with him and Catriona.

Spent **HOURS** blacking in the stitching on my combats with a marker, as suggested by D. They are the absolutely only thing I have that's right for cycling on the heath (excruciatingly cool, but practical at the same time). And if I do say so myself, they look well wicked. I'm also wearing the bat top Disha gave me (partly because I **ADORE** it, and partly for luck). I doubt that I'll sleep much tonight, but at least my chimes will soothe my troubled, restless heart.

SATURDAY 10 MARCH

I'm writing this now, **BEFORE** my date with Elvin, even though I still have scads more to do to get ready. But as I finally drifted off to sleep last night, floating on the delicate sound of my chimes like a bamboo leaf on a warm spring breeze, it struck me that this could be a v momentous day. This may be the day I *Fall in Love* for the first time. (Which, as everyone knows, is the Most Important Day of Your Life!!!) If it is, then I will Never Be the Same Again. Think of it! I got up this morning and did the things I do every morning. I washed, dressed, and put on my makeup, as per usual. I had a cup of tea and a bowl of cereal, as per usual. Nan was arguing with her only son, Justin was stuffing his face while he read the paper, and the Mad Cow was talking to the radio. ("Yes," she was saying, "that's precisely what I think.") Everything normal. And all the time I didn't know I was about to *Fall Excruciatingly Madly in Love*. That while I was wiping up the juice that got spilled, My Destiny was brushing his teeth in Crouch End. So Wish Me Luck! The next time you hear from me I may be a woman in *L-o-v-e*.

SUNDAY 11 MARCH

I couldn't write last night, not after the day I had! And not because I am a woman in *L-o-v-e* (it's almost a miracle I'm not a woman in T-R-A-C-T-I-O-N). I feel like a Pawn of Fate. Delete all that crap about God loving me. Nothing in my life is easy. Nothing in my life goes the way it's meant to. (**HOLD EVERYTHING!** I have to get a cup of tea to calm my nerves before I put this

excruciating tragedy down in purple and white. I'll be
right back.)

I'm back! First of all, I should've known this wasn't going
to be the Date of My Dreams from the moment I woke up
and discovered that something had gone RADICALLY
WRONG with my hair in the night. (I reckon there must
be some cosmic law that says that the more important the
occasion, the worse your hair is going to be.) Elvin said
he'd meet me by the station in Hampstead. This ruined
my plan of taking the tube. I didn't want him to see me
coming out of the station, not after all our talk about how
great it is to ride a bike, etc. On the other hand, there was
no way I was riding up Haverstock Hill, even if I could
have done it without bursting a lung. Not only did I not
want to arrive for our first date all sweaty, but also I was a
bit weak since I'd eaten ALMOST NOTHING since
Friday night so I wouldn't feel too fat. Even walking, it's a
bloody steep hill! I was beginning to think that they'd
moved Hampstead (like to Finchley) by the time I finally
got to the top. I was v happy to see that Elvin is a man of
his word (I think reliability is important in a man). He was
waiting outside the tube with his really flash bike (it made
me wish I'd painted mine black and silver, but I thought it
would impress him more if it looked really used). I got on
before he spotted me and rode to the corner. He started
laughing as soon as he saw me. Elvin said he hadn't seen a
bike like mine in EONS. He said it looked like they'd

128

reinvented the solid-steel frame. But he seemed impressed that I wasn't even out of breath. He said I was v fit and must have incredible thighs (Disha agrees that this was a v flirtatious remark).

The first forty-five minutes were **PERFECT**. We went to this little café before we actually started doing any strenuous exercise. I ordered herbal tea. (I felt pretty pleased with myself that I remembered.) Elvin ordered a double espresso. My tea tasted the way the water looks when you wash your knickers by hand, but it didn't matter because I felt about twenty. A sophisticated twenty. I reckon if you're a sophisticated twenty, you can put up with laundry water. Elvin told me some more about the film he wants to make. He wants it to show the side of life that you don't see in Hollywood movies. I said, "You mean, no guns?" and he laughed and said what a good sense of humor I have. It was all smiles and meaningful looks after that. We should've ended the date on minute forty-six, but we didn't. We went outside to get our bikes. Elvin explained the route we were taking (up there, first right, first right, first left—that sort of thing) and I nodded thoughtfully even though I hadn't a clue where we were going. (To tell you the truth, I've always found Oxford Street more interesting than Hampstead Heath. I mean, once you've seen a tree, you pretty much get the idea, don't you?) I watched Elvin take off. He was faster than the traffic. I got on my bike. I hadn't had any trouble riding the couple of meters to the corner the tube station's on (push down on the right pedal, push down on the left pedal, etc.), but for some reason this time I pushed left and pushed right and then I more or less fell over. (I reckon it was nerves because now I was with Elvin. Or sort of with Elvin. Elvin actually shot through a yellow light just before I tipped over. I thanked God. I didn't need any more of an audience than I had.) The next time I managed to stay upright. I was wobbling a bit, but I was also moving forward. Elvin was waiting on the other side of the lights, and as soon as he saw me he set off again. I couldn't go nearly as fast as he was going without being able to fly (I think he said his bike weighs about a pound), but at least I stopped wobbling. Everybody was right: You Never Forget How to Ride a Bike. Unfortunately there's another thing that's true, and that's that England never forgets how to rain. I was just sort of beginning to almost enjoy myself when it started to pour down. I rang my bell so Elvin would know I was having a good time (and also so he wouldn't forget I was there). He turned round and waved. And then he went right and disappeared. I went after him. I couldn't remember if I was meant to take the first left or the first right then, but he definitely wasn't ahead of me, so I went right, where there were more trees and less rain. It was the wrong choice. The only thing in front of me now was DOWN.

*　　*　　*

I don't think I'd ever seen such a v perpendicular hill
before in my life! Aside from the fact that I was more
hurtling than gliding down the hill, I wanted to stop
before I went too far so I didn't have to walk back up. I
touched my brakes. Absolutely **NOTHING** happened. I
touched them again. If anything, I was picking up speed.
This time I squeezed both brakes so hard I thought I was
going to bend the handlebars. I started ringing my bell, but
that didn't slow me down either. I closed my eyes and
REALLY screamed. Elvin said I was lucky not to have
broken anything. He said it was too bad my brother wasn't
with me because he would've loved a photo of my face as
I came down that hill (I made a mental note to tell Disha
not to talk about my family to Elvin until I've had a chance
to prepare him myself).

Being a gentleman, Elvin insisted on coming back with me
to make sure I was all right. This was **FINE** with me.
Sigmund had a group, the Mad Cow was out with Nan,
and Justin's never home on a Saturday unless he's ill. My
spirits rose even more when on the way home Elvin said
that if I wanted, he'd come back next Saturday and fix my
bike for me. I wasn't actually planning to ever get on the
bike again, but I said that would be v kind of him and I'd
even fix him lunch. He reminded me that I had my yoga
class on Saturday afternoon (what a memory!). I said I'd
changed it because Saturdays are just too busy.

And that's when all the good news stopped, because not
only was Justin at home; he was watching a film on the
little telly in the kitchen. Elvin immediately introduced
himself and sat down. Following his practice of
ALWAYS HUMILIATING ME IF HE CAN, Justin
said, "Costello or Presley?" After I told him it was Elvin not
Elvis and he should consider having his ears syringed, I
went to change into something dry. And also do something
about my hair and my makeup. But what did I see when I
looked in the mirror? Not only was I soaking wet and
slightly bruised (my hair looked even worse than it had
when I woke up—I think I may cut it really short and dye
it plum), but **MY FACE WAS STREAKED WITH
BLACK!** I looked at my hands. They were black too. I
looked down at my trousers. They were still black, but the
stitching wasn't. Now it was gray. I even had ink on my
legs!

By the time I got back to the kitchen, Elvin and the
Abominable Brother weren't watching the film anymore;
they were talking about some photographic exhibition
Justin's going to see next weekend! Really!!! As if
anybody's interested. Trust my brother to be mute for most
of his adolescence and then decide to make up for all those
years of silence the first time I bring a potential boyfriend
home. I put the kettle on. I suggested that Elvin and I
could have our tea in my room, but Elvin said he was fine

where he was. I drank my tea and watched the film while Justin tried to bore Elvin to death. I could feel depression descending, but I acted cheerful and normal. I don't want Elvin thinking I'm moody this early on. And also I have to consider my skin. My skin always erupts when I'm depressed—because of the stress. As soon as the film was over, Justin said he had stuff to do and left.

ALONE AT LAST! I wanted to cry out loud with joy! But not for long because then Elvin said he had stuff to do too and better shake a leg. As soon as Elvin left, I went to Justin's room to kill him, but he was already in his darkroom (that locks, of course!), so instead I went to Disha's for the night. (I used to wish that the Paskis would adopt me, but since the Night of the Fire Engines Mr. Paski's been more in the mood to have Disha adopted than take me on.) Disha said what happened with the ink was I didn't use a laundry marker; I just used a colored pen. It's all the Mad Cow's fault because we didn't have a laundry marker, did we? Sometimes I think she does these things on purpose.

Disha says she doesn't remember saying anything to Elvin about my brother taking pictures. She thinks Calum must have. I'm beginning to see some advantages to having a brother who doesn't speak.

MONDAY 12 MARCH

The Chinese film was well wicked! Neither I nor Disha
really likes martial arts films (one time over at Nick's the
boys were all watching a Bruce Lee movie and Disha and
I talked through it because it was sooo cheesy and boring,
and they told us to leave). Fight scenes are as tedious as car
chases if you ask me. But this was different. This was more
like a cross between Jane Austen and *Peter Pan* because there
were two great love stories in it and the people could fly.
And also the fighting was absolutely brilliant and not just
the men, which, if you think about it, is still pretty
unusual. The boys liked it too, even though it was a love
story. There was, however, a bit of an incident. (Didn't I
tell you nothing's ever easy?) The others went to find our
seats while Marcus and I bought the snacks. It was a long
queue, and we started messing around. I was trying to get
my wallet from behind his back and I wound up pressed
against his chest, but when we broke away most of my
purple glitter bat was on Marcus! (Disha says maybe
it's because it got so wet on Saturday.) It wouldn't come
off Marcus though, would it? When we got back to the
others Disha said it looked like we'd been snogging with a
definite amount of *Passion*. Really! At the snack counter?
And also I never got a chance to interrogate David about
Catriona because he left right after the film for some reason.

TUESDAY 13 MARCH

I had to go to the library this afternoon because I got another notice about overdue books. I told the old bag I'd brought them back, and she said not those, the other ones. I said I didn't even remember taking that lot out, and she said one of the most astonishing things she's discovered in her hundred years as a school librarian is the high percentage of teenagers who suffer from amnesia. I said I'd look for them (the books, not the teenagers). When I got home the Mad Cow and Sappho were in session in the kitchen. There was one of those sudden meaningful silences when I shut the front door behind me. "Shhh! The child's home! Don't let her hear what we were saying about sex!"

Anyway, by the time I got to the kitchen they were going again at full volume, but now, of course, it wasn't about sex; it was about food. Simple as peasants, this lot. It's almost unbelievable. I shouted "Hi!" and they looked up, acting surprised to find me in the house. Sappho said hi back, but the MC gave me this sickly smile like she was trying to be brave and asked me if I'd had a good day. Needless to say, it wasn't a real question. Before I could even open my mouth to answer, they went back to banging on about root vegetables. Boring or what? I waited for someone to remember I was waiting to speak. It's just as well I wasn't holding my breath. "Did someone ask how my day was?" I asked loudly. "Well, to tell you the truth, it was pretty damn awful." Sappho reminded the Mad Cow that she was going to do her chart for her and said that maybe they should go somewhere quiet. This was a hint: they wanted me to vanish. I told them not to bother getting up; I was going to my room to commit suicide.

WEDNESDAY 14 MARCH

Disha got her period last night and didn't feel like coming to school today (HER mother is v sympathetic about these things, unlike some). I was on my way to see her this afternoon when I bumped into David. He said he was going to Camden to get his mother something for her birthday, and I said if he wanted some feminine help I'd be glad to tag along. He was excruciatingly grateful (even when it isn't Christmas, boys hate shopping!!!). Now that I finally had him alone, I didn't know how to start about Catriona. Valentine's Day seems a long time ago. So we talked about the film we saw on Sunday (which he didn't seem to remember much), and school and stuff like that, and then I said he seemed to be hanging out a lot with Catriona Hendley lately—dead casual-like. He said, "Really?" He said he's always hung out with her; he's known her since they were six (she seems to have known every attractive male in London since they were little—if

she wasn't so stupid you'd assume she must've planned it).
Then (v tellingly if you ask me) he quickly tried to change
the subject to how chummy Marcus and I seem to be
lately. Since I definitely don't want David thinking I'm
interested in Marcus (in case he says something to
Catriona, who says something to Elvin), I said we weren't
any chummier than usual, and I explained about the glitter.
As I expected, he laughed v loudly, which I took as an
admission that he'd had the wrong impression. It put him
in such a good mood that he treated me to a coffee.

Naturally, the first thing I did when I finally reached the
House of Horror was ring D. I said I reckoned we should set
up in the matchmaking business, since David and Catriona
are obviously on their way to being an **ITEM**. I mean,
David denied it so much he might as well have admitted it.
Disha, however, disagrees. She says I have no corroborating
evidence. I think she's watching too many police dramas.
Disha says Lila hasn't said anything about it, and we all
know what a **BIG MOUTH** Lila has; there's no way she
wouldn't at least drop a hint if things were hotting up
between Catriona and David. And also Lila did say that
they'd always hung out together, like David said. But
I'm the child of a psychotherapist, and I believe in
psychological evidence. Psychological evidence isn't based
on what people say, but on what they *might* be saying.

FRIDAY 16 MARCH

Bethsheba rings at least twice every day, but tonight she rang **FIVE TIMES**! I was the one who had to answer the phone, because I was the only one home except Nan. I didn't want her to answer in case it was Elvin about tomorrow. I don't want him exposed to the darker side of my family life until we know each other better, say in a year or two. (You can bet your last Rolo that Catriona Hendley's grandmother isn't any more embarrassing than the rest of Catriona's incredibly perfect family. Catriona's grandmother isn't a Jesus freak; she's a baroness.)

Anyway, even though I told Bethsheba that Justin wasn't in and that I'd give him a message, she kept right on ringing. I finally unplugged the phone and went to take a bath. As per usual, the Mad Cow yelled at **ME** when she got home and realized the phone was disconnected. What if she'd been trying to get through? What if there'd been an emergency? I said what if she bought me a new mobe so she'd know that she could always get me if she had to, and she said what if I started ironing my own clothes and the moon turned blue?

You can see why people seeking enlightenment usually live in caves by themselves. (If it weren't for the lack of electricity and the snakes and scorpions I might consider it myself.) I really find coping with my family v draining.

I hope I can survive long enough to get my own place. It's not easy to pursue a life that is intellectually stimulating as well as spiritually fulfilling in a house where everybody else is submerged in the **trivial** and the **mundane**. Mobile phones . . . the menopause . . . a little dye in the washing machine—what are these things compared to the great books, the great music, the great ideas? **NOTHING,** that's what. But how can I concentrate on *Higher Things* when I'm constantly being brought down to below ground level by the Bandrys?

SATURDAY 17 MARCH

MEGA DISAPPOINTMENT! Elvin rang this morning to say he can't fix my bike today after all. He said he was **REALLY SORRY** but he had to do something with his father that he couldn't get out of. I told him that, having unreasonable parents of my own, I understood. So I won't find out if we're destined to *Fall in Love* until next weekend.

To cheer myself up, I went over to Disha's. The other Paskis were all out. Since I've got a **WHOLE WEEK** before I see Elvin again I decided to use it constructively and asked Disha to cut my hair—after all, the DP is a time for experimentation. It took **EONS** because at first she was so terrified of taking too much off that she hardly cut it at all. Since Mr. and Mrs. Paski were out we then moved into their room, where there are two MAJOR mirrors, so I could monitor both front and back the whole time. That worked pretty well until Disha got so obsessed with making it TOTALLY even that she nearly exposed my EARS (one of them is slightly imperfect). We called it quits after that. I think it's too short, but Disha says it's v trendy and immediate. (What else is she going to say? That I look like my head's been mown?) We might've had a fight, but then Disha remembered the dope we liberated from Calum's desk. I pointed out that we didn't have any tobacco, but Disha said she had a few fags stashed away. I asked Disha when she started smoking, and she said she didn't really smoke, she just liked to have one now and then when she felt stressed, and she could stop anytime she wanted. I said did she mean like Sigmund (who stops at least twice a year) and we both laughed. We got some snacks and put a film on, and then we got the hash out from under the carpet. We weren't sure how much to use, so we used the lot. I was trying v hard to follow the film, so I didn't notice when Disha fell asleep. I didn't even notice that I ATE ALL THE SNACKS (a family bag of crisps, a family bag of tortilla chips, and an entire packet of custard creams) either. We both decided that this is not our drug. I definitely can't afford something that turns me into a human Hoover. I walked all the way home (the REALLY LONG WAY) because I reckoned I needed the exercise. Stopped off at the shops and bought some hair dye (*Purple Passion*).

SUNDAY 18 MARCH

Privacy being as rare as film stars in our house, I was v excited tonight to more or less have the entire flat to myself. Sigmund was out solving other people's problems, the Mad Cow was with Sappho, Justin had a date with Bethsheba (I know that's where he went because when I asked him where he was off to he told me to mind my own ****ing business. I wonder if I should tell this poor deluded—and possibly blind—girl that Justin wet the bed till he was ten before she gets too involved), and Nan was passed out in front of the telly (just for a change). I've had a couple of things I've been wanting to do that demand solitude. The first was to finally move my diary to a really secure location. Every day I put it somewhere different in my room, and I always stick a hair or a piece of thread between the pages so I'll know if someone's been reading it, but even though there's been no sign of tampering it makes me v nervous. I had such a premonition that the MC was trawling through my room on Friday, wanting to see what I'd written about her, that Ms. Staples asked me something twice before I realized she was talking to me. After class she pulled me aside to ask me if everything was all right because I seemed distracted lately. I told her it was because I was working on a story with a v good but complicated plot. She said she'd love to read it when it's finished. (I hope she forgets about it, or I may actually have to write something, which I'm MUCH too busy to do at the moment. No wonder Catriona sticks to poems. How long do they take?)

So anyway, I finally came up with the perfect hiding place. The garden! It's easily accessible, and since it's always raining no one ever really goes there. Even Sigmund's once-a-year barbecue extravaganza has been permanently postponed because last year he was so determined that the burgers were going to be totally cooked on the barbecue and not finished off in the kitchen, as per usual, that he set one of the deck chairs on fire. The other thing I wanted to do was DYE MY HAIR purple. I did the hair first because you have to leave it on for twenty minutes, so I could hide my diary while I waited. I went to the kitchen and got an empty flowerpot and a smaller pot with a plant in it. Then I wrapped my diary in a lot of plastic, put it in the empty flowerpot, and put the pot with the plant on top. Brilliant or what?!! It was raining, of course, so I stuck a carrier bag over my head so the dye wouldn't drip all over, then I nipped out and hid it in the shrubs. The wind banged the door shut behind me, but I didn't think anything of it. Not until I tried to get back in. That's when I remembered that it locks automatically. (What'd I tell you about being born under a curse? Of all the billions of families in the world, I had to be born to the one that puts a Yale lock on the garden door. It can't be an accident! There **HAS** to be a God. The only thing I don't understand is why He has it in for **ME**!) I couldn't exactly haul myself over the wall and go next door since all I was wearing was one of Sigmund's shirts and a carrier bag over my head, so I banged on the kitchen window and shouted. Sometimes I think if it wasn't for bad luck I wouldn't have any luck at all. The storm was making more noise than I was, and there was no way Nan would've heard me even if she'd been awake, not with the telly blaring away (not unless I was whispering something I didn't want her to hear). I felt like a ghost looking in at her old life, unseen and unheard. As the seconds turned to minutes, I saw my whole life shimmer before me in the steam from the kettle. Well, maybe not all of it, but **A LOT**. Mainly they were happy memories. I saw me and Disha walking in the rain in our frog wellies when we were little, and the beach that summer we went to Greece and the MC got sunburn poisoning (you should've seen her feet—they looked like she'd nicked them from a purple elephant). And also I saw all my friends' faces floating over the stove, smiling. And Elvin! I hadn't even tasted his sweet lips yet and now it would never be. But I thought to myself, well, if I have to die so tragically—before I even reach my prime—at least my last sight is a happy one!

*   *   *

143

Miraculously Nan shuffled into the kitchen before I died of **exposure and drowning**. Of course, then I had to sneak back out again to retrieve my diary since I had so much to tell. The MC wasn't the tiniest bit sympathetic or worried that I might have got pneumonia. All she was concerned about was what I was doing in the garden in the dark. I can see I'll have to keep my diary indoors after all. I can't keep popping in and out. Not when my mother has such a **suspicious nature**.

MONDAY 19 MARCH

The curse continues to work! When I woke up this morning I SCREAMED OUT LOUD when I saw myself in the mirror. I couldn't've been more SHOCKED AND HORRIFIED if I'd grown a second head. (Which is probably the only thing that could be worse than what has happened.) My hair has turned an EXTREMELY vivid magenta. I'm sure it's because of the hours I spent in the garden. There must've been a chemical reaction with something they're putting in the rain. The MC said it was lucky I cut it so short or I might have blinded half of London. I tried not to let her negativity discourage me. I decided to make myself a **Dramatic Statement**. I dressed totally in black and wore my biggest silver earrings (PERFECT for the DP or what?!!). It's a shame my new boots fell apart like that, because they would've been the killer touch. Disha said I still looked v striking. David said he never realized I wore earrings before. Marcus said I reminded him of the girl in The Matrix, except that her hair wouldn't stop traffic.

The MC **ABSOLUTELY REFUSES** to believe that the Abominable Brother has a girlfriend. She reckons he would've told her if he really was going out with Bethsheba. (I don't see why; he doesn't tell her anything else.) I said then why is she always ringing up like he's the talking clock and she doesn't own a watch? She said maybe Bethsheba hasn't realized that Justin isn't interested in her in that way. It's truly amazing that I haven't been permanently struck **DUMB**, living with these people. Like the girl's pursuing Justin? The MC really is losing touch with reality in a v frightening way.

TUESDAY 20 MARCH

Sappho asked how the vegetarianism was going, and I told her it was going well except I seemed to be gaining weight, not losing it like you'd expect. How can you put on weight when you're eating soya burgers, soya rashers, and chicken nuggets instead of hamburgers, bacon, and pork chops? It doesn't make sense. Sappho said, "McDonald's chicken nuggets?" She said there's twice as much fat per ounce in McNuggets as in a hamburger. I was shocked. I mean, it's chicken! How can you have fat in chicken? Sappho says it's chicken the way the Matterhorn at Disneyland is part of the Alps. She says that in America McDonald's chips have beef additives. She read all about it in some book. Sappho says you can't be too careful. Obviously not. It's incredible the things people don't tell you. They don't tell you there are Great Women Artists and they don't tell you there's all that fat in chicken. What else aren't they telling us? If you ask me, life should come with a book of instructions. D agrees. She says if you think about it, adults are **INCREDIBLY** irresponsible, not to mention they lie a lot—even to each other. We can't decide whether adults never had any principles, or if they lost them when they sold their souls for their mortgages and crap like that.

WEDNESDAY 21 MARCH

Disha wanted to know why I didn't go to the gallery with the guys last weekend. I asked her what gallery and what guys. She said some photographic gallery in the West End and Elvin and Justin. She overheard Calum and Elvin talking about it. I said she got it wrong. Justin went to some photographic exhibition on Saturday, but Elvin couldn't have gone because he had to do something with his father.

Disha gave me her "oh yeah?" look. It's one of her more irritating habits. Like Elvin would dump me to go out with Justin, right? What does she think? That they're **GAY**? And why would Elvin lie to me? It's not like we're even going out together yet, is it? I mean, Sigmund's always telling the MC untruths (e.g., last Sunday when he said he was doing something with his dependencies group, he wasn't because one of them rang up to find out if it'd been changed to Tuesday or Wednesday!!!), but they're married. You expect that sort of thing from people who have lived together long enough to feel suffocated.

THURSDAY 22 MARCH

Went for pizza with the usual suspects after school, except for Disha. I thought Disha'd given up on tennis, but she said she had a lesson tonight and wanted to go home and do her homework first. So it was up to me to watch for psychological **SIGNS** between David and the Hendley. And they were there! David and Catriona made sure they didn't stand next to each other or anything (in a v pointed, let's-act-like-we-hardly-know-each-other way!). At first the conversation was monopolized by Nick and Marcus in PlayStation mode, and then David started banging on about the pizza he makes at home. (I hadn't realized he's a New Man. Justin, the Neanderthal, can barely microwave a

147

croissant.) Marcus didn't find it too thrilling either. He started talking to me about some little art gallery near his place that he thought I should see. I wasn't **TOTALLY** listening because I was keeping watch to see if David and Catriona made eye contact. We had a v good time. Marcus did an impersonation of Bart Simpson accepting an Oscar that cracked us up so much we all had tears in our eyes.

I can't believe it! Turns out that the lesson Disha went to wasn't tennis—it was yoga. She said she'd heard me and Ms. Staples banging on about it so much that she got interested. And also she saw something on telly. I said if she was going to join a class, why hadn't she asked me to go too, and she said she had. She said I said I wasn't interested in a class because I had my book and it was cheaper. I don't remember this conversation **AT ALL!!!** Disha said, "And to think you're like this and you've only taken drugs the once. I thought you had to do it for a while before you lost your memory." I still think she's making it up.

SATURDAY 24 MARCH

The devil Nan's always going on about woke up this morning in a really shitty mood and decided to give me a small taste of what hell is like. First of all, I meant to get

up early because I had a lot to do before Elvin arrived
to fix my bike. I wanted to run through my yoga (so if
he asked me what I'd been doing, I could say my yoga).
I wanted to take a shower with the shower gel Sappho
also gave the Mad Cow for the winter solstice (so if he
noticed how good I smelled I could tell him I smelled
politically correct). And I reckoned it might be a good idea
if I didn't greet him in my pajamas so I needed to dress.
And also get everything ready for lunch. But I must've slept
through the alarm, because I didn't wake up till nearly ten.
It took me an hour just to find something to wear, so I
had to skip the yoga. Then when I opened the fridge I
discovered that the Mad Cow hadn't done a proper shop
yet. There was nothing to eat unless you liked bendy
carrots and mustard a lot. So then I had to change into
something I didn't mind sweating in and run to the shop. I
bought cheese, bread, tomatoes, and a large bag of crisps.
Toasted cheese sandwiches are my speciality. That and
peanut butter. As soon as I got home I changed again. I
was still looking for the sandwich toaster (microwaved just
isn't the same in my opinion) when the doorbell rang.
Elvin! Electricity shot through me. I had a big smile on my
face and was already saying hello when I answered the
door. The smile vanished. It wasn't Elvin. It was Bethsheba.

I was a bit taken aback. She wasn't at all what I was
expecting. I was expecting someone rather pathetic who
probably lives under a rock, but she was trendier looking

149

than even Catriona Hendley. And v attractive in an emaciated art student sort of way. She wanted to know if Justin was in. I was too stressed to deal with her, and also if Justin was in his room, I didn't want him coming out while Elvin was here, so I said no. She wanted to know if I was sure. I said he'd left eons ago. Then she started screaming for him from the doorway. There wasn't any response, of course, so then she said to tell him she'd been by and that he should ring her. I went back to looking for the sandwich toaster. Justin strolled into the kitchen with his camera over his shoulder. I said I thought he'd gone out; didn't he hear Bethsheba **SHRIEKING** for him? He said who hadn't? He reckoned the whole road had heard her. He called her Bloody Bumshiva and said he wished she'd leave him alone, and I said why not tell her that instead of pretending not to be home, and he said what made me think he hadn't told her at least a hundred times? I said because he never tells anybody anything, and he said well, here was a first, then. I could tell Elvin that he couldn't wait for him because he had to go out. And as if this wasn't surprising enough (I mean, why would Elvin think Justin was going to wait for him? He was coming to see **ME!!!**), Justin then made a quick exit through the garden. I was watching him heave himself over the back wall when the phone rang. I picked it up because I thought it might be Elvin. It was Marcus, ringing to tell me not to eat lunch because we could get something after the gallery. I said what gallery? He said the gallery I'd made a date with him to see today because there are paintings in it that reminded him of my stuff. I acted all **shocked and horrified** (which I sort of was, though I was also too preoccupied with my date with Elvin to get **THAT** emotionally involved), and said I'd forgotten all about it. I said my nan had fallen again and we were all pretty upset and it had totally put it out of my mind. I said I couldn't go today because my parents were both out (true), and I had to look after my nan (would've been true if Nan were home). Marcus said well, what about next Saturday, and I said OK because the doorbell was ringing. This time it was Elvin (**FINALLY!**). I still hadn't found the sandwich toaster, but he said just a plain cheese sandwich would be great. (I like men who are flexible; I think that's another important quality to look for.) He wanted to know where Justin was and I told him he'd just climbed over the garden wall. I think he thought I was joking at first. I put the lunch stuff on the table and Elvin said he couldn't eat the cheese because it wasn't vegetarian. I said of course it was vegetarian; it was cheese. He said no, they weren't necessarily the same thing. He said cheese isn't vegetarian unless it has a green V or something on the packet to prove that it isn't made with animal glop. (And how was I meant to know a thing like that?) I said **OOPS,** I forgot. I haven't been a veggie that long. Elvin said vegetarians have to be really careful, and, so he didn't think I was **TOTALLY** clueless, I said it was worse for vegans because my aunt's a vegan and she reads the labels on **EVERYTHING** before she eats it, including salt. At last being related to Sappho has paid off!!! Elvin said he admires vegans. He said I had a v interesting family. Since this isn't true, and since even if it were true he wouldn't know it since he's only met Justin, I knew he was talking about me. I pretended to pick something off the floor in case I was blushing.

After lunch Elvin took a look at my bike, but even though he had a bag full of tools it turned out he didn't have the right one with him, so he said he'd come back next week. I thought maybe he'd suggest doing something else but he didn't. After Elvin left, I rang Marcus back, but he'd gone out. I decided to go to Disha's. When I got outside, Bethsheba was sitting on the step like that creepy bird in that Edgar Allan Poe poem. God knows how Geek Boy knew she'd be out there—perception isn't one of his strong points. I told her Justin wasn't back yet and she gave me this Mona Lisa smile and said she knew. Didn't I say someone who was interested in Justin had to be **REALLY STRANGE**?!!

SUNDAY 25 MARCH

Sappho and Mags rolled up unexpectedly tonight with a bottle of organic champagne. Sigmund (who is a **BIG FAN** of the grape) must've known somehow that there was going to be free wine on offer because he was actually home for a change. Psychologists aren't known for their sense of humor either, and Sigmund is no exception (unless it was marrying my mother), but he still tried to make a joke. "What's the occasion? You scalp another white man?" The Mad Cow, Sappho, and Mags all told him to shut up. Sappho said she had a major announcement. Turns out Sappho and Mags are pregnant! Well, one of them's pregnant (I think it's Sappho, but I got a little confused with all the shrieking this announcement caused).

Once things had settled down a bit, Justin decided to make a joke. He wanted to know if it was an immaculate conception. Instead of telling him to shut up the way they did Sigmund, Sappho said yes, and they all laughed hysterically (except for Nan, who said it was blasphemous and made her lips into a straight line). While they were laughing, Sigmund poured himself another glass of champagne (a big one). Then Nan decided she'd given them the silent treatment long enough and got back into the act. She couldn't understand how Sappho (probably) could be preggers when she's One of Them! Things weren't like this in her day. In her day people knew what they were meant to do, and if they didn't want to do it, they didn't make a big deal of it and have sperm injected into them. Sigmund told her not to start (which was pretty ridiculous, since she was already in full swing). Nan said she hoped they were going to have the baby baptized, the poor little thing. Sappho told her what she thought of that idea, and Nan stomped off to pray for everybody (she made sure she took her champagne with her though).

I hope Sappho isn't making a Big Mistake. I mean, she's only just started living with Mags. What if it doesn't work out? (It's never worked out before.) It seems like a pretty major step to take. Disha agrees. She says it's like marrying somebody on the first date. You'd think that someone who's been to university and is so politically sussed, like Sappho, would have a little more common sense, but Disha says that common sense is like the Canary Islands. There aren't any canaries left on the Canary Islands, and there's nothing common about common sense. Sometimes D can be v profound.

Sappho said I should've known about the cheese not being vegetarian because she'd told me often enough. She wanted to know if I ever listened to anything she said, and I said sometimes.

MONDAY 26 MARCH

It never ends, does it? What would everyone do if I weren't around to take the blame for everything? David was in a mood today because Disha and I didn't turn up

154

for his pizza party on Saturday night. I said I didn't know about any pizza party. David said I did and that I said it sounded great when he invited everyone the other day. I don't consider some casual remark made when at least four other people are talking at the same time even close to a *real* invitation. Who could really hear him? And also he was going **ON AND ON** about pizza (it's bread, basically; there isn't *that* much to say), and he didn't make it excruciatingly clear that he meant **LAST** Saturday. Not to **ME**! I apologized abjectly and promised that even if Prince William invited me to a mega do at the palace on the same night I'd be at David's next pizza party. David was appeased. He said OK, it's a date. Next Saturday. Eight sharp. I wrote it on my hand, and later I made Disha write it down on paper so we don't forget.

Tonight when the phone rang Justin said that if it was Bumshiva I should tell her he wasn't home. I was **SHOCKED AND HORRIFIED** that he expected me to lie for him. He said he still had the negative of me sleeping with my mouth wide open and dribbling, and if I didn't want Elvin to see it I should just do what he said. I told him that was blackmail and it made him a criminal and he laughed.

TUESDAY 27 MARCH

It's a world of surprises, isn't it? Came home from school to find the Mad Cow going through Sigmund's office. She had a duster in her hand to make it look like she was cleaning, but she was definitely turning it over. I told her he didn't hide his cigarettes in his office, and she said she wasn't looking for cigarettes; she was dusting. She said it like she wouldn't care if he smoked himself into an iron lung. (I'm not sure what an iron lung is, but it doesn't sound good. I mean, it doesn't sound like something you'd wish on the *Love of Your Life*, or even your husband.) Maybe I'll never get married, if this is what happens. All the *Passion and Romance* goes, and there's nothing left to keep you together but the mortgage. I almost felt like saying to her (woman to woman), "Jocelyn, don't you remember how your blood used to race when you heard his voice? How your skin tingled at his touch? How you used to lie awake, imagining he was beside you? Where did all that passion go?" But I didn't. If she ever did feel like that (which does seem a bit unlikely) she'll have **TOTALLY** forgotten by now.

D agrees that marriage sucks the romance out of a relationship. She says this is why Great Artists and Writers have traditionally been opposed to it. The *Soul* is always yearning to be free, and society's always trying to chain it down. Does that mean that the creative impulse is innately

156

opposed to the needs of society? If man works on rules and the rest of the universe works on chaos, does society go against our **TRUE** nature? Questions, questions, questions!!! Sometimes I feel as if the Dark Phase may give me a permanent migraine. Watched some old *Friends* videos to calm my overworked mind. *Friends* I can understand.

WEDNESDAY 28 MARCH

HOT NEWS FLASH!!! Sara Dancer **DID IT!!!** She went to a party on Saturday and made it with some bloke from New Zealand. I said she'd been keeping pretty quiet about it, and Sara said that even though she definitely felt **LIKE A WOMAN** now there really wasn't that much to talk about. She said she'd had a few beers and didn't remember it all that well. I said I hoped she remembered using a condom and she said no. She said as a topic of conversation condoms hadn't exactly come up. (Just the penis did!!!)

THURSDAY 29 MARCH

Mrs. Kennedy said she wouldn't need me next week, but she wondered if I could mind the twins from Friday night to Sunday the weekend after next. At first I said no. I'm not totally sure about having the twins for long periods of daylight on my own. I'd have to do things with them and keep them entertained, which could be quite draining. And instinct told me that the Mad Cow would object. As you know, she's not v keen on Mrs. Kennedy, but she's even less keen on leaving me with ME on my own for a whole weekend—never mind with someone else's small children. Mrs. Kennedy said she only asked because her mum usually takes them when she needs a break, but she's gone to Australia. Mrs. Kennedy said it was a shame I couldn't do it because she was going to pay me double time, but she certainly wouldn't want to upset my mother after all my wonderful father's done for her. Double time! I don't like maths, but I do appreciate that it can come in v handy from time to time. A quick calculation told me that what Mrs. Kennedy was offering me was **FREEDOM AND PRIVACY** in the shape of a new mobe. So I threw caution to the wind and said I'd do it. I reckon the simplest thing is not to tell the MC. What she doesn't know can't stop me.

FRIDAY 30 MARCH

This afternoon Marcus said he hoped I hadn't forgotten that we're going to the gallery tomorrow. I said of course

I hadn't. (It had **TOTALLY** gone out of my mind, which is understandable considering all the **STRESS** I've been under lately.) I told him I was really sorry but I still couldn't go, because of Nan's relapse and all. Marcus was v sympathetic (unlike anyone I'm related to). He wanted to know why Justin couldn't look after the old bag for a couple of hours and I said oh, come on now, you've met my brother; Justin's too selfish to do anything like that.

SATURDAY 31 MARCH

If Shakespeare's right and the *Course of True Love* is rougher than a trail up Mount Everest, then the feelings Elvin and I are going to experience (if we ever have ten minutes alone) will be the *Truest Love* that's ever existed. I am **THWARTED** at every turn.

First of all, the MC did another one of her vanishing acts this morning without so much as a word to **ANYONE**. God knows where she goes, but it definitely isn't Sainsbury's since she's out **ALL DAY** and doesn't have any food with her when she gets back. It was just as well I shopped for lunch yesterday. This time I bought pasta, pasta sauce with a big green V on it, and a bag of salad at the health food store, so I felt pretty calm about that at least. Nan was taking one of her afternoon naps, and

Sigmund, as per usual, was working his fingers to the bone to pay my bills, so I was feeling V POSITIVE. But then Justin Bandry, the boy who thinks home is where you sleep, wouldn't leave the flat today no matter how much I begged him. I was rushing round, trying to get ready for Elvin, and Justin even made me check to see if Bumshiva was "lying in wait" for him out front. (Melodramatic or what? Men really are the most incredible prima donnas!!!) She was. Justin said that in that case he wasn't going anywhere unless there was a fire. (How TEMPTING is that? If I wasn't afraid it might spread to mine, I'd torch his room!) I said I didn't see why he couldn't go through the garden, which is what he's been doing for DAYS, and he said the man at the back booby-trapped his border so he can't land in it anymore. I told him that in that case he'd better stay in his room or I'd invite Bethsheba in for lunch. I reckoned that would keep Geek Boy out of the way. Which was just as well because the doorbell rang and it was Elvin.

The first thing Elvin said when I opened the door was had my hair always been this color? I said trust a filmmaker to be so observant. He obviously thought this was another example of my great sense of humor, so I laughed too. He wanted to know if Justin had gone over the garden wall again and I said no, he was in his room, but he was excruciatingly busy. Everything was V COZY after that. I got lunch ready while Elvin fixed my bike, just as if we

160

were a real couple. When he was done he came into the
kitchen, all triumphant. I said that was brilliant, cos now
we could finish that bike ride, and he said sure but not
today. Elvin read the label on the salad dressing while I
drained the pasta. He couldn't eat that either, because it
had anchovies in it. I was already thinking about how I
was going to describe the afternoon to Disha, when Justin
appeared, nose twitching (he's got the sense of smell of a
police dog). I gave him every signal I could to make him
go away (eyes, hands, eyebrows, mental telepathy—the
lot), but except to ask when lunch was going to be ready
he **TOTALLY** ignored me. I said should I be putting out
four plates, and he gave me this big cheesy grin and said
not to worry because Bumshiva had left. Elvin wanted to
know who Bumshiva was. Justin started explaining that she
was in a couple of his classes and had this fixation on him
(ego or what?!!), and to my surprise Elvin not only didn't
laugh at this piece of fantasy but acted all sympathetic. I
was tempted to tell Justin what I'd like to do with his
lunch, but I didn't want Elvin to see my harsher side just
yet. Not until we've at least had our first kiss. So I put out
three plates. And guess what? Disha was right about Elvin
going to that exhibition last weekend, because that's all
they talked about while they shoveled my lunch into their
gobs. As soon as they'd finished eating, Justin asked Elvin
if he wanted to see what he was working on in his
darkroom. As sweetly and meaningfully as possible, I told
Justin that Elvin had come over to fix my bike, not look

at his pictures. And what did Elvin say? Elvin said he'd already fixed the bike and he'd **LOVE** to see Justin's pictures. (If Justin shows Elvin even **ONE** of me—even if I look a stone lighter than I really am and am **MIND-BOGGLINGLY GORGEOUS** in it—I swear I'm going to destroy his bloody darkroom.) I know Elvin was only being polite. He probably thinks he has to be nice to my brother even though he's the biggest pain in the bum that ever lived, but I was so **ENRAGED** I had to force myself to remain pleasant. As soon as I heard Justin's door close, I raced outside to see if maybe Bethsheba had come back, but (**NATURALLY!!!**) she hadn't. Just wait till the next time she calls round. We'll see who lies for Geek Boy then. Rang Marcus, but he'd gone out, so I'm going over to Disha's. I don't trust myself to be alone with my brother.

SUNDAY 1 APRIL

Disha, Marcus, Nick, Siranee, and I all turned up at David's at eight o'clock last night, as requested. David opened the door, and then he sort of stood there, half smiling at us as if he thought he was on *Candid Camera* or something. The boys were hungry, as per usual, so they sort of barged in and the rest of us followed. David said something about checking the dough and dragged me into the kitchen with him. I've never seen him so angry. Not even the time he

162

got thrown into the biology pond in his white suit. He wanted to know if this was some sort of April Fools' joke or something. I said, "Um, duh, you invited us over for pizza, remember? I even wrote it down!" David said he was under the impression that he only invited *me* over for pizza. I said, "Really?" He said really. He said now we were going to have to order more pizzas and I could pay for them, which was pretty unreasonable if you ask me. David said he thought it was more unreasonable to invite four people to dinner at someone else's house without bothering to tell him. I told him to look on the funny side. I mean, considering the fact that out of the lot of us David and I are the only two who speak English as our first language, it's pretty ironic that we can't seem to communicate. David said I'm the one who can't communicate.

MONDAY 2 APRIL

I'm still pretty irked by what happened with Elvin on Saturday. I know it's all Justin's fault, but I can't help thinking that Elvin could have shown a little more interest in ME. Disha thinks I may be misinterpreting things. She says maybe by ignoring me he was showing how interested he really is. Disha thinks Elvin feels so comfortable with me that he doesn't think he has to make any special effort and just acts normal. Like we've been seeing each other for eons. But what about *Passion and Romance*? That's what I want to know. I mean, I know lunch for three isn't the same as a candlelit dinner, but he could at least've talked to me a bit!!! Because I was so **HURT AND DISAPPOINTED** I decided to ask Marcus if he wanted to go to that gallery after school one day this week. Marcus said the exhibition was over. He said it like it was my fault.

TUESDAY 3 APRIL

Will I ever find peace from the slings and arrows of Outrageous Fortune? (It's beginning to look like the answer to that question is **NO**!!!) Between school, Elvin, David, Marcus, my family, and trying to keep my sanity and sense of humor despite all of them, I found it v difficult to get to sleep last night. It was raining pretty hard, so even the wind chimes weren't as soothing as usual. I never count sheep (I don't know about anyone else, but I can never get the sheep to jump over the fence), but eventually I was so desperate that I started going through my multiplication tables. I reckoned that should do it, since it's usually only with **SUPERHUMAN** effort that I manage to stay awake in maths. I was soaring through the fives when I heard someone outside. At first I thought it was a cat. Then it made another noise, and I knew that if it was a

164

cat, it wasn't your average sort of cat; it was more like a
PUMA. I was at the window in a flash! There was just
enough light from the other flats for me to make out a **dark
sinister figure** crouched like a v large puma on the garden
wall. All those lectures from the MC about what to do in
an emergency finally paid off. I quickly squeezed through
my door, raced into the kitchen, and dialed 999. Then
I went to wake up Justin. (He's always had more of a
sense of adventure than the parents, and he acts without
thinking.) Justin wasn't asleep; he was working on some
project for college at his desk. He grabbed his camera
and ran to the kitchen. I grabbed his heaviest tripod and
followed. The rest, as they say, is history. Justin was just
stepping out of the garden door with a tea tray over his
head when I got to the kitchen. He shouted something
threatening like "Don't move!" and then he started
snapping. I reckon it was the first flash that caused
the intruder to fall off the wall. I ran into the garden
brandishing the tripod and warning him that the police
were on their way. Justin yelled at me to be careful of his
tripod, and the dark sinister figure roared, "For @#$%'s
sake, Janet, are you trying to kill me?" It was Mr. Burl. My
wind chimes were driving him **BONKERS** and he'd
hauled himself up on the wall to try and cut them down.
He stabbed himself in the calf with his pocketknife when
he fell off the wall.

WEDNESDAY 4 APRIL

Everybody at school was v impressed by the way I tackled
Mr. Burl last night. And also they thought it was the
funniest story they'd ever heard. Not so at home, though.
Sigmund was **APPALLED** by the behavior of both of his
children. He said no wonder Justin's always being injured
in the line of duty. I no longer even try to make any sense
out of what these people say, but I did mutter oh right,
my brother the law enforcer. Sigmund said he meant
taking pictures. Like that black eye. Somebody decked him
for taking his photo. **GET THIS!!!** Apparently the
Abominable Brother is sort of famous for taking photos of
street people (although they don't always appreciate it).
He's even had his work in some gallery. (You really would
think **SOMEONE** would tell me, wouldn't you?!!) All
this time I thought Justin was just really clumsy. And as for
me, Sigmund couldn't decide if I was just incredibly stupid
or if I'm criminally insane as well. The Mad Cow thinks I
should offer to walk Mr. Burl's dog for a week to show
him how sorry I am. The police, on the other hand, said I
did the right thing and that Mr. Burl had no business
skulking around in the dark like that, and I'm with them.
The only one who's shown any pride in my quick thinking
and resourcefulness is Nan. She said it was what she
would've done. She said next time to wake her up too.

THURSDAY 5 APRIL

The stress just doesn't end! I was just selecting my supper
(vegetarian stir-fry dinner or pasta with salmon) when
Disha rang in a **PANIC**! Elvin turned up, looking for
Calum, but Calum was out and Elvin decided that rather
than wait around with Mr. and Mrs. Paski, he'd walk her
to our yoga class. I said what yoga class, and she said the
one I told him we go to together. What a memory! It's
lucky Elvin fixed the bloody bike, that's all I can say. I told
Disha to walk **SLOWLY** and I raced to the yoga center.
I'd already put my mat at the back when they arrived. I
acted well surprised to see them. And then, as if I wasn't
under enough stress already, Elvin decided to stay for the
class to see if it was as great as we said. We started out
with some breathing (easy), and chanting (dumb but
easy), and then even though it was almost night we
Greeted the Sun (not too hard and vaguely familiar). All
was well until we had to stand on one leg and stretch out
our other limbs. Well, we're not flamingos, are we? I lost
my balance and Greeted the Floor. Mary, the instructor,
said she didn't think my lip was cut as badly as the amount
of blood gushing from it would make you believe. You'd
think I'd deserve a quiet night after that, but God wasn't
through with me yet. I had an encounter with the law on
the way home. A motorcycle cop pulled me over for not
having lights on my bike! Sappho's right—they should use
taxpayers' money to hunt down criminals.

FRIDAY 6 APRIL

Ms. Staples wanted to know if I'd finished that story I was working on, since she was hoping to read it over the Easter break. I said not yet. I said I was trying to do some v complex things with plot and style, which was holding me up a bit. I said I was aiming to finish it over Easter, when I had more free time. She said she can't wait.

Came straight home to pack for my secret weekend across the road. Nan and Justin were sitting on the sofa. Geek Boy doesn't usually have any expressions except asleep and awake, but today he actually looked **WORRIED**. In the kitchen the MC and Sigmund were reenacting the war in Kosovo. I asked what was happening. Justin said Sigmund had just informed the MC that he had a conference to go to this weekend and had only come home to get his kit and the MC went **BALLISTIC**. Nan said that even though Sigmund's her son she wouldn't blame my mother if she beat him to death with his electronic organizer. (Spoken like a true Christian, right?!!) I said that personally I couldn't see what she was all wound up about since he was never home anyway. Justin found another expression— contempt—and said he reckoned that was the whole point. Even baby-sitting the twins has got to be less stressful than dealing with this lot!!!

SUNDAY 8 APRIL

I think it was that Scottish poet Robert Burns who said that no matter how well a mouse or a man plans things, they don't always turn out the way they were meant to. He speaks for me. I planned the weekend carefully and pretty flawlessly. I told the Mad Cow that Disha's parents had invited me to their cottage for the weekend (no phone!). She didn't put up any objection. After Sigmund skulked off on Friday and the smoke cleared, I kissed her and Nan goodbye and walked out of the front door with my satchel over my shoulder.

The twins and I spent Friday night alone. It wasn't too bad, because Mrs. Kennedy left a lorryload of food for us and the twins were watching videos in their room anyway, so I spent most of the night on the phone. Disha (heavily disguised just in case she bumped into my mother on the street) came over on Saturday morning. It was just as well Disha was there, because the twins are definitely more active in daylight. They wanted to go outside (which, of course, was **OUT OF THE QUESTION**), so we had to work v hard to keep them occupied. We were both **EXHAUSTED** by lunchtime. And then the doorbell rang. Disha looked at me and I looked at her. I told her not to answer it, in case it was my mother (you never can tell, right?). The doorbell rang again. **DEMANDINGLY**. Paying no attention to anyone else, as per usual, the twins ran out of the flat to answer it. Just in case it was the Mad Cow, I tried to work out a plausible excuse for being at Mrs. Kennedy's and not in Wales as I raced after them.

The good news was that it wasn't my mother. By the time I got down the stairs, the twins had opened the front door to a pair of policemen. It's amazing how policemen always look like policemen, even when they're not in uniform, isn't it? All I could think of was now what have I done? Shane was shrieking that his mum wasn't home. The policeman wanted to know if his dad was in. They weren't after me! I nearly collapsed with relief. "He's in jail," I said from the stairs. The policeman said, "Not anymore, he's not." Can you believe it? Mr. Kennedy's escaped! Once I'd made it clear that neither Mr. nor Mrs. Kennedy was home, more policemen materialized. They couldn't believe I didn't know where Mrs. Kennedy was, so I explained that I hadn't expected a raid, had I? But I did have a phone number. The Mad Cow was so SURPRISED when I arrived home with Disha, the twins, and approximately half the police force of north London that she didn't make a big deal that Disha and I weren't in the countryside. After the police left, the MC said she thought she should call Mrs. Kennedy too, so she'd know the boys were all right and all. So I gave her the list of emergency numbers Mrs. Kennedy'd left. She stared at it for a few seconds, and then she went over to the memo board and stared at the number Sigmund had left for a few seconds, and then she said maybe I should ring; she was going to take a bath. She was in there for ages. Disha thinks I should **REALLY** consider a career in literature, no matter what Ms. Staples thinks of my plots, because you just can't make this stuff up.

Acting **TOTALLY** out of character (and much to my amazement), the MC said she wasn't going to boil me in oil or anything like that for lying to her about going to Mrs. Kennedy's. She said that in future she'd appreciate it if I made some vague attempt to tell her the truth, but all in all she thought that compared to some people I hadn't actually done anything wrong. And also I'd coped pretty well with the cops and all, and at least I was trying to earn money to buy a phone and wasn't nicking cars or doing drugs or worse (whatever she thinks **WORSE** could be!!!).

MONDAY 9 APRIL

LISTEN TO THIS!!! The police think Mr. Kennedy escaped because he found out Mrs. Kennedy is fooling around with another man!!! Is that **DRAMA** or what? It's like something out of a Quentin Tarantino movie, except so far dozens of people haven't been brutally murdered. Just in case, though, the cops have Mrs. Kennedy and the twins in hiding till they get Mr. Kennedy back. Sigmund got home well late last night, after everything had pretty much simmered down. He was v upset to hear what had happened, though he didn't hear it from the MC since she's even angrier with him now than she was on Friday and not only refuses to speak to him but has moved back into her bedroom with Nan!!! Sigmund wanted to know if the police had considered the possibility of Mr. Kennedy coming after HIM, since he's been trying to help Mrs. Kennedy sort out her life. The Mad Cow happened to be within earshot and said the only words she'd spoken to him since he got home, which were that it *had* occurred to her, and she only hoped that Mr. Kennedy was a really good shot. The menopause is giving her a v black sense of humor.

Since it's the Easter holidays and all, and since he seems to have forgotten that we never really finished our bike ride, and since I'm **ABSOLUTELY** desperate for something to do, I rang Elvin and suggested that we pick up where we left off. He said he'd love to. He'd **REALLY, REALLY** love to. But he hurt his hand doing wing fu or chung ku or whatever it is he does, so he's incapacitated at the moment. He'll ring me as soon as the swelling goes down. At last I have something to smile about.

TUESDAY 10 APRIL

Not only is the tension between Sigmund and the MC
GINORMOUS, but Sigmund's acting even more
peculiar than usual. For months we've hardly seen him
because he's always working, but now he's canceled
EVERYTHING and refuses to leave the house. I asked
the MC what she thought was wrong with him and she
said (**AND I QUOTE!!!**), "He's a total jerk, that's what's
wrong with him." **I WAS SHOCKED**. Really. It's one
thing me slagging him off—after all, being critical of your
parents is part of the teenage experience, isn't it? But
Jocelyn's married to him. Also, she's my mother. I don't
think it can be healthy for a child to have one parent
telling her what a total waste of space and air her other
parent is. It feels like it breaks some really major rule.
People on the same team are meant to be loyal to one
another, aren't they?

Most of my mates have gone away for the Easter holidays
(including Disha, whose parents were lent a cottage in
France for a few days and decided to go at the last
minute). So since I'm well **BORED** (there is no phone in
the French cottage and D was forced to leave her mobe at
home) and feeling very **STRESSED** by the war between
the Bandrys, I decided to forgive David for the pizza
incident (time really is the great healer, isn't it?) and asked
him if he wanted to spend the day with me. He wanted to

know who else I'd invited along, and I said no one. We went bowling up Finsbury Park. I told David all about Mrs. Kennedy and the police and everything. He could hardly stop laughing.

WEDNESDAY 11 APRIL

Rang up Sara Dancer to see if she wanted to hang out, but I never got a chance. SIT DOWN AND GRASP THIS!!! Sara Dancer thinks she's PREGNANT!!! Her period's DAYS late. I said don't be ridiculous; you can't get pregnant from just ONE time, and Sara wanted to know what I was doing during sex education—having one of my out-of-body experiences? I said but THE FIRST TIME? That really does seem a bit harsh. Sara said it's not like learning to skate or something like that; you don't need a few tries before your body gets the hang of it. I asked her what she's going to do and she said get a pregnancy test, so, since I had nothing better to do anyway, I went with her to buy it. She insisted on going somewhere where it would be IMPOSSIBLE for us to bump into anyone who knows either of her parents, which largely left us with the options of Mayfair and Stoke Newington. Mayfair's easier to get to. I am *très* happy that I'm not the one who needs a pregnancy test, but I have to say that the whole experience made me feel v grown up—

like a heroine in some depressing realistic novel. We got
a bit lost coming back and ended up caught in all the
tourists wandering round in confusion outside the V&A
with their cameras and their guidebooks. Sara and I were
discussing the fact that we haven't been in the V&A since
primary school when I suddenly noticed a familiar face
in the middle of a clutch of Japanese tourists who were
having their picture taken on the steps of the museum!
"Good God," I cried, "there's my brother." Sara wanted to
know who his dishy friend was. I said what dishy friend
and she said the one taking everybody's picture. CLAMP
YOUR MOUTH OVER YOUR DENTURES!!!
It was Elvin! He was holding the camera with TWO
HANDS!!! Which suggests that either he's made a
MIRACULOUS RECOVERY or he was LYING
TO ME!!! I told Sara I didn't know who he was. I was
MUCH TOO STUNNED to speak!!!

I decided to have a few words with the Abominable
Brother tonight. I asked him what he thought he was
doing, hanging out at the V&A with Elvin, who, after all,
is meant to be MY friend. Justin wanted to know if there
was something about him that attracted insane women or
if we were all insane.

I've been thinking A LOT about Sara Dancer. I decided
that at our age pregnancy is a bit like death. You never
really think it's going to happen to YOU!!! And also

175

although I'm sure there must be **TONS** of Great (or even just excruciatingly good) Women Artists and Writers who have also been terrific mothers, I couldn't think of any offhand, so I flipped through you, dear diary, to see if I could find any. I couldn't. As an experienced child minder, I know how demanding and time-consuming even children who don't need their nappies changed can be. When would you have time to **CREATE** if you had a baby? How could you devote yourself to your work if you were tied to the schedule of an infant? Sara Dancer wants to be a fashion designer not an artist, but I reckon it's not **THAT** different. You still need *Peace and Quiet* to get your ideas and all. Plus fashion designers have to go to lots of shows and celebrity parties and stuff like that, which is hard to do if you're breast-feeding.

THURSDAY 12 APRIL

I can't tell you how relieved I was this morning when Sara rang to say the test was negative. She sounded pretty relieved too. She said if she'd known it was going to be negative, she would've bought some condoms while we were in the chemist's.

I was just getting ready to settle down to writing my story when Marcus rang to say he's returned to Ye Olde London.

He asked me to go to the Tate Modern with him, so I said I'd been dying to go but somehow had never got round to it. It was all right. The building's pretty cool. But Marcus and I agreed that even though we're *Young and v Avant-garde* we're not really into modern art. Marcus says *Soul* has been replaced by mere cleverness. I was v impressed. I thought that was a v profound perception and said so. Marcus said what did I think, that he was just another extraordinarily handsome face, and I said no, I never thought that. (Sometimes we really crack each other up!!!) We got v bored of **soulless art** in a very short time, so we went out for coffee. I told Marcus all about Mrs. Kennedy and the police, of course, and he laughed even more than David had.

To show you exactly how **TENSE** the atmosphere is at home and how desperate we all are for some neutral conversation, Justin actually asked me how I liked the Tate Modern at supper. I said I thought some of it was pretty cool, but that on the whole I felt that modern art had replaced soul with mere cleverness. Justin said he'd read that piece in the *Guardian* too.

177

SATURDAY 14 APRIL

Nan's all wound up because she read in the paper that according to some poll nearly 50 percent of the population has no idea why we celebrate Easter. I said I thought it had something to do with the founding of Cadbury. Both Justin and the MC laughed, which is pretty much a first for one of MY jokes. Nan said she just hoped I *was* joking.

EASTER DAY

Instead of the Easter Bunny, the Easter Bethsheba turned up at the door with a v peculiar-looking hard-boiled egg for my brother. She said she made it herself. I said it looked like it'd been cooked in tea and she said it was, in Darjeeling. Then she wanted to know if Just was back from Greece yet. (So **THAT** explains why she hasn't been haunting our road lately!!!) It took me a few seconds to absorb this. I was about to say oh yes, he's back and he's sitting in the kitchen right now, when Nan suddenly loomed up behind me and shouted right in my ear that something had gone wrong with Justin's flight and we had no idea **WHEN** he was getting back. Bethsheba said oh, but before she could say anything else Nan shut the door very firmly in her face. I said to Nan that I was **SHOCKED** that she'd lied like that. I said is that what Jesus would've done? Nan said no,

178

of course He wouldn't. Jesus would've zapped Bethsheba like a fig tree or turned her into salt.

The MC said that so we could all eat the same thing she was declaring Easter a no-meat holiday and she made fish. You'd think that even Sigmund could carve salmon without too much trouble, but you'd be wrong. He was just about to make the first cut when a car backfired in the street. He hit the floor as though he'd been shot. Everybody thought it was **HILARIOUS**, except Sigmund, who said it was obvious none of us read the papers or we'd realize just how violent a society we live in.

MONDAY 16 APRIL

There was some jubilation in the Rancho Bandry tonight because Nan's finally gone home. Sigmund was so excited that he actually volunteered to drive her, but the MC said she was going out anyway and she'd take her. Sigmund said what about supper, and the MC said that she reckoned a fifty-five-year-old man with three psychology degrees should be able to manage supper on his own. Fortunately I don't have to sit around half the night while Sigmund tries to find the pasta because Disha's finally back and I'm going over there. I feel like someone being released from prison. Or a bird released from its cage. It wouldn't've been so

bad if I could at least have talked to her on the phone.
God knows how anyone survived before the telephone was
invented. I may have to name my firstborn Bell.

TUESDAY 17 APRIL

I can't tell you how good it was to see D!!! I feel like I've
been living in the **wilderness** without her. Thank God there
was no one home when I got back. I don't think I could
BEAR to interact with my family right now. It's only
after finally talking to someone who understands me and
thinks and feels as I do that I realize what a strain I've been
under this past week.

Life really is full of **SURPRISES,** isn't it? Hang on to
your wig—YOU'RE NOT GOING TO BELIEVE
WHAT'S HAPPENED NOW!!!

After I filled you in on recent events, I started working
on some sketches for art. (I wish I'd gone to see those
paintings with Marcus. Which of my styles is it?) Anyway,
I got pretty immersed in that. (Art is all-consuming,
after all.) I heard Justin come home (he was yelling at
someone—presumably Bethsheba—to leave him alone),
and then I heard Sigmund come in (he was singing some
old song). Next time I looked up it was nearly seven. I was

famished. I went to the kitchen to see how long it was till supper. Sigmund was sitting at the table, drinking a glass of wine and smoking a cigarette and staring into space. I asked him if he was planning to feed us anytime tonight. He told me to get the take-away menus. "Where's Mum?" I asked. He said didn't I get the letter she left me in my room? I said I hadn't seen any letter, but I went to look just to keep him happy. I reckon I must've been in what Sigmund calls denial, because it didn't even occur to me that the MC had abandoned ship (well, it wouldn't, would it?). I suppose what I vaguely reckoned was that she must've taken a sudden holiday. After all, it's a well-known fact that middle-aged women who are sick of their boring lives often go on holiday to Greece and have affairs with gigolos, waiters, or fishermen. (It's almost romantic in a depressing sort of way.) And also menopausal women are known to be impulsive and unpredictable too. The letter was on top of my chest of drawers, under some stuff I'd decided not to wear. She hasn't gone to Greece. She's gone to Hackney to stay with Sappho and Mags!!! You could've knocked me down with a paper clip. **REALLY!!!** The first time I read it, I thought it was a joke until I got to the end and realized there wasn't any punch line. The second time I read it, I didn't know what to think. It might as well have been written in code for all the sense it made. Then, obviously unsettled by this unexpected and shocking news, I made an **UNPRECEDENTED** move!!!

* * *

I showed my letter to Justin. He had one too, though he didn't seem as shocked and surprised as you'd think. The letters are pretty much the same. They both say that the Mad Cow's sorry to leave us like this, but she's been feeling very unhappy and confused lately, and having Nan around was too much added stress, so she's decided she needs a break. She'd be thrilled if we wanted to call her, but she can understand if we're angry and upset and don't want to speak to her just yet. She said if Justin and I were younger she wouldn't have gone, but we're old enough now to be able to get on without her for a while. I said to Justin, "I don't get it. She didn't need to leave to get away from Nan. Nan's gone back to Clapham." Justin said she didn't leave because of Nan; she left because Sigmund's such a jerk. I said but he's always been a jerk, and Justin said, "Wake up, Janet. The man Mrs. Kennedy's been cheating with is dear old Dad." I was so gobsmacked I didn't know what to say.

Right after the take-away Justin sloped off as usual and Sigmund, clutching his wine and muttering about how the MC could at least have left him the car, staggered off to the Bunker. I don't know if they thought I was going to clean up the mess from supper, but if they did they were REALLY deluded. As soon as I was alone I rang D to tell her what'd happened. As one would expect, Disha was SHOCKED AND HORRIFIED. She said imagine Mrs. Kennedy (who looks like she was invented for SEX) having it off with Sigmund (who looks like he was invented to wear old clothes)!!! And also D said she'd always thought of my mother as being so **STABLE** and family-oriented. And what day was that? Disha said no really. Who did I think kept everything together? Sigmund can't even find the coffee without help. And then D remembered that she had said the MC seemed tense, which is true. I said I still reckoned that leaving me with Sigmund and the Abominable Brother is **V DRASTIC**. D said at least I have to admit I have an interesting life. She says if I don't become a major novelist I should consider writing for the soaps!!!

WEDNESDAY 18 APRIL

At first I was v calm and philosophical about the MC leaving home. And, anyway, I was pretty shocked by Sigmund's behavior—you expect more from a psychotherapist, especially if he's your father. But D and I have already discussed how everyone has a secret self, so I wasn't totally unprepared. In reality we are on our own in this life and have to learn to deal with that and be independent and responsible. (That's one of the really good things about being in the DP: you're not looking at the world through the rose-tinted glasses of a child. You appreciate how **deep and painful** life can be.) I could tell from my reaction that the last few months have **REALLY** matured me. But tonight I was left alone in the kitchen with the dirty dishes (**AGAIN**) and it finally hit me what the MC's done!!! She's **ABANDONED ME**!!! Me, her only daughter!!! If you ask me, she might as well've left me in a skip with a note pinned to my nappy on the day I was born. In fact, it would've been a **KINDNESS**!!! At least it would've saved me all those years of **DELUSION**—of thinking I was wanted, cared for, and loved! I mean, what does it matter what she wrote in her letter? She didn't give one nanosecond's thought to how this would **AFFECT ME**!!! If that's not **MEGA SELFISH** I don't know what is. I burst into tears. I just sat there at the table, surrounded by the empty containers of fast food, weeping like an orphan, my *Soul* howling. **HOW COULD SHE DO THIS TO ME?** Eventually I pulled myself together. After all, I am adult enough to accept the fact that I am **ON MY OWN**.

THURSDAY 19 APRIL

I'm going to get a T-shirt made that says **Home Is Hell**. When I got up this morning, not only were all the dirty dishes, etc., exactly where they were last night, but Sigmund was still in the Bunker playing Bob Dylan at a volume more appropriate to dance music. Loyal friend that she is, D came round to console me. She wanted to tidy up, but I said I reckoned Sigmund should do it, since it's his fault the MC left. Neither of us could stand the **doom and gloom** or Dylan for long, so we arranged to meet Marcus and David for lunch so I could get my mind off my woes. That didn't exactly happen, since my woes were mainly what we talked about. David and Marcus were well shocked about Sigmund and also about the MC's behavior. They agreed with me that though leaving home is pretty typical for **MEN**, mothers aren't meant to do things like that. If you ask me, it's unnatural for a mother to just walk out on her children without even a little warning. I can understand her abandoning Justin—if you ask me, she waited eighteen years more than she should have—but I'm her **DAUGHTER**. How could she do this to me? Neither Marcus nor David knows the answer to that question. (The only one who disagrees is Disha, who is showing some feminist tendencies heretofore unsuspected. D says she reckons the mistake the Mad Cow made was in not tarring and feathering Sigmund before she left!!!)

Anyway, we had a v interesting discussion about marriage over lunch. I said the thing that really got me was how **SUDDEN** this all was. I mean, my parents argued a lot, but they *always* argued a lot, especially lately, so how was I meant to know it was different this time? That's what married couples do, isn't it? They argue. Everybody agreed. Marcus said his parents once had a four-day argument over the right way to boil an egg, and David said his mother once threw a Weight Watchers chicken dinner at his dad, straight from the microwave. Even Disha agreed that though the government's always telling everybody that they should be married, it's probably a lot less stressful to join an army in combat.

FRIDAY 20 APRIL

Despite the fact that he never spoke to her when she was here, Geek Boy rang the MC tonight, probably to tell her that we're running out of food and there's no washing powder left. (Sigmund, as per usual, was in the Bunker. He seems to be going through all five hundred Bob Dylan albums in chronological order, which means he won't be out till the weekend at the earliest!!!) After he finished grunting into the phone, Justin said the MC wanted to talk to me, but I said to tell her I was busy. In an **UNPRECEDENTED** gesture of sensitivity and diplomacy, Justin put the phone on hold and said I should talk to her or I'd hurt her feelings. I said what was he trying to do, make me cry? What about **MY** feelings? Then he said I was acting like a child!!! Is that rich or what? I said I wasn't the one who ran away from home.

I'd **LITERALLY** just hung up from talking to D when the phone rang again. I practically jumped!!! It was Sappho.

She said the MC was really hurt that I wouldn't talk to her. I said she wasn't the only one who was hurt. How did she think I felt? Sappho said maybe I should try to put myself in the MC's place, and I said that was not a location I ever wanted to be in.

As you know, I was v traumatized when I saw Elvin at the V&A with my parents' other child. But I have had time to think about it and I realize I may have overreacted. Just because Elvin didn't **LOOK** as if he were in pain doesn't mean that he wasn't. Riding a bike and holding a camera aren't exactly the same thing, are they? And maybe he was suffering when I spoke to him on the phone, but his hand started to heal rather spectacularly after that. So I decided to put it behind us, and after I talked to D I rang up Elvin. As a Serious Filmmaker (and an older man) I reckoned he might have some valuable advice for me during these difficult times. His mother said he wasn't in. I said could she tell him Janet rang. She said Janet who? I said Bandry. And do you know what she said?!! She wanted to know if I was Justin's sister!!! Maybe I should encourage Geek Boy to visit India for a couple of years. He'd love India. It's absolutely **FILLED** with poor people who live on the street.

I couldn't get to sleep so finally I decided to see if Sigmund had left any wine in the fridge. I reckoned a glass of wine would help me relax. It was one in the morning, but the light was still on in the Bunker. At first I thought Sigmund had thoughtfully turned his stereo down really low, but then I realized the sound I could hear was him talking on the phone so I tiptoed down the hall to listen. I reckoned he was talking to Mrs. Kennedy. He wasn't. He was talking to Mrs. Bandry!!! Even more AMAZING, he was begging her to come home. I can only assume it's the car he's after.

Everybody was going to David's tonight to watch videos, but I stayed home. When you have a major upheaval in your life (like your female parent running away and your father having it off with a neighbor), it makes you introspective and reflective. Not for me the bright lights of Hollywood and the innocent chitchat of my friends over snacks and fizzy drinks. The crisps would have turned to ashes in my mouth. My mood demanded the comforting glow of candles, the warm scent of sandalwood, and anguished jazz squeezed from the *Soul*, the notes flowing through the night like blood.

SUNDAY 22 APRIL

Sigmund has emerged!!! He doesn't look great, but at least he's turned off the stereo and he says he's going to go back to work tomorrow. Apparently Mr. Kennedy's been apprehended. I said did this mean Mrs. Kennedy was back

and I'd be baby-sitting the twins on Thursday, and
Sigmund just shook his head v slowly but didn't say
anything. I'm taking that as a no.

Bethsheba was back in her usual position on the front
steps when I got home from D's this afternoon. Since
I'd more or less forgotten about her, I was v surprised.
She said she'd been trying to ring Justin for days, but the
phone was always engaged so she decided to come over
in person. I said she should ring him on his mobe because
there were other people in the flat besides Justin who also
needed to use the phone. I said anyway, I was under the
impression that they'd broken up, and she said no, it
was just a misunderstanding. She said I must know how
difficult Justin can be. **TELL ME ABOUT IT!!!** I told
her if she was waiting for Justin to get home she was
going to have a long wait because he'd gone round to our
aunt's. She wanted to know where Sappho lived and I told
her. If you ask me, it serves Justin right. If he spent more
time with his own friends he wouldn't be spending time
with **MINE**!!!

If somebody doesn't do the dishes soon not only are we
going to run out of plates and cutlery—we won't even be
able to have a cup of tea!!!

I was watching telly tonight to take my mind off all
my problems. (I don't believe one can be a **TOTAL**

INTELLECTUAL all of the time; there are times in life when simple amusement is necessary, which I reckon explains why so many Great Writers and Artists are also alcoholics.) I must've sat on the remote because suddenly the set switched itself on standby. That was when I realized that Sigmund was on the phone in the Bunker again. Stealthy as a cat, I moved towards his door. This time I was ABSOLUTELY sure he was talking to Mrs. Kennedy because he kept saying the L-word. And then I heard him say my mother's name. I couldn't make out what else he said, but at a guess it was probably that he thought there was someone outside the door because he suddenly yanked it open. I said I was looking for my earring and he believed me.

MONDAY 23 APRIL

Justin threw a major wobbly when he got home this afternoon. He marched into my room without even knocking. I said excuse me, but you can't just barge into a person's room like that, and he went DEEP red and started shaking like a Chihuahua. Then he started screaming!!! (He's always been v volatile and emotionally unstable, but if he keeps this up he'll have a heart attack before he gets out of art school.) He wanted to know what was wrong with ME!!! I said ME? What did I do? He said I was the

MORON who told Bumshiva where he was yesterday. Was I OBLIVIOUS? Or did I really live on my own planet? Didn't I see that Bumshiva's a mad, deluded creature who's been stalking him? It was just as well I was already lying on my bed or I would've collapsed from laughter. If you ask me, the Abominable Brother's been watching too many movies. Stalking! I mean, really, get a life. It's pretty obvious that the girl isn't working with a complete deck or she wouldn't be interested in Justin in the first place, but STALKING?!! People who stalk aren't trendy art students; they're usually balding losers with bad dress sense and worse breath. Justin said it wasn't funny. He spent the night at Sappho's because even though he told Bethsheba to go away she stayed outside the house and he didn't want to end up trying to get home from Hackney with her in the dead of night. I said I was under the impression that he and Bethsheba were back together, which was why I told her where he was, and he asked me who told me that. I said well, who did he think? He said I was a con man's dream. Wait till he finds out I gave her his mobile number.

Disha says it's possible that Bethsheba really is stalking Justin. She says she thinks certain sorts of stalking can happen to anyone, like measles or something. She says you'd have to have an **obsessive personality,** but artists often do. I said give me a BREAK. Who could get obsessive about a boy who shops in Oxfam and always smells of developer? Disha said apparently Bethsheba.

TUESDAY 24 APRIL

Nan rang last night to find out why no one's rung her to see if she's all right. Since the only person who would think to ring her isn't here anymore, I admitted that the MC had run away from home. Nan said she always knew something like this would happen, right from the moment Sigmund turned up at the church in a wedding coat and high-tops. She offered to come back and look after us. Personally this struck me as a reasonable idea, since Nan believes in Victorian values like meals and household maintenance, but Sigmund looked like this was all the good news he needed for the rest of his life and lied and said we were doing just fine on our own—he's not **INCOMPETENT,** is he? (I couldn't hear Nan's answer, but even though she's old she isn't exactly stupid!) Then he said it wasn't as if the MC'd left for good; she was just taking a leave of absence. I just hope the MC knows that.

WEDNESDAY 25 APRIL

There are some disadvantages to being a motherless child that I haven't thought of before. For one thing, there's the food. I'm the first to admit that the MC's one of the worst cooks to ever make lumpy gravy, but at least she does cook. Now that she's living it up in Hackney, nobody

can be bothered to go shopping, so we're still living on
take-away. (Take-away's all right for a couple of days,
but you'd be **AMAZED** how quickly the charm wears
off. I mean, it's not what you'd want as a steady diet.
Especially not when your choice is pretty much pizza or
pizza if you don't want to do the dishes.) So, since no
one's shopping, we're not only out of food, but stuff like
detergent and bog rolls as well (we're reduced to using
newspaper—I can't tell you how **GROSS** that is). And
also I had a report to type up for history, and even
though Sigmund can type almost as well as the MC he
REFUSED to do it for me. It took me **EONS** with
only two fingers! The other thing is that the health and
sanitation standards of the flat have slipped so much that
it's getting v hard to find things, and if you put something
down you have to check first that you're not putting it in
something disgusting. I said to Sigmund, didn't he think it
was time he found the Hoover, and he said why didn't I
find it? (Yeah, right! If he thinks I'm going to be his
SKIVVY he can think again.) I hope he is right and the
MC will come back once she's calmed down or I may have
to move to Hackney too!!! I don't think I could survive
indefinitely with Sigmund in charge.

Disha says to look on the bright side. I asked her what that is.
Disha says that this is meant to be our year of spiritual and
intellectual growth, and I'm definitely doing that. And also it's
pretty dark. I said that if I get stuck living on my own with

Sigmund for the rest of my life it's going to be more like a black hole than a Dark Phase. But I can see she has a point.

THURSDAY 26 APRIL

I told Disha how selfish I think the MC is being, and she said have I thought about how I'd feel if I were in the MC's place? I said she was beginning to sound like Sappho, and she said no REALLY. What would I do if I found out my husband was running around with another woman— cook him supper? I said not likely. If I cooked him supper it would only be to dump it over his head. D said EXACTLY!!! She said if I'm going to be pissed off with anyone, it should be Sigmund.

FRIDAY 27 APRIL

Disha's got a point. Sigmund's always telling me I'VE got a long way to go before I'm an adult, but if you ask me so has he. He doesn't DO anything! He just goes to work and then he comes home and goes back to the Bunker to listen to Mr. Doom and Gloom. (I should've dumped all his Dylan albums in the bin while he was out.)

*   *   *

194

I decided to break down and ring the MC tonight. It's ironic considering how she drives me crazy, but I'm really starting to miss her. And besides the general quality of life descending quickly into Third World levels, I don't know where my PE kit is and I got yelled at again by Mrs. Wist today. The MC sounded surprised to hear from me. I said I wasn't angry with her (which is more or less true, though I'm still v irked). I said I'd been thinking about it and if I'd found out my husband was running around with another woman I would've gone too. And then I asked her when she was coming back. She said, "For God's sake, Janet, I've only just left." I said no, really. I said if she didn't want to live with Sigmund anymore (and who could blame her?), wouldn't it make more sense to make him move out? The MC laughed, but not AT me (for a change!), more like in surprise. She said my Dark Phase must really be changing me because I'm actually sounding more mature. If you ask me, it's the MC who's changing (I've ALWAYS been v mature for my age), but I didn't say that to her. I said it's a well-known fact that children of divorce grow up suddenly (I heard it on *Oprah*).

SATURDAY 28 APRIL

Disha was hauled away for the weekend by her parents, and the usual suspects (David and Marcus) are doing something male and juvenile together tonight, so I sat myself down and went into *Creative Mode*. It's true what the poets say about it being a REALLY rotten wind that doesn't blow some good somewhere, isn't it? With the exception of people like Tolkien and Jeffrey Archer, lots of writers use their own lives for the basis of fiction, but up till now I'd always felt that my life wasn't BIG enough for that yet. But after what D said about not being able to make up the stuff that happens to me, I decided to give it a try. It's about a girl whose self-centered father uses her to mind his lover's children while they go to cheap hotels, and then the lover's psychotic husband breaks out of prison to avenge himself on the self-centered father, but when the girl captures the psychotic prisoner and becomes a hero, her mother finds out what's been going on and leaves home. I'm calling it "Reasons Never to Get Married."

SUNDAY 29 APRIL

There wasn't any milk in the flat this morning, so I had to go out and get some. AGAIN. I'm going to start keeping a record. Anyway, it's not even eight in the morning and the first thing I see when I step outside is the girlfriend from hell! Since I got all that grief from Justin for just talking to Bethsheba, I decided to ignore her. She called my name, but I kept right on walking. When I got back with the milk she was standing in front of our door. I told her Justin was still sleeping, and she said how nice it would be if she could have a cup of tea while she waited. I told her there was a café nearby. She didn't budge. I said would she mind stepping aside so I could get into my own home, and she started crying and going on about how she LOVED Justin and how if only she could talk to him they could patch everything up. (Talk about drama queen!!!) Not only was I DYING for a cup of tea, but I was going to have to dig a cup out of the sink and wash it before I could have one, so I was less than MEGA sympathetic. I told her that as far as I could see, Justin had even less interest in her than he did in translating Mansfield Park into Sanskrit. I advised her to get a life.

That's when she went for me! (Literally!!!) I know this may sound naive, but I really wasn't expecting to be attacked on my own doorstep. Which gave Bethsheba the advantage. She lunged straight at me and knocked me over. (If you ask me, it's a miracle I wasn't wounded.) It's just as well Sigmund's a light sleeper. He charged out in nothing but his boxers (which is not a pretty sight—if photographs of Sigmund in his boxers were given out in sex ed there'd be a whole lot less pregnant teenagers in this country, believe me), shouting like a kung fu warrior. Of course, it wasn't Satan's spawn he was shrieking at. It was ME—the innocent victim!!! What the hell are you doing? Yadda yadda yadda . . . What I was actually doing, besides trying to push the stupid cow off me, was open the milk so I could try to drown her. Sigmund got us both inside and then he went to wake up Justin, but Justin had already escaped through the garden despite the booby traps. Sigmund, of course, was **TOTALLY** oblivious to what had been going on, but Bethsheba was excruciatingly happy to fill him in. Anyway, Sigmund was all Mr. Concerned Parent and Comforting Shrink, while I (of course!!!) got stuck with making the tea and washing out **THREE** cups, etc.

Eventually Bethsheba calmed down enough to say she was sorry for trying to cut my promising life short, but she was in a v emotional state (um, duh . . . really???) and she couldn't believe I told her to **GET A LIFE** when that was what she had. Neither Sigmund nor I knew what she was on about. We looked at each other, and then we looked at her again and Sigmund said, "Pardon? I'm not certain I understand—" and Bethsheba started crying again. **HANG ON HARD TO ANYTHING THAT ISN'T CEMENTED DOWN!!!** Bethsheba, through a churning ocean of tears, said that what she meant was that she's carrying Justin's child! Even Sigmund didn't have an answer for that one. He just sat there like a beached fish, staring at her. I took advantage of this moment of **SHOCK AND HORROR** to pretend I had to go to the loo (not that either of them noticed). I walked straight out of the front door and went to Disha's. (What would I do

WITHOUT HER? I ask you!!!) D called it the Attack of the Killer Cow. She said did I really think Justin would be stupid enough to get Bumshiva knocked up and I asked her if she'd met my brother. I was going to stay over at D's, but in the end I decided to come home and work on my story. It's so **ABSOLUTELY** true that suffering fuels creativity, isn't it? Let's face it: shallow, happy people write Burger King jingles, but deep, unhappy people write *War and Peace.*

MONDAY 30 APRIL

Justin stayed at Sappho's again last night and the Mad Cow brought him home this afternoon. She said she reckoned it was time the four of us sat down and had a **SERIOUS** talk. Sigmund said too bloody right and immediately started going on about Justin being a disgrace. The MC wanted to know what he was on about, and when Sigmund explained she and Justin both fell about laughing, which made Sigmund go into morally superior mode (which is probably his favorite). He said he was shocked that the MC, of all people, would condone Justin's irresponsible behavior. Justin stopped laughing long enough to say that he wasn't like Sigmund and didn't indulge in irresponsible behavior. Sigmund said that getting your girlfriend pregnant and then dumping her like a hot potato was pretty irresponsible in his book. Justin said first of all Bumshiva'd **NEVER** been his girlfriend and that second of all she **WASN'T PREGNANT**; she was just insane. Sigmund said, "That's what you say." Justin said it was. The Mad Cow had already heard the whole tortured tale from Justin (obviously), and she **TOTALLY** believed him. Sigmund got all haughty and raised an eyebrow and all like he'd completely forgotten he was meant to be trying to encourage the MC to like him again and said **REALLY?** The MC said **REALLY**. She said if Bethsheba actually was preggers it was either an immaculate conception or the father was someone we didn't know. Sigmund asked her how she could be so sure, and the MC said because Justin wasn't a compulsive liar like the only other male in this family!!! I just sat there, observing all of this like a Great Writer would, but I have to admit I was v impressed by my mother. I'd never seen her like this before. Then she said that anyway, Bethsheba's histrionics weren't what we had to talk about. You could tell from the way he immediately started nodding and looking v serious like someone on Newsnight that Sigmund thought this meant she was ready to come home for good. But I was watching the **NEW** Jocelyn Bandry and I had my doubts (and also I noticed she didn't have a suitcase with her). You should've seen Sigmund's face when the MC said she was coming home, but only because he was moving **OUT**. (If he doesn't stop looking like a dying fish I may have to change his name to Trout!!!) Sigmund wanted to know where this brilliant idea came from but the MC just smiled and gave me a look.

TUESDAY 1 MAY

I gave Ms. Staples my story today. It's over **TEN PAGES**. Ms. Staples said no wonder it took me so long to write. I said I **KNOW** how busy she is and all (apparently teachers, like whales, are an endangered species!!!), but I would **REALLY** appreciate it if she could read it as soon as she has a chance. Now that my creativity has been turned on, it needs **FEEDBACK**. Ms. Staples said she'd do her best.

WEDNESDAY 2 MAY

I'd like to think that the new Jocelyn Bandry owes something to me and the Dark Phase. I mean, it's possible, isn't it? She saw me struggling to live deeply and meaningfully and she was inspired. She looked at her own life and she saw its shallowness and triviality, and she was finally ready to face the pain and remake herself. The Dark Phase has **DEFINITELY** affected Disha. I have always known that I will never have a better friend than Disha

Paski—not if I live to be a **MILLION** (though, really, who would want to?)—but now she has surpassed herself. How? I hear you ask. And this is how. To stop my torment Disha took direct action. She just came right out and asked Calum if Elvin was interested in me or not. Calum said or not. Disha said she was wondering because Elvin had sort of made a play for me, and Calum said, "Oh, that." D wanted to know oh what. Turns out Elvin was hoping that if he got friendly with me he could get Justin to help him with his film. My only consolation is that Elvin's stupid film is also the reason he was cooing round Catriona. Because of her father. He was hoping he could get it on telly. I'm **DEVASTATED**! Mine is a trusting nature. I can't believe someone could be so duplicitous. Disha says well, live and learn—that's what life's all about, isn't it? (She really has **MATURED**!!!)

THURSDAY 3 MAY

NOTHING lasts for ever, that's the truth. Last week I was a motherless child, and now I'm a fatherless one. Sigmund moved out tonight, although, as Justin says, it isn't as if he's gone **FAR**. He's got a flat in Kentish Town. The MC's saying this is a trial separation, but Sigmund couldn't have been halfway up the road before she was rearranging their bedroom. Already the living standards have risen. There's bog roll in the bathroom and we had meatballs and spaghetti for supper. It wasn't as bad as I remember, but that could just be because I've been on the Sigmund Bandry Starvation Diet. Now that Elvin has proved not to be a Man of Principles but a 𝕾𝖓𝖆𝖐𝖊 𝖎𝖓 𝖙𝖍𝖊 𝕲𝖗𝖆𝖘𝖘 𝖔𝖋 𝕷𝖔𝖛𝖊, I've started eating meat again. I mean, really, why not?

David rang tonight to see if I wanted to go to a film on Saturday night. I said yes. He said just you and me, right? I said of course. At least I know that David is an honest person and interested in ME—not my brother. And also (since I'm not COMMITTED to anyone yet) I've already arranged to go ice-skating on Sunday with Marcus.

FRIDAY 4 MAY

I AM DEFINITELY ON MY CREATIVE WAY!!!
Ms. Staples was v impressed with my story. She says it's funny, insightful, and ORIGINAL. She even wants to publish it in the school magazine. She did say we'll have to sit down and discuss it IN DEPTH, of course. She says she still feels I have a problem with implausible plots.

I said it's not MY problem—it's LIFE'S.

PLANET JANET
IN ORBIT

For Chiqui D

FRIDAY 13 JULY

Let the bells of **FREEDOM** ring! The last day of school
finally arrived! As you know, it's been a **GRUELING**
year of hard work and personal development (with all the
stress and slog of GCSEs), but though I'm pleased with how
much I've grown and matured, I'm also très glad it's over.
A person can only take so much graft and growth, and then
she really needs to **RELAX**. So it was all tears and hugs
at the institution today. Farewell, dear friends. See you in
September. Though we won't see **EVERYONE**, of course.
Siranee, Alice, and Sara Dancer are all going to different
colleges in the autumn. It seems like only yesterday that we
were nervous Year 7s who thought taking the laces out of
our trainers was très cool and were awed by the sight of kids
smoking behind the science building, and now it was the last
time we'd ever walk through those gates together unless in
memory. [Note to self: Youth really does go **QUICKLY**,
doesn't it?] Because my father is **OBSESSED** with Bob

Dylan, I know all of his billions of songs by heart, and it's just like he says: Everything passes and changes. Ms. Staples said she was V IMPRESSED with my efforts this year and that I deserve to have some fun (at least SOMEONE appreciates me!). She said I was going to have to work even harder next year, but she was looking forward to having me for A-level English. I said likewise. I said I didn't know how I could have got through this year without her *Support, Inspiration, and Encouragement*. She said hearing something like that makes working sixty hours a week for a fraction of the salary of a spin doctor worth it. She said I should write to the Prime Minister and tell him, since he seems to think education is only about test results.

Disha's father has pretty much recovered from the trauma of the 𝕹𝖎𝖌𝖍𝖙 𝖔𝖋 𝖙𝖍𝖊 𝕾𝖒𝖔𝖐𝖊 𝕬𝖑𝖆𝖗𝖒, so I'm invited to go to Greece with her family in August! They're renting a house on some idyllic island untouched by time (except that there's electricity, etc.). I said I thought it sounded terminally COOL. After all, GREECE is the cradle of Western Civilization. Disha said we'll be on a beach, not in Athens, and anyway, she doesn't think Greece is civilization's cradle—it's more like the nursery. I said so Rome's the cradle, but they're pretty close to each other, aren't they? And she said actually it's Iraq that is the cradle of Western Civilization—from when it was called Mesopotamia. Neither of us is sure how a beach holiday fits in with the Dark Phase, so we've agreed to take a short (and much-deserved) break. After all, even God rested on the seventh day. We'll continue to think DEEPLY and be creative, of course, but we're going to forget about jazz and Albert Camus for a while and ENJOY ourselves. (To tell you the TRUTH, I never finished *The Outsider*, even though it's pretty short, and I always lose track of what the song is in jazz unless there are words.) Disha said we should look on this as ANOTHER BIG STEP ON THE LADDER OF LIFE. She said she thought it could be a v broadening experience. Apparently there was a story in the paper about a teenager who fell in love with a waiter at the hotel where she went on holiday and then ran away from home to go back and marry him. (Disha's always reading newspapers. I don't usually bother because everyone knows that they never tell you the truth, and if there's one thing the Dark Phase has taught me, it's that there's enough lying in everyday life without looking for MORE!) Disha said what if we fall in love in Greece? I said I didn't reckon either of us was about to fall in love with a waiter.

Not everyone's going away for the summer. Marcus and David are staying in London (poor sods!). Marcus gets to sleep till noon and play video games all night, but David's dad is making him work in China Gardens, his take-away (no gardens, and miles from China Town, never mind

Beijing). We all commiserated with him, of course, but—
if you ask me—riding around on a scooter isn't exactly
slave labor.

SATURDAY 14 JULY

Oh, how I wish Ms. Staples was my mother instead of
Jocelyn Bandry. It just isn't fair. Of course, I know Life isn't
fair (yet another thing the DP has taught me!), but it does
seem to me that my life is more unfair than most. If there
was any justice in this world, Ms. Staples would be my
parent. Ms. Staples has a *Passionate Soul* and a *Questing
Spirit*. She also truly appreciates me (unlike some **BLOOD
RELATIVES** I could mention). Ms. Staples would let me
go to Greece and expand my cultural horizons. She'd say
I **MUST GO**—my *Spiritual Growth* demands it. The
Mad Cow said, "I thought you were getting a summer job."
(It's incredible, isn't it? She can't remember the simplest
thing I asked her to do for me yesterday, but some passing
remark made **MONTHS** ago, she remembers!!!) I said I
didn't recall being date-specific. She said not only can we
not afford for me to go away, but if I don't start earning
some money soon, I'll finally get my chance to see what
Oxfam looks like on the inside—because there'll be **no
NEW clothes** this autumn! (I ask you, what sort of
mother would let her only daughter go to school in **RAGS**?)

She said anyway, the house is going to feel really empty with Justin gone and she'd like my company. I said did that mean Justin's finally been arrested? She said it meant Justin was taking some time off to travel, didn't I listen to **ANYTHING** anyone says? I said only the important stuff. Apparently Justin's tired of taking pictures of poor people in London and is going to South America to take pictures of them there. I asked how it is that she has money to send Geek Boy wandering all over the world to bother the peasants but no money to send me to Greece to expand my cultural horizons. She said Justin's paying for the whole thing with the money he got from his photographs. I swear he does this stuff just to **IRK** me!!!

Disha tried to cheer me up over this **CRUSHING BLOW** (as you know, she's very loyal). She said that, personally, she wishes she could stay in London with me. What's the big deal about sitting on a beach all by yourself? I pointed out that she'd be all by herself if she did stay here because **I HAVE TO WORK**. She said I don't have to work **ALL** the time though, do I? I said I would if the MC had her way. It's just as well slavery was abolished or she'd've sold me off years ago. Disha said slavery still exists. I hope no one tells my mother.

MONDAY 16 JULY

I GOT A JOB! Can you BELIEVE IT?!! (The MC can't.)
And I'm not working in Woolies or anything like that, either.
(Which, of course, was what the MC suggested. Imagination
is not her strong point—assuming, of course, that she
actually has one.) I was going past this V TRENDY
Mexican restaurant in the neighborhood and thinking how
nice it would be to eat there sometime (it's way too sophisticated and upmarket for my family) when I noticed the HELP
WANTED sign in the window. As you know, I'm very outgoing, have megatons of personality and like to help people,
so I reckoned it was the *perfect* job for me. Also, I'd much
rather work in a place where you might bump into an actor
you recognize than somewhere like Woolies—where the
only person I've ever bumped into is the security guard—so
I just went right in. The owner's name is Mr. Saduki (he's
dark and has a mustache, so I reckon he's Mexican even
though I thought they were all named things like Lopez).
I was prepared to lie about having experience (on the
grounds that I've spent YEARS putting food on the table
and clearing it away again), but he didn't even ask. All he
wanted to know was when I could start. I said I was available
for immediate employment. He said all I had to do was get
my uniform together (I supply the white shirt and black skirt
or trousers and he throws in the string tie with the silver D—
for Durango) and he'd put me on weekday shifts till I learned
the ropes. I said I'd have it sorted by tomorrow. He said

214

and no trainers: you have to wear black, low-heeled shoes.
Neither black, low-heeled shoes nor white shirts have ever
formed part of my essential wardrobe, of course, so I raced
home to get some money off the MC to go shopping. Can
you believe it? She said she'd **LOAN** me the money, but
I have to pay it back out of my wages!!! (There's just no
end to this woman's ability to sink to new depths of bad
parenting.) I said since she's the one forcing me to work,
I'd've thought paying for my uniform was the least she could
do. She said no, loaning me the money was the least she
could do.

TUESDAY 17 JULY

So now I know where slavery still exists—in **DURANGO**!
My feet feel like I loaned them to someone else—someone
who's just walked across the Himalayas in too-small shoes
(they may **LOOK** comfortable, but, as we all know,
appearances can be **EXCRUCIATINGLY** deceptive!).
And there's more to this waiting-on-tables lark than you'd
think. [Note to self: Don't **EVER** for even one second
consider becoming an actor, as they all work as waiters until
the big break comes, which is a pretty depressing thought if
the big break never turns up!] You not only have to write
everything down and fetch it and all; you're meant to do all
this v quickly and with a cheery smile (and you can't stop

smiling just because you've got a customer with the personality of Margaret Thatcher). And then there are the Kitchen Staff, who, I notice, Mr. Saduki kept pretty quiet about yesterday. There are three of them and they all look like they've got form, probably v recent. Not that this has made them grateful for a chance to go straight and make an honest living. They've all got MAJOR attitude problems and do nothing but grumble and snap your head off. It's all pretty strenuous and stressful. Not only are my feet ABSOLUTELY KILLING me, but my face aches from smiling so much! Also, the other waiter on my shift comes straight from hell. Her name's SKY! (If you ask me, it should be BOSOM, since her breasts enter the room at least a minute before the rest of her!) She's a complete KNOW-IT-ALL in the Catriona Move-Over-God Hendley mold. I tried to ignore her, but it was très difficult since she spent the entire day TELLING ME WHAT TO DO. By the time I limped into the Staff Room (otherwise known as the Broom Cupboard) at the end of my shift to get my things, I'd decided I wasn't coming back. But God finally took pity on all my suffering. One of the waiters on the next shift was in there reading a newspaper (maybe they're not as big a waste of time as previously believed!). I thought *My Heart had Died and Gone to Heaven*. My first thought was: *So this is what humans are meant to look like!* His name's Ethan and he's Australian (most of what I know about Australia comes from those beer ads and a documentary I saw on how badly the Aborigines were

216

treated, but, of course, I said that I'd always wanted to go there). He's only just started too, but he's been a waiter for over a year. He's almost twenty, and looks like he spends a lot of time outdoors (surfing, etc.). In addition to being so good-looking, he's practically a walking advert for God: Ethan's extremely nice, v sophisticated, and staggeringly mature (it wasn't a tabloid he was reading!). All I can say is **THANK HEAVEN** I never made up my mind about getting serious with either Marcus or David!!! Can you imagine the **agony** if I wasn't **FREE**?!! Have decided to give Durango a second chance.

Sappho was looming in the living room when I got home. (And when I say **LOOMING**, I mean it. I've never seen anyone **SO PREGNANT**—she looks like she's carrying triplet elephants.) Sappho wanted to know how I like the Working Life. I said I don't think it's a patch on the Life of Leisure. After that, all she talked about was indigestion and back pain, etc. (all of which are apparently integral parts of pregnancy). It was dead boring so I went to my room to think about Ethan, which is a lot better than thinking about morning sickness!

WEDNESDAY 18 JULY

The only reason I didn't burst into tears and **WALK OUT** when the man who ordered the Chihuahua Chicken yelled at me so much that I knocked his water over (For God's sake—chicken . . . beef . . . what's the difference? They're both full of hormones!) was the thought that I was going to see Ethan again. Even when Miss Bazooms took over, I didn't lose it. Not even when she told the bloke I was **NEW** and hadn't caught on yet in this *très* patronizing voice. *You'll see that face again,* I told myself. *Be cool.* . . . God must be feeling a bit guilty about me, because for once this demonstration of maturity and self-discipline was actually **REWARDED** instead of punished. Ethan was right where I left him yesterday! His smile nearly turned me to mush, but I rallied enough to ask if he was waiting on tables because he wants to be an actor. He said no, he's waiting on tables because he wants to be a waiter. His *Passion* is travel (he's already been to India!), and being a waiter means he can always get a job. I said I'm going to South America after my A-levels, as I believe that experiencing a new culture is worth *très* more than anything you can get from books, and he agreed. He said South America is his next destination too! He wanted to know where I was planning to go in South America. I know there are quite a few countries down there, but the only ones I could think of at such short notice were Mexico (because I spend half my life filling tiny cups with

218

pickled chilies, etc.) and Colombia. I said Colombia, because Durango is as close to Mexico as I ever want to get! He said he thought that was very brave of me— because of the gorillas. I said I didn't know they had gorillas in South America; I thought they were only in Africa. He thought this was **HYSTERICAL**. By the time he stopped laughing, I'd worked out that he meant guerrillas as in soldiers, not gorillas as in large primates (I must've been paying more attention to **HIM** than what he was saying, which is understandable!), so I acted like I'd meant it as a joke. Ethan said that, all kidding aside, he thinks it's important to have a sense of adventure. I totally agreed.

Had to wash my shirt **BY HAND** tonight because I got something red on it (if you ask me, dark **PINK** would be a much better color for our uniforms). I only hope it doesn't rain, since the Mad Cow refused to put on the heating just to dry my shirt, because it's **THE MIDDLE OF JULY**. I bet if it was Justin, she would've cranked it up as high as it would go. Maybe I should've bought more than one shirt. [Note to self: When you have children of your own, don't treat them the way your mother treats you! Be nice to them!]

THURSDAY 19 JULY

NEWSFLASH!!! Mr. Saduki isn't Mexican; he's from Pakistan. Of course, this piece of information came from Sky (which is where she acts like she's talking to me from). Trying to be friendly, I asked her if she thought Mr. Saduki brought the blankets and crap he's got on the walls from Mexico with him, and she said did I mean the Mexico that's next to India? Sky said she reckoned Durango's the closest Saduki's ever been to Mexico. She thought it was **ABSOLUTELY HILARIOUS** that I didn't know he was from Pakistan. I said well, he looks Mexican, and she said he also looks Pakistani and that if I'd ever done any traveling (as *she* has, of course) I'd know that. [Note to self: Discuss with Disha the fact that people from opposite sides of the world can look so alike.]

I live for the end of my **Day of Toil** and my few stolen minutes of *Bliss* with Ethan. If it weren't for him, I wouldn't put up with this crap for a single second!!! (You wouldn't believe how **RUDE** and **SNOTTY** a lot of customers are. Today this woman made me take her meal back **THREE TIMES**!!! It took so long, she could've gone to **Mexico** for lunch!) Ethan said he overheard the blokes in the kitchen talking and he thinks the reason Mr. Saduki wasn't too bothered about me not having any experience is because half his staff quit last week and he's desperate. I said thanks for the compliment and laughed (which was the first time I'd laughed **ALL DAY!**). Ethan said he likes a girl with a sense of humor! Which is **ME**, of course. Everybody says I should be a comedian. I said it's too bad the chef didn't quit. The chef, whose name as far as I can work out is Gonzo, has already told me off **FIVE TIMES**. Ethan said not to take it personally: chefs are known for being temperamental because of the stressful, creative nature of their work. I didn't want to start disagreeing with him before we'd even had one date, but I don't see what's so stressful or creative about wrapping some beans up in a pancake. I definitely think I'm about to *Fall in Love*!!!

Today I got something green on my shirt! [Note to self: If you ever work in a restaurant again, make sure you choose a country whose cuisine isn't so colorful. Like Tibet. All they eat in Tibet is rice.] If I have to wash my shirt out **EVERY NIGHT**, it's going to be in shreds by the end of the month. As soon as I get my wages, I'm back to the West End for more white shirts. I wonder if they have any that are stain-resistant.

FRIDAY 20 JULY

So how was **YOUR** day, Janet? Bloody awful. I wasn't even supposed to be working today but someone was ill, so (out of the goodness of my heart) I said I'd do an extra shift. This was a MAJOR MISTAKE. First of all, turns out it's Ethan's day off. I was so DEVASTATED I nearly burst into tears. Naturally, since I was so traumatized, Sky was on top form. (There must be a place people like her and Catriona Hendley go to learn how to be a real cow—NOBODY could be born that way!) I couldn't fill a salt cellar today without being told I was doing it wrong! Saduki adores Sky, of course. Even if it was possible to look ANYWHERE and not notice those breasts, he wouldn't (I'm not even sure he's ever seen her face!). He's just a phoney Mexican. The second reason this day was the bottom of an *abyss of misery* is because I've worked my feet to a pulp for nearly AN ENTIRE WEEK—and what do I have to show for it? ABSOLUTELY NOTHING. (Well, almost absolutely nothing.) I've got my tips, but they're not exactly what I was expecting. I thought you were meant to earn a fortune waiting on tables, but I don't have enough to buy a single white shirt, never mind anything I ACTUALLY WANT!!! Apparently they keep your first week's wages, just in case. I said just in case of what? Saduki said in case I break something. The only thing I'm likely to break in this job is my back or SOMEBODY's neck. Anyway, I got home tonight feeling about as down as you can get without actually falling through the earth. I really could've done with a nice meal and some pleasant company. DREAM ON! Of course, I'm all on my own. Since my paternal

222

parent moved in with Nan, the Mad Cow must be bored
having no one to argue with, because she's **NEVER** home
(even in the summer, she's got her reading group and her
yoga and some class that sounds like Pontius Pilate).
Also, now that Sigmund's gone, my maternal parent is
taking a new interest in her appearance (I don't have the
heart to tell her it's way too late). Most women her age
go in for plastic surgery (which, in the MC's case, would
be **TOTALLY UNDERSTANDABLE**), but she's
decided on a permanent diet instead. Which means there's
no real food in the house. So I microwaved myself a
couple of her diet dinners (they taste all right, but there's
not much to them), since even though I'm allowed to eat
as much as I want at the restaurant, I wouldn't touch the
crap they serve if I was starving. (I actually saw Gonzo
making barbecue sauce out of Coca-Cola and tomato
ketchup, which was enough to put me off restaurant
food for life.)

Rang Disha. She had chicken and homemade chips
for supper (at least someone's mother still believes in
cooking!). D says the tips'll be better when I start doing
night shifts because people drink more and that makes them
generous. She couldn't talk long because her father wanted
to use the phone and she no longer has a mobe because
her mother threw it in the toilet. (Now Mrs. Paski's going
through the **BIG M**. It just never ends, does it?)

*   *   *

When I heard Sigmund getting ready to leave the bunker, I went out to say hello. The deal is that he can use the bunker for his clients, but he has to have the Mad Cow's permission to come in the flat. (Usually I avoid him like spots because I'm still pretty pissed off with him for fooling around with Mrs. Kennedy and destroying our unhappy home, but I was **REALLY** desperate for some *Companionship and Sympathy*.) I might as well have gone out on the street and waylaid some total stranger. Sigmund didn't even ask me how my day was or if I had terminal blisters or was on the verge of **EMOTIONAL AND PHYSICAL COLLAPSE** or anything like that (I ask you, how can it be possible that people **PAY** this man for his sensitivity and understanding?!!). He wanted to know if we'd heard from Justin!!! I said **ALREADY**? He's only been gone a few days! Then he talked about himself, of course. Apparently Sigmund moved into his new flat yesterday, so now I can visit him anytime I want. (That's typical, isn't it? I have to wait on strangers hand and foot just to have some spending money, and he's got a flat!) I said the anticipation had been practically **KILLING** me. Could he book me in for my twenty-first birthday? He thought I was joking. Then I asked him if he could lend me a few quid because I **DIDN'T GET PAID**. Dr. Tell-Me-Your-Problems-I'm-Here-to-Help said **NO**. He said he's penniless because of the new flat and giving the MC money. Apparently it's not easy to support two households (pass me the handkerchief!). I said he

124

should've thought of that before he decided he needed two women.

I'm too horrifically fatigued to write another word, so I'm going to bed. Though, with my luck, I'll probably dream about giving the Texas Tacos to the bloke who ordered the Fajita Tijuana and being asked what language I DO speak since it's obviously not English. (I said MEXICAN!)

SATURDAY 21 JULY

D rang this morning to say that the trip to Greece is off! (She's not sure why—she doesn't listen to her parents any more than I listen to mine.) I was v sympathetic, of course, but, to tell you the truth, this piece of news cheered me up no end. Apparently feeling better about your own miseries because of someone else's is pretty common. Sigmund explained it to me once (God knows WHY). It's called *schadenfreude*, which is German and obviously has something to do with Freud (all of Sigmund's soul-numbing explanations have to do with Freud!). Disha wanted to go shopping to cheer herself up. She has to rethink her summer wardrobe, since she's staying in London (i.e., anoraks and umbrellas rather than swimsuits and flip-flops). I wanted to support my local best friend, of course, but I didn't really feel like going. (I mean, what was the point? I for one do not think shopping is a spectator sport.) So I asked the Mad Cow if she'd let me have some dosh. Since the MC's a teacher and not a psychotherapist, like Sigmund, I don't expect her to be kind and understanding— and, as per usual, she didn't let me down. Apparently she's trying to pay off her credit cards before she becomes another of the government's victims of debt. I said what about the money she gets from Sigmund? Surely some of this is meant to be for ME—or does she have other children she's supporting that I don't know about? She said half the stuff on her cards was FOR me (which can't possibly be true— we all know it's easier to get the truth out of a politician than money out of Jocelyn Bandry!!!). Was about to ring D back and say I was too FATIGUED to go shopping when I had one of my BRAINWAVES. JUSTIN!!! For the first time in nearly seventeen years, I was happy he's my brother. My Parents' Other Child has always been the sort of nerd who saved half his Easter egg till June and then lorded it over his baby sister because she'd finished hers by Easter Monday. This obsessive-compulsive behavior has always IRKED me, but now I reckoned it could be an advantage. Most people blow all they have on their holiday and then have to walk home from the airport, but not the Sharer of the Bandry Gene Pool. I knew there was no way he wouldn't have left some money to come back to. AND I WAS RIGHT. It was in an old brown jar mixed in with his chemicals in his darkroom (the world of international espionage lost the greatest agent since James Bond when

I decided to become an artist or a writer or whatever!!!).
There was **FIVE HUNDRED QUID** in it!!! I feel I'm
doing him a **MAJOR** favor. If he doesn't watch out, he's
going to end up one of those old men who live in **poverty
and squalor** till they die and then the police find a fortune
under the pee-stained mattress. And besides, it'll all be back
in the jar before he comes home, so what's the difference?
I know Karl Marx isn't popular any more, but I'm with him
on this one: From each according to his ability; to each
according to her need. My need's pretty **GINORMOUS**
right now. Also found Justin's mobe in an old camera bag.
Took that as well for emergencies, since the MC says they'll
be **skiing in hell** before I get another one after what happened
LAST TIME. Disha and I had a great time (I really don't
see why anyone would want a hobby like trainspotting
when shopping's so rewarding). I got **SIX** new white
shirts so I can do them all in the machine at the end of
the week, two more black skirts and two more pairs of
black trousers (ditto, one laundry), and a bunch of stuff
I **DESPERATELY NEEDED**. Ran into Marcus and
David. They'd been buying CDs. (I've noticed that though
boys may hate shopping the way real humans hate bad hair,
they're perfectly willing to do it if they're getting something
for themselves. Sappho says men are genetically more self-
centered because of not being mothers, though the MC is
obviously the **EXCEPTION** to this rule.) They wanted to
know why they hadn't heard from me since term ended,
and I said because I've become a wage slave, haven't I.

Though in my case it's more of a non-wage slave! Marcus said at least David gets paid for delivering chow mein.

I swear you can't turn your back on the Mad Cow for ONE MINUTE these days. While I was shopping, Sappho came over, chopped all the MC's hair off and DYED IT!!! And not blond or black or even what it used to be before it started going gray (mousy brown) like a normal person would. She dyed it PINK! I said didn't she think she was a little old for pink hair, and she said you're not old till you're dead. (How some people delude themselves!) Then I said I thought the school had rules about things like that (I've certainly never had a teacher with pink hair!), and she said if I hadn't noticed, it's SUMMER. I said how could I notice when I have to WORK ALL THE TIME? I reckon the MC's going through her midlife crisis now. D agrees. She says her uncle bought a sports car when he turned fifty. I said being seen in public with an old woman with pink hair is not the same as swanning around in a Jaguar. I wouldn't mind that. Disha said I would if I'd been with her uncle— he backed it out of the showroom and straight into a police van.

The sales assistant I asked about stain-resistant shirts was well sarky. She wanted to know if I'd ever heard of soap and water. I said I just thought that since this is THE TWENTY-FIRST CENTURY and scientists can put human ears on mice, one of them might have come up with something more useful, like clothes that stay clean. She said I was in Top Shop not **The Twilight Zone.**

The MC came snooping around my room and noticed my new gear. She wanted to know where I got the money. I said Sigmund gave it to me. She said she thought he was meant to be broke. I said some people are willing to make sacrifices for their children.

I think I'm getting corns. As if I don't suffer enough!

SUNDAY 22 JULY

Disha had to go to a gathering of the clan today and none of the lads were home, so I broke down and went over to see Sigmund's new flat. It's in Kilburn, which, if you ask me, is one of the most depressing areas in London (and not in a **Spiritual Angst** sort of way, in a what's-the-point-of-living sort of way—all cheap shops and **gloom**). Sigmund's flat is in this old, gray building behind the bingo hall (see what I mean?). The intercom doesn't work, the hall smells of damp, and the carpet on the stairs looks like it's been there since World War I. Sigmund's flat is at the top (needless to say, there is no lift). It took him a few minutes to get his breath back after we got up the stairs, and then he gave me the Grand Tour (which isn't going to make Thomas Cook lose any sleep, believe me!). First stop was the hall (about the size of my wardrobe—*sans* the clothes and shoes, of course); next was the bedroom (and **BED ROOM** pretty much sums it up); after that came the sitting room (ditto, an accurate description of what you can do in it); then the kitchen (stand-in, not eat-in); and finally the bathroom (the window's **INSIDE** the shower!). All of the furniture came from Nan's. The only remarkable thing in the entire flat was the pair of gold drop earrings on the shelf in the bathroom, where Sigmund keeps his rubber ducks (unless he's started cross-dressing, they definitely aren't his, so he must already have a new girlfriend!). The entire tour took all of one minute. (It would've been even quicker if Sigmund had remembered the trick to opening the bedroom door.) And there isn't any heating—unless you count the fireplace. He asked me what I thought of the flat and I said I was speechless, which he took as a compliment. Sigmund said he was lucky to get it at a price he could afford. I said I was surprised they hadn't given it to him. The **GOOD NEWS** is that there's no space for me to stay over. I wouldn't be surprised if it's got bugs. Sigmund made me coffee in his new coffeemaker (it was a good thing I was there or he would've forgotten to put the water in!!!). My cup was from the Queen's first jubilee and his was a souvenir from Blackpool (obviously it's not just the furniture that came from Nan.) The only thing he could find to eat were two stale chocolate biscuits. I said, FOR ME? You shouldn't've gone to so much trouble! Sigmund lit up a fag with his coffee. I said I thought he'd given up smoking again, and he said that he had but there's no way he can stick to it when he's under so much stress. I said in that case maybe he should just admit that he's never going to quit, since the only people who aren't stressed are **dead**.

For once the MC was home when I got back. I said I thought Sigmund had a girlfriend, and she said, "No change there then." She wanted to know what the flat's like. I said it's like a squat—only he has to pay rent. She said he has no one to thank but himself. He made his bed and now he's got to sleep in it. I said it wasn't really a bed; it was Nan's old army cot (does this mean Sigmund and his new girlfriend have to DO IT on the table? She must be a lot smaller than Mrs. Kennedy!). All of this made me think. Only a few months ago, Sigmund lived in a flat with central heating and beds and matching dinnerware, and now look at him! He's only one step away from living in a doorway if you ask me.

Disha rang as soon as she got home from the relatives. I told her all about Sigmund and Kilburn and the possibility that he'll end up sleeping in front of Marks and Sparks. D said that's Life, isn't it? You never know what's going to happen next. I said I know that's true in a general sense, but anyone could've told Sigmund what would happen if he got caught fooling around with Mrs. Kennedy like that. Disha said the reason Sigmund didn't think that sleeping with Mrs. Kennedy would destroy his life is because nobody really believes they're going to get caught. She said, Didn't I remember that politician who dared the press to discover him fooling around and then took some blonde he wasn't married to on his boat? She said it was all over the papers. She said it was a bit like me and my gym teacher: I always give the old bag the SAME EXCUSE for not playing hockey and then I'm surprised when she doesn't believe me. I said I didn't think it was the same thing at all. I said I thought it was much more like people not giving up smoking (as Disha said she could do WHENEVER she wanted!), because even though the cigarette packets are plastered with warnings like **Danger of Death**, they think they're not going to get cancer. Disha said that if I meant her, the only reason she didn't quit was because she hadn't realized how HARD it was going to be. I said I didn't see why not—it's not like she hadn't been TOLD. Sigmund's been giving up since I was in primary school.

MONDAY 23 JULY

Saduki's got me working Mondays now too (I can't refuse or he'll stop asking—also, I've got to put something away so I can put Geek Boy's money back before he returns from the Third World). So it was another day, another dozen enchiladas. The only good thing that happened was that I saw Ethan. I'm happy to tell you that, unlike the phony Mexican and the Borstal Boys in the kitchen, Ethan shows **NO INTEREST WHATSOEVER** in Sky's anatomy. In fact, he shows no interest in Sky **AT ALL**! (Because Sky thinks she's the Sun to everybody else's Planet, she always comes into the Staff Cupboard when we're in there, making a big deal of getting her stuff out of her locker and banging on about how **HARD** she works. But Ethan pretty much ignores her.) Even today when she leaned over him to get something (and practically **SUFFOCATED** the poor bloke in breasts), he kept right on talking to **ME**!

Sigmund was let into the flat tonight because just as he was slouching off to the mean streets of Kilburn, Geek Boy rang up. Usually the male progeny doesn't say more than three words a week, but when he's ringing from **THOUSANDS** of miles away on **SOMEONE ELSE'S** phone bill, he doesn't shut up. Since the MC and Sigmund were fully occupied, I took the opportunity to have a long soak to try and ease my aching muscles. (Must

233

find out what essential oil is good for **Physical Torture**.) The parents were still on the phone when I got out of the bath. Not only that, but they'd opened a **BOTTLE OF WINE!!!** (In case you think this is normal procedure in the Bandry household, let me assure you that no one **HAS EVER** opened a bottle of wine because they were talking to **ME!**) So, of course, by the time they did finally hang up, they forgot they only communicate in monosyllables now. Sigmund told the MC she was looking **TERRIFIC** (which is **NOT** what he said to me when my hair went red!), and the MC asked him how he was settling into his new flat. Except that they weren't yelling at each other, it was almost like old times—the two of them **IGNORING ME**, as per usual. So I decided to join in the conversation. I asked how Justin liked South America, which seemed like a perfectly reasonable question to me. They both started laughing. I asked what was so funny about that, and the MC said only someone who had totally left the Earth's orbit wouldn't know where her only brother is. I said so long as he's not near me, I don't really care. Apparently he's in Mexico. I said, That was what I said: How does he like South America? Sigmund said Mexico isn't **IN** South America. I said, What did they do, move it? It's **SOUTH OF THE BORDER**, isn't it? The MC said maybe I should've done a GCSE in geography after all. I asked her if she was aware that drinking made her particularly unfunny. Vacated the premises **IMMEDIATELY**, of course. Looked Mexico up in my atlas. Unless the lads at *The Times* made a mistake, it looks as though Mexico isn't in South America, after all—even though they do speak Spanish.

I knew the truce couldn't last. They got into one of their screaming bouts and Sigmund left, slamming the door. He didn't even bother saying goodbye to me, although I went all the way to Kilburn to see him yesterday (on the bus!!!). When I came out in search of sustenance, the MC told me what the fight was about (even though I hadn't actually asked). Apparently she wanted some money from him and he said he didn't have any, so she reminded him that he'd just given me a small fortune and he denied it. The MC says you can trust a thief but never a liar. I said that since Sigmund's reputation as a liar has been pretty well established, she couldn't say she hadn't been warned.

TUESDAY 24 JULY

Ethan said he really envies my brother. I said, You mean because he's related to me? And he laughed and *Gave Me a Hug*!!! It was THE MOST AMAZING FEELING I've ever experienced! A trillion stars exploded in my heart! ELECTRICITY flowed through every cell in my body. (I'm certain I was GLOWING, but there isn't a mirror in the Staff Cupboard, of course, so I couldn't check.) Now I know what people mean when they say they could *Die*

Happy! I wanted him to *Hug Me Forever*!!! I was so swept away by *Passion* that I sort of bounced off the wall when he let go, but I don't think he noticed since he was still all wound up in Mexico. He wanted to know how long Geek Boy's going to be away, and I said I reckoned he'd come back when he ran out of poor people to photograph. Ethan said he could be there YEARS in that case. Which is the best news I've had in months.

Nan came over tonight. You'd think a person's mother would be on his side when his marriage breaks up, but not Nan. She says the day Sigmund moved out of hers was the happiest she'd been since D-Day. She says she thanks God every night for finally finding Sigmund a place to live. He was driving her nuts. She said she doesn't know how the Mad Cow put up with him for so long.

WEDNESDAY 25 JULY

D met me after work today so she could get a look at Ethan. Ethan got to his feet the instant we stepped through the Cupboard door (he's not just another *Astoundingly Beautiful* face—he's a GENTLEMAN as well, which makes a pleasant change from the teenage Neanderthals we normally associate with). We didn't have much chance for a chat, though, because Sky barged in, and the Cupboard

136

wasn't big enough for the six of us (me, Disha, Ethan, Sky, and Sky's anatomy). Went home with Disha to discuss the situation. D was **TOTALLY** bowled over by Ethan. She wanted to know if I was **CERTAIN** he doesn't have a girlfriend, since it's hard to believe someone hasn't snapped him up. I said he hasn't been in London that long. And anyway, he's obviously **DISCRIMINATING** and wouldn't date someone just because her breasts are the size of a life jacket. D says if he doesn't ask me out soon, I should ask him. I said I'm still a bit **traumatized** from my experience with Elvin. D thinks I'm overreacting. She said that not only does Ethan not know my brother, but my brother's in Mexico, so Ethan can't be flirting with me because he wants to meet Justin. I said that was true, but being older and wiser does make one cautious. D doesn't think that's true. She says all being older and wiser means is you recognize your mistakes faster because you've made them before. Sometimes she's so **DEEP,** I think she must have had several past lives.

Sigmund was waiting for me like a lion waiting for an antelope when I got home tonight. He wanted to know why I told the MC he gave me money. I said I didn't. I said she must have misunderstood me. So then he wanted to know what I **DID** say. I said I'd told her I'd borrowed it and she must've thought I meant from him. He said that wasn't the way the MC told the story. I said, Well, you know what she's like: she never really listens, does she?

THURSDAY 26 JULY

I can't see Saduki making it to old age, not with his temper. His blood pressure must be higher than the Post Office Tower. I had **ONE FOOT** through the door today when he started. In case I hadn't noticed, he's running a restaurant not a social club and unless my friends are planning to order a meal, they're **NOT TO COME AROUND**. I said my friends valued their health too much to eat at Durango. It didn't stop there of course. I was tempted to quit on the spot, but then I wouldn't see Ethan again unless I came in as a customer and **THERE'S NO WAY** I'd ever do that.

FRIDAY 27 JULY

This truly is **THE SUMMER OF MY DISCONTENT!!!** You're **NOT GOING TO BELIEVE THIS!** (I can hardly believe it myself.) I said I'd work today because it's pay day. And guess what? The Dorito Bandito (which I feel is an appropriate name since he doesn't come from Mexico any more than Dorito tortilla chips do!!!) not only deducted the cost of the tray of **DIRTY DISHES** I dropped but charged me for his stupid tie **AS WELL!!!** (Sappho's always banging on about the Working Poor, and now I know what she means!) I asked him when he was going to give me some night or weekend shifts so at least I could make some **MEANINGFUL** tips. He said when I stopped mixing up orders and trying to drown the customers. And if you think I got any sympathy for all this from the MC when I got home, you probably believe in Father Christmas. She said **WELCOME TO THE REAL WORLD, JANET.** She reminded me that I still owe her for the first shirt, black trousers, and those torturous shoes. Fortunately she was getting ready to go out. Women the MC's age need at least two hours to prepare for public appearances, so by the time she surfaced from that, she'd forgotten about the dosh, and God knows the sight of her **TOTALLY** shoved it out of my mind. Not only was she wearing **MAKEUP** (she'd better not have used **MINE!**); she was also wearing **ORANGE** combats and a white shirt covered with dragons. She looked like she'd been tattooed! I asked her if she was going to a fancy-dress party and she said as a matter of fact she had a **DATE!** I said who with? The strongman from the circus? She said with the same guy she went out with last week and the week before. Apparently she's met some bloke at her yoga class. I said I hoped he was color-blind, since her trousers clashed with her hair. She said fashion is fascism. I said tell that to Naomi Campbell.

Talked to D on the mobe till gone midnight and still no sign of the Mad Cow. And she's always on at **ME** about

being **RESPONSIBLE**. You'd think she'd ring to say
if she's going to be back **REALLY LATE**. I know
there isn't much chance of it in that outfit, but what if
I was worried that she'd been hit by a bus? She has **NO
CONSIDERATION** for anyone else. [Note to self: If
I ever do have children, I will always give them the time
and understanding they need and put them first like you're
meant to.]

SATURDAY 28 JULY

No sign of the MC when I got up this morning. For a
change it wasn't raining, so Disha and I went to the park.
Just because we're stuck in the concrete city doesn't mean
we have to be the **ONLY** people in the world not to have
a tan. We brought beach hats and sunglasses and flip-flops
so we could pretend we were on the white sands of the
Mediterranean. D and I discussed **LIFE** and things like that
for a while (D said that even though he **HUGGED** me,
maybe Ethan was just shy about asking me out—after all,
hugging's a natural, accepted thing and even the Queen
hugs people now and then). Then we plugged ourselves
into our Discmen and gave ourselves over to the worship
of the Sun, Giver of Life. I was sort of dozing off a
bit, imagining I was on a deserted beach with a certain
Australian, when something touched my foot. I reckoned it

was a dog. I'm wary of dogs since the time one came over all cute and friendly and then attached itself **TO MY LEG** and got all excited. (It was très **EMBARRASSING**.) I sat up to chase the dog away and **NEARLY PASSED OUT** with joyous surprise! It wasn't an oversexed spaniel; it was one of those little dogs that look like gremlins—and with it was **ETHAN**!!! Apparently the dog belongs to his landlady and he helps her out by taking it for walks. (Didn't I say he was a **GENTLEMAN**?) He said I was looking a little pink, but I assured him that I don't burn. I asked if he remembered Disha and he said how could he forget her? (**CHARMING** or what?) D and I watched the dog (whose name is Fifi even though she's definitely not a poodle) while Ethan went off and got us all ice creams (which is not the sort of thing you really want to be eating when you want to look your best, because it drips, but I couldn't say no!). He hung out with us for **AT LEAST AN HOUR**! It was **TOTALLY INCREDIBLE**. I can't even remember what we talked about, I was so *Hypnotized by Love* (though there could've been a bit of **lust** involved as well since he is **SO GORGEOUS**!!!). He only left because he had to go to work. As soon as he left, Disha started nagging me again to ask him out before someone else gets her hooks into him. I said I'm working on it.

The MC said I should put something on my face because it looked a bit pink. I reminded her that I don't burn. Asked her what time she got in last night and she laughed and

241

said **THIS MORNING**!!! I said I took it that meant she'd had a good time. She said they had a lot to talk about (we all know what **THAT** means!). I said I just hope she practices **SAFE SEX**. She said, Where would I be if she did?

SUNDAY 29 JULY

Woke up to discover that my face looks as though it's been **GRILLED**. Fortunately it only hurts when I smile (which isn't something I do too much round here!). Went straight to the MC to see if she had any magic potions for sunburn. I said it has to be something that works really **FAST** because I've got to go back to **Hell's Kitchen** tomorrow. The MC said she can't guarantee anything, but she gave me something so it won't blister. Thank God it's pissing down so I don't feel tempted to go to the park in case Ethan's walking the mutt again.

Marcus and David asked me and Disha to go to a film with them. Since it meant sitting in the dark most of the time, it didn't matter that my nose makes me look like Father Christmas is going to ask me to lead his sleigh, so I said yes. (I wore sunglasses so everyone would assume I'd just got back from some incredible holiday.) The film was OK.

242

(They picked it, which is never an indication of Intellectual Content.) Some of us talked about our jobs. David hates his as much as I hate mine. He says I'm wrong about riding a scooter being fun. Apparently it's all whining customers and dicing with death. (Yesterday some crazed motorcycle courier with some sort of vendetta *deliberately* ran him up on the sidewalk!) David said almost every adult he can think of hates their job. [Note to self: Our lives are but a drop in the ocean of time and yet we spend them delivering cold rice and waiting on people who don't leave tips!] David says his uncle used to get really happy when Friday came around but now it just depresses him because it's so close to Monday. [Another note to self: This may be the destiny of most people, but it's not going to be mine!] Had everyone HYSTERICAL with my True Stories of Being a Waitress. (Marcus says I should write a book! I may discuss this idea with Ms. Staples—the school magazine could do with a little humor, since it tends to be dominated by the whining poetry of Catriona Hendley.) The MC was out, as per usual, so Disha came back to mine and stayed the night. D said that even though we always have a good time with Marcus and David, after a conversation with Ethan, talking to those two is a bit of a comedown. She said it's like having a gourmet meal one night and a pot noodle the next. I agreed with her, even though I couldn't remember what it was we'd talked about with Ethan (but it was obviously GOOD!).

*   *   *

Spent most of the day mucking about with the MC's new collection of makeup, looking for something to make my face look less bright. At least the pain's going.

TUESDAY 31 JULY

Another day that was dreamed up by Satan when he was in a **REALLY BAD** mood. First of all, **EVERYONE** noticed the sunburn. Saduki muttered something about mad dogs and Englishmen, and Sky said I looked a bit like a racoon—only red. Then I had an argument with Gonzo because he said I had the writing of someone who was educationally challenged (he should know!). Then I had an argument with Saduki because he said I was over-filling the salsa bowls (they're not even **BOWLS**—they're thimbles!). **THEN** I leaned over to reach for something and my brand-new shirt ripped down the arm (and it cost nearly twenty quid!). **ALSO**, I didn't even have a nanosecond alone with Ethan today because Sky was stuffed into the Cupboard with us the whole time.

The MC got on the phone after supper and never got off, so I went to my room and rang D on Geek Boy's mobe. D says it might be the bleach that made my shirt tear like that. I said how can something everybody uses all the time

244

be so destructive? D said lots of things are. She said maybe I should go easy on the bleach. But **HOW CAN I**? I'll be buying a new white shirt every other day at this rate. The MC was still nattering away when I came out for a soothing cup of bedtime tea. God knows who she was talking to: the only ones who talk that much are Nan and Sappho (I know it wasn't Nan because neither arthritis nor Jesus was mentioned, and it wasn't Sappho because neither vomit nor pain came up in the conversation).

WEDNESDAY 1 AUGUST

Ethan said he had something he wanted to ask me. But before he could ask it, Miss Bazooms barged in and **THAT ENDED THAT**. D agrees with me that that's practically the same as asking me out. Now I just have to survive the *long and lonely* night and hope he manages to ask me tomorrow. The rain and my *Longing for Love* made me feel thoughtful and melancholy tonight. Decided to start writing some poetry. I reckon poems may be more my thing than stories since you don't have to worry about plot or motivation or continuity or any of that crap. And also, they're much more open to *Inspiration*, which it seems to me is what *Art and Literature* are about. If I wanted to slog my brains out at something that I never got right, I'd be a mathematician. So far I've only got the first line: *How brief is youth and, oh, how filled with pain.* I'm not **TOTALLY** sure what it's about yet, but it was inspired by my feet (which will probably *never* heal).

THURSDAY 2 AUGUST

Still haven't had a chance to hear what Ethan wants to ask me (**OH, WHAT COULD IT BE?!!**), so I said all casual like that we should go for a coffee sometime when we're not working, so we can actually finish a conversation. He positively jumped at the chance! He said what about tomorrow? He said we could meet at that place by the canal after I get off work. I said I did have plans for the evening but I could probably squeeze in a quick cup before. (This isn't true, of course, but I don't want him to think I'm not popular.) I've decided to act really surprised when he asks me out—like it never entered my head that he might be interested in **ME**. Then I'll hesitate and say maybe it isn't such a great idea and how there are always articles in magazines about not mixing romance and work. Then I'll let him persuade me that I'm wrong. I plan to wait at least a week before I tell him how terrific I think he is (but I will kiss him on the first date—I don't want to play too hard to get).

FRIDAY 3 AUGUST

I'm beginning to think that the **ONE** thing you can count on in Life is that nothing is **EVER** going to go the way you want it to. Really. Maybe I should just quit while I'm ahead and become a nun or something. I mean, being a nun isn't really that bad, is it? You get a place to stay and food and a bunch of other nuns to do good deeds with, etc., and you know you're never going to experience **heartbreak and despair** (nuns are married to Jesus, and Nan says He never lets anybody down). Ethan was already at the café when I got there. I acted like I hadn't seen him at first, even though he stood out like a Jaguar in a car park full of Fords. (He looked **INCREDIBLE!** Every female in the place was looking at him, even the ones with lads.) We ordered cappuccinos and chatted about this and that. When I couldn't stand the suspense anymore, I said, "So what did you want to ask me?" About the only thing that went according to my fantasies from that point on was that I acted surprised. **I WAS SURPRISED.** It isn't **ME** he wants to go out with—it's **DISHA.** I couldn't believe it! My best friend? Is he thick or something? Couldn't he tell I fancied him? He wanted to know if she had a boyfriend and also if I'd ask her if it was all right to ring her. I could've said she did have a boyfriend (someone **INSANELY** jealous with a black belt in karate), but I decided that was v immature. Also—even though I find it **GALLING** that he's sometimes right—Sigmund says that most people are

247

honest only because they're afraid of getting caught, and I was worried Ethan might find out the truth (the way my luck's going, it's practically **INEVITABLE**). Also, Disha Paski, as you know, is the most loyal friend a girl could have, so I know she'll turn him down flat (which he certainly deserves). I said I'd ask her. Ethan said I was a real mate (but not the sort I'd had in mind!). The MC was glued to the telephone from the minute she got home, so, sadly, asking D if Ethan can call her will have to wait until tomorrow (I don't see why I should *pay* to ask her). Decided to take a candlelit bath to cheer myself up. Stayed in the bath so long I was **TOTALLY** shriveled. So now I know what I'm going to look like when I'm an old lady. I just hope I get a boyfriend before then, since I'm obviously not going to after!

SATURDAY 4 AUGUST

Hung out with Disha, David, and Marcus today. Marcus just got his license (he lost a year of school when he was in primary, so he's older than us), so we went for a drive in the country. It started pissing down while we were still stuck in traffic. We got as far as *near Oxford* and then we left the motorway to find a quaint country teashop (the lads had been without food for two whole hours and were starving, of course). The English countryside looks pretty attractive in pictures and old films, but let me tell you, it's different when it's right in your face. Even if we'd had any visibility in the rain, it wouldn't've mattered, because you never knew what was around the next bend (another car, a dog, a cow . . .). After we nearly hit the cow (and it wasn't just me and Disha who screamed), Marcus started going so slow we might as well have walked. We passed quite a few churches (though it could have been just one church, since we seemed to be going in circles) but no quaint country teashops. Disha said it's because the English village is almost dead. Most of them don't even have a post office anymore. I said did the Prime Minister know about this, and she said that preserving the countryside wasn't a priority of his. In the end we went back on the motorway and stopped at a service station for tea (which isn't something I'd recommend to tourists, since they'd think they'd never left the airport). Came home.

Marcus says I should get my license—I'm going to be seventeen on 27 October after all. Marcus says that with all the money I must be earning I could get myself a car to run around in. I said with what I'm making I could hardly afford a bicycle. But it's not a bad idea (driving, not another bloody bicycle).

Couldn't say anything to D about Ethan when we were with the lads, of course, and by the time we got home, it'd gone out of my head completely. Tomorrow is another day (which can be either good news or bad news, can't it?).

Asked the MC if I could have driving lessons for my birthday. She said did I realize that in order to **DRIVE AND SURVIVE**, you had to be able to do more than one thing at a time and occasionally stop talking so you can concentrate? I said I'd never known it to stop her talking. Then she wanted to know if I had any idea how much lessons cost. I said no. She said well, when I paid for them, I'd find out. I don't see why I should **PAY** some stranger to teach me to drive when there are two qualified drivers related to me by blood. The MC is obviously out of the question (not only is she way too highly strung but we can barely cross the road together without an argument!), so I rang Sigmund to ask him to teach me. Once again demonstrating the caring and understanding nature of the professional psychotherapist, Sigmund said **NO**. He said he was still recovering from teaching the MC.

SUNDAY 5 AUGUST

There seems to be no end to the surprises Life has in store for me (I just wish one or two of them were **GOOD**!). Sappho and Mags were coming over for Sunday lunch, and since a real meal (even a vegan one with all the interesting stuff taken out) is something of an event in this house these days, I said I'd be here. Had a **WELL-DESERVED** lie-in and then talked to Disha for a while on the mobe. (Forgot about Ethan again.) By the time I got off the phone, I could hear activity in the kitchen, so I went out to say hello. Mags and Sappho were at the table as expected. But there was a bloke with an apron wrapped around him, stirring something on the cooker—which *wasn't expected*. (He looked like an old folk singer—beard, wire-rimmed glasses, an earring, and one of those ethnic caps that are popular in the Himalayas and places like that.) I didn't think anything of it because, even though they're lesbians, Sappho and Mags know a lot of men, and I assumed they brought him along because he was hungry. (Though I did think someone could've **WARNED ME**! What if I'd come out in my underwear?!!) As soon as the MC saw me, she started shrieking, "Here's Janet!" like she was a talk-show host and I was the guest. She grabbed hold of the pot-stirrer and dragged him away from the cooker. "Janet, this is Robert Hotspur!" I said, "Hi." Sappho laughed and said, "You have no idea who Robert is, do you, Janet?" I said, "How could I? I only just walked into the room!" The MC did her Bridge-About-to-Collapse sigh and said that Robert is the bloke she's been dating! (To him she said, "What'd I tell you about our Janet? She's not in this world." Which I felt was v cheeky!) I maintained my cool and said that (as per usual) no one had told me he was coming. Robert said he and Joss (!!!) felt it was time he got

251

acquainted with everyone (except Nan and Sigmund, of course!). Robert said he'd been looking forward to meeting me. I said and *vice versa*, even though that isn't strictly true since I didn't really know he existed. He said he'd heard a lot about me. I said I hoped it was all good and he said SOME of it was. Apparently Robert's a solicitor, but not the sort who makes TONS OF DOSH (which is the sort of bloke we could do with in this house, if you ask me!). Robert works for one of those groups that are always trying to save the planet and all the oppressed people who live on it (Greenpeace or Friends of the Earth—something like that). This made lunch a *très* jolly affair since Robert spent most of it banging on about human rights abuses round the world. Sappho (our very own Rebel Queen) couldn't've been more delighted if she'd just found out she was having twins. The MC and Mags were pretty mesmerized too, but I found it *très* boring for something so incredibly depressing. And I was right about the folk singer bit. After lunch he brought out his guitar! I couldn't believe it! He sat there in OUR KITCHEN playing and singing some *très* depressing song about a dead hobo. I was still recovering from that when he went on to depressing Bob Dylan songs. (Disha's right about being older but no wiser. The MC has obviously learned NOTHING from her mistakes!) When the rest of them started SINGING ALONG (!!!), I said I was really heartbroken to break up the party but Disha was expecting me. Walked right into a bicycle in the hall on my way out. It was plastered with stickers (SAVE THE RAIN FOREST . . . SAVE THE WHALES . . . SAVE ANYTHING YOU CAN GET YOUR HANDS ON, etc.) so I assume Robert has something against cars and public transportation as well as most governments on the planet.

D was surprised to find out my mother has a boyfriend. I said well, how did she think I felt? And Sigmund's going to be well irked when he finds out—the male parent's always wanted to grow a beard, but the MC wouldn't let him. Then I said, "Speaking of boyfriends . . ." and told her about Ethan. Disha was **TOTALLY GOBSMACKED**. She said but she hardly knew him. Also, I was the one with the crush. I said it wasn't really a crush, I just thought he was v attractive. I'm not a jealous person, as you know—and I'm more mature than many people old enough to be my parents—so I said it was fine with me if she wanted to go out with Ethan. I expected her to say no—or at least to argue. She said **REALLY**? I said of course; it wasn't as if we were going out with each other or anything—he's just a mate. And even though he's très attractive, I'd realized that what I thought might be chemistry was just the smallness of the Broom Cupboard. D said, "All right then, give him my number." I said, "Pardon?" She said, "Well, he is gorgeous—and if you don't want him . . ." If you ask me, she could've put up a bit more of a fight.

The MC wanted to know what I thought of Robert. I asked if he ever talked about anything besides man's inhumanity to everything that pokes its head above the ground, and she said of course he did. Apparently he's a very intelligent bloke with many interests. It's too bad songs about dead hobos is one of them, if you ask me.

MONDAY 6 AUGUST

Buskin' Bob was back last night. He banged on all through supper about the **evil** in ordinary things you find around the house. Apparently there are a number of companies **NO ONE** should buy from because they aid and abet repressive regimes, or exploit the poor, or are determined to destroy the planet. It's a surprisingly long list (and I was wearing at least two of them). After supper he and the MC started going through the cupboards to see what she shouldn't buy anymore. Couldn't take it, so I went to my room and rang D. This proved to be a bit boring too, since she was trying to decide what to wear on her date with Ethan (if you ask me, she's jumping the gun a bit—he doesn't even have her number yet!).

TUESDAY 7 AUGUST

The more I think about it, the more I realize that Ethan choosing Disha is the best thing that could have happened. I'm really v lucky. It's an **ENORMOUS** relief to have seen the real Ethan before it was too late. (Look how long it took the MC to see the real Sigmund!) I mean, aside from the lack of chemistry (which everyone knows is **CRUCIAL** to a real relationship), it would never've worked between us. He's not at all artistic or creative, for one thing—which is something that's v important to me. And for another, he doesn't really have an active sense of humor. He laughs at my jokes, of course (only my parents don't), but he never really makes any of his own. And today, instead of being **STUNNED** by his eat-your-heart-out-Keanu-Reeves good looks, I noticed that he has hair on his earlobes (how gross is that?). Gave him Disha's number and by the time I got home, he'd already rung her and made a date! I reckoned he must've called on his mobe from the gents', since Saduki **DOES NOT ALLOW** personal phone calls on the Durango phone. I said, "It's not v romantic, ringing someone from a urinal, is it?" Disha said, "Maybe he was standing at the sink."

Discovered a bowl of rotting vegetables on the kitchen counter tonight, but when I went to throw it in the bin, instead of thanking me for helping out in the house like she's always nagging me to do, the MC shouted at me to put it back where it was! Apparently it's organic waste for the compost heap. I pointed out that we don't have a compost heap. She said we do now. I assume that the box of bottles next to the fridge means we recycle now too.

THURSDAY 9 AUGUST

Went to wash my hair and discovered that my shampoo has been replaced with something with **NETTLES** in it! Went straight to the MC to demand an explanation. She said, Did I realize that my shampoo had animal urine in it? I said that was ridiculous. Who would put piss into something that was basically soap? She said the company that made my shampoo, that's who.

FRIDAY 10 AUGUST

MC out with Buskin' Bob and Disha out with Ethan. Now that I don't even have my few minutes with Ethan to look forward to (I mean really, what's the point? It's not like he's a real mate like David or Marcus), the only conversations I have in the day are about tacos and cutlery shortages and other hot topics in the world of catering.

*   *   *

Invited Sigmund in for a cup of tea before he went home. He wanted to know whose guitar was propped up in the corner (it'll be his natural straw toothbrush that's moved in next!!!). I said Robert's. He said, "I'm Robert." I said, "The other Robert who's intimate with my mother." Sigmund hadn't been told **ANYTHING** about Robert. He wanted to know if the MC was seeing a lot of him, and I said, "Well, that is his guitar. What do *you* think?" Then, of course, he wanted to know what Robert's like. I said not only is he musical, but he's very intelligent, has a lot of interests, and has dedicated himself to making our planet a better place.

Sappho says my shampoo does have piss in it. Once again I was v sorry I'd brought it up because she was off like a horse at the Derby. She said remember when I was a vegetarian and discovered that McDonald's chicken nuggets had twice as much fat as their hamburgers and that in America they used to put beef additives in their chips? Did I think it was just *them*? And what about sugar? Did I know how many things I think are savory actually have **SUGAR** in them? I said well, if everybody knows all this stuff, why don't they do something about it? She said it seems to her that's exactly what Buskin' Bob is trying to do.

Went into the kitchen for a cup of tea to take to bed with me while I wrote and remembered that I'd been ordered to **GET ALL THOSE DISHES OUT OF THE SINK**. Really didn't feel up to it—but also didn't feel up to another hysterical scene (the *Power of Love* DOES NOT include chilling out hormonally imbalanced women!). Luckily had one of my brilliant ideas. Stuck them all in the broom cupboard and it only took a minute! Sometimes I think Sappho's right and it really is hard to believe that God isn't a woman.

SATURDAY 11 AUGUST

Came out to breakfast this morning to find Buskin' Bob tucking into a bowl of muesli (yes, **REALLY**!). He was dressed (thank God), but he didn't have any shoes on. The MC told me not to look so shocked. I said I wasn't shocked; I was just surprised, since I hadn't been told he was staying over. The MC gave Robert the sort of long-suffering look she used to give Sigmund. I went to the cupboard to get my cereal but there wasn't any. I said I thought she'd been shopping and she said she's not buying anything made by Nestlé anymore because of the Third World (I didn't ask). She said I could have muesli (what am I—a horse?). I fixed myself some toast (**WHOLEMEAL**!). I could feel Robert watching me while I was waiting for the toaster. He wanted to know what brand my trainers were. Sadly, I made the mistake of telling him. He went on for sixteen minutes (I timed him!) about sweatshops and things of that ilk. When he finally shut up, I said, "Thank God I'm wearing cotton and not fur or we'd be here till lunch." This was another BIG MISTAKE. Apparently the other place besides Durango where slaves are still used is in the cotton industry. Thank God, the phone rang in the middle of this fascinating insight into corporate greed. Saved by the bell!!!

It was Disha to tell me about her date. Apparently there has never been such a brilliant night in the history of dating. Ethan's handsome, Ethan's smart, Ethan's kind, Ethan's funny, Ethan's sensitive . . . I asked if he'd hired her to be his press agent and she laughed. I asked if that meant she'd be seeing him again. She said she'd like someone to try and stop her. Apparently he feels the same about her. They've got another date this afternoon! [Note to self: Ask Sigmund what the opposite of *schadenfreude* is. You know— when you're *not* happy about something good happening to someone else.]

Rang Marcus to see if he wanted to have another go at finding the Last English Village, but he's been banned from using the car. I said, What'd you do, drive into a police van? He got a parking ticket. Apparently his dad HAS NEVER had a parking ticket in his life! So Marcus is back on the buses of London until he pays his father back for the fine—which is pretty much like saying he's not going anywhere.

*   *   *

Tonight Sigmund rang to say he's been thinking about me learning to drive and he's decided he'll give me lessons after all. It'll be something we can do together. I joked that the last time we did something together was the father-daughter three-legged race at the school fête when he broke his ankle. He said he reckoned we were both older and wiser now (which, if Disha's right, means that this time it won't take twenty-four hours before he realizes he broke his ankle!).

SUNDAY 12 AUGUST

Disha spent the day with Ethan **AGAIN**. I asked her if this meant she was in *Love*, and she said she wasn't sure but whatever it is feels fantastic (not if you have to listen to it, it doesn't). My morale and energy levels depleted by my **LONG** and **TEDIOUS** hours in Hell's Kitchen, I gave in and went to visit Sappho and Mags with the MC (Buskin' Bob must've been out saving the mongoose or something). They've both gone so mad about this baby that they've turned the spare room into a nursery! Which, of course, we had to examine every centimeter of. (I'd rather be doing the tour of the Kilburn squat!!!) Then we had to look at every item of clothing they'd bought for this kid, including the nappies (how fascinating is that?!!). Has every woman I know suddenly taken leave of her senses? Sappho dragged me into the kitchen to help her make the tea. It was a ploy,

of course. What she really wanted was to know what I
thought of Buskin' Bob. I said he seems OK. She said she
and Mags think he's terrific. I said then it's too bad one of
them couldn't have him as a boyfriend. I reckon he'd be
v useful in choosing politically-correct baby gear. Sappho
said I sounded a bit put out. I said I **AM NOT PUT
OUT**, but just because the MC's besotted with the
Corporate Avenger doesn't mean that I have to be. I said one
woman's knight in shining armor is another woman's
repetitive stress syndrome. I was v glad when our visit was
over. Though not for long, of course. Now that I'll be
learning to drive, I feel I should start paying close attention
when someone else is driving. The MC said if I was going
to be a back-seat driver, I could at least sit in the back.
(It's incredible, isn't it? Buskin' Bob tells her what's wrong
with her toothpaste—**A LOT** apparently!—and her
washing-up liquid and she's off buying crap made from
wild herbs, but if I just say one little thing about not paying
enough attention to what's up ahead she goes berserk!)
I turned my attention to the car itself after that—which is
why I noticed we were almost out of petrol. She was totally
humiliated last time she ran out of petrol and called the RAC
for a tow truck because she thought something was wrong
with the car. Since I'd already been told off once for trying
to help, I let her go past two petrol stations before I asked
why she didn't stop. She said she was boycotting Esso.
This had **ROBERT** written all over it, of course, so I
didn't ask for any of the gory details. We drove on. But trust

Buskin' Bob to pick the biggest chain in the universe to boycott! The MC said he didn't choose it, Greenpeace and Friends of the Earth did. I said it didn't seem to me there was any point, since it wasn't going to do any good. She said that's where I was wrong. Many companies, including Nike and McDonald's, have changed their policies because of public pressure. I said, well, I didn't see why she couldn't go to Esso just this once—as it was an **EMERGENCY**. She said I was old enough to understand the importance of principles. Apparently principles, like puppies, are not just for Christmas. You don't just have them when they're convenient. (I never noticed that this bothered her before!) We ran out of petrol at a traffic light about five minutes after it started pissing down. Then—even though it was **ALL HER FAULT**—she made me get out of the car and help her push it to the curb! This is the first time I've been grateful it's a Mini and not a real car.

MONDAY 13 AUGUST

Now when Saduki asks me if I'll work an extra shift, I automatically say **NO**. Before, I always said yes because I wanted him to think I was keen and hardworking so he'd put me on nights. But now that Ethan and Disha are **AN ITEM**, I don't see the point. I hear enough about their relationship from her without getting it from him too.

Rang D to see if she wanted to do something, but
SURPRISE, SURPRISE she's already doing
something with Super Waiter. [Note to self: I will
NEVER abandon *My Best Friend* for a man. I think
it's v immature.] I said, Didn't she think she should slow
down a bit? I mean, she doesn't want to get really serious
about someone from Australia. What if he goes home? Is
she planning to move *there*? She said WHY NOT? I can
think of quite a few v good reasons, a lot of which are
poisonous spiders. I reminded her of that advert. I said that
personally I'd think twice about living somewhere that sees
itself as a nation where a man would sleep with his best
friend's wife but not drink his last beer. Then I said, "What
about sex?" She said, "What about it?" I said, "You know,
has he asked you yet?" She said, "I've only been going
out with him for a couple of days, for God's sake." I said,
"Exactly. But already you're thinking of emigrating." She
said I didn't understand!

Went to the V&A with Marcus. He says he likes the V&A
because he finds it v inspiring, but if you ask me he likes it
because there's no entrance fee. Marcus wanted to know if
I'm *absolutely* certain I don't want to go on a proper date
sometime. I said I'm positive. I said I value his friendship
too much to risk ruining it by exchanging saliva. What
I didn't tell him was that Ethan and Disha have opened
my eyes (in more ways than one!). Marcus doesn't inspire
the feelings in me that Ethan obviously inspires in D.

Apparently Ethan makes Disha feel like dancing among the stars. Marcus makes me feel like having a nice cup of tea— and maybe a couple of biscuits.

Nan came over for supper tonight to meet the Eco Balladeer. As per usual, Nan immediately went into Jesus mode. Buskin' Bob didn't blink. He said he reckoned that if Jesus were alive now He'd be a vegetarian, ride a bicycle, not buy anything that isn't fairly traded, boycott all companies that support oppressive regimes, and grow His own vegetables (now who does that remind me of?!!). I expected Nan to argue, like she usually does, but instead she **TOTALLY** agreed! (I looked out the window to see if the moon had turned blue, but it was raining.) Apparently Nan's joined some new Bible group that sees Jesus as a rebel. Nan said Jesus had a lot to say about wealth and money, etc., and was v anti-materialistic. Robert said all the Great Teachers were like that because they understood what is truly important. (I thought Nan was going to hug him on that one!) Nan said that the more she learns about Christ and His teachings, the more she realizes that it's easier to call yourself a Christian than actually be one. Robert said this was **TOO TRUE**, and called her Rose! (I didn't even know that was her name. The MC always calls her Mum; Geek Boy and I always call her Nan; and Sigmund calls her either Mother or—when she's not in earshot—the Thirteenth Disciple.) Nan said her Bible group is really opening her eyes to the injustices in the world. Buskin' Bob said that between

30,000 and 35,000 children die every day of preventable poverty-related causes. He said he reckoned that if Jesus came back now, He'd be an anti-globalist. Nan said she didn't know about that but He'd certainly be pissed off.

TUESDAY 14 AUGUST

I was just congratulating myself on finally getting the hang of this waiter lark (I'd been on **ONE WHOLE HOUR** and I hadn't mixed up an order, dropped anything, or had an argument with **ANYONE**!) when Marcus and David strolled in. (Of all the joints in all the world, right?)
To tell the truth, I was actually glad to see them. But wary. I sidled up to them in my best professional waiter mode and asked them what they thought they were doing. David said they thought they were having lunch. I said not in Durango they weren't. Marcus said it's a free country. Not according to Robert and Sappho, it isn't. But I wasn't about to argue that right then. I said if they gave me **ANY** trouble, they'd only live long enough to regret it. Marcus said they weren't trying to get me fired, they just thought it would be a bit of a laugh. I gave them the table way at the back by the kitchen, tucked in behind the fireplace so Saduki wouldn't see them. David asked me what I recommended. I said the Thai place across the road. This made us all laugh. Marcus said there must be

SOMETHING on the menu that was good, and I said that none of the beverages had been known to kill anyone yet. Then David spotted Sky. He said, "She's a bit fit! Are they real?" I said, "What, her feet?" (She has ENORMOUS feet as well!) That made us all laugh too. Marcus and David agreed that all the blokes in the kitchen looked like they had rap sheets as long as your arm. David said he hoped none of them had been charged with poisoning, and Marcus said you definitely wouldn't want to send anything back. More laughter. For the first time since I started, I actually enjoyed myself. And they gave me the biggest tip ever! I was feeling almost happy by the end of my shift—but happiness is v fleeting, isn't it? The Dorito Bandito grabbed me as I was leaving. He said what did he tell me about my friends coming by? I said they were eating. He said I'm not meant to FRATERNIZE! I took exception to this, of course. If you ask me, the whole deal with being a waiter is that you fraternize. I'm meant to make the customers feel that they're on to a good thing and not suspect that Satan's chef and his henchmen have been done for criminal damage. I said that as far as I could work out, I was the person who made people glad they'd come here instead of staying home and cooking for themselves. Saduki wouldn't listen, of course. Blah blah blah. I was practically shaking with the INJUSTICE of it all. So I QUIT!!! Just like that! I threw his stupid tie at him and said, "In the words of Bart Simpson, I'm outta here!" It was a truly liberating moment. It wasn't until I got home that I wondered if Sappho has had more of an influence on me than I'd thought.

Disha said she was proud of me for lasting as long as I did at Durango. She said Ethan said Saduki makes Captain Bligh look caring and compassionate. I said now that I'm freed from my bondage, we can hang out more, and D said, "Um." I said, "What does that mean? Only if Ethan's abducted by aliens?" D said it's just that she doesn't have that much time to see him, since he works so much, etc. And he gets a bit funny when she suggests hanging out with someone else. I said what do you mean funny? She said **YOU KNOW**. I said you don't mean **JEALOUS**? **OF ME**? She said not really jealous, but she can tell he doesn't like it. He thinks I'm a bit of a flirt!!! If you ask me, she's making it up. She just doesn't want me to think she's the sort of **shallow and superficial** person who dumps her mates the minute she's got a boyfriend (the sort of person she **USED TO SAY SHE HATED**!!!).

Nan rang tonight, wanting to know what I thought of Buskin' Bob. I said he's all right. Nan likes him. She said he seemed like a man of principles. I said if he had anymore principles, I reckon he'd have us living in a tree.

THURSDAY 16 AUGUST

The MC wanted to know why I wasn't going to work again today. I said because I didn't feel that the pittance I earned being a servant justified the grueling labor and constant humiliation. She said, "You mean you were fired." I said, "Actually, I quit." I said I felt the Dorito Bandito was hostile and vindictive toward me because I have **NORMAL-SIZE** breasts. She said, "What about that boy?" I said, "What boy?" She said, "What was his name? Eden? Elijah? Evan?" (Can you believe it? Jocelyn Bandry, who **NEVER LISTENS TO A WORD I SAY**, remembers some passing mention of Ethan I once made!) I said I didn't know what she was on about. She said she had the impression from the fact that I never stopped talking about him that I fancied him. I asked if she ever got tired of jumping to the wrong conclusion.

Hung out with Disha a bit tonight (since she's **ALWAYS BUSY** in the day either seeing Ethan or waiting to find out if she's going to see him). More insights into his perfectness. (I even got a *detailed* description of what it's like to **KISS** him! Apparently it's like kissing a chocolate mousse. I said I hadn't realized she'd spent so much time kissing puddings.) I'm v happy for D and I've completely lost the little interest I had in Ethan, but to be honest, it really is exhaustingly boring. I mean he's just a lad—it isn't the Second Coming. I'd rather listen to Robert bang on about the **evil** of the pharmaceutical companies (which **IS NOT** one

of his shorter lectures) than hear one more thing Ethan said
about anything. David phoned to say he knew somebody
who was having a barbecue, but Disha didn't want to go in
case Ethan got a chance to ring her from the toilet at work.
I know I could've lent her the mobe, but I don't see why
I should pay for her to tell him how much she misses him
because she hasn't seen him in six hours. I didn't want to go
to the barbecue without D, since the only person I'd know
would be David and I reckoned he'd be off with the other
boys playing video games or something. But I didn't want to
sit around the house with the MC and Buskin' Bob either, so
I forced myself to go. David wanted to know if Disha was ill
or something, since it's rare to see me without her. This isn't
true, of course. I go plenty of places without Disha. David
said yeah, but they're all toilets. After the barbecue (which
didn't actually feature anything COOKED because no one
could get the fire going in the rain), we ended up playing
Pictionary. I was partners with David. You'd have to be
psychic to guess any of his words. One of his drawings
looked like a pyramid. I tried pyramid, but that wasn't it.
It wasn't a triangle, a tepee, or Mount Everest either. He
drew what looked like a head peering over it. I tried
Egyptians and Aztecs. I tried blood sacrifice and religion. I
tried Peeping Tom. It was a cheese grater. (The head was a
biscuit!) After that, I prayed for All Plays so at least I could
look at someone else's drawings. We were all laughing so
much, it took hours. I said to David that I haven't laughed so
much for WEEKS. David said I should hang out with him

more, especially now that Disha and I have had the operation
and been separated.

FRIDAY 17 AUGUST

Since I'm unemployed, the MC made me do the food
shopping with her. (First she made me help her put the
mountain of bottles in the car so they don't fall all over the
place every time you go near the fridge!) We set off with
the bottles rattling round in the boot, but we didn't go
to the superstore as per usual (where they have a bottle
bank!)—we went to the street market (where they don't
have a bottle bank, of course!). It was like stepping back in
time, all sweat and rotting vegetables. I said, "Don't tell me
you're boycotting supermarkets too." She said, "Yes. The
big chains are squeezing out the small, local shops and
farmers." I said well, that was **PROGRESS**, wasn't it?
We don't make our own soap anymore either. (**NOT
YET AT ANY RATE!!!**) She said and their business
methods leave something to be desired. I said I didn't
think they sold diet meals in the market and the MC said
she isn't buying them anymore because Robert doesn't like
the company that makes them either. Also, real food
doesn't make you fat. At this rate we're going to be
growing our own vegetables in the back garden and
brushing our teeth with sand.

SATURDAY 18 AUGUST

Nearly had a heart attack at supper tonight. There was a
SLUG in my salad! Buskin' Bob said that proved the
vegetables we bought at the market were organic and not
grown in a hothouse on chemicals. (Well, **THANK
GOD FOR THAT**!) The MC said that maybe from now
on when she asks me to wash the lettuce, I'll do more than
just wave it toward the tap. Was still recovering from this
when the MC asked how I'd like to go away for a week
before school starts. For one insane moment, I forgot who
I am, who I'm related to, and how God treats me. I was
suffused with *Joy*! I said of course I wanted to go away.
Hadn't I worked my fingers to the bone and my feet to
wood pulp all summer? Didn't I deserve a break?
I **LONGED** to leave the stresses of the city behind for
even a few short days and really relax and enjoy the long
hours of sun! I asked where we were going. The beaches
of Greece? The mountains of Spain? The olive groves of
Italy? The theme parks of America? The answer is: *none
of the above*. The answer is: the isolated Wilds of Wales.
Robert's got a cottage (of course—he probably built it
himself from wood he found in skips!). The MC banged on
about the cottage and how Robert was bringing Marcella
and Lucrezia because they really love getting into the
country (I didn't know he had dogs. I'm **ASTOUNDED**
he hasn't brought them around—he brings eveything else
he owns here!), but I wasn't really listening. I was too

DEVASTATED. I said of course, my going did depend on whether or not I got another job. (I reckon I can get SOMETHING even if it only lasts long enough for me to wave them goodbye.) The MC said if I get a job, I can stay with Sappho and Mags while she's away because she doesn't like me being on my own (she doesn't say that when she stays out ALL NIGHT, does she?). What a choice—nesting lesbians or the Eco Warrior and his lover! Things just get better and better and better, don't they?

MONDAY 20 AUGUST

Marcus's parents went out last night, so he invited everybody around for a Waiting-for-Your-GCSE-Results party. He reckoned it'd be a hoot to order a takeaway from China Gardens. Disha didn't want to come. I said I thought Ethan was off with his Aussie mates for the day and she said eating pesticide-free food must be improving my memory. She said she just didn't feel like hanging out. She had a lot to do. I said, Don't tell me you've got to wash your hair, and she laughed. Had a good time even without female support. David was happy to see us. He said usually he's greeted with scowls and mutterings about how he must've come via Norway. David said that if Marcus wants to make some money to pay his parking ticket, he can get him a job with his dad because they're short-handed right now. I said didn't you have to be Chinese to deliver takeaway chow mein and David said Marcus could keep his helmet on.

TUESDAY 21 AUGUST

Have decided to go to Wales after all. I don't think I could survive a week of talking about nothing but heartburn and natural childbirth (I never thought I'd say this, but oh, how I long for the days when Sappho's conversation was all about politics and feminism and what a mess men have made of the world!). And, anyway, I haven't found a job. The MC said I might have better luck if I actually *looked*, but I pointed out that unless it's around here I probably wouldn't make enough to cover my bus fare. She said I could always be an Avon lady. I said yeah, right. I might as well just end my life now.

WEDNESDAY 22 AUGUST

Sigmund took me out to supper tonight. He said it was because I'm leaving on Friday and he won't see me for over seven days, but I'm not fooled. (Not only has he gone **WEEKS** without seeing me, but the last time he took just me out for a meal I was in primary school and we went to McDonald's.) I reckoned he wanted to chill me out about my impending GCSE results, which I have to admit I found rather touching. It isn't like Sigmund to be so *Empathetic and Sensitive*. And I was **RIGHT**! It isn't like him. What he wanted was to pump me for info on Buskin' Bob. (Adults always have ulterior motives.) To tell you the truth, I feel a bit ambiguous about this. (Things really aren't black or white—our minds and hearts are fogged and gray!) On the one hand, Sigmund behaved like a total idiot and pissed everybody off. On the other hand, he is my father—and he doesn't make you feel like you're torturing some innocent child every time you put on your trainers. He said Nan had a lot of good things to say about Robert (which is more than she ever has to say about anyone else—esp. Sigmund!). Sigmund said he was très sorry about what happened with Mrs. Kennedy and all, but he never meant to hurt anyone. [Note to self: Why do people **ALWAYS** says that when the obvious result of their actions is that they hurt someone? It's like dropping 500 megaton bombs on a city and saying you didn't mean to kill any civilians!] Sigmund says that now that he's realized the error of his ways, all he wants is for the Mad Cow to be happy. He should've thought of that before too, if you ask me. I said, Well then, he has nothing to worry about, does he? She's happy as a pig locked in the green-grocer's (**ORGANIC**, of course!). He said he had hoped that he and the MC would get back together in time—

214

once he'd given her some space. I said he did science at university; he should know how Nature hates a vacuum. If you leave any space, something will fill it (in this case an Eco Warrior armed with a guitar). I said and anyway, what about his girlfriend? Sigmund wanted to know what girlfriend that would be—the one who doesn't mind sharing an army cot? I said the one whose earrings were in his bathroom. He said ever since I was little, he's hoped that someday I'd learn to be observant, and now he's got half his wish. Apparently the earrings belong to the MC. He keeps them to remind him of what he's lost!!! If he hadn't looked so serious, I would've laughed. I mean, really. How much more of a reminder does he need than living in Kilburn?

THURSDAY 23 AUGUST

The papers are full of hair-raising stories of **GCSE Stress and Teenage Suicides**, etc., but I was feeling v laid-back about the whole thing until this morning when I woke up at 3 A.M. in a panic attack and couldn't get back to sleep. My predictions were all good, but what if something went horribly wrong (**LIKE IT OFTEN DOES!**)? Would my brilliant future be ruined forever because mine is a *Creative, Artistic Mind* that has trouble with quadratic equations? Would all my *Hopes and Dreams* be dashed forever on the rocky shores of French grammar? As you can imagine, the MC was très sympathetic as per usual. She said there was no use worrying about it now. Then, seeing that this didn't exactly **CHEER ME UP**, she said the worst that could happen was I'd have to do some of them again. I said I didn't want to **DO THEM AGAIN**—it was bad enough having to do them the first time. Went to school with Marcus to collect our results. Once the envelope was in my sweating palms, I couldn't open it. Marcus couldn't open his either. So I opened his and he opened mine. Smiles and shrieks of *Teenage Jubilation* all around when we discovered that our young lives hadn't been blighted for evermore! I nearly kissed him I was that excited!

The MC said I don't have to bother packing Justin's mobe as she doesn't reckon it'd work where we're going. I said what made her think I had Geek Boy's mobe and she said call it a wild guess. She spent most of the night phoning the train stations of London trying to get a timetable. The deal is that since Buskin' Bob has to pick something up in Oxford on his way and the Mini can't go more than a few miles without something falling off it, we're going to take a train to the nearest town with a station and he'll collect us. I said on what, his bike? She said not to be ridiculous. He has a Land Rover. I couldn't've been more surprised if she'd said he had a private jet. Disha's parents have a Land Rover and it's well cool. Am almost beginning to look forward to this holiday, even if I will be out of telecommunication. At last I'll have some truly private time to take stock of myself before the new school term overwhelms me. After all, a lot has happened in a few short weeks (as in my mother's having sex and my best friend's become Zombie in Love). And Nature is very conducive to *Thought and Reflection*, isn't she? Must remember to pack lots of candles and incense to get me in the proper mood for *Thought and Reflection*.

FRIDAY 24 AUGUST

Life really is stressful, isn't it? Up, down. Up, down. One minute you're happier than a slug in an organic lettuce patch and the next it's all gloom and doom again. Yesterday the world was my oyster and tonight it's back to being a pit of tar. Anyway, just to show how quickly Life can turn on you, I'm writing this BY CANDLELIGHT!!! (Thank God I brought them, right?) Apparently Buskin' Bob's cottage does have electricity but NOT AT THE MOMENT. What it also doesn't EVER have is heat, which is unfortunate if you ask me, since although it's August (a summer month in the rest of Europe!), it's pissing down and freezing cold. (Oh no, we don't want to go to Greece; we want to stay in the sodden British Isles!) So not only am I writing by candlelight but I'm wearing two layers of clothes and am wrapped in a blanket as well. I am totally shattered and exhausted and possibly in a state of clinical shock, but I have to tell someone what happened. Since there's no one around here but sheep (and the MC was right—the mobe doesn't work!), you, Dear Diary, have been chosen. The train journey was a nightmare, of course. We could've got to Greece quicker. We had to wait ages for our connections and half the time they got canceled!!! It was DARK by the time we staggered off the train and into the rain. [Note to self: If privatization is such a brilliant idea, why doesn't anything work properly anymore?] There was only one car in the car park. I said I couldn't believe Buskin' Bob wasn't here, and the MC said of course he was here, what'd I call that? I said that didn't look anything like Mr. Paski's Land Rover and she said that was because Robert's is a classic (as in the First One Ever Made). I said, "But there are three people inside!" And the MC said of course there were three people inside, Robert had Marcella and Lucrezia with him, didn't he? They aren't dogs. Apparently Buskin' Bob Hotspur has reproduced!!! I asked her why she didn't tell me Robert was bringing his daughters (or even that he had any!), and she said she did. I said I thought she said Robert was bringing his dogs (I mean, really, who gives their children names that make them sound like bottles of wine?). The MC did her sighing thing. She said Marcella and Lucrezia are the WHOLE POINT of the holiday since he doesn't get to spend as much time with them as he'd like. I said, And what am I

278

meant to be? The bloody child-minder? She said of course not. She reckoned we'd be COMPANY for each other. (If you ask me, it's like putting somebody in jail and saying, "Well, at least you've got plenty of people to hang out with.")

So here I am. I haven't actually SEEN the cottage because of the lack of light, but I can tell it's really old from the way it leans to one side. (It's hard to understand why anyone would go to a five-star resort when they could come here!) The MC said to stop griping, because everything will look better in the morning. I can only hope that for once in her life she's right.

SATURDAY 25 AUGUST

(SOS from the hut at the end of the universe!)

The MC was wrong, of course. Not only does NOTHING look better this morning—it looks SIGNIFICANTLY WORSE. I wouldn't even call this a cottage—it's more like a HUT. And it's practically vibrating with spiders (which you're not allowed to kill, of course). Also, it's totally filthy. (Apparently Robert doesn't just want to save the whale; he wants to save dirt and cobwebs as well!) I can appreciate the idea of getting back to Nature (it is a common theme in music, literature, and art, after all), but if we got any further back, we'd be in a cave.

The primitive living conditions aren't the **WORST OF IT**, though!! The worst of it are the Hotspur progenies. Exhaustion rendered them pretty quiet last night, but today they're wide awake. If there'd been a crystal ball handy at their births, the parent Hotspurs would have been totally justified in drowning them straight off, if you ask me. I have **NEVER** come across such totally obnoxious children—and you will remember that I am related by blood to Justin Bandry and live next door to Jupiter (who was banned for life from the local swimming pool because he pushed a little girl in when he was only four). Marcella's not even a teenager yet, but she looks older than I do (here is **ABSOLUTE** proof that children are growing up too fast nowadays, just like the magazines say!). She *never* stops talking. Either she's banging on about herself (**ME! ME! ME!** and **I! I! I!**) or she's criticizing everyone else (esp. her father). Lucrezia's nine and totally demented. One minute she's laughing and skipping about like she's been hitting the organic white wine and the next she's transformed herself into the 𝔐onster 𝔗hat 𝔄te 𝔚ales. The only positive thing I can say about Lucrezia is that she's refusing to talk to anyone but her father—and she only shouts at him. (In my humble opinion, Buskin' Bob should spend **LESS** time saving the planet and **MORE** time looking after his children.) I tried to discuss this with the MC but all she'd say was that Marcella's just at that age (I said, "What? ELEVEN?") and Lucrezia has problems (which is like saying the army has a couple of guns).

Buskin' Bob and the MC went out to look for birds in the rain. The Hotspurettes wouldn't go. I wouldn't go either, but I didn't get a chance to refuse. It was assumed that I'd stay in the hut with them (child-minder or what?!!). Since there's no TV—even if we had electricity—I went to find a book. Other people leave mysteries and bestsellers in their country homes for imprisoned guests, but not Buskin' Bob. It's all stuff about politics, etc.! Found something called No Logo. I thought it might be a novel set in the fashion industry, but it isn't. Apparently it's "a convincing analysis of the superbrand." Started to read it anyway, since it's the only book he has that doesn't give me a headache just seeing the title.

SUNDAY 26 AUGUST

Question: What's WORSE than being stuck in the Wilds of Wales in a primitive shack with NO ELECTRICITY and two of the most IRKSOME children ever born?

Answer: Being stuck in the Wilds of Wales in a primitive shack with NO ELECTRICITY and two of the most

IRKSOME children ever born and having to sit around the fireplace every night singing "Where Have All the Flowers Gone?"!!!

MONDAY 27 AUGUST

Robert's book is actually pretty interesting. It says at one time it cost Nike $5 to make shoes it then sold for at least a hundred. And that's not all!!! It also says that Nike once paid a mega-famous basketball player **$20 MILLION** to advertise their gear—which was more than it paid **ALL** its workers in Indonesia in the same year! That is a bit off, isn't it? This is obviously an example of the injustices Nan was banging on about. Must ask her if she's read this book. (It could solve the problem of what to get her for Christmas. I reckon she's probably got enough candles by now, and Robert's copy's in pretty good nick. I'm sure he'll never miss it—not when he's got global warming and starving Third World farmers and all those political prisoners to worry about.)

TUESDAY 28 AUGUST

Lucrezia walks in her sleep (**OF COURSE**—how could
I have failed to guess that?!!). After our nightly hootenanny,
the Deadly Duo went to bed and the MC, the Eco Warrior,
and I settled down to play Scrabble. (You can't play games
with Lucrezia because after about two seconds she gets
pissed off and flings the board in the air.) [Note to self:
Just because a person worries about endangered species and
how many trees are being chopped down in the Amazon
doesn't mean he can't be **V COMPETITIVE.**] We were
debating whether or not *bazooms* was a real word when
Lucrezia suddenly marched down the stairs. I knew right
away she was asleep because she wasn't howling about
anything. Apparently it's v important not to wake a
sleepwalker suddenly (though no one in their right mind
would wake Lucrezia whether she was walking or not—let
her sleep, it's the only time she isn't making a scene).
While Robert took Lucrezia back to bed and the MC made
sure all the doors were locked, I took the opportunity to
get some decent letters. I feel the least they owe me is
winning one lousy game of Scrabble.

WEDNESDAY 29 AUGUST

Woke up in the middle of the night to find Lucrezia Hotspur **IN MY BED**!!! Not only that, but she had *all* the blankets and her foot was in my stomach. It's a miracle I didn't wake her up **SUDDENLY** by screaming with terror (which was only because I can't believe that even a psychopath would find us out here—never mind come out in this rain). Robert said I should move the chest of drawers in front of my door from now on to keep her out. Personally I'm for leaving the front door not only unlocked but **WIDE OPEN**!

THANK GOD this week is nearly over! It was another **RED-LETTER DAY** here at **Camp Despair**. Marcella informed me that my taste in clothes is v passé (she's not even a teenager, for heaven's sake—what does **SHE** know about style?), and Lucrezia attacked me!!! Really—as in went for me with a sharp instrument! All I said was that I don't like Marmite and she threw a knife at me! I've seen her hit Buskin' Bob (once with a hairbrush and once with a free-range egg!), but I never expected her to go for **ME**! I said to the MC that they must have obedience schools for children—like the ones they have for dogs—and the Mad Cow said it's not that Lucrezia's badly behaved (!!!), it's that she has a syndrome. I said she should give it back. The MC (or Joss, as she's known here in **Camp Despair**) said it wasn't a joke; poor Lucrezia's v ill. She's on drugs. If you ask me, it's a shame they don't work.

THURSDAY 30 AUGUST

Robert **INSISTED** that we go for a walk today (he bribed us with a pub lunch and all the crisps we could eat—no matter who made them!). We all got into our anoraks and wellies, etc., and then Lucrezia remembered that the rain was going to melt her and threw herself on the floor, screaming. It took Robert over an hour to convince her that the acid in the rain wasn't going to turn her into a Slush Puppy (and who told her there's acid in the rain to begin with, I wonder?!!), by which time the rest of us had taken off our anoraks and wellies and pretty much resigned ourselves to more brown rice for lunch. The pub turned out to be **MILES** away, and most of them were uphill and through mud. I was numb from the cold and the wet, of course, and muscles I'd forgotten I had were screaming in agony, but unlike the Deadly Duo, I was too depressed to complain. All I could think of was Disha and Ethan in some warm, dry place, snogging and telling each other how wonderful they are. By the time we got to the pub, they'd already stopped serving lunch! I reckon Robert knew he was about to have a mutiny on his hands because he bought whiskies for him and the MC and **COKES** for us. I said, "Listen! Can you hear that? It's the sound of principles crashing to the ground!" Apparently no one thought I was funny. (I wish I'd asked David or Marcus to come—they would've thought it was hysterical!) All was well for the few minutes it took Lucrezia to decide that her bag of crisps was smaller than everyone else's and throw a major fit. You could tell that the good folk of the Welsh countryside aren't used to this sort of behavior because **EVERYBODY** stopped what they were doing and stared at us. (And they didn't look concerned that some poor little girl was being cruelly tortured by her father—they looked really irked!) Nothing would calm her down, of course. Robert said he'd take her outside while we finished, but the MC said that was ridiculous (it didn't seem ridiculous to me), so we all left. Halfway back to the cottage, Lucrezia started up again because she hadn't finished her Coke. [Note to self: **NEVER EVER HAVE CHILDREN!**]

FRIDAY 31 AUGUST

Buskin' Bob drove us back to London. I'd've preferred to have taken my chances with the rail service but, as per usual, wasn't consulted. So I got to bounce around in the back with the Hotspurettes (it's like riding in a wagon pulled by mules). Marcella talked the whole way (of course) and Lucrezia got carsick (**TWICE!**). Then we broke down. It was lucky someone had a mobile phone with her—not that anyone thanked me. It took ages for the RAC man to come. Then we had to stop in Oxford because that's where Robert's daughters live with their mother the actress and their stepfather the property developer—in a mansion (the ex–Mrs. Hotspur obviously **DOES** learn from her mistakes, unlike some women!). When we finally rolled up to ours, I nearly kissed the door to our flat, I was that happy to be home! I said, "Well, at least we won't be seeing them again too soon," and the MC said, "Not till next weekend." I said, "We're going **BACK** to Wales?" She said, "No, Robert's got the girls for the weekend, and I thought it would be nice if they all came **HERE**." She thought it would be **FUN**!!! I reckon she was an Inquisitor in a previous life. I said I hoped she didn't think the Borgia Sisters were sleeping in my room. She said of course not. They could kip in Justin's. Isn't that just like Life? A week ago, I thought there was nothing in the world that could make me want My Parents' Other Child back home, and now that something is practically moving in with me!!!

SATURDAY 1 SEPTEMBER

Couldn't get Disha last night, so I rang her first thing this morning. Told her I'd really missed her (which was true, but I didn't mention that I'd missed **EVERYONE**—even Nan!). D said she missed me too. She's still in *Love*, but Ethan's working a lot—and he has his own friends and all. I said, **AND YOU DON'T**? I said why didn't she hang out with the lads while I was away—they're always good for a laugh. She said she didn't fancy it on her own. I said you used to. She said so how was your holiday? Do anything exciting? I said not so you'd notice. I said, So do you want to do something today? and she said she was going to Camden Market with Ethan. She said why didn't I come too; then after Ethan went to work, I could spend the night at hers. I said I thought he didn't like me because I'm such a **FLIRT**!!! She said of course he likes me. I'm blowing what she said out of all proportion and taking it out of context. Since Ethan's showing no signs of going back to Australia (or anywhere else) at the moment, I reckon that if I want to see Disha, I'm going to have to get used to seeing her with him, so I said yes.

SUNDAY 2 SEPTEMBER

The way Disha and Ethan hang on to each other, you'd think they're afraid of falling over if they let go. It was like walking around with some alien creature with two heads. And it takes **HOURS** to get through the market like that. I've never thought of Disha as the quiet, retiring type, but today Ethan did most of the talking. Blah blah blah, the restaurant . . . blah blah blah, back home . . . blah blah blah, his travels . . . (He was almost as bad as Marcella!) Whenever I tried to have a conversation with Disha, he'd start hugging her or something equally distracting, so in the end I gave up. Ethan wanted to know if I'd heard from my brother and I said I didn't hear from Justin when we were in the same house, so I didn't expect to hear from him when he's thousands of miles away. He said (**AGAIN**) that he wished he could go to Mexico, and I said I did too. Disha (a girl who has always defended Sappho and her views!) pouted and asked what about her. Ethan laughed (which I reckoned you could pretty much interpret any way you wanted). At last he had to go and get ready for work (talk about **THE LONG GOODBYE**—you'd think they weren't going to see each other for years!) and Disha and I went back to hers. It was like old times after that—at least for a while. After supper D and I locked ourselves in her room with the candles and the incense, and although there was a lot of talk about Ethan, of course, we also managed to discuss *Life, the Universe, and Everything Else* as well. Had Disha in hysterics with my *Tales of Camp Despair*. She said she didn't understand why I'd said I didn't do anything exciting since just being with Lucrezia Hotspur sounded pretty exciting to her. I said only in the way that being in combat is exciting. Disha said maybe Sigmund could tell me what sort of syndrome she has. I asked if she thought we were as self-absorbed as Marcella when we were her age and D said it was possible, but, frankly, I don't think so. Then Disha said I'd better hope the MC and the Eco Warrior don't get really **SERIOUS**—as in decide to move in together. Then Lucrezia and Marcella would be like my sisters. I said I've already got one sibling I don't want; there's no way I'm taking on two more. I said speaking of getting serious, what about her and God's Gift to the Catering Industry? I said if **SEX** was in the offing, she'd better make sure it was **SAFE** because there's been a lot in the mags lately about **SEXUALLY TRANSMITTED DISEASES** making a big comeback. She said what was I trying to insinuate about Ethan? I said I wasn't trying to insinuate **ANYTHING**!!! All I meant was that the diseases that used to be so popular amongst prostitutes, sailors, and kings, like syphilis and gonorrhea, are spreading like wildfire (or like syphilis and gonorrhea!). She said sex wasn't an issue yet because the room Ethan rents is right off his landlady's kitchen and they're not likely to do anything with Mrs. Spader cooking and singing along with Capital FM in the next room, are they? All was well till the bewitching hour of midnight, when Ethan rang. I'd never seen Disha move so fast. (Not even that time we thought the house was on fire!) The second she heard the phone, she was off like a fox with a pack of hounds after it. I got into bed and lay down to wait for her to come back. She was gone so long that I fell asleep. I would've slept till the morning if she hadn't woken me up when she got back. I sat bolt upright, I was that startled. I thought maybe the house really was on fire this time. Disha said there was nothing to panic about. She just wanted to tell me that Ethan said he loves her. I said so now can I go back to sleep?

*   *   *

Have been thinking about what Disha said about the Deadly Duo becoming **MY** relatives. Just the thought makes my blood turn to **POLLUTED ICE WATER**! How could I be so **BLIND**? People like my mother have no sense of *True Passion or Adventure*. They crave security and routine—not a white-knuckle ride on the Kayak of Life. Obviously the MC's going to want to replace the rut she was in (married to Sigmund) with another rut (cohabiting with Buskin' Bob) ASAP. And equally obviously, I can't let that happen!!! It's enough that Fate has saddled me with Geek Boy as a brother without adding the Deadly Duo as sisters. (I could leave home, of course—they always need volunteer workers in Africa—but I feel it's important to wait till I've at least decided whether I want to be a writer or an artist, because I'm certainly not going to be able to even think about that if I'm walking sixty miles a day to get drinking water, am I?!!) There's nothing for it—I have to get the MC and Sigmund **BACK TOGETHER**. And très **FAST**!!! I know the MC's still pretty pissed off with him, etc., but they *were* married for a long time—that's got to count for something. And she already knows what a pain he can be. There aren't going to be any surprises like with Buskin' Bob. (Sappho says the reason people put up with politicians who lie to them and cheat on their expenses and take money from big corporations is because they're afraid that the ones who replaced them would be even worse. I reckon it should be the same in marriage. And **DEFINITELY** in the Bandry marriage!!!)

Marcus had everyone around tonight because his parents have thrown caution to the wind and gone away for the weekend. Disha said she had something to do with her parents. She missed a really good laugh. We played Trivial Pursuit, and David (who, I have to admit, has a v interesting and original mind) **ABSOLUTELY** excelled himself! One of his questions was what *craft* (as in **SHIP**) did Neil Armstrong take to the moon. David thought it meant craft as in **HOBBY**! He rejected knitting, woodwork, pottery, and jewelry-making and said **BUTTER-CHURNING**! He reckoned butter-churning was small and portable enough. Marcus wanted to know where David thought the astronauts were going to keep the cow! Game ended due to hysteria!!!

MONDAY 3 SEPTEMBER

Had a word with Sigmund about Lucrezia tonight (partly because I'm curious and partly because I want to start him thinking that everything isn't as perfect between the MC and Buskin' Bob as he believes!). Sigmund said Lucrezia sounded as if she might be *a bit* autistic. (She isn't *a bit* anything, if you ask me—she's totally out of control!) I didn't think girls could be autistic. I said Sappho says that it's men who are autistic, and he said that's not what Sappho meant. What she meant was that some male behavior also happens to be autistic behavior (well, that's what I said!). Sigmund can't say good morning in less than an hour, so you can imagine how he went on about autism, its symptoms and theories (obsessive behavior is one of the signs!). When he finally ran out of steam, I asked if I could spend next weekend at his. He made a big joke of pretending he hadn't heard me right. He wanted to know if I'd lost a bet or something. He said he'd heard I thought Kilburn was located somewhere on the bum of the universe and that he lived in a squat (Jocelyn Bandry really has a BIG MOUTH). I said I didn't say it *was* a squat, I said it was *like* a squat because it didn't have central heating. I said I just thought it'd be nice if we spent a little quality time together. Since when was that a CRIME? He reminded me that he didn't have a spare room or even a sofa. I could tell that my having the cot wasn't really an option, so I said I'd bring my air bed. Just hope I can get HIM to blow it up!

Talked to Disha after Sigmund left. Asked her if she had a good time on Sunday. She said she did all her ironing! I said I thought she was going somewhere with the old folks and she said oh, right, there was a change of plan. I said she should've rung—we had a brilliant time at Marcus's. Disha said she didn't think of it. [Note to self: Is *Being in Love* like having a lobotomy?]

WEDNESDAY 5 SEPTEMBER

All is hectic preparation for the start of school. Am really looking forward to going back despite the incredible academic pressure that will be on me for the next two years. Found a v interesting article in the paper about all the **STRESS** teenage girls are under and how much they worry about **EVERYTHING** (their looks, their weight, their clothes, their popularity, their grades, etc.) and left it out where the MC would see it—in case she has any thoughts about me working *and* doing my A-levels. Instead of being sympathetic, all she said was that she thought there were more important things to worry about than the size of your nose or whether you're wearing last week's T-shirt. If you ask me, her new role as Consort to the Eco Warrior isn't improving her parenting skills any.

Actually got Disha to emerge in daylight today to do some shopping for our return to the corridors of education. (Though **NOT FOR LONG**, of course. She was meeting Ethan before he went to work. God forbid twenty-four hours should pass without them seeing each other. It's practically a miracle she survived the sixteen years before I introduced them!) Both of us fell in love with this *très* cool orange top in Gap. I, of course, couldn't buy it because orange makes me look jaundiced, but Disha *wouldn't* buy it. I said why not? It's totally **YOU**. She said because it's orange. I reminded her that orange is one of her favorite colors, and she said but Ethan **HATES** orange. I said well, that was good news then, since Ethan doesn't have to wear it. She laughed, but she still wouldn't buy the top. I said but *you* like it. She says that she doesn't dress for *her*; she dresses for Ethan. I said you mean like he dresses for you? I can just picture him getting up in the morning and thinking, *Now which T-shirt would Disha really like? Should I put on my green socks or my blue ones?* She said boys were different. I said that was true. Boys can piss standing up without ruining their shoes. [Note to self: Is *Being in Love* like having a lobotomy *and* being on tranquilizers?]

Disha left me to meet the Man Who Hates Orange, so I took the bus back on my own, which to tell you the truth was fine by me. All D talks about is Ethan, the Ninth Wonder of the World. It's unbelievable! A few short months ago, she was my *Soul Sister* and now she's more like the Soul Sister of Britney Spears. Since I'd been **WARNED**, I had my book with me. The book says that big companies don't just sell *things* like shoes or cars anymore. They sell ideas, lifestyles, and attitudes. (That's why cars have names like Renegade and Cherokee and Picasso, etc.—not Henry or George.) It says that whereas a car is just a machine to get you from one place to another, a Renegade is a **STATE OF MIND**. Personally I think the author may be stretching it a bit. Anyway, I was mulling all this over when I heard a truly irritating voice that I recognized immediately. I looked up. Catriona Hendley and Lila were sitting two rows in front of me. I could tell they didn't know I was there because they were having the sort of private, intimate conversation you have on buses full of strangers. Apparently Catriona got more than a tan during the holidays. She got a secret boyfriend as well! Lila was gushing about *How Romantic* it all was. Catriona said her parents would absolutely kill her if they ever found out. I leaned forward, hoping I could find out who the unlucky lad is, but **AT THAT VERY MOMENT** the girl in front of me started talking on her mobe, so all I could hear was **HER** telling her friend she was on a bus, etc. (Some people are **SO** inconsiderate. There really should be a law!)

Told the MC about Disha not buying the orange top. I should've known that a woman who won't even buy my favorite ice cream anymore because of her boyfriend wouldn't be too sympathetic. She said Disha just wants to please Ethan because she's in love. Then the MC said it was a good thing I didn't buy the top, because Robert has a lot to say about Gap. I said Robert has a lot to say about **EVERYTHING**!!!

Must get Disha to pump Lila for more information on Catriona's *Secret Love*!

THURSDAY 6 SEPTEMBER

Got sent to the corner shop for TP this morning. For the first time I actually noticed the names of the different brands. One was called **FREEDOM** and another was **FESTIVAL**. Made me think about what I was reading yesterday. Maybe the book has a point after all. I mean, what do Freedom or Festivals have to do with TP? Why not just call it Bog Roll or Something to Wipe Your Bum With?

Went to Hampstead Heath with Marcus today. As you know, the Heath holds some bittersweet memories for me because of Elvin—as well as some painful ones because that's where I crashed that stupid bike and nearly tragically ended my young life!—but I don't believe in living in the past. (I mean, what's the point? It's **GONE**.) Marcus wanted to know whatever happened to Disha Paski. I said **WHO**? He wanted to know if we'd had a fight. I said no, what's happened is that Disha's in *Love*. He said here he was thinking she was in quarantine or something, since he's hardly seen her all summer. I said tell me about it. Marcus said, "We're not jealous, are we?" I said of course I wasn't jealous (jealousy is an ignoble emotion, if you ask me). I'm just fed up with being treated like last year's favorite Christmas present. Marcus wanted to know why he hadn't met this bloke. Isn't she meant to introduce him to her mates? To tell you the truth, I hadn't thought of that.

I explained that Ethan works a lot, etc. He said the Prime Minister works a lot too, but you can bet his wife's met his friends. Marcus doesn't think it's normal. Sappho was having a cup of ethically correct tea with the MC when I got back. I asked them what they thought about Disha not bringing Ethan around to meet her mates, etc. Sappho wanted to know if I was a wee bit jealous. I said of course I'm not jealous. I just don't think it's **NORMAL**. Flying against all past behavior, the MC actually agreed with me on this one! She doesn't think it's normal either. The MC said she's introduced Buskin' Bob to **EVERYONE** she knows. Sappho finally admitted that we had a point. She said when she started dating Mags, she even introduced her to people she didn't know.

FRIDAY 7 SEPTEMBER

The MC wanted to know where I was going with my air bed and my overnight bag. I said I was going to my father's. She remembered him, didn't she? She wanted to know when I had been planning to tell her I wasn't going to be around at the weekend. I said I did tell her but because she never listens to anything I say, she obviously didn't hear me. Even though you'd think she'd know by now that guilt doesn't work with me, she said what about Marcella and Lucrezia? They'd been looking forward to seeing me again.

298

(Oh, and I THEM!) I said I felt that spending some time with my father was more important. She said I'd never shown any interest in spending time with my father before and I said that he's never lived somewhere else before. Also, I think he's LONELY. And he isn't getting any younger, is he? Men his age have a tendency to suddenly drop dead. How would I feel if Sigmund had a heart attack next week and I'd missed my last chance to see him because I was listening to Marcella tell me which of her friends she'd fallen out with this week? I left très quickly before she could think of a comeback.

Sigmund took me to see a film tonight and then we picked up a pizza on the way home. I was going to get him in a nostalgic mood by reminiscing about all the good times we had as a family, but I couldn't think of any. So instead I told him all about our week in the wilderness at Camp Despair (except for the bits where the Mad Cow and Buskin' Bob were all lovey-dovey). I've never made him laugh so much! He asked if Robert REALLY played "Where Have All the Flowers Gone?" every night? I said did the moon wax and wane? He said, "Well, your mother likes him." Since part of this visit is to start sowing the seeds of doubt about Buskin' Bob's suitability for the MC, I said I didn't think the Mad Cow's judgement could be totally trusted. After all, she was V HURT by Sigmund running around with Mrs. Kennedy like that and she needed to regain her sense of herself as a woman (I read this in the color supplement). I said in that state she'd go for any bloke whose knuckles didn't actually scrape the floor. Sigmund looked thoughtful at this, but since he'd determined to be **UNDERSTANDING**, he said that from what he'd heard they did seem to get on v well. I said there had been a couple of shouting matches in the Welsh wilderness. A spark of Hope shone in his eyes. He said **REALLY**? I said yes, really (these were between Marcella and Lucrezia or between Lucrezia and anybody else, but I didn't see any reason to mention that).

Sigmund refused to blow up my air bed on the grounds that a man who's been smoking cigarettes for over thirty years needs all the breath he can get. I said he should've thought of that before he started. He said he wishes he had.

SATURDAY 8 SEPTEMBER

I'm having such a good time with the paternal parent that I'm beginning to think it's almost too bad that Sigmund didn't get a two-bedroom flat after all. It's *v Peaceful and Quiet* here behind the bingo hall—though to be honest the West Bank would probably seem pretty *Peaceful and Quiet* without the Hotspurettes. Also, unlike Buskin' Bob, Sigmund is still buying from Proctor & Gamble, Unilever, Coca-Cola, Colgate-Palmolive,

Nestlé, etc., so he got all my favorite things in. And tonight he took me to a v cool restaurant (in Kilburn!) where we ate on this little indoor balcony. We played backgammon when we got back to the squat because he hasn't got around to getting a telly yet. Since I had a few hours to spare, I asked Sigmund what he thought about someone not introducing her mates to her new boyfriend and vice versa. Sigmund wanted to know who we were talking about. I said just someone from school. He said you mean Disha? I said yes, otherwise known as **Zombie in Love**. Sigmund wanted to know if perhaps I was a little jealous. I said NO, I just found it distressing the way she was changing because she has a boyfriend—also, I didn't think it was normal to keep him away from everybody else. Sigmund finally admitted that he thought it was a bit off too, especially for someone with Disha's extrovert personality. He had a lot of psychobabble to back him up, of course. Is she afraid that he won't like her friends and think less of her? Is she afraid that he might like her friends more than he likes her and think less of her? Is she **jealous and possessive** and doesn't want to share him because of her own insecurity? None of this sounds like Disha to me. I've never known her to be **jealous** or **possessive**, and she isn't insecure. She may not ooze confidence the way a slug oozes slime (as Catriona Hendley does) but she's v together. Sigmund pointed out that I'd never seen her in this sort of situation before (which is true, of course—she's always been completely sane). Was mulling over Sigmund's words when the truth hit me the way an asteroid hits a planet! Maybe the reason D's keeping Ethan to herself is because she feels guilty—you know, for more or less stealing him away from me. That would make sense. The magazines are right: it definitely helps to discuss things with someone else. I was really glad I had talked to Sigmund—even though he's always wrong.

SUNDAY 9 SEPTEMBER

The Mad Cow was in the kitchen with Sappho and Mags when I got home (I made certain the Hotspurs were on their way to Oxford before I appeared!). I asked the MC how the weekend went, and she said it was fine. I know she was lying because Sappho patted the MOUNTAIN and said that after hearing about Lucrezia she almost hoped it would be a boy (which is the same as a normal woman saying she almost hoped it would be a woolly mammoth). The Mad Cow said the girls were v disappointed not to see me, and I said I was practically heartbroken. I said there'll always be another weekend, and she said there would be. Not if I can help it, there won't.

MONDAY 10 SEPTEMBER

Someone should write to the Prime Minister and let him
know that not all British Youth are disillusioned and
apathetic about their education. My friends and I are
absolutely **ECSTATIC** to be back at school again. David
and Marcus said that having nothing to do but play video
games and watch telly is like having nothing to eat but
crisps and sweets. David said he's seriously thinking of
dedicating himself to going to school for the rest of his life.
He reckons that next to doing a mindless job (as in riding
a chow mein scooter), going to school is like a holiday.
Only Disha's a bit down, because now that she's at school
all day and Ethan's at work all night, she's not going to see
so much of him. I said she should take a photo of him—
then she could see him whenever she wants. She said I'll
understand what it's like when I *Fall in Love* myself (all
I can say is I *sincerely* hope not!). But when Marcus asked
her what she did with herself over the holiday, she went
all coy and said oh, this and that. David said he heard she
was in *Love* with some Australian. Disha blushed and
gave **ME** a look as if I'd told some government secret or
something. David wanted to know when we were going to
meet this Wizard of Oz. Disha gave me another accusatory
look and said, "His name's **ETHAN** and Janet's met
him." David said he meant everybody else. Disha said
Ethan works most nights, so it's v difficult. Marcus said his

bedtime isn't nine anymore, so he can't see any problem—
not unless this bloke's a vampire.

Catriona Hendley had THE MOST BRILLIANT
HOLIDAY OF ANY HUMAN WHO EVER
LIVED (and, as per usual, was physically incapable of
NOT talking about it). Last summer Catriona and Mummy
and Daddy went to Canada (which, of course, was the most
brilliant holiday ever *that year*!), but this summer they "did"
Singapore, Malaysia, Fiji, Australia, Hawaii, Bali, etc. I said
what did she "do," bore them to death? Also as per usual,
she ignored this barbed comment and banged on about
where she went and what she did when she got there.
She did yoga on a mountaintop overlooking the ocean.
She went swimming with dolphins. She went sailing and
surfing. She watched the sun set over the rice paddies. She
went topless on the tropical beaches of Kuta. Up until then
everyone had been nodding and wishing she'd hurry up
and finish, but when she said the bit about going topless,
all the boys looked up with genuine interest (AS IF,
right?). She told David that her holiday experience had
given her a fuller understanding of Asian culture. David said
his experience delivering cold rice and prawn crackers had
given him a fuller understanding of Asian culture too.
I noticed she didn't mention anything about a MAJOR
ROMANCE. This must be even more secret than I
thought. Catriona Hendley doesn't get so much as a new

hair clip without making certain everyone else knows about it. Reminded Disha that she's got a Mission!

TUESDAY 11 SEPTEMBER

Had to go to the library after school to return some books from last term. (What a palaver! Mrs. Higgle actually came into English **AFTER ME**! Everyone was shocked. I don't think any of us have ever seen her **OUTSIDE** the library before!) Anyway, when I came out, Catriona was walking towards the main gate with Mr. Plaget. I could tell she was still banging on about rice paddies at sunset because of the glazed look in his eyes. Mr. Plaget saw me and asked if I'd had a good summer. (I reckoned it was a case of Janet to the rescue!) Normally I would've told him I'd had a v crap summer and was excruciatingly grateful to the State for giving me something to do other than work my toes **NUMB**, but since he was with Catriona I lied and said it was **ABSOLUTELY BRILLIANT**.

Suggested to Disha that we have a really mega joint party to celebrate our birthdays (she's 22 October and I'm 27 October) since seventeen's practically eighteen (and eighteen's just a step away from twenty-one, so it's something to make a big deal of). Especially if Buskin' Bob is right about the state of the world. If things are as bad as he says, there may not be anything to celebrate by the time we're twenty-one. I also pointed out that it would be a perfect opportunity to introduce Ethan to everybody in a relaxed and casual way. She said he'd probably have to work that weekend. (So as well as being in *Love* she's psychic, since no one actually picked a date!) She said anyway, she just wants to celebrate quietly with Ethan!!! I said hang on, what about me? We always do *something* together. She said not to be like that. I said *like what?* And she said YOU KNOW (but I don't, of course!). [Note to self: Isn't it ASTOUNDING how small the world gets when your brain's been fried by love?] So I'm having the party on my own. I'm going to invite EVERYBODY (even people I loathe, like Catriona Hendley). And since it's so near to Halloween I'm going to make it a fancy-dress party. The MC will only give me a pittance towards it, of course, so I'll have to hit the Justin bank to get everything I'll need. Does a day pass when I don't THANK GOD that my brother's gone to Mexico? Only when the Deadly Duo stay over.

WEDNESDAY 12 SEPTEMBER

BIG NEWS at the Institution! The school's been given a whack of lottery money and some of it's going to the school magazine because Mr. Cardogan—the head, otherwise known as Old Woolly Jumper—feels that there should be more to education than textbooks and tests (which is more than the government does!). So now, instead of coming out once a year, it'll come out every **MONTH** like a proper journal. Ms. Staples says this will mean a lot of work and **ENORMOUS** dedication, but she knows that we can do it. We're having a meeting Friday afternoon to plan the layout, etc. Have decided that despite my many academic pressures I'm going to volunteer for either Editor-in-Chief or Fiction Editor. Ms. Staples wanted to know if I'd written any more stories over the holiday and I told her I'd moved into poetry because I feel it's more emotionally direct. She said she can't wait to read some of my poems. Since I haven't exactly written a whole poem yet, I said they're still too rough to show.

THURSDAY 13 SEPTEMBER

Not only has *Love* destroyed Disha Paski's ability to socialize and choose her own clothes, but it's badly affected her investigative skills as well. She didn't get **ANYTHING** out of Lila. She told Lila all about being in love with Ethan and then v casually mentioned that she'd heard Catriona was also in love. Lila wanted to know where she heard that. Disha said around. Lila said it was news to her. This is such **INCREDIBLY UNTYPICAL LILA BEHAVIOR** that I can only assume there is something **REALLY** wrong with this bloke. Disha said maybe Lila was telling the truth and there isn't any bloke. Maybe I mistook what Catriona said. I said there was nothing to mistake in **MUMMY AND DADDY WILL KILL ME IF THEY FIND OUT**. I said since the Hendleys are media people and *très* liberal and all, I reckon this could mean that he's either **MUCH OLDER** (like over twenty) or even that he's **MARRIED**! Disha said not to get carried away. She said there could be *dozens* of reasons why Catriona doesn't think her parents would approve. I said like what? He's got two heads? He's an arms dealer? He's in prison? She said no—maybe he's a squatter or a protestor or a Womble or an anarchist or something like that. Catriona does like to think of herself as being v cutting edge, doesn't she? I said **A WOMBLE**? A Womble's a fictional character that lives on Wimbledon Common. She said not that kind of Womble, the kind that wears a white boiler suit and goes to all the anti-globalization demos. (I could ask Buskin' Bob for more details on this, of course, but I don't like to encourage him.)

SATURDAY 15 SEPTEMBER

If the truly *Creative Soul* is destined to suffer then I must
be the reincarnation of Leonardo da Vinci or someone like
that, because I've certainly got the suffering bit down! Wait
till you hear what's happened **NOW**!!! We had this
GINORMOUS meeting yesterday about what sort of
magazine we want to have and what we're going to call it
and put in it, etc. (We're calling it *Speak Out! The Students' Voice*
and we decided that it has to have a popular side as well as
a cultural one or it'll just end up underneath budgie poo.)
After we decided all that, Ms. Staples wanted to know if
anyone was interested in the **V DEMANDING** job of
Editor-in-Chief. Catriona Hendley's hand shot up like it'd
been fired from a missile launcher. Not only did Catriona
want it, but she'd actually written a statement of Editorial
Policy **AND** *jotted down a few ideas* (three pages of them!!!).
Ms. Staples said she was impressed by Catriona's
organizational skills (being able to put on her makeup
AND rule the world at the same time) and gave her the
job. I could've argued, of course, but I decided to let
Catriona have it. I don't want to waste all my precious time
ORGANIZING, mine is a creative not a managerial
spirit, after all. I thought I might take the post of Fiction
Editor instead but while I was still mulling it over, Ms.
Staples gave it to David! So I volunteered to have my own
column (which I reckon is almost as good as being an
editor—maybe even better really since you don't have to

read a lot of other people's work). I said I'd been thinking of doing a series of humorous articles on working as a waiter, which would give my fellow students a good laugh as well as a vivid idea of what it's like in the world of the Wage Slave (and would make them as happy as I am not to be part of it). Ms. Staples thought it was a brilliant idea but reckoned that it's more a single article than a series. She said she wants me to be the main feature writer. That way I can do timely articles and interviews as well as humorous pieces. I know she meant this as a compliment and all, but being the main feature writer isn't the same as being one of the editors or a regular columnist. I mean, I don't get to make any decisions or tell anybody what to do, I just get to WORK. Ms. Staples said a magazine is NOTHING without good writers. Big deal, right? I mean, the world is nothing without the people who clear the rubbish and sweep the streets, but you never hear about them, do you? All you hear about is the people who boss them around and make all the money. It's the same with history. History's all about kings and queens and generals—not about the people who built the palaces or did all the work in them or actually had their limbs blown off, etc., fighting the wars. I mean, you never see a blue plaque for a cook or a cleaner or the maid who emptied the bedpans, and yet what would've happened without them? (The Royal Family and their friends would've starved to death or died of the stench, that's what would've happened!) I thanked Ms. Staples and said I'd think it over.

SUNDAY 16 SEPTEMBER

Disha stayed over last night. She wasn't here ten minutes
when she decided she'd better text Ethan to tell him
where she was. I said I thought her mobe had gone in the
loo. She just blew all her savings on a new one, as it's
IMPOSSIBLE to be in *Love* and be tied to a landline.
She said just think about it. If Romeo and Juliet had had
mobes, they would never have killed themselves. I said it
was more likely that they'd never've got together in the
first place because she would've been talking all the time.
So the girls' night in was periodically disturbed by him
texting her or her texting him. Then, as per usual, he
rang her at midnight after his shift. After a few hours of
listening to them cooing at each other, I asked her to go to
the bathroom to talk to him so I could get some sleep. If
you ask me, *Love* may be great for the person who's in it,
but it sucks for her friends.

This was the first time Disha met Buskin' Bob, of course.
She thinks he's rather good-looking. I said and on what
planet would that be, precisely? She said no, really. She
thinks he's nice. I said that *Love* is obviously eating away
at her brain (like syphilis)! [Note to self: Can *Love* be
considered a sexually transmitted disease?!!] She said I'm
just being defensive, which is understandable since I don't
like the idea of some other man replacing my father
(which isn't true—I'd be **DELIGHTED** if Harrison

311

Ford replaced him). Disha said at least Buskin' Bob cooks and stuff like that. I said just because he knows how to wash up doesn't mean he doesn't have his **dark** side. Let's not forget that his first wife booted him out. Disha said Sigmund's first wife booted him out too.

MONDAY 17 SEPTEMBER

I think Ms. Staples must've noticed that I was a bit unhappy about not having a fixed position on the mag, because she took me aside after English today. She said she'd been thinking of ways to give the magazine more popular appeal and she thought she'd come up with something. (For one wild moment I thought she was going to dump Catriona, but—sadly—that wasn't it.) She wondered how I'd feel about doing a Personal Advice Column. I said I'd never thought about anything like that because Fiction's my thing, of course. Ms. Staples said that's what makes me **PERFECT** for the job. She reckons that with my writer's empathy and my sense of humor I'll be able to write a column that gives sound advice and is entertaining at the same time. I admitted that I've **DEFINITELY** had my share of problems in the last year (and probably someone else's!), so I do have plenty of experience in **suffering and angst**. On the other hand, even though my father's a psychoanalyst, I never really listen to him, so I don't really know the theories, etc. Ms. Staples says that isn't necessary. This is a school magazine not the *Observer*. And she thinks that the people who know all the theories don't necessarily know what goes on with people any more than the rest of us. I said that's v true of my father—most of the time he knows even less. Ms. Staples says all I need to do is be **SENSIBLE**. Which, of course, I always am. The more I think about it, the more the idea appeals to me. After all, I am **EXTREMELY** qualified for the job because of my family and my almost-broken hearts, etc.—and it should be good practice for my mission to bring the MC and Sigmund back together as well! Also, it isn't going to be too strenuous (answering a couple of letters), so it won't interfere with my own *Creative* work. I'm going to call it **HELP!** and my name's going to be Aunt Know-It-All (which is both funny and serious). Ms. Staples said it's v important that I keep my anonymity, so she and I are the only ones who'll know who Aunt Know-It-All really is. I can't even tell Disha! (This would've been a problem a few months ago, but since I hardly see her and the only thing she's interested in is the Wizard, it's as easy as eating a packet of crisps!) Spent most of tonight writing my request for problems. See what you think of this:

Stressed out? Depressed? Picked on? Nagged? Misunderstood? Worried? Insecure? Do your parents ignore you? Your friends take you for granted? Your teachers give you a hard time? Do you find the world difficult to understand? Well, weep no more! **HELP!**

has arrived!!! No matter what your problem—be it a lost love or a few gained pounds—Aunt Know-It-All will show you how to solve it. Send your questions or even just your general thoughts about life on our planet to Aunt Know-It-All c/o **Speak Out! The Students' Voice.** Auntie K is here for YOU!

Since I'm not Catriona Hendley, I don't want to boast, but I do think it's pretty good. Showed it to the MC (I don't reckon she counts as telling). *As per usual,* she was as supportive and encouraging as an attack of fighter jets. She said **TALK ABOUT THE BLIND LEADING THE BLIND!** Personally I thought that was a bit harsh. After all, even **SHE** has admitted that I've matured a lot over the last year (thanks to the Dark Phase and Male Duplicity). Also I **AM** a teenager. If you were a teenager, who would you rather get advice from—**ME** or someone who can't even remember what it feels like to be **FORTY**?

TUESDAY 18 SEPTEMBER

I got to school early this morning so I could run off my flyers and put them up before classes started. And were all my efforts rewarded? Is there a pot of gold at the end of the rainbow? The answer to both those questions is **NO**. When I went to collect my post this afternoon there wasn't **ONE LETTER** for Aunt Know-It-All!!! As accustomed as

I am to the **DISAPPOINTMENTS** of Life, I couldn't believe it. I really thought I'd have to hire a cab to get them all home! Ms. Staples said I have to give my potential readers a chance. Like at least overnight.

The MC was out tonight, as per usual, so I invited Sigmund in for a cup of tea. After we exhausted the topics of the weather, school, and his flat, he wanted to know how everything was going. I said oh, fine, just fine— quietly and rather sadly as though I wanted to spare him the really bad news. With the instincts of the professional psychoanalyst, Sigmund immediately asked me what was wrong. I said, "Nothing." He said, "You can tell me; I'm your father." I sighed and looked v reluctant. And then I said it was just that the MC and I had been talking about how different the flat is without him. (This is technically true. She was banging on about missing Justin—which, if you ask me, is like missing a migraine—and how the house didn't feel the same with him gone, and I said **AND SIGMUND TOO** and she more or less nodded.) Sigmund said, "Really?" I said yes. I said the MC seemed très sad. He looked a bit misty at that, though he said it was because the tea was too strong.

WEDNESDAY 19 SEPTEMBER

Still no letters! What's wrong with the students in this school? Are they all on Prozac? Everybody knows that this is meant to be one of the most **traumatic and stressful** times of a person's life. You can't open a paper or magazine without reading some terrifying tale of teenage **suffering and woe**. The pressure . . . the changes . . . the insecurities . . . the fear . . . the doubt . . . the raging hormones!!! If you believe the Sunday supplement, at least half of us are thinking of hurling ourselves off the nearest bridge!!! But not at my school. From the **OVERWHELMING LACK OF RESPONSE** I've had, you'd think my classmates were all in nursery school with nothing to worry about but lunch. Don't any of them go home and cry? Don't any of them lie awake all night in the dark listening to Led Zeppelin? Don't any of them go home and read the color supplements? They can't all have perfect families. They can't all be happy with their bodies. They can't all be accepted by their peers. It's **ABSOLUTELY** impossible that every alcoholic, addicted, abusive, and sociopathic parent in the country lives **OUTSIDE OF LONDON**!!! I mean, really, what are the odds? Ms. Staples said it's still too early to panic. She said after all, there's a lot going on in the world and even teenagers have more to think about than themselves. As proof that I *do* listen to what people say (even Buskin' Bob!) I pointed out that there's *always* a lot going on in the world. I said aside from the constant warfare and injustice, etc., between 30,000 and 35,000 children died *every day* of preventable causes related to poverty, but it's never stopped anyone from worrying about their hair or whether their hips are too big. I said I didn't really have A BIT OF TIME, did I? The first issue comes out in a month!

Was so upset that I confided in David (I don't reckon telling him counts anymore than telling the MC since he's a boy and therefore limits his verbal communications to only what is necessary). David said not to worry. If the fiction submissions are anything to go by, I'll be drowning in letters by the end of the week. He said Catriona alone has already submitted SIX poems for the first issue of the magazine, most of which must've been written on her holiday since there's a lot about beaches and sunsets over the rice paddies. He wanted to know where my poem is. I said I was working on it.

As part of my plan to reconcile the parents I had a little chat with the MC tonight. Got her laughing by reminding her of the time Sigmund set fire to the deck chair when he was doing his annual barbecue. She said only Sigmund could burn a deck chair in the rain. I reckoned I heard an affectionate note in her voice, so I told her Sigmund really missed her and said he was hoping they'd get back

together someday. She laughed and said well, you never can tell, can you? Let's not forget the Restoration!!!
I consider that v hopeful!

THURSDAY 20 SEPTEMBER

Catriona reminded me that the deadline for copy for the magazine is in two weeks and she hopes I'm planning to write something. What about my idea about being a waiter? She really thought that could be v *droll*. She said she's often thought of doing a job like that just to see what it's like. She said that since she intends to be a journalist she feels that sort of experience would be good to help her identify with The People. I asked what she meant. The People **WHO WORK**? Catriona said my sense of humor is just what the mag needs and that it would be **A CRYING SHAME** if I didn't have something in the very first issue. I explained that I have a lot on my plate at the moment, and also that I feel there are more important things in the world than a high-school magazine. I asked her if she had any idea how many children die *every day* of poverty-related causes, and she said 33,000, but none of them were from around here.

After school Marcus helped me make my birthday invitations on his computer. I brought along a photo of me when I was just born to work into the design. Marcus said he always knew I must've been a beautiful baby. I said all babies are beautiful. We put the baby picture at the top and over it we wrote: FROM THIS . . . and under it we wrote: TO THIS . . . And under that we put a photo Marcus took of me this afternoon. Then at the bottom we wrote: COME CELEBRATE SEVENTEEN YEARS OF PROGRESS AT JANET BANDRY'S COSMIC COSTUME BIRTHDAY BASH. Then Marcus did something with the computer and put stars and moons and comets, etc. all over. I think it's **ABSOLUTELY BRILLIANT**! I know my party's not till the end of October, but I don't want to do it all at the **LAST MINUTE** (the way the MC always does). If I give out the invitations now, everyone will have plenty of time to respond and I'll have plenty of time to prepare (and Ethan will have plenty of time to arrange his work schedule!).

Told Sigmund that the MC said she thought there was still a chance they could patch things up. He said really? What about Robert? I said everything passes, everything changes, doesn't it?

FRIDAY 21 SEPTEMBER (Only five weeks and one day till my party!!!)

Everybody was **WOWED** by my invites—even the Hendley. Apparently she **LOVES** dressing up (I love her dressing up too—at least I won't have to look at her face). I told her she should bring her boyfriend. She said what boyfriend would that be? I said I'd heard rumors. She said not about her, I hadn't, but she gave Lila a **V DIRTY LOOK**!!! (Everybody knows what a **BIG MOUTH** Lila has!!!) David couldn't believe I made the invitations myself. I said I had a bit of help from Marcus. David said he should've known. I said why, because the last time David and I worked together on the computer at school I wiped half the magazine from the hard drive? David said that wasn't what he meant at all. Then he said if I want, he'll help me revise for my driving theory test when the time comes. I snapped up the offer. I obviously can't count on any help from *Disha in Love.*

Unlike Catriona Hendley, David really does have amazing organizational skills (possibly due to being the son of a restaurateur) and has arranged for us all to go bowling tonight with Siranee, Sara, and Alice! We haven't seen them since July, so it should be a hoot. Asked Disha if she and Ethan wanted to come since it's his night off, but she said they already had plans. I said can't they be changed? What are you doing, dining with the Queen? Disha

laughed. I said just remember you and the Wizard of Oz
are coming to my party. She said of course they are . . .
unless he has to work. I said he could always come late:
I'm expecting it to go on for quite a while!

Sigmund left a present for the MC tonight! It's a book he
borrowed from her when they first met. (Sigmund usually
gives the MC things like electric toothbrushes, so I reckon
this counts as a *Romantic Gesture*—another FIRST!) It's
not the *same* book, of course (that fell out of his backpack
when he was cycling down Marylebone Road in the rain
and got run over by a number 18 bus). He wanted her to
know he hadn't forgotten about it!!! I showed it to her as
soon as she came in with Buskin' Bob. She said it was about
time—he borrowed it nearly twenty years ago and she'd
never even finished it. But after Buskin' Bob left, I heard
her ring Sigmund to thank him and she was so nice and
pleasant that at first I thought she was talking to someone
else. They went on for approximately twenty-seven minutes,
which is something of a record since he moved out
(especially since none of it was shouting and screaming!).
I definitely consider this another hopeful sign!!!

Still no letters for Aunt K! What am I going to do if she
doesn't get any?!! I haven't bothered writing anything else
for the mag because I thought solving everybody's problems
would be enough to start with. The last thing I need is
Catriona pretending to feel sorry for me because I missed

out on the **FIRST** issue. David said I could always do an interview if I really have nothing to submit. I said **AN INTERVIEW**? With **WHOM**? It's not like our school is filled with Fascinating Characters or Hollywood Stars. David said how about Mr. Tulliver the caretaker? I said and what would I interview him about? The best way to get old socks out of a toilet? David said Mr. Tulliver used to be in the SAS and has lots of interesting stories about killing people and living on grubs and tree bark, etc. And to think that most journalists want to interview the likes of Spielberg or Madonna—they don't know what they're missing!!!

Have to get ready for bowling. More anon.

SUNDAY 23 SEPTEMBER

It's been **GO! GO! GO!** all weekend. Siranee, Alice, and Sara all wanted to know where Disha was on Friday night. I said Disha was in the *Arms of Love*—which seems to be a lot like being in solitary confinement. Siranee was v surprised by this news. So was Alice. Alice said Disha's the last person she'd have expected to behave like that because she's got a boyfriend—it's something she'd expect more from **ME**! (Can you believe that?!! I was too **GOBSMACKED** even to defend myself!!!) Sara, however, wasn't at all surprised. Sara watches a lot of daytime telly and says the talk shows are absolutely chock-a-block with women who totally turn themselves inside out for men: have their breasts enlarged, dye their hair, become weightlifters, move to islands off the coast of Africa, etc!!! And it's not just the unattractive, desperate women either! Like AIDS, it can happen to *anyone*!!! [Note to self: Ask Sappho if this could possibly be genetic.] On the brighter side, the bowling was a hoot and a half! Marcus and David were good, of course—they have well-developed hand muscles from playing so many video games—but it was Siranee who hit so many strikes that the man in the next lane asked her if she wanted to join his bowling team. After that, everyone came back to mine to watch a film. Ended up getting two videos because we couldn't agree (the males, of course, wanted something violent and not too intellectually taxing, and the females wanted something with character and plot). We couldn't agree on which one to watch first, either, so we played charades instead. The MC and Buskin' Bob came in just as we were starting and wanted to join in. I was still recovering from this shock when I realized that the others were moving around to make room for them! I said pardon me, but fraternizing between my family and my friends is something I tried to discourage (and have done since primary school when the MC first began embarrassing me in public). The Mad Cow and Robert acted like I was making a joke. In the end, it wasn't as bad as I'd feared. There was plenty of hysterical laughter all around. (No one could decide which was funnier—David miming *lap dancer* or

Buskin' Bob miming *Bridget Jones's Diary*!!!) Marcus, David, Siranee, Sara, Alice, and I had such a good time that we decided to hang out again last night and watch the videos. Alice said I should ask Disha to come. I said, "You ask her." (Alice did ask her and Disha said she was busy—for a change!)

MONDAY 24 SEPTEMBER

Aunt K finally got two letters today!!! Not that it was exactly worth the wait. I know beggars can't be choosers, but these girls would never be selected to go on *Jerry Springer*! Their letters practically redefine **dull and boring**. I swear they could put a starving tiger to sleep. Told David how DISAPPOINTED I am. I said I want exciting problems—abusive uncles, incestuous relationships with brothers and cousins, tortured teens worrying about their sexuality, children driven to the edge by parents who make them scrub the kitchen floor with a toothbrush every morning before school . . . But what do I get? I get *fat thighs* and *I had a fight with my mom*. David said maybe Life is more about imperfect bodies and domestic rows than you'd think from watching telly. [Note to self: If television isn't a reflection of reality, what is it?] At least the letters were easy to answer. (*Half the people in the world have fat thighs—it's not a handicap unless you want to be a catwalk*

324

model, and EVERYBODY fights with their mother.) I can only hope the next batch is better!

TUESDAY 25 SEPTEMBER

Discussed the **shallowness and drabness** of most people's lives again with David. He said maybe I should jazz up the letters a bit to make them more exciting. It's tempting, but I don't think it'd work. I mean, the person who wrote the letter will know that it isn't what (s)he said and then Aunt K will lose her credibility. David said anyway, it's still early days yet. Something juicy might be just a letter away. Not today it wasn't.

Sappho and her BUMP (otherwise known as Mount Everest!) came over for supper. Sappho says she isn't sure she and Mags are doing the right thing having a child when the World Situation is so bad. I said things have always been this bad (there are a lot of history programs on the telly, so I know what I'm talking about!) and I didn't see what the problem was. I said it was all right in the past if you were rich or a lord, or something, but everybody else got hanged or shipped to Australia if they so much as nicked a crust of bread. (I found myself thinking that hanging was a better idea so at least their descendants couldn't come back and brainwash your *Best Friend*!) Sappho agreed that life on

Earth has never been a picnic for most people, but she said this is the closest we'd ever come to actually destroying the planet. I said well, that's progress, isn't it?

WEDNESDAY 26 SEPTEMBER

As you know, I don't usually hang out with Disha after school anymore because she's always off to meet Ethan before he goes to work, but today he had something else to do, so I went over to hers. Mrs. Paski said it seems like she never sees me anymore. I said that's because she doesn't. D and I hung out in her room. It's amazing how she can get Ethan into conversations that have **ABSOLUTELY NOTHING** to do with him. If we talk about school, she says, "Ethan says when he was in school blah blah blah." If we talk about clothes, she says, "Ethan says that clothes blah blah blah." If we talk about parents, she says, "Ethan says that his parents blah blah blah." Mentioned in passing that it must be possible to get through just one whole sentence without bringing Ethan into it—she used to, didn't she?—and she got all snotty. She wanted to know if I was still cheesed off that he asked her out and not me. I said I was **BORED**, not jealous.

THURSDAY 27 SEPTEMBER

Two more deadly dull letters for Aunt K. The first was from someone who wanted to know if it was true you can't get pregnant the first time (*Answer: No, it isn't true. Aside from the Virgin Mary, who got pregnant* WITHOUT *a first time, women have been known to get pregnant without even realizing they had sex!*). The second was from He Loves Me So Much, whose boyfriend is **v possessive and jealous** (*Answer: Jealousy is not a sign of affection; it's a sign of insanity!*). Ms. Staples said I should try to remember that though I think the problems I'm sent are dull and humdrum, to the people writing they're dire and HUGELY important. I said it just proves that subjective reality is really unreliable, doesn't it? Then she reminded me that my copy's due in next week. The SOONER, the BETTER. She said if I was having trouble getting my material together she could always give me a hand. I thanked her, but said that I'm here to GIVE help, not take it!

FRIDAY 28 SEPTEMBER

At last! Just when I was beginning to think I was living in a cereal commercial, a REALLY INTERESTING letter came for Aunt K today. It's from someone who's worried that her best friend might be seeing one of her teachers!!! Worried Mate's friend told her she met this bloke at the gym she goes to. She said he was one of the trainers and his name was Fred. Worried Mate wanted to get a look at this bloke, of course, so she decided to surprise her friend at the gym one afternoon and get a glimpse. Her friend wasn't there. The person on the desk said her friend hadn't been in for weeks. And **THERE AREN'T ANY TRAINERS NAMED FRED**!!! Worried Mate asked her friend what was going on and her friend told her to **MIND HER OWN BUSINESS**!!! Now she won't talk about Fred **AT ALL**. Worried Mate says they've **NEVER** had any secrets from each other before, so she knows this has to be something really **MAJOR**, like a teacher or a married man. This is the sort of problem that makes an Agony Aunt's day!

Nan came over for supper tonight. It's almost a shame that Buskin' Bob isn't her son; they get on so well. The two of them banged on about the inhumanity of man toward man (and toward every other thing on the planet as far as I can tell) through the whole meal. Apparently Nan's new Jesus group doesn't just sit around reading the Bible all the time; they believe in **DOING** as much as **PRAYING**. So Nan's becoming a Christian activist!!! (The Prime Minister worries a lot about hardcore anarchists—just wait till he has to deal with **HARDCORE GRANS**!!!) Nan said that since she had **PERSONAL** experience of the **horror** that is war she's even joined a Christian peace group. They believe that the **Thou Shalt Not Kill** commandment should be taken literally—as in you shouldn't kill anyone. She says she reckons that she knows exactly what Jesus would do if He were here now—and it wouldn't be to bomb innocent people who have already suffered enough.

SATURDAY 29 SEPTEMBER

Helped David sort through the fiction submissions for the magazine today because he was a bit overwhelmed (maybe in the rest of Britain the teenagers are all couch potatoes, but at our school at least half of them are writing stories either about *Falling in Love* or saving the world from an alien invasion). To thank me, David took me to lunch at that conveyor-belt sushi restaurant in the West End. It's v high-tech and très trendy. The sushi wasn't bad, but I didn't get much to eat because it's v difficult to hold a conversation and keep up with the dishes drifting past at the same time— it was all right for David because he mainly listens. I told David about Worried Mate's letter. I said if only I had more like that, my first column would be **ABSOLUTE DYNAMITE**. David said it's too bad I can't write to myself, what with all the problems I've had/have in my life. If he hadn't had a mouthful of raw tuna at the time, I think I would've kissed him!!! I told him he was a genius. Why didn't I think of that before? All I have to do is write letters myself. The first one's going to be about how I'm feeling about *Disha in Love*. (She'll never recognize herself—she's

much too self-absorbed.) I don't consider this dishonest, because if I wasn't Aunt K I probably would write to her about this situation (God knows, there's nobody else I can talk to about it without sounding JEALOUS—which after much soul-searching I absolutely know that I'm not!).
I CAN'T WAIT to hear what I say!!!

SUNDAY 30 SEPTEMBER

Thinking about abandoning both art and literature to pursue a brilliant career in psychotherapy instead. I DEFINITELY have a talent for it (must have got more from Sigmund than just small earlobes!). It's taken me ALL DAY, but I've written an excruciatingly interesting letter and the reply. Here's what I said to Last Year's Christmas Present (that's ME!):

> Dear LYCP, First off, you have nothing to apologize for. Of course you're feeling a bit hurt and rejected because your best friend has abandoned you for her new boyfriend. Think of all the hours, days, and years you've spent together. All the Kodak moments and secrets of youth you've shared. It would be strange if you didn't miss her. Especially the way she's carrying on! It's never pleasant to watch someone you respect and admire turn into a zombie right before your eyes. But it's a sad fact of life that many women do change when they get a boyfriend. All of a sudden they're interested in football

and how many megabytes their computer has, and they won't
wear pink because it reminds HIM of some medicine he was
given as a child. They stop seeing their old friends not just
because they're OBSESSED with their New Love, but because
they don't want anyone to tell HIM that football puts them to
sleep and half their wardrobe could belong to Barbie. But what
you're feeling is NOT jealousy. It's SORROW and
HURT! What you have to understand is that, in the words of
the poet, nothing lasts forever—and nothing lasts less time than
a passion built only on physical attraction. In time your friend
will come to her senses and be back to her old self. Before you
know it, the two of you will be sitting around, laughing about
what a dork he is!

I feel better already! It's so good that I decided to write a
second letter. This one's from Scared of My Own Shadow.
It's meant to be from someone who has been so affected
by all the things there are to worry about in the world that
she's afraid to go anywhere or do anything. It takes all the
strength she has to go to school. Not only is she afraid
of all the things everybody else is worried about (car
accidents, plane crashes, tornadoes, cholesterol, etc.) but
she worries about pianos falling out of windows and things
like that. Aunt K says:

It's a known fact that most accidents happen in the home and are
caused by tea cosies. And it's not just killer tea cosies you have to
worry about either. A man in Putney was watching cricket on

the telly one Saturday afternoon when two men broke into his flat and shot him in the leg and he bled to death (they were after someone else). So put on your jacket and get out of the house. Home is the last place you want to be.

MONDAY 1 OCTOBER

Handed in my copy for **ISSUE ONE** to Ms. Staples today, who immediately turned it over to our Editor-in-Chief—who has decided to let Power go to her head! Apparently Catriona (she may write poetry but obviously has the soul of a bureaucrat!) was a bit bothered about the letter from Worried Mate. She reckoned that Old Woolly Jumper, the teachers' unions, and the Minister of Education might be upset about accusing a teacher of professional misconduct. I pointed out to Ms. Staples that no one was accusing anybody of anything. All Worried Mate was saying was that she thinks it might be a teacher because her friend's being **SO** secretive. Also, it's not like this sort of thing doesn't happen all the time, is it? There are precedents! But Ms. Staples said she wasn't certain we should start out with a major controversy. What if we edited the letter a bit to leave out the part about the teacher? I could tell that, besides not wanting to be sued or lose her job or anything like that, Ms. Staples wanted to appease Catriona and not let her feel that she isn't in charge (blessed are the peacemakers, as Nan would say!). I said I wasn't sure that was ethical. And how can my readers be encouraged to write about their real problems if we won't print them? Ms. Staples said I had a point. She said in that case what if Aunt K suggested one or two other reasons why the friend was lying, etc. I said I could live with that.

TUESDAY 2 OCTOBER

Question: HOW BLIND IS A GIRL WHO WILL NOT SEE?

Answer: VERY!!!

Just as I was drifting off to sleep last night I practically fell out of bed when a new thought hit me like an out-of-control juggernaut! Suddenly I **KNEW** why Catriona didn't want to publish Worried Mate's letter. And not because it might upset Old Woolly Jumper either! Because it's **ABOUT HER**!!! I mean, really, how many girls can there be in *one* school who are secretly dating a man they don't want their parents to find out about? (Especially in my school—I read the letters!) Told Disha I've been giving more thought to Catriona's *Secret Love* and it occurred to me that it might be a teacher. Disha said, "Which teacher?"

I said I hadn't got as far as thinking about **WHO** it might be; it was just a thought. Disha said if anyone fancied a teacher at our school it would have to be Mr. Plaget, since he's young, single, and attractive. All the other male teachers are either old, married, attractive only if they're being compared to trolls, or all three. That's when another lorry of thought crashed into me and my brain lit up like Piccadilly Circus! I told D about seeing the Hendley and Mr. Plaget leaving school together. Disha said **SO?** Was a student and teacher walking together meant to be **UNUSUAL?** Disha doesn't believe that Mr. Plaget would put his career on the line to date Catriona, esp. with her media connections. Since my own personal experience includes Sigmund putting his marriage on the line to date a woman with twins and a psychotic husband, I find this less impossible than D does. But it is v shocking!!! I've always liked Mr. Plaget. I would've thought he's too smart to fall for someone as obnoxious as the Hendley. But Disha is right about one thing—there is no one else! Must keep a sharp eye out! [Note to self: Why do even intelligent men always fall for the wrong women?]

FRIDAY 5 OCTOBER

The *Roller Coaster of Love* has finally started its descent! (And **NOT A MOMENT TOO SOON**, if you ask

334

me.) Disha and Ethan had a fight!!! She was all quiet and moody at lunch, and then she asked me if I wanted to sleep over. I said I thought she always saw Ethan on Friday nights and that's when she said they're not exactly speaking. I asked her what happened, and she said it was something that wasn't worth discussing. As soon as we got to her room she lit up a cigarette. I reminded her that she doesn't smoke anymore. She said she didn't usually but she was feeling a bit stressed. I said I didn't see how getting lung cancer was going to make her feel less stressed. I said, "So are you going to tell me what's wrong?" and she said, "**NOTHING**." Then she started to cry. I said she ought to be angry, not miserable. She wanted to know how I could say that when I didn't even know what had happened. (Well, I **WOULD** know if someone would tell me!) I said because she isn't the sort of person to argue over something stupid like how to boil water. (Sigmund and the MC have had several fights about that one!) So it must be something Ethan did. She said it wasn't really anything he did—it was more that they have different views of things. I said well, of course they do. He's a boy and she's a girl—what did she expect?

SATURDAY 6 OCTOBER

Got home to find the MC scrubbing around the bathroom taps with a toothbrush. I asked if this was some sort of post-menopausal symptom or if the Queen was coming around. She said Marcella made an unkind remark about her housekeeping standards last time and she didn't want it repeated. I said you mean the Hotspurettes are coming HERE? AGAIN? She said she'd told me. Wanted to go back to Disha's but the Mad Cow mooed and PUT HER HOOF DOWN (right on ME, as per usual!). I tried to explain that Disha's in a state of emotional turmoil brought on by love and needs me. The MC said that Disha can look forward to many unhappy years of emotional turmoil brought on by love, so I'll have plenty more opportunities to be supportive—today it's her turn. She said she'd told them I'd take them to Camden Market. Apparently they'd like that. (Please note that she didn't tell ME I was taking them to the market and obviously doesn't care that I won't like it. And I thought it was the stepchildren who were meant to be treated like second-class citizens!) Immediately rang Disha and got her to come along. She said at least it would take her mind off her aching, breaking heart. Which wasn't true, of course. If you ask me, there's nothing short of a nuclear war that could take Disha's mind off her bleedin' heart. She was in ABSOLUTE Zombie Girl mode all afternoon. She wasn't crying (miraculously!), but she looked like that was only because she had no tears left. She clutched her mobe the

336

whole time we were out, just in case Ethan rang to apologize (but for **WHAT?!!**). And she didn't really speak (unless you count the occasional grunt and nod—which I don't). Being terminally **SELF-ABSORBED** themselves, the Deadly Duo didn't notice Disha's state. Marcella kept up a running commentary on everything we saw (the child's like walking background music!), and Lucrezia held up her end by throwing a **MAJOR** hissy fit because she wanted to buy a blue top like the one Marcella bought in green, only they didn't have it in blue. Walked off and left her to it but she came straight after us, screaming that **EVERYONE ELSE** gets what they want! (How can this child possibly be related to Buskin' Bob?) I said that actually it isn't true that everyone else gets what they want. I said that **MOST OF THE PEOPLE** in the world don't even get what they really need—never mind what they want. She said I sounded just like her father and kicked me! Through all this Disha was constantly testing her phone to make sure it was working and said nothing. Only when we were leaving the market did D say it seemed to her that Lucrezia has some behavioral problems. I said she couldn't imagine how grateful I was to have her point that out to me. Disha went home (presumably to cry, or at least moan in anguish, in the privacy of her room), and the Deadly Duo and I went to get a video. Lucrezia got to pick because she screams loudest. (Marcella says there's no point arguing with Lucrezia because even if you win she'll ruin it for you. I asked if she doesn't find her sister **EXHAUSTING** and she said yes. I felt really sorry for Marcella even though she never stops talking. I know how much I suffer from being the sister of Justin Bandry—but on the list of Most Irksome Siblings in the Universe he's **WAY** below Lucrezia Hotspur. He's like a goldfish next to her shark!) Marcella and I played backgammon after supper while Lucrezia watched her film and Buskin' Bob and the MC sat in the kitchen drinking wine and singing "Big Yellow Taxi" and "He's Only a Hobo" over and over. (I'm surprised the neighbors don't call the cops—I was v tempted to call them myself.) I learned a lot about Marcella's mother the actress and her stepfather the entrepreneur. Apparently they're v busy **ALL THE TIME** (being on telly and making money). That's why the Deadly Duo go to boarding school in the week. Marcella said that although Buskin' Bob is a pain in the bum about what you can eat, etc., at least he hangs out with them. I said what about the guitar? Marcella said she's learned to live with it. If you ask me, it's like learning to live underwater.

TUESDAY 9 OCTOBER

Catriona was banging on about her costume for my party today. She's coming as a belly dancer—even though she doesn't actually have a belly. (It's a good thing I didn't decide to have a Middle Eastern theme for my party or *all* the really slim girls would've come as belly dancers and

I would've wound up being an aubergine!) Anyway, the Hendley's monologue reminded me that I haven't done anything about my own costume yet! I'm going as Trinity from *The Matrix* (thanks to the Dark Phase, **BLACK** is something I can do!). Disha doesn't know what she's going to be yet. I said it is only a little over **TWO WEEKS** away you know. She said that was plenty of time. I said only if you're planning to come as a twenty-first-century teenager. Marcus and David are being *v secretive* about their costumes. They both want theirs to be a surprise.

WEDNESDAY 10 OCTOBER

Woke up in the middle of the night with **THE MOST AWFUL** thought in my head. What if the MC invites Buskin' Bob to my party? Even worse—what if he decides he's the entertainment? (One chorus of "Where Have All the Flowers Gone?" and my social life wouldn't be toast, it'd be the crumbs at the bottom of the toaster. I could never live it down!) Had a word with the MC over the organic muesli this morning. She gets all huffy if you say anything even the teensiest bit critical of Buskin' Bob, so all I said (très casually) was, was she planning to see him next weekend? She said he's taking the Deadly Duo camping and since she has no intention of leaving the party without a chaperone she's not going with them. (Apparently she made that mistake when Justin was my age and came home to find the police on the doorstep. I think she's making it up. I have NO memory of this AT ALL! You can see what I have to deal with here, can't you?) Then she wanted to know why I wanted to know. I said no reason.

THURSDAY 11 OCTOBER

The *Roller Coaster of Love* has peaked again. Apparently Disha and the Wizard of Oz have made up (oh, JOY!!!). She was all bubbly and happy and talking again today. Of course, since she only seems to have one topic of conversation when she isn't depressed into silence, it was all about Ethan. Blah blah blah . . . I think I liked it better when they'd fallen out.

A few more letters are trickling in to Aunt K but none of them are any more riveting than the first lot. *Dear Aunt K, My parents won't let me have a nose job . . . (Answer: Save the plastic surgery for when you're over forty and really need it.) Dear Aunt K, There's a boy I like who seems to like me but he hasn't asked me out, so I'm not really sure how he feels. What should I do? (Answer: Ask him out. You'll know from his reaction exactly how he feels.) Dear Aunt K,*

I've tried every diet there is but I'm still a size fourteen. Should I have my lips sewn together? (*Answer: I can tell you from personal experience that dieting makes you fat, so the first thing you should do is stop doing that. And if you sew your lips closed and get a cold, you'll die because you can't breathe. Being a size fourteen is a lot better than being dead.*) Both David and Ms. Staples say not to worry about the meager (in every sense of the word!) letters, as once the first issue hits the stands I'll be deluged. I said I hoped so. At the moment I'm being dampened to death.

FRIDAY 12 OCTOBER

I swear to God Nan spends more time at ours now that her son's in Kilburn than she did when he lived here! She rolled up tonight with a sign that says THERE IS NO SUCH THING AS A GOOD WAR and her overnight bag. Turns out she's spending the night at ours because she's going on some demo tomorrow. I said wasn't she going to feel a bit out of place among all the squatters, hardcore anarchists, and travelers who usually show up for these things? Nan said why should she? I said because she's OLD. Nan said even old people have a right to their opinion. That's what democracy is all about. I said I didn't really see the point in taking to the streets, then. The government was elected to do its job and that's what it's doing. I said that's what democracy is all about too!!! Nan says it can't do the job **SHE** elected it to do if it doesn't know what she thinks.

SATURDAY 13 OCTOBER

Even though I haven't exactly got back into the Dark Phase, I'm happy to be able to say that my personal growth and development continue at a rapid pace. Had a completely **NEW** experience today (and for once it wasn't all bad!). Without consulting **ME**, the MC decided that we should **ALL** go on the demo with Nan. I said I had a lot of homework and really couldn't waste time being arrested. The MC said she didn't see any problem since I never do it till Sunday night anyway and we'd be released by then. She said wasn't I meant to be a writer for the school magazine? She reckoned an article on an antiwar protest would be more interesting than writing about what the cafeteria was serving for lunch. I had to admit that she had a point. Especially if I **DID** get arrested. And since Disha and the Wizard are back together, I wasn't going to be hanging out with her. Rang Marcus to see if he wanted to come (he did). Then rang David to see if he wanted to come too. David wanted to know if I'd already asked Marcus. Then he said he'd wait for the next demo. I asked how he knew there'd be one? He said because this one wasn't going to do any good. I haven't seen so many policemen in one place since I watched that documentary on the Miners' Strike. (God knows where they all are when you really want one—there certainly weren't any about the time Mr. Burl's scooter was nicked!) I was **ASTONISHED** at how many old people were there (and some of them were even older than Nan!). I was expecting riot police with shields and horses and clubs, etc. like they put on for May Day, but it was all pretty civilized. No incidents of violence—unless you count the balloon filled with tomato sauce Nan threw at a police van (she missed). Nan was cautioned by a copper who was shocked that a woman who had been through the war would behave like that. Nan said she was behaving like that *because* she'd been through the war. Marcus thanked me for asking him along. He thinks the MC, Buskin' Bob, and Nan are all brilliant (another first!). He said he wished his family would show more interest in politics instead of just watching telly and destroying the house with DIY projects.

SUNDAY 14 OCTOBER

Had a brainwave (I really should do the Mensa test— I have to be at least **NEAR** genius!). I don't reckon the parents are ever going to patch things up if they're never together, and they're never together because either she's out or Robert's sitting in the kitchen strumming his guitar. But next weekend Robert will be in a tent somewhere with the Deadly Duo, so I rang Sigmund and invited him to the party. He was **THRILLED**. He kept saying, "You really want me to be there?" I said of course I did: the MC would need some company.

MONDAY 15 OCTOBER

Since Disha was **OTHERWISE ENGAGED**, got Marcus to come to the goth shoe shops of Camden with me to look for just the right combination of leather and metal. Marcus said he hoped I appreciated that this is something he would only do for **ME**, since boot shopping is just below torture on the list of activities he tries to avoid. He was pretty good for the first hour, but by the time we hit the third shop he was starting to grumble. He said he didn't know why I had to try on every pair of boots I saw—especially since they were all basically the same. I explained that they were only the same to the untrained eye. Finally found the **PERFECT** pair (in the last shop, of course!). They're v futuristic. Marcus couldn't believe how much they cost. He thought I was mad to spend that much on a pair of boots I'm never going to wear again. I said that was the beauty of it. Since I'm not wearing them out in the street, I can return them after the party and get my money back. Marcus says he admires my mind even though it scares him a bit.

TUESDAY 16 OCTOBER

David wanted to know why I didn't ask **HIM** to go shopping with me. I said because he hates shopping. He said so does Marcus. Also, *The Matrix* is one of his all-time favorite films, which qualifies him to choose the right boots. Marcus is a Jackie Chan fan, which obviously disqualifies him. I said if he wants, he can come with me after school next Friday to get in the supplies for the party. He said he wants.

WEDNESDAY 17 OCTOBER

Mr. Belakis managed to wheedle some of the lottery loot out of Old Woolly Jumper so the A-level art classes can have a real exhibition in the spring and invite guests besides our parents. I saw that artist Tracey Emin on telly once and apparently she got a load of money for her bed—which, if you ask me, just looked like it hadn't been made in a while. I reckoned I could get even more for my bed and really **SHAKE UP** the Art World (not only

345

hasn't my bed been made in a while but the headboard's been set on fire at least three times—and it has the name of every boy I fancied in primary school scratched into it). But Mr. Belakis says he prefers Inspiration to Installation. He's given us all a project to form the focus for the exhibition, which is something about our families. Marcus is doing a ginormous canvas depicting the history of his family from their beginnings in Africa to winding up in England. My family's history isn't nearly as interesting as Marcus's (no slave trade, no Jamaican rebels, no poor immigrants with all their possessions in a cardboard box and a picture of the Queen), so I'm doing a family portrait. I was going to do just my immediate family (the Mad Cow, Sigmund, me, and possibly Geek Boy—if I can find a photo of him where he doesn't look like a throwback to our primal past), but Mr. Belakis said that including my un-immediate family would be a good challenge for someone of my talent and potential. Think I'll do Sappho now, since pregnant is easier to do than an infant.

THURSDAY 18 OCTOBER

All I can say is, we **DEFINITELY** live in stressful times! (It's a wonder the whole planet isn't on drugs, if you ask me!) Marcus and I stayed after school again to work on our

346

art projects. Mr. Belakis rushed off afterward, but before
Marcus and I left to get the bus, I went to the ladies' while
he took the art-room key to Mr. Tulliver. (I didn't really
have to go, but I knew that by the time I got home—
public transport being what it is—I'd be desperate!) I was
repairing the damage the ravages of the afternoon had done
to my face—Marcus and I had been laughing so much that
my eyes had run—when I knocked my mascara off the
counter and it rolled under the sink. I bent down to pick
it up and **GASPED OUT LOUD**!!! Right in front
of my eyes, stuffed behind one of the pipes, was a
SUSPICIOUS PACKAGE! (You really never think
it's going to happen to **YOU**, do you?) It was small
and in a brown bag. I didn't panic, of course, but I was
CAUTIOUS (there's been a lot on the telly about just
this sort of thing!). I put all my makeup back in my case
and raced out to get Marcus. Marcus, of course, is an artist
not a fighter, but he didn't hesitate for a nanosecond—he
went straight in! (It was a side of him I'd never seen before
and I was v impressed!) Marcus thought it was too small
to be a bomb. I said if you can put a bomb in the heel of
a **SHOE** (which apparently you can), the package could
probably hold **TWO** bombs. Marcus was all for removing
it and seeing what it was (is that **FEARLESS** or what?),
but I reminded him that that's **EXACTLY** what you're
not meant to do. The office was shut by then, but the news
is always on at ours (so Buskin' Bob can keep up with the
injustices each new day brings), so I knew exactly what to

347

do. I rang 999 on my mobe. I said I had reason to believe that there was an explosive device in the ladies' of the main building at the Bere Road Secondary School. The police said to wait outside and they'd be RIGHT WITH US. All I can say is, I don't know how the police reckon time but it's not the way the rest of us do. HOURS PASSED. Marcus kept looking at his watch and telling me how many more minutes had passed. Five . . . ten . . . twelve-and-a-half . . . fourteen . . . twenty . . . I was just about to ring the coppers back when Mr. Tulliver rolled up. He wanted to know what we were doing, standing there like we were waiting for a bus. I told him about the suspicious package. Mr. Tulliver is fat and bald and doesn't look like he was ever in the SAS (unless it was as a cook), but like Marcus he didn't hesitate. He said this was just the sort of thing he'd been trained for and vanished inside. When another EON had passed, Marcus decided to go after him. I said I was certain we would've heard the bomb go off if Mr. Tulliver's training had let him down, but Marcus said maybe it wasn't an explosive; maybe it just leaked a lethal gas and poor Mr. Tulliver was passed out on the floor of the ladies'. I said we weren't in an episode of *Batman* but Marcus wouldn't listen. He didn't come back either. By the time the police finally turned up (no lights or siren—you can only wonder what they consider an emergency!), I was feeling V ANXIOUS but I remained calm and explained about the suspicious package and the two brave men who had gone to investigate (and who, for all I knew, were BOTH passed out on the floor of the ladies'!). The first cop wanted to know why I thought it was a bomb. I said well, what else would I think it was, stuffed behind the sink like that? The second cop wanted to know if the rest of us could hear laughing. I'd never heard Mr. Tulliver's laugh before. (Well, I wouldn't, would I? He's usually fixing something or fishing something out of the biology pond in a professional manner.) But I recognized Marcus's. I said maybe it wasn't laughter; maybe it was hysteria. It was laughter. Mr. Tulliver and Marcus came striding toward us. Mr. Tulliver was holding up the paper bag and both of them were laughing so much there were tears in their eyes. Marcus said I should've seen Mr. Tulliver in SAS mode. It was so much like a film that Marcus hadn't even been frightened, he'd just stood by the door watching him sneak up on the bomb—ready to run. Only it wasn't a bomb . . . it was a packet of cigarettes. The coppers said that if they had a quid for every bomb scare they'd investigated in the last few weeks, they could take early retirement. Marcus wanted to know how many bombs they *had* found, and the coppers said that so far the cigarettes were the only things they'd discovered that would actually light.

FRIDAY 19 OCTOBER

Marcus thinks I should include the Hotspurs in my family
portrait. I said that though it's true you can't get much
more un-immediate than Buskin' Bob, Marcella, and
Lucrezia, I have my doubts about them still being in the
family by the time of the exhibition. Marcus wanted to
know what made me say that. He thought they all seemed
pretty well embedded in the family. I said he shouldn't
always go by appearances.

SUNDAY 21 OCTOBER

Spent the WHOLE day sorting out my costume for the
party. I'm going to look so cool, people who come near
me are going to need a jumper! Got a cheap black wig in
the market as I'm not risking dyeing my hair after what
happened last time.

MONDAY 22 OCTOBER

The first issue of *Speak Out!* hit the stands today!!! It looks
FANTASTIC!!! Ms. Staples said we should all be proud
of ourselves (something you DON'T have to tell Catriona

Hendley twice!). It was sold out by lunchtime. I heard
quite a few people talking about MY column! Everybody
thinks the teacher in Worried Mate's letter must be Mr.
Plaget. They all want to know who Aunt K is, of course.
Even Disha was nagging me. A few short months ago I
might have weakened and told her, since I've never had
any secrets from D, but now that she's keeping me at a
distance, I found it easy to lie. I said I had NO IDEA.
I said it was something Ms. Staples cooked up and NO
ONE on the magazine knows who it is but her. Then,
very casual like, I asked her what she thought of the letter
from Last Year's Christmas Present. She said she hadn't read
it. She said she'd read the one from He Loves Me So Much
and didn't think much of the advice, so she'd stopped after
that. She said it didn't seem to her that Aunt K knew v
much about *Love*. I said that didn't mean she didn't know
a lot about insanity.

Gave D her birthday present at lunch since she was
meeting Ethan straight after school for their PRIVATE
celebration. Got her that top we saw in Gap. I said I knew
she couldn't wear it now, but, judging by what you read
in magazines, there's a good chance she'll have another
boyfriend in her lifetime and he might like orange.

TUESDAY 23 OCTOBER

I could hardly believe it but when I checked the mailbox
this afternoon there were four letters for Aunt K! (This
represents a definite deluge!) Ms. Staples said hadn't she
told me this would happen? I said I'd never really doubted
her but she knew better than anyone that the *Creative
Spirit* is v sensitive and easily demoralized. (Great artists
and writers are known for self-mutilation, suicide, and
drinking themselves to death—and what is that but the cry
for help of a *Delicate Soul*?) Ms. Staples said she never
really thought of writing an agony column as requiring
a great amount of *Creativity* (so even she has her
limitations!). I said I didn't really see much difference
between writing a story, a poem, or a letter to Spotty
and Desperate. Not that these new letters are any more
interesting than the others, of course. I really do
understand that to a person with dandruff or wobbly
thighs there isn't anything much worse that could happen,
but reading all these letters has made me realize anew how
shallow and trivial the lives of most people are. (And
I thought it was just MY family!) Ms. Staples said my
column has certainly generated a lot of interest. I said good
advice is much more relevant to people's lives than poems
about dusk in Indonesia, isn't it? She said not only among
the student body. Apparently Old Woolly Jumper wants a
word with her.

WEDNESDAY 24 OCTOBER

As you know, I have nothing but respect and admiration
for Ms. Staples, so you can imagine how **SHOCKED**
I was today to discover that she's a snitch! She told Mr.
Cardogan who Aunt K is! She said she had no choice. So
the upshot was that I had to go and see him!!! Old Woolly
Jumper and I are not unacquainted, of course, but our
meetings have always been about things like lateness and
talking at the same time as a teacher. Mr. Cardogan started
out by telling me how brilliant the magazine is and how
proud he is of all of us. Then he went on to praise my
column for being so practical and down-to-earth. He said
he was pleasantly surprised. I said, "Really?" He said he'd
always thought I had a rather flamboyant imagination.
I said having a *Passionate Heart and Soul* didn't mean
you don't know how to change a fuse. He said he also
liked my sense of humor. I was just starting to think that
I'd been worried over nothing when Old Woolly Jumper
let me have it. He wanted to know if I was aware that
there were rumors **FLYING ALL OVER THE
PLACE** since my column came out. I said a school is like
a village—there are always rumors flying about. He said
not about one of his teachers going out with a student,
there aren't. I said if he'd read my column, he'd know that
Aunt K pooh-poohed the whole teacher idea and suggested
that the mysterious boyfriend might be something much
worse, like a traveler or a Womble. He said he accepted

that I wasn't personally responsible for the gossip but he would appreciate it in future if I stuck to things like diets and skin care. I said would Life? Would Life content itself with the odd spot and the need for garlic? I said I didn't think so. He said he'd like us both to try. I said I'd see what I could do, of course. But I have **ABSOLUTELY** no intention of letting Aunt K be threatened or bullied by the reactionary forces of the Establishment. Freedom of the press is at stake!!! Disha wanted to know what Old Woolly Jumper wanted. I said he was wondering if I would like to do an interview with him for the magazine.

On a more positive note, Aunt K had **FIVE** more letters today! One Fat Bum, one Small Breasts, one My Boyfriend Would Rather Hang Out with His Mates Than with Me, one The Only Films My Boyfriend Wants to See Are Thrillers, and one My Boyfriend Says I Talk Too Much (*Answers: Learn to live with it* and *Dump him*). It made me think once again about how *très* **IRONIC** life is. I mean, I've worked really hard for years (or at least months!) trying to write fiction with little success (though Ms. Staples did have a lot of good things to say about the story I wrote in the spring)— and now here I am excelling at **NONFICTION**. What if it is genetic? What if I've inherited psychoanalytical skills from Sigmund (even though he doesn't really have that many) when my *Heart and Soul* cries out to be a novelist—or maybe an artist or poet? Am I to be **thwarted and frustrated** because of a mere accident of birth?

There **MUST** be a blue moon tonight! Got Disha to come with me, David, and Marcus after school to the new très trendy café by the canal as a late birthday treat for her. (Apparently Ethan's working.) You can sit outdoors (**YES**—even in **ENGLAND**!!!) all year long because they've got heaters and umbrellas. Marcus said you have to hand it to British ingenuity and David said he reckoned it was more likely to be American technology because Americans like to improve **EVERYTHING** but the British have always just muddled through and made do. We were mucking about, having a few laughs, when I thought I saw Ethan walk past. I said, "Hey, there's Ethan!" David and Marcus both swung around like turnstiles, but Disha said it wasn't him. I said I was sure it was and she should go after him and bring him over, but she was **ADAMANT**. She said she thought she'd be able to pick her own boyfriend out of a crowd. Marcus said he was beginning to doubt that this bloke actually exists. David said maybe he's the Invisible Australian. Disha said she had to go.

THURSDAY 25 OCTOBER

It's a sad and galling fact of my life that ever since I was little, the small, dull minds of my relatives have constantly accused me of having **TOO MUCH IMAGINATION**

355

(as if there is such a thing, right?). Even Disha Paski (you remember her—she used to be my best friend in the universe) has been known to suggest that sometimes I get carried away. Well, they can scoff **ALL THEY WANT**— guess what I saw today? Something that will force the doubters to think again about my instincts and judgment, that's what!!! David and I went to the high street after school to get me a driving handbook. We were walking back to mine when I saw Mr. Plaget's Beetle stopped at a light (you can't miss it—most of it's orange!). I was just about to wave when I realized who was sitting beside him! Oh, yes! It was none other than Catriona of-course-I-don't-have-a-boyfriend Hendley!!! She was smiling and shaking her hair about the way she does. I pulled David into a doorway so they wouldn't see us. He wanted to know what was wrong with me. I said I'd just seen Catriona in Mr. Plaget's car. David said, "**AND?**" and I said I had reason to believe that Catriona was the girl in Worried Mate's letter. David said, "And why is that?" I said, "Call it a hunch." He said he'd rather call it a wild guess and that it was bad enough that people are whispering about poor Mr. Plaget without me joining in. He is **ABSOLUTELY CERTAIN** that Mr. Plaget is not going out with Catriona or any other student. I said maybe, but you don't have to be Einstein to work out that two and two makes four, do you? David said actually Einstein flunked maths, so he probably wouldn't've worked it out. David said the fact is that Catriona's in Mr. Plaget's advanced calculus class and

356

it's not a big deal if he gives her a lift. I said I still thought it was v suspicious. David wanted to know if I remembered when I thought *he* was interested in Catriona? I said *oh, that.*

The driving manual is nearly **FOUR HUNDRED PAGES LONG**!!! I really think that's a bit harsh. I mean, how can anyone be expected to remember **EVERYTHING** that's in it? (Especially someone who's doing her A-levels!! There is only so much space in the human brain, after all!) You'd have to have a photocopier memory.

Love's Roller Coaster has done another deep dive. Disha rang in tears again tonight. (She'll dehydrate if she doesn't watch out!) She had yet another fight with Ethan. I asked what it was about this time. She said, "**NOTHING**" (between sobs!!!). Which, of course, is what she always says. I said I really didn't think this was the way a relationship was meant to be. Not unless you'd been married for a while. I said was she sure she was in *Love* and not just having a **nervous breakdown**? Disha said nothing that was really worth having was ever easy. I said a lot of things that weren't worth having (like AIDS) weren't easy either. Disha said that's what she loves about me, I always make her laugh. I said it didn't sound to me like she was laughing—unless it was through her tears. I said why won't she **TELL ME** what's going on? She said it's really no big deal. Also, I wouldn't understand (she obviously doesn't know **WHO**

357

she's talking to!!!). And she already knows what I'd say. I said I don't see how *she* could know when I don't.

FRIDAY 26 OCTOBER

Marcus has finally paid his father back for the parking ticket, so he took me shopping for party supplies in the car this afternoon. It's so long since I've been in a real supermarket that the lighting, etc. practically made me **SWOON**! It was weird to be totally engulfed in food and not actually be able to smell any of it. Marcus said he never noticed. I started reading the labels on everything (it's **ASTOUNDING** how even someone with a strong character like mine can be influenced without even realizing it!). Marcus wanted to know what I was doing. I said I was just checking for sugar and GM soya, etc. Marcus said I was mad. He said even crisps have sugar in them and if I kept that up we wouldn't have **ANYTHING** to eat. Dropping Buskin' Bob's standards, we filled a whole trolley with unsuitable soft drinks and snacks!!! Then we went to the party shop and got balloons (black and purple) and streamers (also black and purple). And then we went to the cheap place across from the tube to get prizes. The MC noticed the carrier bags right off. She immediately started going on about how I was destroying the market stalls and small grocers of London.

I said, "It's my party and I'll buy where I want to."
Marcus thought that was **HILARIOUS** but the Mad Cow
didn't even crack a smile. Marcus said he'd come round
tomorrow to help me blow up the balloons, etc. I decided
not to mention that David is coming too in case he gets
in one of his moods. (I don't know why it's women who
have a reputation for being temperamental—I find blokes
v touchy!)

Told Disha about seeing Catriona with Mr. Plaget. Disha
thinks I should dedicate my brain to science. She said
it'd distract them from human cloning for centuries
trying to work it out. I said David saw them too (which
he would've if he'd been looking). I said they seemed to
be having a good time. D said he was probably just giving
her a lift, which isn't a crime in this country yet. I said a
lift to *where*? Disha said a lift *home*.

Sometimes it almost surprises even me how I'm always
right (though I do realize, of course, that I'm lucky to be
so intuitive!). This afternoon Disha discovered that Lila
and the Hendley have had a **MAJOR FALLING-
OUT**!!!! I'm willing to concede that Mr. Plaget *might* just
have happened to give Catriona a lift home because she
broke her foot leaving the school grounds or something,
but not when at the **VERY SAME TIME** Catriona and
Lila have stopped speaking. I mean, really—how can that
be a coincidence? Catriona must've worked out who

Worried Mate is. Disha said that wasn't what Lila told her. Lila said it was over something Lila borrowed that she can't find to give back. Pull the other one, that's what I say. David, of course, agreed with Disha. He asked if it had ever occurred to me that the letter might not be about Catriona? I said no.

SATURDAY 27 OCTOBER

It's been GO! GO! GO! all day, but I have to STOP for just a few minutes to tell you what happened now because I'm V UPSET!!! (Now I know how that woman who found a tarantula in her bunch of bananas must've felt! Surprise doesn't even BEGIN to cover it!) David, Marcus, and I were putting up fairy lights in the living room (Marcus's idea—so they'll look like stars!) when the phone rang. It was Disha. She said she was REALLY, REALLY sorry but she's not going to be able to come tonight because she's got the worst period pains any woman has ever had since time began. I couldn't believe she was using the old cramps excuse on ME OF ALL PEOPLE!!! I practically invented it! I said why didn't she just take a painkiller? She said she's been eating them like sweets but they don't help. I said what about a hot-water bottle? She said that didn't work either. I said what about Ethan? Wasn't he looking forward to meeting everyone? She said had I forgotten that

they'd had a fight? And anyway, he has to work. I said so
why can't she come on her own? She said because she's got
the worse period pains any woman has ever had since time
began. I was TOO hurt and angry to argue. I said well,
thanks for the birthday surprise and slammed down the
phone! Then I burst into tears. David and Marcus were
v comforting. David said maybe Disha really is in pain
(she would be if she'd told me to my face!). I said yeah
and maybe there's a flock of pigs flying over London.
I said I knew she was lying. David said not to let this ruin
the party for me. He gave me a hug. Marcus said you've
still got US. He gave me a hug too. I put on a brave face
and said of course I wouldn't let the petty insanity of Disha
Paski destroy my big day. But I was lying. How can I enjoy
myself when my *Best Friend* has dumped me ON MY
BIRTHDAY?!! I know, of course, that you can't rely
on anyone in this world, but I never dreamed that included
Disha! I'll get dressed and put a smile on my face, but
I'll be crying on the inside. (The dark, bitter tears of
wisdom!)

SUNDAY 28 OCTOBER

The party was an INCREDIBLE, GINORMOUS
success!!! *Everybody* said so. The decorations were brilliant,
the costumes were brilliant, and there was a lot of food.

Even Catriona Hendley was v enthusiastic! (Which could be because she won the prize for Best Costume, as two of the judges were men—even though one's an **EXPERT** on human behavior and the other has his mind on **HIGHER THINGS**. I reckon this is evidence in favor of the Nature over Nurture argument!) Anyway, guess who David came as? **NEO FROM THE MATRIX**! I was **COMPLETELY SURPRISED**. But I was even more surprised when I saw Marcus. He came as the bloke from *The Matrix* too! (And if you think I was **STUNNED**, you should've seen their faces when they saw each other!) Of course, this being Life on Planet Earth, it wasn't all gaiety and laughter—there were a few tense moments. The first was when I went into the kitchen to show the MC my costume and discovered the three Hotspurs drinking tea (they all looked like they'd been through the wash!). I said I thought they were going camping. The MC said maybe I hadn't noticed but it'd been pissing down since last night. Their tent collapsed and they had to come home. (Since I didn't want to start a fight right then, I didn't point out that this **ISN'T** their home!) This was followed by some high drama because, even though it was agreed that the Deadly Duo would watch telly in Justin's room and not bother me and my guests, Lucrezia went **BERSERK** because she wanted to come to the party. So we didn't all end up with migraines, I said she and Marcella could come for *ten* minutes. Then she went even more berserk because she wanted to wear a costume. This time it was the MC who caved in like a sandcastle and said she'd see what she could find. (Lucrezia came as a lampshade!) The next tense moment was when Sigmund turned up with a bottle of champagne. Sigmund was as surprised to see Buskin' Bob and his progeny as everybody else was to see him! Using the skills he's developed over decades of professional psychoanalysis, Sigmund asked the MC why she was looking at him like that. She said because she hadn't known that he was coming. (BOTH of them then glared at ME, of course! I sometimes think the only reason they had me was so they'd have someone to blame for every little thing that goes wrong.) I said it is my SEVENTEENTH BIRTHDAY, you know, and, unless the Mad Cow had some **dark secret** to reveal, Sigmund is my father. Sigmund started muttering that he didn't want to be in the way (something that has never bothered him before), but Buskin' Bob (obviously très affected by being in a collapsing tent in a monsoon with Lucrezia) made the first joke I've ever heard him make (possibly the ONLY joke he's ever made!). Robert said he wasn't going to let a man with a bottle of champagne leave. Not after the weekend he was having. Sigmund sat right down. He loves to hear other people's problems even when he isn't being paid by the hour. [Note to self: Is this because it's his job or because it makes him feel better about the mess he's made of his own life?]

Rang Disha first thing this morning to tell her what a BRILLIANT time we all had. (I know this may sound a

wee bit petty, but I asked Aunt K and she said it would be
wrong not to, since true friendship is based on honesty.)
Disha said she'd thought I was angry with her. I said I was
a bit irked but I got over it. Anyway, I was more **HURT**
than angry. I said I just don't understand why she's being
so weird. She said she's not being weird; I just don't
understand how hard it is being in *Love*. I said I hadn't
realized it was meant to be *hard*—I thought it was meant
to be fun. If she's anything to go by, I don't really want
to find out what it's like. Disha said the party sounded
really excellent. She was sorry she missed it. She said she
supposed everybody wondered where she was, and I said
no, they were getting used to her not being around.

Sigmund gave me my first driving lesson today! (We hadn't
gone around the block when he wanted to know what the
rattling sound was—he thought the exhaust was falling
off again. I said not to worry, it was just the bottles for
recycling in the boot.) All things considered, I thought it
went v well. I feel I have a natural talent for driving as well
as for literature, art, and problem solving. Sigmund took
me to a deserted car park on an industrial estate behind
King's Cross where I could drive around without having
to worry about anybody hitting us (London drivers are
NOTORIOUSLY bad). There's more to this driving lark
than you'd think, though, especially if your parents are old
fogeys who still drive a manual! It's just as well there were

364

no other cars about as it was all très intense. Nonetheless, I've already mastered starting and stopping. (I'm particularly good at stopping because changing gear is v tricky and you have to do things with your feet and your hands all at the same time.) I did suggest that maybe it was time the Bandrys joined the age of technology and got an automatic, and Sigmund said he'd sooner get a new daughter than a new car. (Whoever said psychoanalysts don't have a sense of humor? The man's practically a laugh a line!) While we were waiting for the Mini to recover from having its engine flooded (apparently MY fault!), Sigmund said he'd had a good time at my party (all things considered!). I said, "You mean all things like Buskin' Bob considered?" He said more like the fact that no one had known he was coming. Sigmund said Robert seemed like a nice bloke. I said you're just saying that because you think your professional reputation would be damaged if it got out that you'd like to feed Robert's liver to the wild dogs of Clapham. Sigmund said no, he really likes Robert. He thinks he has some v sound ideas. I said and which one would that be? I said he'd feel differently if Buskin' Bob had had his guitar with him. Sigmund said it looked to him like the MC was v keen on Robert. He certainly didn't get the impression she was thinking of dumping him and getting back with the father of her children any time this millennium. I said you can never tell with women, though, can you? They're enigmas. He said, "Speak for yourself!"

Invited Disha around tonight but she's too depressed to
enjoy herself. She said she's never felt like this before. Can't
eat . . . can't sleep . . . thinks about him all the time . . . I
said it sounded to me like she's ill. She said only with
Love. If you ask me, *Love* should come with a
Government Health Warning.

MONDAY 29 OCTOBER

Since it's half-term, this was day two of my driving lessons.
I only stalled four (possibly five) times **AND** I got into
THIRD GEAR! Got a little confused with the lights and
the indicators and couldn't find the horn, but all in all I
made quite a bit of progress for a beginner. While we were
driving around the car park, Marcus rang to see how it was
going and Sigmund went **WILD** because I answered the
mobe. I said but it was ringing. He said **YOU DON'T
TALK ON THE PHONE** while you're driving. I said
was he *blind*? **EVERYBODY** talks on the phone while
they're driving. He said well, they shouldn't. Especially if
they can't drive. And then (despite his **PATHOLOGICAL**
lack of interest in his youngest child) he suddenly
remembered that I don't have a mobe and wanted to know
where it came from. I said I bought it with the money
I made in the summer, didn't I? Once he'd calmed down,

I asked him when he thought I'd be ready to take to the road and he said as soon as I'd mastered only stopping when I mean to. The MC invited him in for tea when he brought me back!!! (I knew she'd soften once she got used to having him about again!) I left them alone, of course, but I did hear her ask him how it was going. He said about what you'd expect! Didn't I say I was a natural?

You'd think it'd be *easy* to return a pair of boots, wouldn't you? I mean you go to the shop, you give them the boots, and they give you your money back. Could anything be SIMPLER? Apparently the answer to that question is: YES—crossing the Channel in a washing-up bowl. You wouldn't believe the palaver! First of all, the sales assistant gave me this ginormous hard time because I'd lost the receipt. I said look at them—you know they came from here. He said he knew no such thing. He said they could've come from another shop on the road. I said, "But you were *here* when I bought them. Don't you remember? I was with a v tall boy with plaited hair." He said there was more than one v tall boy with plaited hair around here and he saw at least five of them a day. I said that he was being COMPLETELY unreasonable and that my stepfather was a solicitor so I *know my rights*. That convinced him! He said he wouldn't give me cash but I could exchange them for something else in the shop. Compromise is, of course, très important in Life, so I accepted this offer even though I'd rather have the dosh. Went to the back where they keep the clothes. I had a pair of black trousers with tons of pockets and zips in my hand and was debating whether or not I think corduroy's going to come back in when this bloke came up behind me and told me to get into the changing room. I said, "Hang on a minute! I haven't decided what I'm trying on yet!" He said, "**NOW!!!**" and gave me a poke. I said, "**OI!**" and turned around pretty sharply, of course. He was wearing a ski mask and **POINTING A GUN AT ME!** Then he said, "This is a holdup," just like in films. [Note to self: Does Art imitate Life, or is it the other way around?] There were three other girls in the shop and they were being herded to the changing rooms by another geezer in a ski mask. (God knows what thieves did before skiing became a popular sport!) As soon as we got in the changing room, the other girls started crying. I didn't see the point. I mean, it's not going to make the robbers change their minds, is it? The only effect crying hysterically might have is to annoy them so much they shoot you. And I really wanted to try on the black trousers. I don't think the robbery took too long. One minute I was surrounded by weeping women, and the next they were charging back into the shop to greet the police. I was grateful. It was way too crowded (and too distracting!) to really see what my bum looked like with that lot in there sobbing away. I was still studying myself in the mirror when someone started shouting through the curtain for me to come out. I said

368

I was just in the middle of something. He said he was a police constable and he needed to take a statement. I said right, I'd only be a minute. He said, "NOW!" (He sounded just like the bloke with the gun.) So I never got to exchange the boots because the assistant was all involved with the cops. Took the boots home and stuck them at the back of my wardrobe. I don't seem to have much luck with boots. I wonder if that means something. Maybe I should ask Sappho.

I sat down with all Aunt K's new letters tonight to write her replies so I'm ready when the copy's due in next week. Of course, they're less **INSPIRING** than watching lettuce rot—weight, skin, jealous boyfriend, etc. (Once again I have to ask myself: Where's the *Passion*? Where's the **conflict**? Where's the blood and mud of **LIFE**?) I started to doze off. But just as sleep was trying to save me from terminal boredom, I was struck by yet another **BRILLIANT** idea for a problem that resonates with *Passion* and **conflict**! (I will admit that I probably wouldn't have thought of it if Rose Bandry the Thirteenth Disciple wasn't my grandmother. How can they say I never listen?) This beats the pants off Even After All He's Done Should I Take Him Back? (*Answer: NO! Give someone else a chance to ruin your life!*) Anyway, here's a **REAL** and excruciatingly dramatic problem—and it isn't anything that could wind up Mr. Cardogan either!

Dear Aunt Know-It-All,

My brother just announced that he's gay. My father says that according to the Bible, homosexuality is an abomination and has thrown my brother out of the house. Is this true? Does this mean I shouldn't have anything to do with my brother either?

Answer: Yes, it is true that Leviticus says homosexuality is an abomination. Leviticus says a lot of things: that anyone who consults the dead should be stoned to death and that only God can own land, and then there's a lot of detailed information about how to make animal sacrifices. I hope your father is making the proper blood offerings and growing a beard or he'll be in trouble even if he never speaks to your brother again. As for you, you have to make your own decision, but keep in mind that the Bible (though not Leviticus, of course) also has a lot to say about compassion and not judging others. If you do choose to join your father, I might know where you can get a nondefective goat.

TUESDAY 30 OCTOBER

Disha got tired of crying over Ethan in her room and came to the Body Shop with me today to help spend some of my birthday dosh. (Even Buskin' Bob can't have anything against Body Shop, so I'm safe there.) Ran into Lila, former best friend of Catriona Hendley! This was my chance to get the story firsthand. Asked Lila where the Hendley was. Lila said she didn't know because they weren't actually speaking to each other at the moment. I asked her what had happened. She said Catriona's pissed off because Lila borrowed a jacket of hers to take on holiday and never gave it back. I said oh, really? Then she went into a long saga of why she couldn't give it back (because she left it in San Francisco), why she couldn't replace it (it's irreplaceable), and why she's pissed off with Catriona (because Catriona's pissed off with her). I could tell she was making it up as she went along. When she finally stopped for air, I asked her what the name of the gym Catriona goes to was, as I was thinking of doing an aerobics course. Lila acted all bewildered and said she didn't know Catriona belonged to a gym. After Lila went off, I said to Disha, "**SEE**?" She said, "See what?" She said Lila told me exactly what she'd told *her*. I said but it isn't the truth. Disha said I only have my word for that. I said no sane people argue over a jacket, for God's sake. Disha said it's been known to happen. I said well, what about the gym? Disha asked if it had ever occurred to me that maybe Catriona **DOESN'T** belong to a gym? That maybe the letter in the paper wasn't about **HER**? I said now she sounded like David!

David came around this evening to help me study for my driving theory test. We wound up in **HELPLESS FITS OF LAUGHTER** because some of the multiple-choice answers were so stupid (e.g., What should you do before you set out in the fog?—b: Top up the radiator with antifreeze!). Also, I got a lot of the questions wrong. David said, "For God's sake, Janet, it's always the first answer." I said but that didn't always seem right to me. David said to think of the test like a school exam. They're not asking you to think, just to memorize the right answer. Buskin' Bob was watching the news (which, for Robert, is NOT a spectator sport—he actually talks back to the box!) when David was leaving. No sooner had the door shut behind David than Robert stopped arguing with the presenter to talk to me. He said, "So is David your boyfriend?" (God knows why he's obsessed with MY love life—you'd think he had enough to keep him busy with his own!) I said I'd already told him we were just good friends. He said we were laughing a lot. I said in my experience the sign of a relationship is when everybody *stops* laughing. Also, I think it's v immature to jump to conclusions like that.

WEDNESDAY 31 OCTOBER

Went to the zoo with Marcus today. Marcus doesn't like to go INTO the zoo because they're too much like jails— though their standards are higher than human jails, of course—but you can see quite a bit from outside. We both like the elephants best. We were strolling back talking about Life, etc., when who did I spy with my little eye but Queen Catriona. She said she couldn't stop to talk because she was meeting someone. I asked who. She said nobody I know and dashed off! I wanted to follow her. Marcus wanted to know why. I said so I could see who she was meeting. Marcus said, "Who cares who she's meeting?" I said I did—in case it was Mr. Plaget. Marcus said, "OK, I give up. Why would she be meeting Mr. Plaget?" I told him my theory. Marcus thought this was possibly the funniest joke I'd ever made. He said sometimes he thinks I have a really interesting mind and sometimes he just thinks I'm not really from this planet. He said Mr. Plaget has a girlfriend. I said it has been known for men to cheat on their girlfriends. Marcus said, "You haven't met Mr. Plaget's girlfriend, have you?" [Note to self: How is it possible that men, who are prone to violence and a love of power, etc., can be so trusting and gullible at the same time?] By the time we finished this discussion, the Hendley had vanished, of course. Marcus was relieved. He didn't want to play spy; he wanted to get something to eat since it'd been at least three hours since his last MAJOR intake of food. So we headed for the high street. We were just about to go into a café when I heard what sounded like a sewing machine, and when I glanced around, Mr. Plaget's Beetle went past. I punched Marcus and said, "Do you see that? It's Mr. Plaget!" Marcus said, "So?" I said, "He's obviously on his way to meet Catriona." Marcus said he was going the wrong way. I'd never realized what a nitpicker he was before. (It's just as well I don't really fancy him!) Marcus said he'd decided that I do have an interesting mind, but only because I'm totally in orbit.

*   *   *

The MC waited till I got back from the zoo to tell me that
Buskin' Bob and the Deadly Duo were coming around to
celebrate Halloween with us. I said not US—I'm going out.
(We're all going around to David's to watch horror videos
and eat black and orange food. Except Disha, of course.) The
MC said I wasn't going anywhere until I'd taken Marcella and
Lucrezia trick-or-treating! You could've knocked me over
with a small pumpkin! I said I really would recommend
hormonal treatment, as she's obviously lost the plot in a
major way. She said that was nothing to what I was going
to lose if I didn't do this. I said that frankly I was surprised
Buskin' Bob would let his daughters go out begging for
sweets when there were so many starving children in the
world. The MC told me to put a sock in it. Then I said that
since Marcella looks like she's going to be thirty on her next
birthday, I didn't see why they needed me. The MC wasn't
having any of it. She said she doesn't care how old Marcella
looks; she's only eleven and there's no way she and Lucrezia
are roaming around London on their own. Rang Marcus for
support, since I reckoned David would be busy with the
orange food coloring. Marcus said we should wear our Matrix
costumes for a laugh. Marcella was dressed as Morgan le Fay
(what else, right?) and Lucrezia was a unicorn. (Marcus was
v admiring of her head, which, amazingly enough, Buskin'
Bob made!) Since there are always tons of people in our
neighborhood dressed in black and metal, I don't think
anybody noticed that Marcus and I were in costume, but

374

everybody noticed the Deadly Duo. (Heads **TURNED**!)
Even though Marcella talked the whole time about her friends
at school (yawn yawn!) and Lucrezia kept walking into things
because she couldn't actually **SEE** out of the unicorn head,
we had a good time because Marcus had us all laughing. (If
I'm ever on 𝕯𝖊𝖆𝖙𝖍 𝕽𝖔𝖜 or something like that, I hope Marcus
is with me, or at least that he's a regular visitor.) And the
Deadly Duo made out like corporate executives. Even people
who didn't know it was Halloween went scuttling off to find
them something when they saw them. Marcus reckoned we
should hit the goth hangout before we took them back
because the goths are v into 𝕳𝖆𝖑𝖑𝖔𝖜𝖊𝖊𝖓 on a permanent basis. I
said that was fine with me. Ms. Staples says you shouldn't
rely on coincidence when you write fiction, but, if you ask
me, **LIFE** is built on coincidence. We were just about to
turn off the high street when I saw a couple with their arms
wrapped around each other going into the trendy pub on the
corner. I **GASPED OUT LOUD**!!! Marcus said, "Now
what?" I said, "Look over there! That's the Wizard of Oz!"
Marcus is an artist, so he has an eye for detail. Marcus said,
"But that's not Disha. It looks like that waitress from
Durango." It more than looked like her! It was Sky! I'd
recognize that chest anywhere. Marcus said so, did Disha
break up with the Wizard or something? I said not yet.

Was so distracted during the horror-film fest that I didn't
scream **ONCE**! How could I? Reality is much more
terrifying than any special effects. What are ghouls dripping

ectoplasm and ax-wielding psychopaths compared to discovering that your best friend's boyfriend is a two-timing creep? Also, I was **TORN APART** by a Significant Moral Dilemma! Should I tell Disha about Ethan and Sky or not? I don't want her to be the **LAST** to find out, but on the other hand I don't want her to go into **DENIAL** (which Sigmund says is more common than the cold) and get angry with **ME**. David, Alice, and Siranee all agreed that Disha has a right to know if her boyfriend is two-timing her but they don't think I should say anything. I said but you just said she should know the truth!!! Alice said that was just the point— I don't know what the truth is. All I have is circumstantial evidence. I pointed out that **A LOT** of people have been electrocuted on circumstantial evidence, and Alice said but not in Britain. I then reminded them that I had more than circumstantial evidence—I had a **WITNESS**!!! But the pressure to conform is obviously more **POWERFUL** than the truth. Even though he'd seen **EXACTLY WHAT I SAW**, Marcus sided with the others! He said he knows how it *looked* but that doesn't mean that's how it *is*. It could have been completely innocent. I said but it could also have been completely **GUILTY**. Marcus said that's why he thinks I should have more proof before I get Disha all wound up. But it doesn't stop there! David insisted on walking me home. In case you think this was because he's concerned for my safety and would be devastated if I became a Crime Statistic, it wasn't. He

wanted a Private Word! I said you mean you can't stand it
anymore and want to confess your undying love for me?
David laughed. He said he thought I should chill out on
the Disha thing. He said, "You know what you're like,
Janet!" I said, "No, what AM I LIKE?" He said I have
the mind of a fiction writer, not a journalist. I said and
what's wrong with that? David said I have a TENDENCY
to jump to conclusions. Like with Worried Mate's letter.
I said I didn't jump to conclusions with that; I deduced.
He said well, I deduced WRONG. He happens to know
who wrote that letter and it wasn't Lila. I said, "OH,
REALLY? And how do you know that?" And he said,
"BECAUSE I WROTE IT!!!" This time I laughed!!! I
said and why would he do a thing like that? Apparently he
was trying to HELP ME. Because I was so disappointed
with the letters I was getting. I was practically struck dumb
with shock and disbelief. I mean, just look at all the
trouble he could've caused! (Perhaps David's not as très
intelligent as I thought!) I said that from now on if I
WANT his help, I'll be sure to ask him. I said also, that
doesn't change the fact that I SAW Ethan with another
woman, does it? The Eyes Don't Lie! David said the Eyes
Lie All the Time. He said he'd really like to visit my planet
sometime but he's not sure that he'd want to live there.

THURSDAY 1 NOVEMBER

Was still thinking about Disha when I went to bed. Tossed
and turned all night long on a mattress of **worry and care**.
Should I? Shouldn't I? Should I? Shouldn't I? Woke
up exhausted. To show you how **ABSOLUTELY
DESPERATE** I was, I actually brought it up over
breakfast. Marcella was still in bed and Lucrezia was
busy spreading organic butter on her toast (which takes
hours because it **CAN'T** touch the crust and has to be
completely even!), so I could actually get a few seconds of
attention. I said Aunt K had a letter from a girl who'd seen
her best friend's boyfriend with another girl and didn't
know what to do. I said since Buskin' Bob and the MC
were both pretty old, I reckoned they might have some
worthwhile advice (for a change!). Buskin' Bob said it was
a tricky problem (which was obviously **NEWS TO ME**).
He said that just because you do something for a person's
own good doesn't mean you're going to be thanked. Aside
from the fact that I **DON'T ACTUALLY KNOW** what
this girl saw (hah!!!), the friend could get more than she
bargained for. Robert said that in ancient times they used
to kill the bearer of bad news—which seems to me to be
taking **DENIAL** a step too far! The MC was right behind
him, of course. She wanted to know if I remembered the
time Sigmund tried to help a woman who was being
roughed up by her boyfriend at a bus stop and the two
of them turned on him! (The answer to that question is:

NOT EVEN VAGUELY!) I said so they were saying she shouldn't tell her? The MC said no, what they were saying was that Don't Know What to Do shouldn't jump in boots and all, the way I always do!!! She said Don't Know should be aware that she might get a black eye for her trouble. Even though I KNOW WHAT I SAW, all this NEGATIVITY shook my confidence a bit. [Note to self: Do humans have basically the same nature as cows—stay with the herd and go where they go? How have we ever made any progress?!!] Just in case I only thought I saw Ethan with Miss Bazooms, I asked Disha if she had a good time last night. D said in the end Ethan couldn't get off work so she watched some crap on the box on her own. I said she should've come over to David's. She said and how was she meant to talk to Ethan when he rang her after his shift? I said had she thought of using her mobe? She said she knows how much that irks me.

FRIDAY 2 NOVEMBER

The Hotspurettes ARE STILL HERE!!! I asked the MC when they were going home and she said SUNDAY. I said God knows why Buskin' Bob thinks he doesn't see enough of them—some of us see FAR TOO MUCH! The MC said they were staying for the Guy Fawkes party. I said what Guy Fawkes party? She said she'd told me. But she never did. The only things she tells me are what not to wear, eat, or wash my hair with. Apparently the whole clan's coming—Nan, Sigmund, even Mags and Sappho (even though Sappho has **ALWAYS REFUSED** to participate in Guy Fawkes before because she thinks it's barbaric to burn people in effigy— and also she thinks Guy Fawkes was set up and reckons it wouldn't necessarily have been such a bad thing if his plot had succeeded because at least it would've spared the country James I). I said well, what a shame that I wasn't going to be here for it, since I already had plans. She said to change them—Marcus can come around here instead. I said what made her think it was Marcus I had plans with and she said it was one of her wild guesses.

SATURDAY 3 NOVEMBER

Marcus didn't even flinch when I asked him about coming around here. (Unlike most artists, he doesn't shy away from family life.) He even turned up early because he didn't want to miss anything! (He needn't have worried.) All I can say is that if Guy Fawkes had had Lucrezia Hotspur on his team, the whole course of British history would've been different. You'd think a child who's afraid of rain and getting so much as a **SMIDGEN** of butter on the edge of her toast would be terrified of fireworks, but, sadly, that isn't the case. Lucrezia **LOVES** them. She loves them so much that while the rest of us were inside with the mulled wine (or fruit juice if you're Marcella or Sappho), she decided to start without us. It's amazing no one noticed she was gone (the lack of shrieking was a dead giveaway!). The first we knew anything was amiss was when Nan went to fetch the box of fireworks (she's always in charge because of her War Experiences) and she couldn't find them. Sigmund asked if she was sure she'd looked in the right place, but Buskin' Bob leaped to his feet like he was on springs, shouting, "OH MY GOD! Where's Lucrezia?" We got to the garden just in time to see Mr. Burl's garden shed go up like a rocket. (Fortunately Mr. Burl wasn't home.) Mags and Marcus got it out before the fire brigade had to be called. Marcus said that's what he loves about my family: there's never a dull moment. I said maybe not, but there are a lot of dull hours, days, weeks, months, and years.

SUNDAY 4 NOVEMBER

Sigmund took me for a drive this afternoon. (Or rather, I TOOK HIM!!!) When we got in the car today, Sigmund said that we were going to leave the block. I said, "Really? You think I'm ready?" Desperate to convince me that he does have a sense of humor, Sigmund said no, he was beginning to doubt that I'll ever be truly ready, but he was bored with driving in slow and dangerous circles for hours.

He said he reckoned we'd be safe enough if we kept to the back streets. I admit that we got off to a bad start because I didn't see the **NO ENTRY** sign (he was yammering away at me, "Look! Indicate! Maneuver!"—I felt like I was in the army!). So, of course, we went the wrong way up a one-way road. He said, "BACK US OUT." I said, "I don't do backwards." At first he was ADAMANT that I had to do backwards, but he gave up that idea when I nearly hit the BMW. So then we had to change places (which in a real car is no big deal, of course, but in a Mini is like climbing out of a tin), so he could back us out. After that, he was all ATWITTER! Not only did he hang on to the dashboard the whole time and yelp a lot, but he kept his legs straight out as if he was trying to brake even though we were only doing about five miles an hour because the back streets are one long speed bump. I told him he was making me nervous. How could he expect me to concentrate if he was going to undermine my confidence the whole time? I reminded him that this was exactly what happened when he was teaching the MC. From what I'd heard, he yelled at her even more than he yells at me. I said I would've thought a professional psychoanalyst would have more patience. I was still talking when Sigmund shouted, "JANET!" and grabbed the wheel. It's true that in times of stress (like when you're peacefully driving along and someone suddenly BELLOWS in your ear) your brain goes on automatic and your instincts take over. Because I was raised with Justin Bandry, who spent my childhood

382

stealing my things, my instinct when someone tries to take
something away from me is to hold on v tight. (This seems
très reasonable to me.) Anyway, that's what I did. Sigmund
pulled one way and I pulled the other. We hit a skip.
Sigmund said he will *never* complain about speed bumps
again. Think what could've happened if we'd been going
any faster!

MONDAY 5 NOVEMBER

Another sleepless night of grappling with my Moral Dilemma.
I can forget about seeing Ethan and Sky for hours at a time in
daylight but as soon as I get into bed it comes back with a
VENGEANCE. Sigmund came in for a cuppa after his last
client, which is becoming a pretty regular event. He doesn't
even wait to be invited anymore. As per usual, he didn't
notice my anxious state (the dark circles of sleeplessness . . .
the pale complexion of moral torment). I was tempted to ask
him what *he* thought about Don't Know's problem but
changed my mind since being a Cheater himself he might be
prejudiced in Ethan's favour. (I know he's meant to be an
Objective Professional, but birds of a feather **DO** flock
together, don't they?) So instead I asked him if he thinks that
humans are ruled by the herd instinct. He said yes. Sigmund
says that humans have made progress more or less in spite of
themselves. He says that change has come about because one

or two visionaries have had the courage to challenge the
established ideas of their times—and have usually ended up
imprisoned, murdered, or branded heretics for their trouble.
I said if he was trying to comfort me, he hadn't succeeded.
He wanted to know if we had any biscuits.

WEDNESDAY 7 NOVEMBER

Yet another night of turning and tossing and troubled dreams.
(In one I was waiting for a bus with a herd of cows when
suddenly one of them turned into Disha and decked me!)
Should I? Shouldn't I? Should I? Shouldn't I? Sigmund's always
banging on about dreams being the subconscious mind trying
to work out problems, and for once I think he may be on to
something. When I woke up this morning I finally had the
solution to my soul-ripping problem: write to Aunt K! Then
when the letter comes out, I'll show it to Disha and see what
she thinks. *What would YOU do, Disha? Would you tell her or not?*
Whatever D says is what I'll do! This way I can't possibly make
a mistake. Aunt K's reply was easy (*Your friend already has one person
close to her who's lying—don't make it two!*), but it took me a while
to get Don't Know What to Do's letter right so that she seems
sympathetic and not interfering. Was nearly late for school
again. Handed in my copy to Ms. Staples. She wanted to know

when I was going to write a feature piece for the magazine. I said what with my academic work, my social life, my emotional growth, **AND** sorting out everyone else's problems, I really haven't been able to fit it in. It's astounding to me that the Prime Minister ever has time to practice his guitar!

THURSDAY 8 NOVEMBER

D invited me around to hers after school. She and Ethan have had another fight (now, there's a change!). Disha said it was all her fault—she was annoyed because they were meant to hang out on Saturday and he couldn't make it after all. I said well, maybe she had a **RIGHT** to be annoyed. After all, they'd made plans, hadn't they? Disha said it wasn't Ethan's fault if he had to work, was it? I said I thought he was a waiter, not a policeman. Also, **MAN DOES NOT LIVE BY BREAD ALONE**. Disha said try telling that to the Ethiopians. Disha said she doesn't feel it's right that she gets fed up with Ethan's work schedule—esp. when she knows there's nothing he can do about it. Apparently loving someone else should make you less selfish and très more *Thoughtful and Understanding*. I said, "You mean like the way Ethan's so amazingly *Thoughtful and Understanding* of you?"

She said I didn't know what I was talking about since I'd never been in *Love*. I said well, maybe I'm not the only one who doesn't know what she's talking about!

FRIDAY 9 NOVEMBER

Decided to veg out in front of the box while the MC was fixing supper. (As you know, I'm not really a telly person—especially since it's all reality TV nowadays. I like a little more intellectual stimulation than watching a bunch of people in a house annoy each other—I get enough of that in my daily life—but this is such a strenuous and demanding term that sometimes I need to MINDLESSLY RELAX.) Was so whacked that though I don't usually watch the news because it's SO depressing—no wonder Buskin' Bob sings about dead hobos; it's almost light relief!!!—I didn't even have the strength to lift the remote and on it came. There was an award-winningly boring interview with some bloke from the government [Note to self: Why do politicians NEVER answer the question they're asked—even if it's repeated several times?], so I drifted off. I was thinking about Life and staring at the screen when I realized I was watching some fanatical protest types having a scuffle with the police. One of the fanatics looked familiar. I turned up the sound. A bunch of people had climbed over a fence at an air base and hung up an antiwar banner. The woman being hauled off by the coppers was Nan!!! I yelled for the Mad Cow. She didn't seem v taken aback to see her mother-in-law being nicked. She said Nan's arthritis doesn't seem to be giving her any trouble, does it?

SATURDAY 10 NOVEMBER

Sigmund came to take me for another driving lesson. Found him in the kitchen drinking tea and eating chocolate biscuits with the MC. The two of them were laughing like hyenas about Nan's run-in with the LAW. Sigmund said he never expected to be putting up bail for his mother. It was meant to be angry young men who wound up in jail, not angry old women. I said, "Welcome to the twenty-first century."

I was doing really well with my driving today when all of a sudden we turned this corner. I said that's a roundabout up ahead. Sigmund said I was one hundred percent correct and to take the right-hand lane. He said it was gratifying for him to discover that the education system hasn't failed me like it has so many others. I said, "But I don't do roundabouts." He said, "You do now." He said the important thing was not to panic. Just remember what he told me. I didn't see how I could do that when I had NO RECOLLECTION of him telling me anything, but I said I'd try. Got onto the roundabout without too much trouble (Sigmund did a bit of yelping but the other driver didn't beep his horn or shake his fist or anything of that ilk, so it was just Sigmund overreacting as usual), but then I couldn't get off it! It was really surreal. We just went around and around and around. Sigmund was yelling that I had to move left but I couldn't move left because there were already all these cars there. They just kept coming like they were on some berserk assembly line. I was actually DIZZY by the time I finally made a break for it. (And you should've heard all the horns honking then!)

No sign of Buskin' Bob at all this weekend! And today when we got back from my lesson the MC asked Sigmund if he wanted to stay for supper. Sigmund said yes. He said he felt as if he'd just crossed the Atlantic on a raft pursued by sharks and needed some adult company (which seemed to mean the MC!). She made his favorite: macaroni cheese with crushed crisps on top. He's never really grown up, if you ask me. I reckon that Peter Pan probably lived on macaroni cheese and chocolate biscuits too! (But without the white wine and fags.) I wonder if anyone's ever done a scientific study on the relationship between food preferences and emotional maturity. (One of my favorite foods is smoked salmon, of course!) Just to prove that CHANGE really is

the nature of the universe, we had a v pleasant family meal
with no singing or lectures on **Corporate Greed**.

WEDNESDAY 14 NOVEMBER

Forget Thorpe Park. If you want a real white-knuckle ride,
Love is obviously the thrill of choice. Disha's roller coaster is
swinging madly among the clouds again. She was brighter
than a spotlight today because she and the Wizard are back
on. It's no wonder her brain has turned to slush; she must
be exhausted from all the toing and froing. [Note to self: Is
Love anything more than a faulty light switch in the electrics
of the heart?] Disha said the good bits are more than worth
the bad bits. Also, what can she do—she's in *Love*? I said I
didn't realize it was meant to be a terminal disease. I said she
sounds like one of those old American blues songs sung by a
woman who's going to end up with a broken heart as well
as a few broken bones. Disha thought I was joking. She said
she prefers the love songs about being complete and blissed
out and never having any meaning in your life before you
met him. I said I didn't see how a **VIRTUAL STRANGER**
could do all that. (Esp. one who has hairy ears!) I said if she
hadn't met Ethan, she would've met someone else and be
saying the same things about **HIM**. Disha said I'm wrong!
She said she would probably have gone her whole life
without ever *Falling in Love*. I said I couldn't believe that

the survival of the species depended on a chance meeting like that. If it did, there'd probably only be about six humans alive and they'd all look alike and need help getting out of the rain. Disha said what about all those women after the World Wars who always remained true to the soldiers they loved who never came back? I said I reckoned that after a World War, they wouldn't have had much choice, considering how few soldiers actually did come back. I said what about *Sleepless in Seattle*? Tom Hanks finds *True Love* twice. D said that some people's destiny includes two *Loves of Your Life*—but not hers.

THURSDAY 15 NOVEMBER

David says it's ironic that I can sort out everybody's problems but Disha's. I said I thought it would probably help if Disha realized she *has* a problem.

SATURDAY 17 NOVEMBER

Today's driving lesson was cut short by a flat tire. First Sigmund went mad because I didn't realize we had a puncture and kept driving. I said I thought he wanted me to concentrate on getting down the road without hitting

anything. Also, how was I meant to know we had a
puncture when the only smooth ride in the Mini is when
you're parked? Then he went mad because he had to take
the bottles out of the boot to get to the jack. Sigmund said
it doesn't count as recycling if you never actually take them
to the bottle bank. I said not to tell me; I was just the
child. Then he had another fit because the jack wasn't in
the boot. I said the MC moved it to make room for the
bottles (which was true except for the bit about the MC,
since she doesn't do *anything* if she can get me to do it, but
I don't see why I should take the blame—I'm completely
in favor of just throwing the bottles in the bin like we
used to!). As soon as we got back to the **House of Horror**, he
started yelling at the MC about the jack and the bottles,
etc. It really was like old times. If Justin had been there
grunting and pawing the ground, I'd've thought I'd been
dreaming the whole separation. Went to my room for
some peace and quiet.

SUNDAY 18 NOVEMBER

Apparently Sigmund woke up this morning knowing that
today was the day I should learn to park. I said I knew how
to park; you just pulled into the space. He said he meant
parallel parking. I said I never intended to use it. He said I
might have to. All I can say is **LET'S HOPE NOT**!!! He

made me drive all the way to Dollis Hill because the streets are wider and not as busy as around ours. If you ask me, they put the curb too close to the road. It's virtually impossible not to hit it or go over it. Was **TOTALLY SHATTERED** by the time I finally got into the space, what with all the yelling and screaming (and clinking of the bottles in the boot). Sigmund wanted to know how I could be seventeen and not know the difference between **PARALLEL** and **PERPENDICULAR**. I said I did know the difference but I didn't think it really mattered with the Mini since it hardly sticks out at all. He said he can't wait till I get to hill starts. He said perhaps in the future we should bring the mobe with us after all so I'll be able to ring for the ambulance when he has a heart attack.

Despite yesterday's argument about the recycling, it looks to me like my little plan is working *très* brilliantly. As soon as we got back to the **House of Horror**, Sigmund went straight into the kitchen for yet another cup of tea!!! The MC didn't bat an eyelid! She said, "Bad Day at Black Rock?" Sigmund said teaching me to drive made the Gunfight at the OK Corral look like a church picnic. I laughed too. I do feel it's important for them to have their little jokes if they're going to patch things up.

TUESDAY 20 NOVEMBER

Mr. Belakis kept the art room open after class so Marcus
and I worked on our art projects all afternoon. I was going
to do one of those traditional portraits with everyone
posed in their good clothes, but though my family
members don't think very much, they do move about a
lot, so I'm making it more active. Marcus was v impressed
with my depiction of Nan lobbing the balloon at the police
van. We got so absorbed in our work that the only three
cars left in the car park when Mr. Belakis finally threw us
out were Mr. Belakis's Volvo, Mr. Plaget's Beetle, and Mr.
Tulliver's Kawasaki. Ran into Catriona on the way out. Even
though nobody asked her, she insisted on telling us how
she'd had to stay late to work on the magazine **AGAIN**.
Apparently the job of Editor-in-Chief is **NEVER DONE**.
She said I must be deliriously happy that I'm just a feature
writer—or will be if I ever write a feature. I said I was. I
said I feel there are **FAR MORE** important things in life
than correcting punctuation.

SUNDAY 25 NOVEMBER

Since Marcus is about to start the part of his painting where
his grandparents come to England, he wanted to check out
the light on a rainy autumn afternoon, so we went to the

park. Apparently his grandparents used to hang out there when they first came over because the trees reminded them of home. (Either my image of Jamaica is COMPLETELY wrong or Marcus's grandparents were v lonely!) Ran into Mr. Plaget under an umbrella. We would've walked right past him but I recognized his ratty old sneakers (mathematicians don't care about their appearance—Einstein used to turn up for important dinners in his pajamas). The Beetle had broken down and he was taking a shortcut home. Marcus wanted to know if I didn't think that was a little odd. I said not at all. Our car was as old as Mr. Plaget's and it was ALWAYS breaking down. Marcus said not that—the fact that Mr. Plaget was walking home instead of ringing the RAC. I said I thought that was pretty rich coming from him since he's always telling ME not to leap to the wrong conclusion. I said there could be a dozen reasons why he was walking. Marcus said he'd buy me a coffee if I could name even five. I had a mocha latte.

FRIDAY 30 NOVEMBER

It's been one of those six-of-one, half-a-dozen-of-the-other days (and which days aren't, right?). The first part was très brilliant. The second issue of the mag sold out by lunchtime. EVERYBODY was talking about Aunt K. Even Old Woolly Jumper gave me a knowing smile when I passed him in the corridor. That and the **ASTOUNDING** progress the Old Folks Not Quite at Home are making (no Buskin' Bob **ALL WEEK!**) have certainly shown those naysayers like my mother, who didn't think I was a gifted problem solver! It wasn't until the afternoon that the day sort of fell apart. As you can imagine, I was feeling v confident with all the positive feedback. Read out the letter from Don't Know What to Do to Disha at lunch. I said I thought it was a tricky situation. What would she do? Disha said she'd tell her. (She said this with **NO HESITATION!**) She said it was the duty of a *Best Friend* to tell the truth— esp. about something like that. So I told her about seeing Ethan with Miss Bazooms on Halloween. Did she fall into my arms sobbing with gratitude? Did she cry out **OH, THANK GOD, AT LAST I KNOW THE HORRID TRUTH**? Did she thank me for being the *Best Friend* a girl ever had? **NO, SHE DID NOT!!!** She went **COMPLETELY MAD!!!** First she was pissed off because I'd taken so long to tell her!!! She said she supposed I'd told everyone else I know and we were all laughing at her behind her back. And then she was pissed off because I'd told her at all. She said that at best I hadn't seen what I had seen—that I'd **LEAPED TO THE WRONG CONCLUSION AS PER USUAL**—and that at worst I was making it up because I'm jealous of her happiness. I said what happiness would that be? She was usually depressed. She said I should mind my own business **FOR A CHANGE!** She said hadn't I learned my lesson from my mistake about Catriona and Mr. Plaget? (I knew I shouldn't've told her about David writing the letter. She's always been a very TOLD-YOU-SO sort of person.) I said this was different. She said it wasn't. She said I've been trying to throw a spanner in the works ever since she started seeing Ethan! I said I had not. Also, I wasn't the only one who saw them. Marcus, Marcella, and Lucrezia saw them too. She said and that means what? She said Marcella's self-obsessed, Lucrezia's on drugs, and Marcus would say anything I told him to say. I said he would not (I couldn't really argue with the other two objections). I said I was sorry—I was only trying to help. After all, it's my duty as a *Best Friend*, isn't it? Disha accepted my apology, but after that the atmosphere was a bit like Frosty the Snowman BEFORE the thaw. Decided to go around to Disha's after school to patch things up. (I can see now, of course, that I should've left well enough alone. But I didn't.) Ran into David and Marcus on the way and they invited themselves along. I reckoned she'd be nicer to me if they were there, so I didn't argue. Mrs. Paski was just going out when we got there. She said Disha and Ethan were in the kitchen and told us to go on through. You'd think I'd turned up with a herd of wildebeests from the expression on D's face, but Ethan acted like we were long-lost friends. *Oh, Janet, it's been ages. . . . Oh, David and Marcus, I've heard so much about you. . . .* So it was all blah blah blah until Disha started dropping hints that they wanted to be alone. As soon as we got outside, David and Marcus had a go AT ME, of course!!! They said Ethan

396

seemed like a nice bloke. David said didn't I say you were overreacting? Got so embroiled in this conversation that we were at the corner before I realized I'd left my schoolbag in Disha's kitchen. Ran back to get it but I only got as far as the front door. There was such an almighty **ROW** going on inside that for a second I thought I'd stepped back in time and was listening to Sigmund and the MC! It was Ethan mainly. He was all **INCENSED** that there was something going on between Disha and **MARCUS**!!! Or maybe Disha and **DAVID**!!! Or maybe Disha and **BOTH OF THEM**!!! I don't know if it's me, but **JUST** when I think I know how peculiar people can be, they get worse. Then the **PENNY FINALLY DROPPED**! This explains everything! Why Disha and Ethan never hang out with the rest of us . . . why she didn't come to my party . . . why she ran off that time we were having coffee with the lads because Ethan walked by, and then they had another fight . . . **HOW COULD I HAVE BEEN SO BLIND?** It was right there in front of me all the time and I didn't see it!!! Sigmund was **WRONG** (as per usual). It isn't Disha who's **jealous and possessive**—it's the Wizard of Oz! [Note to self: People often accuse innocent others of doing what they're doing themselves—i.e., Ethan being jealous of Disha when all the time he was the one who was cheating. Is this to divert attention from themselves or is it because they assume everyone else is just as bad as they are?] **I WAS TOTALLY GOBSMACKED!** I just stood there with my jaw hanging like a chandelier. I felt like I'd been superglued

391

to the Paskis' front step. But not for long!!! I was still trying to **ABSORB** everything I'd heard when the door started to open (Ethan's voice may carry over miles but his footsteps are silent as a moth's!). It's a bloody good thing that I'm used to thinking on my feet, that's all I can say! I was in Mrs. Paski's herbaceous border faster than a flea on a cat! Ethan slammed the door behind him (so anyone who'd missed his shrieking would know he was angry) and strode down the path. I wasn't breathing but I was praying. I reminded God that my Nan is a v close friend of His and begged Him to make Ethan go in the opposite direction to Marcus and David. For once, He was listening! The first thing the lads said when I got back to them was, "Why have you got leaves in your hair?" The second was, "SO WHERE'S YOUR BAG?" I said it was a Hostage to Love!

Tried ringing Disha when I got home but her mobe was off and no one answered the landline. I kept calling, "Disha! Disha! It's ME!" on the answering machine but she wouldn't pick up. All I got was Mr. Paski's voice telling me to please leave a message and someone would ring me back as soon as possible. I suppose she could've suddenly had to go to Moscow or been kidnapped by pirates because D didn't ring back. I left six messages and then gave up. (It makes you think about progress, doesn't it? Here we are at the pinnacle of civilization and all it means is that you get to humiliate yourself by leaving messages for someone who's probably standing right there staring at the answering machine while

398

pretending to be too busy to talk to you!) This is what happens when you listen to others!!! If I'd told Disha what I knew about Ethan right off, I could at least have saved her a couple more weeks of needless suffering. But OH, NO— I succumbed to peer pressure like everyone else. Have been in a deep and reflective mood all night. I can't believe that all this drama and trauma has been going on for months and Disha didn't tell me! I'm her *Best Friend*!!! She's always told me EVERYTHING!!! And when I say EVERYTHING, I mean EVERYTHING! (Who was the person she rang when the string broke on the tampon that time? That's right, it was Janet Bandry!) I feel like we're in a play together, but we're working from different scripts.

Marcus just rang to see if I'd talked to Disha. I said she doesn't seem to want to talk to me! He said I shouldn't take it personally. After all, she just had a MAJOR fight with her boyfriend so she's probably too upset to talk to anyone. I said she's always just had a major fight with her boyfriend. Also, I'M HER BEST MATE! Marcus said people in *Love* don't have best mates until after the relationship's over (which even in my distraught state I thought was a très profound thing to say—must remember it for Aunt K!).

SATURDAY 1 DECEMBER

Woke up with a **GINORMOUS** sense of responsibility re Disha. I felt it was time we had a **SERIOUS** conversation about her and Ethan. I had to make her see that Ethan's jealousy doesn't mean that he loves her—it just means he's **jealous**. Also, she's obviously in desperate need of some female support. Didn't even ring to tell her I was coming to collect my schoolbag, but just turned up at her door. Mrs. Paski said that D was still in bed but it was about time she rose to greet the day and I should go up. Disha was dressed but lying on her bed as if it was made of nails, smoking a cigarette. She was all red-eyed and gloomy (for a change!). I said if she didn't stop puffing away like a chimney in winter, she's going to have a lot more to worry about than just love, and she gave me this **UGLY** look and said, **"WHAT DO *YOU* WANT? HAVEN'T YOU DONE ENOUGH ALREADY?"** I said, "What's that supposed to mean?" She said, "Bringing Marcus and David around like that when you knew it was a Friday and Ethan would be there." I said I had forgotten about that (which was **TRUE!**). I said and anyway, I didn't think it would be a big deal since I'd **HAD NO IDEA** that the reason she never brought Ethan around was because he's jealous and possessive. Disha said, **"WHAT MAKES YOU SAY THAT?!!"** (**IT ABSOLUTELY DEFIES BELIEF!!!**) I told her what made me say that. I said that since I'd heard them arguing yesterday I'd been v worried about her. I said it sounded to

400

me like Ethan has some unresolved issues (as in *he's out of his mind*). She said so now I was an EAVESDROPPER as well! (I didn't ask as well as what?!!) I said I wasn't eavesdropping; the way they were screaming, I would've heard them in Iceland. We went back and forth like a tennis ball at Wimbledon and then she TOLD ME TO LEAVE! She said she never wants to speak to me again EVER—not even if we're reincarnated as giraffes a thousand years from now and I know where the best trees are. Came home and cried all afternoon! This is the most MEGA fight we've had since I lost her brown velvet shirt when we were fourteen.

SUNDAY 2 DECEMBER

Have been in a funk ALL DAY. Only left my room to eat and get a cup of tea, etc. Every time the phone went, I thought it might be Disha ringing to apologize but it never was. I'm beginning to understand why Sigmund's not better at his job. I mean, he really couldn't be, could he? People are a lot less predictable than the random movements of the cosmos. You have more chance of winning the lottery than understanding your *Very Best Friend in the World*.

MONDAY 3 DECEMBER

Despite the fact that I'm taking a break from the Dark Phase, if my life gets any darker, I'm going to have to walk around wearing one of those miner's helmets so I can see where I'm going. Disha **DISSED** me so completely today that I almost thought she'd suddenly gone blind (which I suppose she has—though not *literally*, of course). *Hi, Marcus* . . . *Hi, David* . . . *Hi, Total Stranger That I've Never Spoken to Before* . . . She didn't even come to lunch. She told David she was on a diet and was going to spend lunch period in the library feeding her mind instead! (She'll be behind the bike shed stuffing her sarnies into her face more like!) It's not so much the silent treatment as the nothing-at-all treatment. I have ceased to exist. I put a brave face on it, of course, and acted like I didn't notice (and that if I *did* notice, I wouldn't care), but inside, a **dank, chill wind** was howling through my heart and soul. It's only the knowledge that I'm **RIGHT** that got me through the day.

WEDNESDAY 5 DECEMBER

Day Three of Nothing at All. Waiting for Disha to come around is obviously like waiting for a 46 bus in a storm.

Only with Disha I can't just walk home; I'm stuck here with
rain dripping down my neck and soaking into my shoes.

THURSDAY 6 DECEMBER

Too depressed even to open Aunt K's post. I mean, what's
the point? Maybe Mr. Cardogan was right and there's a lot
to be said for spots and fat thighs. At least there are things
you can do about physical problems (i.e., eat fresh fruit and
vegetables and have liposuction) but I'm beginning to think
that the only good advice about personal relationships you
can give anyone is: **Abandon hope, all who enter here**!!! Either
that or GET A DOG.

FRIDAY 7 DECEMBER

Not even a pile of letters for Aunt K could cheer me up
today. Ms. Staples was with me when I picked up Aunt K's
post and she noticed that I stuffed it in my bag without
even counting it. She wanted to know if something was
wrong—I've seemed moody and distracted all week.
I said it was just Life. She said that sounded like a Bob
Dylan line. (My God! Things are worse than I thought if

I'm quoting Bob Dylan!) I said well, he is something of a poet, isn't he? I said I reckon it's a bit like Great Minds thinking alike—you know, poets think alike too. She said she still hasn't read my poems. Well, how could she? I haven't written them yet. (But you do have to admire Ms. Staples's memory. It's *months* since I mentioned the poems. You'd think someone over thirty would've forgotten it by now.)

SATURDAY 8 DECEMBER

There's nothing like driving around the back streets of north London with an unstable psychotherapist to take your mind off your problems. *Clutch . . . Brake . . . Faster . . . Slower . . . Watch out for that . . . Watch out for this . . . Signal, Janet. Signal, Janet . . . Janet, the gears . . . No, not the bloody windscreen wipers!!!* He just never stops! And I was **DEFINITELY** not in the mood for it today! I mean, I'm doing my best, but there's a lot to remember. It's not as if I don't have a **LIFE!** Also, it wasn't as if I was making **GINORMOUS** mistakes. They were all really piddly (signal right, turn left, etc.). Then this motorbike nearly plowed into us (they really do come out of **NOWHERE!**). Both Sigmund and the rider lost it completely. Sigmund was screaming at me on one side and 𝔇𝔞𝔯𝔱𝔥 𝔙𝔞𝔡𝔢𝔯 was shrieking on the other. Neither of them would calm down, so I got out of the car and left them to it. Had to walk home since I wasn't about to go back and ask Sigmund for the bus fare. The MC wanted to know where he was. I said back on Camden Road as far as I knew. He turned up eventually. My Father the Role Model said that if he had an addictive personality, he'd probably be shooting up heroin by now (and they wonder why I can be a bit dramatic at times—where do they think I get it from?). I said he does have an addictive personality—he's hooked on cigarettes, isn't he? He banged his head on the fridge. The upshot is that he **REFUSES** to give me any more lessons! I ask you, what sort of example is that meant to be for me, just quitting like that? But, as I've said before, Life isn't all one thing or another. Stomped off to my room to recover from this trauma. Decided **ANEW** that **I NEVER WANT TO BE LIKE MY PARENTS**. I mean really. No wonder Sigmund's stuck in Kilburn on an army cot, with his attitude. Decided that though there's nothing I can do about the small earlobes, that doesn't mean I also have to inherit Sigmund's lack of fortitude and determination. Decided I would **FORCE** myself to write Aunt K's replies to the more practical problems at least and went back to the kitchen for my schoolbag. Arrived just in time to hear the MC invite Sigmund around for Christmas!!! Sigmund said what about the other Mrs. Bandry and the MC said of course

405

Nan was invited; it wouldn't be Christmas without her. Despite the fact that "it wouldn't be Christmas without Nan" translates as "it wouldn't be Christmas without a major fight between Sigmund and Nan," I couldn't help feeling pretty chuffed about this. Obviously things are going the way I intended between the parents! Set to work on Aunt K's column with new enthusiasm. Wrote myself another letter about Disha and signed it I Was Only Trying to Help.

SUNDAY 9 DECEMBER

Sappho turned up this afternoon with a suitcase. I said don't tell me Mags threw you out; I didn't know that happened in same-sex couples. Sappho said *everything* happens in same-sex couples, including arguments over who never fills the ice-cube trays, but that she hasn't been given the old heave-ho. Mags's mother is v ill, so she had to go up north to be with her. I said so you decided to move in with us because you're afraid if you fall on your back while you're on your own, you won't be able to get up again? As per usual, I laughed alone. The MC said just wait till I'm pregnant and see how funny I think it is. As I'm v discouraged about even *Falling in Love* at this point, I told her it could be a long wait. Apparently there are a lot of things Sappho can't do around the house because of her ginormous size and all her aches and pains—and Mags doesn't want her to be on her own in case the baby is early. Then they sprung the **REALLY BIG** surprise on me. Sappho's having my room! I said why couldn't she kip in Justin's, and the MC said because Justin only has the futon and not a bed, and we couldn't expect Sappho to sleep on that (which isn't true, of course—I could expect her to). So I had to move into the Black Hole of Wooster Crescent. It took me all afternoon just to make some room for my stuff and get rid of the boy stink (apparently not noticed by the Deadly Duo—probably because Marcella was talking too much and Lucrezia was shrieking).

MONDAY 10 DECEMBER

When I finally get around to writing the Story of My Life (after I've lived it a bit more), this part is going to be called **Janet Bandry and the Chamber of Horrors**! I swear to God, Geek Boy's room is **haunted**! I couldn't sleep because I was worrying what's going to happen when the Mad Cow is really old and needs someone to look after her. (I hope she's not expecting me to drop my life and rush to her side like Mags. Not after the way she treats me!) Anyway, because I was awake, I heard all these weird sounds. I **KNOW** I heard groaning and creaking and am

extremely certain that I heard chains rattling as well!
(I almost feel that I should've expected this, since if
anyone fits the description of The Unquiet Dead, it's my
brother.) The MC says it's all in my mind. I pointed out
that I never hear strange sounds in my room. Also, the
Chamber still reeks in a v unnatural way. The MC says it's
just the darkroom. Well, that's all right then. It isn't the
smell of terror and doom—it's the smell of poison in the
air! The MC wanted to know if I thought I was ever
going to grow out of over-dramatizing everything. I
said probably soon—when I die an ugly and tragic death,
suffocated by toxic wastes.

TUESDAY 11 DECEMBER

Another night in the Chamber of Horrors! (If I end up
dropping out of school and becoming a government
statistic, we all know WHO'S TO BLAME!) Woke up
to the sound of stealthy footsteps and the mournful moans
of a restless soul in endless pain. Any ordinary person
would have pulled the duvet over her head très rapidly,
but not I! I decided to prove to the Mad Cow that the
ghost wasn't in my mind, but in our flat. I switched on
the reading lamp over the futon and leaped into action.
For the first time in my young life I was glad my brother
is as far from normal as the Earth is from Jupiter. Normal

people have makeup and books and stuffed animals, etc., in their rooms, but Geek Boy's got cameras! I grabbed the one on top of the chest of drawers, turned the light off again and made for the door. I expected to see the eerie glow of a troubled spirit, but the hall was dark. **THOUGH NOT SILENT**!!! I could hear the low moans of perpetual torment coming from the linen cupboard. I'm not saying I wasn't frightened; my heart was pounding like an oil pump! But Life is frightening, isn't it? You never know what's going to happen next— and I've experienced enough to know that there's no reason to expect that whatever it is will be **GOOD**. But I believe that you can't **TRULY LIVE** if you don't take chances. (If you can be mown down by hired killers while you're watching cricket, then there's really nothing to stop you going after a ghost, is there?) I tiptoed down the hall. I stopped at the linen cupboard. I raised my camera. I yanked open the door and pressed the button in one brave motion. There was a flash of light. Sappho, who was sitting on the toilet with her head in her hands, looked up pretty sharply and screamed. To her credit, she took the whole incident a lot better than the MC. Sappho thought it was pretty funny. Also, she understood that since I wasn't used to sleeping in Geek Boy's room, I was understandably confused about which door was the linen cupboard and which was the bathroom. The Mad Cow said that as I've lived in the flat since I was four she reckons I should know that much. I said it isn't my fault

409

that I'm not in my own room. Also, who expects anyone to be roaming around the flat in the dead of night, moaning? The MC said it was lucky for me there was no film in the camera. She said wait till Robert and your father hear this one!

WEDNESDAY 12 DECEMBER

I always thought you're meant to glow when you're pregnant because you're fulfilling your Biological Destiny, but it turns out this is yet another myth. Sappho walks around like her arms are on backwards, and her skin's the color of Buskin' Bob's organic soya milk. If you ask me, she looks like she's fulfilling that other Great Biological Destiny—dying. I said was she sure this pregnancy's **NORMAL**? I've heard of women taking off ten minutes from plowing a field to have a baby then going straight back to work, but Sappho's exhausted just walking to the bathroom (where she spends an inordinate amount of time, if you ask me). Sappho said there is no such thing as normal for everyone—just normal for **YOU**. Apparently Sappho has a friend who went to the hospital with acute stomach pains and came back with a seven-pound son—and she'd never even known she was

knocked up! I said well, Life is JUST FULL OF
SURPRISES, isn't it?

The only person to appreciate my courage and intrepidity
in pursuing the ghost without a thought to my own
personal safety is Nan. Nan said I would've been useful in
the war as a SPY! Sigmund said only if I'd been working
for the Germans.

THURSDAY 13 DECEMBER

At last something good has happened to me!!! Justin's
NOT COMING HOME!!! Well, not yet at any rate.
God knows, no one told me he was meant to come back in
December, but today the Mad Cow had a postcard from
him saying he's having such a brilliant time among the
poor of hungry Mexico that he's staying on. I can't tell you
what a relief this is. I've still got some of Geek Boy's ill-
gotten gains but not so little that he wouldn't notice
there's a bit missing if he came back now.

It's just as well Disha's not speaking to me because it would
cost me a bomb on the mobe since Mags and Sappho talk on
the landline every night and it goes on for hours (maybe
Sappho's right about lesbians being no different from

straight women!). Apparently Mags's mum isn't making a miraculous recovery. The Mad Cow and Sappho were talking about what might happen (as in, maybe the old lady's going to that Great Bingo Hall in the Sky), and Sappho said at least her will is all in order. Can't help wondering if the MC's will is in order. What if it isn't? What if she leaves everything to Justin? I just hope I don't get the car.

FRIDAY 14 DECEMBER

This afternoon I casually remarked to the MC that the flat was going to be a bit crowded over Christmas, what with Sappho staying and all. The MC said she feels that at Christmas it's a case of the More the Merrier (which is not something she's ever thought before!!!). Apparently she's worked it all out: Sappho and Nan can have the double bed in her room, I can have my room, the Deadly Duo can sleep on their air beds on **MY FLOOR**, Sigmund can sleep in Justin's room, and she and Robert will take the sofa. I said **PARDON**? I said when did the Hotspurs get back in the frame? The MC said as far as she knew, they were never out of it. I said well, I hadn't heard any catchy tunes about dead hobos being played in the flat recently. The MC said that was because Robert's been away with work. She said it as though I should've already known this, which, of course, I didn't. She said where did I think that

postcard on the fridge from Malaysia came from? I said
Malaysia obviously (though to be **ABSOLUTELY** honest
I never looked at it twice—I reckoned it was from Geek
Boy). Then she started laughing. She wanted to know if I'd
thought she and the Eco Warrior had broken up. I said
well, it had occurred to me as a possibility. I said Sigmund
had been around quite a bit lately, hadn't he? She said
Sigmund has always been around quite a bit. She said the
only person who stopped speaking to him for a while was
ME. She says she doesn't want to ban him from her life;
she just doesn't want to live with him anymore. I said I
still think it's a bit much having him stay here with her
new boyfriend. It won't be v comfortable for him. She
said Sigmund doesn't mind—he likes Robert. Then
ANOTHER DASTARDLY thought occurred to
me. I asked if this meant I was supposed to buy presents
for Robert **AND** the Deadly Duo too? The MC wanted
to know if it was just *her* I don't listen to or if it was
everybody. I said it was just her. She said I was there when
we all decided to have an Oxford Christmas this year. As
per usual, I had no idea what she was on about. I said
I didn't see how *we all* could've decided anything when I
knew nothing about it. She said there's nothing she can do
if I'm going to continue having Out of Body Experiences.
I was sitting right *there*, in *that* chair and I nodded as if I
was listening, so—as far as *she's* concerned—I was told.
I said so I give up, what's an Oxford Christmas? Nan says
Jesus does a lot of sighing in the Bible because the blokes

He hangs out with frustrate Him, but I doubt He sighs more than my mother. After she finished SIGHING, she practically screamed at me, "Not OXFORD, Janet! OXFAM!" I said, "What? You mean Oxfam *the charity shop*?" She said, "PRECISELY." The idea is that instead of spending hundreds and hundreds of pounds on pointless presents and tons of food that you don't need (half of which gets thrown out, apparently) and all the other commercial crap associated with Christmas, we're going to give the money we would've spent to Oxfam to help the hungry and oppressed and have a simple dinner and exchange small gifts, preferably ones we made ourselves!!! She might as well have said we were getting a donkey and walking to Bethlehem. I said, "You're joking, right?" She said no. I said but I thought I was getting a new mobe! The MC said not unless she can knit me one, I'm not. I said this was all Buskin' Bob's idea, wasn't it? She said she didn't think the idea that Christmas is about the birth of Christ and not about seeing how much money you can spend originated with Robert. I said it did as far as I was concerned.

SATURDAY 15 DECEMBER

This may be the season of *Peace and Love and Goodwill to All Men* in the rest of the world, but in this house it's all systems as usual. (There certainly isn't any goodwill toward ME!) Got up this morning to find the Mad Cow in one of her less attractive MOODS. Apparently the Abominable Brother asked her to send him the rest of his savings—only it isn't where he said it would be. Of course, she immediately blamed her only daughter! I said that since Justin's South of the Border and therefore probably on drugs, it's unlikely that he remembers *where* he hid his dosh—IF he actually left any behind. She said to pull the other one. I pointed out that as I'd worked my fingers to the bone all summer, I had no motive for taking Geek Boy's money. Rising to her title of Queen of the Nitpickers, the Mad Cow said that I hadn't worked all summer; I'd only worked a few weeks. And she'd never known me to need a motive to spend money. I said I couldn't believe that she was accusing me, the baby girl she'd longed for, of stealing. And she shook the empty jar in my face and said she'd hate to have to dust it for fingerprints. I said it wasn't like I'd nicked it or anything—I'd only borrowed it. She said then I could give it back—NOW. Which, of course, I couldn't, could I? I said if he put his money in the bank like normal people, I wouldn't've been tempted. She said she'd lay out the money for him but she's charging me INTEREST. I said I didn't think that was showing much Christmas Spirit

and she said that taking things that don't belong to you
wasn't showing much Christmas Spirit either.

Rang Marcus to see if I could go around to his for
Christmas, but turns out his family's going to stay in a
lighthouse somewhere off the coast of Scotland till New
Year's Day (he doesn't have a clue as to why—neither of
his parents has ever shown any interest in the sea). As yet
another example of how unpredictable the male of the
species can be, Marcus thought the Oxfam Christmas
sounded like a brilliant idea (probably because he doesn't
have to do it). He said he's pretty fed up with the gross
commercialization of Christmas too. He said things are so
out of control he wouldn't be surprised if they had Harry
Potter advent calendars. What did Harry Potter have to do
with Christmas? It was about the coming of Jesus not
Harry Potter. Somehow, when Marcus says this kind of
thing it isn't as annoying as when Buskin' Bob says it.
I completely agreed. I said did he remember that Christmas
when Birds Eye paid for the lights in the West End? At
first everybody thought it was meant to be the Dove of
Peace swinging over Oxford Street, but turned out it was
the Birds Eye logo. So it was actually the Dove of Peas!
Marcus thought that was hilarious. He said he'd be très
relieved if his family decided they should all make their
own presents—then he wouldn't have to go shopping.
He says shopping takes *years* off your life.

SUNDAY 16 DECEMBER

As much as I like the idea of not having to spend any
money on Christmas presents (especially since I'm **IN
DEBT**!), I am v busy as per usual and don't see when
I'm going to have the time to make anything. Also, I don't
know what I *can* make—unless it's a gag for Lucrezia. (I've
got that book for Nan, which I reckon is all right since I
didn't actually **BUY** it. So that's one down.) I asked
Sappho if she had any ideas. She got out this book she
bought in that cheap shop in Camden. It tells you what
you can make out of stuff you find around the house and
is full of things like papier-mâché jewelry boxes, bottle-top
earrings, and coasters made of dried macaroni and beans.
(You can see why it was sold for pennies—I'm surprised
they weren't giving it away.) I pointed out that I'm a
Creative Artist, not a craftsperson. Sappho couldn't see
the difference. She said well, why not knit everybody a
scarf (something only a hippie would think of!)? I said I
couldn't knit. Ditto crochet. Woodworking, pottery, and
metal sculpture are also out. As are candles since the time I
poured hot wax all over the cooker. Sappho said, "You're
always talking about your poetry—why not write
everybody a poem?" I said that was a typical layperson's
attitude. I said you don't just sit down and *write* a poem.
Just one poem takes months, not a couple of weeks. Also,
you have to be in the mood. Sappho said what about
biscuits? I asked if she was offering or just hungry? She

said no, really. Why don't I make homemade biscuits? My question was: Why would I want to do that? Apparently I'd want to do that because homemade biscuits are special and a *Gift of Love*. And they don't require Inspiration. I said I didn't see what was so special and *Full of Love* about something you can buy for 59p in Safeway (assuming you're *allowed* in Safeway). Sappho said that was the point, wasn't it? What makes them special is that I make them myself. I can decorate them with colored sugar so they look really Christmassy. She says the cheap shop always has really nice gift boxes and tins for under a quid, so after they eat the biscuits they can still use the container. I said I thought she was forgetting one teensy thing — which is that my culinary skills pretty much start with a cup of tea and end with a hard-boiled egg (I've given up on soft-boiled). Apparently biscuits are dead easy.

MONDAY 17 DECEMBER

Disha's still avoiding me like I have some **MAJOR** communicable disease. She was all over Catriona Hendley at lunch like honey on a spoon. I wish there really was an Aunt K to console me. (I mean, one who isn't **ME** — *oh, physician heal thyself*, right?) I just can't believe that the bus of friendship has moved on without me. Especially over an **AUSTRALIAN** with hairy ears.

TUESDAY 18 DECEMBER

Since I haven't come up with any more ideas on what
inexpensive and easy presents I can make for Christmas in
the Third World, I snuck into the supermarket after school
today to check out the baking section. You wouldn't
believe what they want for this tiny little tub of green or
red sugar! Unless it was hand-dyed by Father Christmas,
it's **ABSOLUTELY OUTRAGEOUS**. And forget the
other stuff like the chocolate bits—you'd think they were
made out of gold and they're not even made out of
chocolate! (I can't stop reading labels now—no matter
how hard I try.) Was on my way back to Green Army
Headquarters when who should I see with her arms loaded
with shopping but **SKY**?!! (I've always said there's
NOTHING spiritual about her, haven't I?) I believe
I was divinely inspired because, instead of turning right
around and acting like I hadn't seen her, I actually accosted
her. Blah blah blah . . . How are you . . . ? Blah blah
blah . . . Been Christmas shopping . . . ? Blah blah blah . . .
It was all pretty mindless and excruciatingly boring. But
then Sky said something about Durango and I said (and
this is where *Divine Inspiration* comes in), "Oh, are you
still working there? I thought Disha said you'd left." Sky
wanted to know who Disha was. I said, "You know,
Ethan's girlfriend. She's my best mate—he met her
through me." That was the moment when I finally
understood why Justin always lugs a camera around with

419

him. Oh, how I wish I could've photographed Sky's face when I said those magic words "Ethan's girlfriend." Not that I'm likely to ever forget it, of course, but it'd be nice to show people. Sky wanted to know what I was on about. She said, "I'M ETHAN'S GIRLFRIEND." I pretended to be all flustered and shocked (acting is definitely another of the many career possibilities open to me). I said I thought they hardly knew each other, and she said they kept quiet about it at work because of Saduki and all his rules. I was still stammering apologies and muttering about me and my big mouth as Sky stalked off with **Blood in Her Eye**! It is definitely the season to be jolly! I was half tempted to get David and Marcus and race around to Durango to watch the fireworks.

WEDNESDAY 19 DECEMBER

(There is a Father Christmas!!!)

I was having an absolutely fascinating conversation with Sappho tonight about **Birthing Horror Stories** (thirty days in labor . . . twenty-pound babies . . . quadruplets two days apart . . . the sorts of things that make a young girl long to be pregnant) when the doorbell rang. Normally I'm not that eager to drag myself all the way down the hall to find out it's a family of Jehovah's Witnesses or some bloke selling tea towels, but I was pretty worn out by Sappho's tales of **suffering and pain** (you'd think having a baby would be easy—I mean, EVERYTHING does it; how can it be so hard?). You can imagine my SHOCK and SURPRISE when I opened the door to find DISHA PASKI standing there! She was wearing the orange top I gave her and had a package wrapped in silver paper with a purple ribbon around it, and she was crying. I said well, it was nice that she was so glad to see me. She said she was sorry for everything, especially for DOUBTING ME. She met Ethan tonight and Sky suddenly jumped out from behind a building and let rip. Disha said she couldn't believe that all this time Ethan was two-timing her by two-timing Sky. It really is true that we're at the mercy of our feelings. Here was my chance to be v sarky and get even, and what did I do? I STARTED CRYING TOO!!! I said I was sorry for not being more sensitive (though I don't know how I could have been when she never told ME anything!). Disha said I was right about Ethan's jealousy but she hadn't known how to handle it. Being a rabid feminist, Sappho doesn't usually have any time for weeping women, so it must be her impending motherhood that's changed her because Disha and I weren't halfway down the hall before she came shuffling out of the kitchen wanting to know what was wrong. I said nothing; everything was all right now. Sappho offered to make us tea! (Which means it truly is the *Season of Miracles*!!!)

THURSDAY 20 DECEMBER

Buskin' Bob has returned from saving Malaysia with a new hat (batik) and a tan. He was in the kitchen **POPPING CORN** when I got back from Disha's this afternoon. I said he did know you can buy it in bags already buttered and salted, didn't he? And he said it wasn't for eating; it was for stringing. I said **PARDON**? He said strings of popcorn are much nicer than environmentally unfriendly tinsel on the tree. If you ask me, this is a matter of personal taste. I like tinsel and I don't care if takes three billion years to decompose either. To add insult to aesthetic injury, he expected **ME** to do the stringing! I said I had a previous engagement and went over to Marcus's.

FRIDAY 21 DECEMBER

Today's the winter solstice, which is Sappho's Big Holiday. She turned on all the fairy lights that are still up from my party and it looked well cool. (That was the highlight.) Next Sappho put on a CD of some pagans chanting. Then she lit some incense and candles and read a poem about a tree, and then we had sweet cider and oatcakes. That was about it really. (You can understand why people turned to Christianity, can't you? The food and the music are très, très better.) Since the solstice isn't over-commercialized like

422

Christmas, Sappho bought our presents. I got a postcard book of Frida Kahlo paintings (because I once mentioned her to Sappho). I was hoping for another diary. Was saved having to pretend to be too enthusiastic because the incense made Sappho nauseous and she wobbled off to the loo as soon as she gave out her gifts, and spent the rest of the night vomiting. [Note to self: Did the Virgin Mary have to go through this?]

SATURDAY 22 DECEMBER

The MC had a party to go to tonight and Sappho was beached on the sofa, so I decided it was a good time for biscuit making. I'd already picked my recipe (Basic Sugar Cookies). First I had to dye the sugar for the tops with food coloring. Then I had to melt the margarine to get it soft enough to mix with the flour. After that, I discovered that we were right out of vanilla flavoring, so I had to use a dollop of the Christmas sherry instead. And then I had to **ROLL OUT** the dough, which is v time-consuming and not as easy as it sounds. The first lot stuck to the counter. The second lot stuck to the table. Asked Sappho, who said you're meant to roll it on a *floured* surface. I said well, why didn't it say that? And she said it did. Had to move all the small appliances to the floor to make enough room on the counter. And something went horribly wrong with the colored sugar. First of all, the colors weren't too brilliant. Also, it turned into a paste! I'd been at it for hours, so I wasn't about to do it all over again. Spread it on with a knife. Put the baking sheets in the oven, set the timer, and went to take a quick shower since I was COVERED in flour. When I came out of the bathroom the flat was filled with smoke, the alarm was shrieking away, and Sappho was hanging out of the back door being sick in the garden. (I don't know why they call it Morning Sickness; she does it morning, noon, and night!) The MC was at the sink with a tea towel across her face looking v unfestive. Of course, she blamed ME! She wanted to know what I was trying to do—BURN THE HOUSE DOWN? I said I was making my Christmas presents, wasn't I? WHICH WASN'T MY IDEA. I'm perfectly happy to have a commercialized and materialistic Christmas like everybody else. Also, now I'm going to end up giving everyone empty boxes.

SUNDAY 23 DECEMBER

The gods of burnt biscuits left me no choice—I've had to give in and buy presents for my *extraordinarily extended* family. I reckoned that as long as I got really inexpensive little things, I couldn't be accused of rampant materialism or contributing to the commercial bloodbath that is Christmas. Disha went with me to the cheap shop beloved of Sappho. (Not only is it cheap, but a lot of the stuff comes from China or somewhere like that. According to Robert, most of it is handmade by blind prisoners and orphans. So, if you ask me, that means it's v close to being homemade.) It was brilliant. I got something for **EVERYONE** (even Sappho's baby). And for a lot less than a T-shirt! Was so chuffed I treated Disha to lunch in the West End so we could do some shopping for ourselves while we were out. Waiting for the bus is usually très boring and irksome, but today it was **DISGUSTING** as well. There was **VOMIT** at every stop. D said that's how you know it's Christmas—that and the lights and the manger, etc. We had a brilliant time. Everybody always bangs on about how **IMPORTANT** friendship is, but it's true! It's only now the real Disha Paski has reclaimed her body that I realize how much I missed her while she was the **Zombie of Love**. Disha says the same. She says being in *Love* was très exciting and all, but now that it's over, she wonders what it was really about. She says she was out of her mind most of the time because of Ethan's jealousy. You won't believe this—she **ACTUALLY** wrote to Aunt K!! Disha was But I Love Him! She said Aunt K was right (of course!) but at the time Disha thought she was v offhand and dismissive. I said I didn't think that was true at all. I said that Aunt K was just demonstrating her incredible knowledge of human behavior and she should've listened to her. Nearly got into another fight! (Disha's still très defensive.) D said Aunt K may be right **NOW**, but at the time Disha didn't

425

realize what a deceitful creep Ethan was; she thought he was the *Love of Her Life*. I said so Love Is Blind. Disha said and deaf and dumb as well.

Got back to find that Robert and the Deadly Duo had arrived. The MC made me drag the tree in from the garden, of course, while she and London's Answer to Bob Dylan sat around singing about holly and ivy and drinking environmentally-friendly mulled wine! Marcella wouldn't help, because: (a) she didn't want to get dirty; (b) she'd just done her nails; and (c) she prefers artificial trees (I wonder if it's possible that **NEITHER** of them are actually Buskin' Bob's). Perverse as always, Lucrezia **INSISTED** on helping, then got a microscopic needle from the tree stuck in her hand and practically had to be hospitalized! Was exhausted by the time we got it inside. Since the fairy lights are still up and it doesn't look like anyone's going to take them down, we at least didn't have to go through the drama of putting them on the tree. Marcella doesn't like our ornaments, and Lucrezia was still **SUFFERING UNSILENTLY**, so I got volunteered to do the decorating while Buskin' Bob went off to get the popcorn. That's when he discovered we have mice (or possibly rats—something that likes popcorn, anyway). The MC came after me like a nuclear warhead! She was all atwitter because in searching for mouse holes she found the dishes I put away in the broom cupboard and is holding them responsible for the **INFESTATION**. (Shows how much she cleans up—that was **AGES** ago! And she says I'm a lazy cow!) Blah blah blah . . . She actually stood next to me while I washed them, with her arms folded across her chest! I said you better watch out or your face will stay like that. Let me assure you that having a boyfriend has done nothing for her sense of humor!

More trauma while the MC and the Eco Warrior continued to scour the kitchen for mouse holes. Lucrezia and Marcella locked themselves in the bathroom for safety from the rodents of London. Of course, it was Cinderella Bandry who had to race to Woolies for tinsel. What would any of them do without me?

Asked Marcella why she came here, to the Third World, for Christmas when she could've stayed at home with her artificial tree. She said because the Actress and the Entrepreneur have gone on a cruise. Also, she doesn't mind about no presents, food, crackers, or other festivities because they celebrated early at her mum's, so she got all the stuff she wanted and they even let her have a glass of champagne. Here, if she wants a glass of water she'll probably have to go to the well for it.

CHRISTMAS EVE

Sigmund had to fetch Nan this morning. I said I'd be happy
to go with him and do the driving, but he REFUSED.
He said he thought Nan was way too old to survive a
journey with ME, even if she was a spy in the war. I went
along for the ride anyway (he wouldn't even let me drive
going, on the grounds that he's too close to seeing another
year in to risk it!). Even if it meant being squashed in the
back with Nan's bags, it was better than staying at home as
Robert had everyone stringing cranberries (apparently not
on the mouse menu) instead of the popcorn. I noticed that
one of Nan's bags was filled up with placards. I said what's
this, have you got a job advertising the January sales?
Apparently there's a Peace Vigil tonight. I said Christmas
Eve's an odd time to have a demonstration—everybody's
going to be at parties or getting drunk or whatever. Nan
says Christmas is peace. Sigmund said tell that to the
Vietnamese (whose present from President Nixon was to
have Hanoi flattened by bombs, apparently). Of course, as
soon as the Mad Cow clapped eyes on the placards, she
decreed that I should go to Parliament Square with Nan
(it's obvious that the MC was an Absolute Monarch in a
former life and I was a serf). I said you mean that while
everybody else in the world is watching television and
eating chocolates, I'm going to be standing in the rain with
Nan, trying to keep my candle from going out? The MC
said that was precisely what she meant. D was already off

visiting the family, but Marcus isn't leaving town till the morning so I decided to see if he'd come with me. If you asked most boys whether they wanted to spend Christmas Eve standing in the cold and the rain with a bunch of fanatical Christians, they'd say no, right off. But not Marcus. Artists are meant to be moody and temperamental, but even though Marcus is an excellent painter (Mr. Belakis says he's a dead-cert for Saint Martin's), he has a v patient and flexible nature—more like a fisherman than a *Creative Spirit*. Marcus said of course he'd come. He said it was better than watching Toy Story again—and he always likes to do new things. So off we went on the bus with Nan and her placards. There were a few more people down at Parliament Square than there were in the manger in Bethlehem—but not many. (And not a shepherd or king in sight!) My first thought was that they must all be homeless, but it turned out most of them were Quakers. Nan made straight for this old geezer with a golden lab. It was wearing a sign that said LET LOOSE THE DOGS OF PEACE. The old geezer was wearing a bowler hat and carrying an umbrella with a peace symbol painted on it. If you ask me, he looked like one of those blokes who walk around with signs saying that the world's about to end, so I tried to stop her, but it turned out he's the **PRIEST** that runs Nan's Jesus group, the Very Reverend Jerym Noad. The dog's name is Luke. Both of them seemed pretty pleased to see Nan (which must make a nice change for her). Nan latched onto them and more or less forgot about me and Marcus. Marcus said it looked like my gran's got a beau. I said he must be mad. My nan hasn't dated since the war. Also, she's **WAY** too old for that sort of thing. Marcus said well, they seemed pretty close, and I said that was because she was sharing his umbrella. Anyway, for a few hours we just stood around trying to keep our candles from going out (as predicted by Janet Bandry!). Then a couple of people started singing "O Holy Night" and then a few more joined in until everybody was singing—even one of the coppers! It was like being in church—except for the rain and the fact that nobody was just pretending to sing; they were all belting it out like they really wanted God to hear them (or possibly the Prime Minister, though you can bet he wasn't hanging around Parliament on Christmas Eve). I moved closer to Marcus because it was cold, etc., and he put his arm around me. It really is true that you **NEVER** really know what's going to happen next. I turned to Marcus to say that I could murder a hot cup of tea and (wait for it!) . . . **HE KISSED ME**!!! Right there in front of Big Ben! I said, "What's that for?" He said, "It's Christmas," and held up a piece of mistletoe he'd brought with him. So I kissed him back.

CHRISTMAS DAY

Unless I go senile like my mother, as I get older I'm going to remember this Christmas for the rest of my life. I couldn't fall asleep because I could still hear everyone singing at the *Vigil* in my head. Also kept thinking about Marcus kissing me in front of Big Ben. (Is this the start of *Something*? Or is it the end of a *Beautiful Friendship*? If we start going out, will we hate each other by the spring? If we don't hate each other and end up getting married—after my career as whatever is established—will our children all have one eyebrow too?) I was finally sort of drifting off when I heard someone stumbling about in the hall. (The bulb went out ages ago, but as per usual the MC's too lazy to do anything about it. Not only is Love blind, but it wants everyone else to be blind as well.) I ruled out Father Christmas straight away. Then I ruled out the Mad Cow, Sigmund, and Robert because I could hear them all snoring (it's like sleeping with hogs, I swear!). I also ruled out Sappho (wrong direction, she'd be heading for the loo) and Lucrezia and Marcella (because I could see them). I reckoned it must be Nan, because everyone knows that old people are too close to death to sleep much. So I got up and tiptoed out of my room in case she was going to make a cup of tea. Nan likes me well enough (I am her only granddaughter, after all), but she's never been exactly overjoyed to see me before. "Praise the Lord!" cried Nan. "Janet, I need your help!" I said for what? To make tea? She said to ring for an ambulance—she had to get back to Sappho because the baby was coming. Being Nan, I wasn't sure what baby she was talking about. I mean, it could've been the Baby Jesus. (Also, it was très **LATE** and I was shattered.) Nan wanted to know how many babies I thought we were expecting and I said you mean *Sappho's* baby? It's coming here? *Now?* Nan said it probably wanted to be near its mother. I said wouldn't it be faster to get Sigmund to drive her to the hospital and Nan said Mary may have ridden on a donkey, but there was no way Sappho was going to the hospital in the Mini. Making phone calls is one of my natural talents, so I raced to the kitchen and rang the hospital. Then I went to tell Nan the ambulance would be here in probably less than an hour. Sappho was on the bed. (She wasn't screaming the way women having babies on telly do, which I put down to the fact that she's a rabid feminist and doesn't like to seem weak or girly.) I've never seen anyone look pale AND flushed at the same time before. She looked like she'd just run ten miles. Except that her legs were wide open! (I couldn't look! I've seen someone giving birth on telly, but it's not the same as in your own home with a blood relative!) Nan said that less than an hour was probably a bit too late. The baby was coming right this minute! I said but doesn't someone have to deliver it? I didn't think they could just come on their own. Nan said she was an experienced midwife (is there no end to this woman's talents?). She said she delivered many a baby in the war. (I'm going to have to check in the library and see if what I was told in school was wrong and it was Nan who won World War II!) She told me to go and boil water (I still don't know WHY!). Sappho yelled at me to ring Mags. So I raced off to boil water and ring Mags. When

I got back from that, a scene of **gory horror** met my eyes. Nan was pulling this bloody, goppy-looking thing out of my aunt! [Note to self: In the story of the Nativity, there is NO mention of blood or goo or anything like that. Mary always looks like she got the baby in the market.] "Push!" ordered Nan, and Sappho (who usually won't do anything anyone tells her to) pushed. IT WAS SO GROSS. I know birth's meant to be a miracle and this brilliant thing, etc., but all I could think was, what a mess! And it didn't even look like a baby. Not a human baby at any rate. (Here is ABSOLUTE PROOF that not all babies are beautiful— it looks like a pig!) Comandante Rose Bandry said to stop being stupid and go and wake my parents. By the time the ambulance finally turned up, we were all in the kitchen having tea, even Sappho and the Piglet. Sappho's naming it Germaine after that writer who's always on the box giving her opinion on everything. I said she did realize everyone would call her Germ, didn't she (which, if you ask me, is putting an unreasonable burden on a child that's already off to a bad start)? But Sappho is oblivious to things like peer pressure. Having got the birthing bit over with, Sappho went straight back to Nobody Tells ME What to Do mode and refused to go to the hospital on the grounds that it was like going to a restaurant after you'd eaten dinner. Was just thinking of going back to bed when Nan's priest and his dog rolled up! (See what I mean about old people and sleep? It was practically dawn!) I asked Nan what THEY were doing here and she said they'd come to share the

fatted lentil loaf with us. She said she thought it was time
Jerym met everybody. I said, "And why's that, then?" Nan
got all coy (which is a sight I've never seen before, believe
me!) and said, "Because he's more or less part of the family,
isn't he?" I said, "Nobody told ME." She said many are
called but they don't all come. If you ask me, this family's
getting way too big. We're going to have to move in with
the Queen at the rate we're going! (Or I'm going to have to
get a bigger canvas!) It wasn't like spending Christmas with
anyone normal, but it wasn't completely DREADFUL
either. The food was all right. The presents aren't going to
make Jennifer Lopez wish she was part of our family, but
they were all right too. Buskin' Bob wrote me a song called
"Planet Janet in Orbit" (which was actually funny—esp. if
you're not ME). The MC made me a photo album with
pictures in it of me when I was little (which was touching
in a sad and bittersweet way—and useful for my portrait).
Nan knitted me this très cool jumper that she copied from a
magazine. Lucrezia made me a bookmark with my name
on it, and Marcella decorated a cigar box with glitter and
sequins and a picture of me, her, and the Little Horror in the
rain in Wales (which I suppose I can incorporate into my
art project, since it looks like I really am stuck with them)
for me to keep jewelry in. And Sigmund broke all the rules
and bought me ten lessons with a proper driving school
because he said his nerves really couldn't take any more.
(And mine could?) Everybody LOVED my gifts.
(Especially Nan! She said she'd been wanting to read that

book. Robert said it was really good; he had a copy himself. Didn't I say he'd never know?) Of course, after we ate, we had to sit around singing for a few hours. I didn't mind it as much as usual, but I think that was because Jerym contributed champagne to the dinner. (I notice Robert didn't tell him he could've fed some child in Africa for six months on what that cost!) Then we had to take pictures so that in years to come we'll think we had a brilliant time. Not only did I have to pose with the Deadly Duo but I had the Piglet on my lap as well. (She pissed all over me.)

BOXING DAY

Went around to Disha's to get away from all the singing and crying at our house. Told her about Christmas Eve and she **WAS ASTOUNDED**! She said you really kissed him back? I said twice. Disha wanted to know if that was it then and Marcus and I are officially an item. I said I've been giving it **TONS** of thought (which I have—when it's quiet enough in the **House of Horror** to think). I said I'd decided that when he gets back, I'm going to tell him that I thought we both got swept away in the moment with the singing and the rain and the clock and all and that it wouldn't be a good idea to add snogging to our personal itinerary. She said that's v mature of me. I said I know.

435

THURSDAY 27 DECEMBER

Disha came over to meet the Piglet today. D thinks she's
cute. I said she's been hitting the Christmas eggnog too
hard. The Piglet's only cute if you're comparing her to the
rest of the barnyard. Showed Disha my Oxfam Christmas
presents. She said I did v well. At least I didn't get any bath
gel or anything like that (she got three bottles of gel, two
of foaming bubbles, and four lots of oil balls!). Disha thinks
it's cool to have things **MADE** for you. It shows people
are really thinking about you. I said they could think about
me in any major department store as well.

FRIDAY 28 DECEMBER

Went with D to exchange some of her Christmas toiletries
today. Lila was in the Body Shop, exchanging some stuff
she'd been given. I said, "You're still not speaking to the
Hendley even in this season of goodwill?" She said she can't
speak to her because she's in Bali. I said, "**SHE'S WHAT?
ANOTHER HOLIDAY?**" Lila said not exactly. She said
Catriona *Fell in Love* with a waiter in the hotel where she
stayed in the summer and has run off to be with him. Disha
and I were both pretty **GOBSMACKED**. But I could see
some good news for me personally in all this. I said so she's
not coming back to school in the New Year? **WHAT A**

SHAME. Lila said she'll be back. The parent Hendleys have gone after her. I said well, you kept pretty quiet about this. Lila said she'd been SWORN TO SECRECY. I said fancy the Hendley falling for a Balinese waiter! Lila said he was Australian. I said well, at least we know it isn't Ethan, and Disha and I cracked up in a major way. Lila said she didn't see what was so funny.

MONDAY 31 DECEMBER

Was just getting ready to go over to Disha's for New Year's Eve (it's becoming our tradition!) when the phone rang. It was Marcus. He said he would've rung me sooner but there's no phone in the lighthouse and this was the first chance he'd had. He wanted to know if I'd been thinking about US. I said a bit. He said he hadn't been able to put Christmas Eve out of his mind. He says it was the best night of his life! And I must know how much he likes me since he's never tried to hide his feelings. He said he thought we should go out properly. He wanted to know if that was what I thought too. I surprised myself by saying yes.

TUESDAY 1 JANUARY

ANOTHER NEW YEAR BEGINS! (I'm not sure
whether I should rush out to greet it or duck for cover!)
Disha and I talked so much last night that midnight came
and went before we even noticed! We certainly had
QUITE A YEAR!!! D said that even though there was a
certain amount of **emotional turmoil** and **pain and suffering**, she
actually found it all sort of exciting. She said at least we've
started to really live. I agreed. I said but I thought that, all
things considered, it was just as well we'd jacked in the
Dark Phase, since Life is dark enough without having to
egg it on.

GLOSSARY

59P 59 pence (Pence are the smallest denomination of money in the U.K., similar to U.S. pennies.)

999 U.K. equivalent of 911

A-LEVEL ENGLISH advanced-level exam in English, usually taken at age 18

A-LEVEL MATHS advanced-level exam in mathematics, usually taken at age 18

ADVERT advertisement

AUBERGINE eggplant

A–Z street map of London

BANGING ON talking endlessly

BIG BEN nickname of the Great Bell of Westminster, the hour bell of the Great Clock, hanging in the Clock Tower of the Houses of Parliament

BIN trash can

BISCUITS cookies

BLACKPOOL a seaside resort in northwest England

BLOKES men/boys

BLOODY very; used as an all-purpose intensifier

BLOODY-MINDED stubborn, pigheaded

BOG ROLL toilet paper

BOMB large sum of money

BOOT trunk of a car

BOTTLE BANK a bottle recycling bin

BORSTAL BOYS juvenile delinquents (Borstal was a juvenile detention center.)

BOX, THE television

BOXING DAY the day after Christmas; a public holiday

BRILLIANT very good, excellent

BUDGIE POO parakeet poo

BUSKIN' performing on the street

CAMDEN MARKET a famous street market in north London; pretty much the goth capital of the world

CAPITAL FM a radio station

CAPITAL GOLD British radio station; plays oldy-moldies from the sixties

CAR PARK parking lot

CARRIER BAG plastic shopping bag

CHANNEL, THE the English Channel; body of water separating England from France

CHEEKY impudent, saucy

CHEESED OFF irritated, annoyed

CHEMIST pharmacy

CHILD-MINDER babysitter

CHILL ME OUT relax me

CHIPS french fries

CHUFFED pleased

CLAPHAM an area of south London

COLOR SUPPLEMENT the magazine that comes with the Saturday or Sunday newspaper

COMBATS fatigues

COOKER stove

COW PAT pile of cow dung

CRACKER a Christmas party favor that gives a satisfying bang when you open it and contains a tissue-paper crown and other trinkets

CRISPS, CRISP WRAPPER potato chips, bag of potato chips

CROUCH END a neighborhood in north London

CUPBOARD closet

CUPPA cup of tea

DEAD-CERT absolute certainty; sure thing

DEMO political demonstration

DINNER LADY a woman who cooks or serves food in a school cafeteria

DISHY very good-looking; cute

DOLLIS HILL a quiet residential section of London

DOSH money

DRIBBLING drooling

DWEEBLE made-up word meaning geek, idiot

EastEnders popular soap opera set in London's East End

ESSO gas station chain

FAIRY LIGHTS Christmas lights

FAG cigarette

FANCY have a crush on; like or desire

FÊTE fair

FIT good-looking, attractive

FIVER five-pound note

FLASH flashy, ostentatious

FLAT apartment

FORM prison record

FROG WELLIES rubber boots with frog faces on them

GARDEN yard

GCSEs General Certificate of Secondary Education exams, usually taken at age 16

GENTS men's room

GET OUT borrow or take out, as a library book or video

GINORMOUS made-up word; amalgamation of *gigantic* and *enormous*; very big

GIVE A TOSS care

GM genetically modified

GOBS mouths

GOBSMACKED astounded

GONE OFF gone bad; spoiled

GREENGROCER retail seller of fresh fruits and vegetables

GUY FAWKES an English conspirator and member of the 1604 Gunpowder Plot, aimed at blowing up Parliament; Guy Fawkes Day is observed annually in England with bonfires, fireworks, and parties

HALF-TERM one-week midsemester vacation

HAVING IT OFF having sex

HAMPSTEAD HEATH heath (open tract of uncultivated land) in north London

HAVE A LIE-IN sleep in; stay in bed later than usual

HEAD headmaster, principal

HERS, HIS, MINE, OURS her place, his place, my place, our place

HIGH STREET Main Street; the main road in a town

HOLIDAY, HOLIDAYS vacation

HOTTING UP becoming more intense

INDUSTRIAL ESTATE industrial park

IN PRETTY GOOD NICK in good condition

JACK IN quit

JELLY Jell-O

JUBILEE, QUEEN'S FIRST anniversary of the coronation

JUMPER sweater

KILBURN area below Dollis Hill; features cafés and inexpensive shops

KING'S CROSS major train station

KIP sleep

KIT clothes and/or equipment assembled for a specific purpose

KNICKERS underpants

LAY OUT give, loan

LIFT elevator

LOO toilet, lavatory

LOOT British magazine and web service advertising used goods for sale

LORRYLOAD truckload; a large quantity

MAD crazy

MARKS AND SPARKS Marks & Spencer, a British clothing and grocery store

MARMITE a savory spread made from yeast

MATES friends

MATHS math

MI5 the U.K.'s security intelligence agency

MINCE ground beef

MIND babysit

MOBE mobile phone/cell phone

NAFF cheesy, tacky

NAPPIES diapers

NATTER chat

NEWS AGENT'S small shop selling newspapers, candy, cigarettes, and such

NEWSNIGHT current affairs program on British television

NICKED stole or stolen; arrested

NIPPED OUT stepped out

NOTHING FOR IT nothing else to do

OFFING, IN THE a possibility

ON ABOUT talking about

ON TOP FORM in good form

OVERGROUND above-ground trains

OXFAM charitable organization based in the U.K.; runs shops selling secondhand clothes and goods as well as fair-trade products made in developing countries

PARLIAMENT SQUARE square outside of Parliament (home of U.K. national legislature); frequent site of demonstrations

PE KIT clothes worn for Phys. Ed.

PETROL gas

PHONE BOX phone booth

PICCADILLY CIRCUS busy junction of five streets in London; the U.K. equivalent of Times Square

PISSING DOWN raining heavily

PLASTICINE a soft modeling material

PLAITED braided

POST mail

POST OFFICE TOWER British Telecom communications tower, a London landmark

POT NOODLE plastic cup of instant noodles

POUND basic monetary unit of the U.K.

PRIMARY elementary school

PRIME MINISTER leader of the party with the majority in the House of Commons

PUDDING dessert

PUSHCHAIRS strollers

QUEUE stand in line

QUID pound(s); five hundred quid is equivalent to almost one thousand dollars

RAC Royal Automobile Club; a road service, like AAA in the U.S.

RANG called

RASHERS thin strips of meat, especially bacon (in this case soya)

REVISE study

RIZLAS brand name for cigarette papers

ROUNDABOUT traffic rotary

ROUNDED ON turned on; started attacking verbally

ROW, ROWING argument, arguing

SAATCHI GALLERY contemporary art gallery in London

SAINSBURY'S large U.K. supermarket chain

SAFEWAY grocery store chain

SALT CELLAR saltshaker

SARKY sarcastic

SARNIES sandwiches

SAS Special Air Service

SHATTERED exhausted

SERVIETTE napkin

SIXTH FORM YEARS last two years of school before university, equivalent to twelfth and thirteenth grades

SKIP Dumpster

SKIVVY servant

SLAGGING OFF insulting, deriding, criticizing

SNOGGING kissing passionately; making out

SNOOKER a variety of the game of pool

SODS pains in the butt

SOLICITOR lawyer

SPANNER wrench

SPOTS acne

ST. MARTIN'S prestigious art school

STONE measurement of weight; approximately 14 pounds

SUSSED knowledgeable

SWANNING AROUND swaggering

TAKE-AWAY take-out

TALKING CLOCK telephone service that gives the time of day

TATE MODERN gallery of modern art in London

TEA COSY padded cloth covering to keep a teapot warm

TELLY television

TENNER ten-pound note

TERM school semester

THOMAS COOK a travel agency

THORPE PARK an amusement park

TILL GONE MIDNIGHT after midnight

TIN, TINNED tin can, canned

TOP SHOP a chain of fashionable, affordable clothing stores

TORY member of the Conservative Party

TRAINERS sneakers

TRAINSPOTTING an obsessive hobby that involves watching trains and recording their types, names, and numbers; often used as an example of an extremely boring activity

TROLLEY shopping cart

TUBE London subway

V very

V&A Victoria and Albert Museum

VEGGIE vegetarian

WARDROBE external closet

WASHING POWDER detergent

WATER BISCUITS thin, plain crackers

WELL very

WELLIES Wellingtons; high, waterproof rubber boots

WEST END shopping and entertainment district of central London

WHACKED exhausted

WHOLEMEAL whole wheat

WICKED cool

WIND UP push one's buttons

WINDSCREEN windshield

WOBBLY tantrum

WOMBLE character featured in a series of children's books and, later, a television show; Wombles are fantastical creatures who live on Wimbledon Common.

WOOLIE'S affectionate term for Woolworth's, a chain of five-and-dime stores that no longer operates in the U.S. but is still in business in the U.K.

YEAR 7S students in their first year of secondary school, for ages 11 to 12

YORKSHIRE PUDDING similar to a popover, baked either muffin style or in a flat pan; traditionally served with roast beef

The stories in this collection were previously published individually by Candlewick Press.

Planet Janet text copyright © 2002 by Dyan Sheldon
Planet Janet in Orbit text copyright © 2004 by Dyan Sheldon

First edition in this format 2007

The Library of Congress has cataloged the hardcover editions as follows:

Sheldon, Dyan.
Planet Janet / Dyan Sheldon — 1st U.S. ed.
p.   cm.
Summary: Sixteen-year-old Janet Bandry keeps a diary as she deals with
an annoying family, school, a quirky best friend, and trying to find herself
through vegetarianism, literature, romance, and her "Dark Phase."
ISBN 978-0-7636-2048-6 (hardcover)
[1. Family problems—Fiction. 2. Interpersonal relations—Fiction.
3. High schools—Fiction. 4. Schools—Fiction.] I. Title.
PZ7.S54144 Pl 2003
[Fic]—dc21   2002073626

Sheldon, Dyan.
Planet Janet in Orbit / Dyan Sheldon. — 1st U.S. ed.
p.   cm.
Summary: Having taken a break from the "Dark Phase" of her life,
Janet records in her diary the trials and tribulations that occur as she finds
a summer job, witnesses the changes in her mother and best friend as they
fall in love, and approaches her own seventeenth birthday.
ISBN 978-0-7636-2755-3 (hardcover)
[1. Interpersonal relations—Fiction. 2. Family life—London (England)—Fiction.
3. High schools—Fiction. 4. Schools—Fiction. 5. Diaries—Fiction. 6. London
(England)—Fiction. 7. England—Fiction.] I. Title.
PZ7.S54144 Plj 2005
[Fic]—dc22   2005050789

ISBN 978-0-7636-3216-8 (paperback collection)

2 4 6 8 10 9 7 5 3 1

Printed in the United States of America
This book was typeset in M Joanna.

Candlewick Press
2067 Massachusetts Avenue
Cambridge, MA 02140

visit us at www.candlewick.com